This Book Is A Gift From

John Fortin

Happy 8th Birthday
3-25-13

© Highsmith Inc. 1999

NICK BRUEL

A NEAL PORTER BOOK
ROARING BROOK PRESS
NEW YORK

For all teachers
everywhere

Page 83, *The Battle at Bunker's Hill*, George Edward Perine after John Trumbull, courtesy of Emmet Collection, Miriam and Ira D. Wallach Division of Art, Prints and Photographs, The New York Public Library, Astor, Lenox and Tilden Foundations

Copyright © 2013 by Nick Bruel
A Neal Porter Book
Published by Roaring Brook Press
Roaring Brook Press is a division of Holtzbrinck Publishing Holdings Limited Partnership
175 Fifth Avenue, New York, New York 10010
mackids.com

Library of Congress Cataloging-in-Publication Data

Bruel, Nick.
  Bad Kitty school daze / Nick Bruel.
    p. cm.
  Summary: "When Kitty's owners have finally had enough of her bad behavior, it's time to ship her off to obedience school"— Provided by publisher.
  ISBN 978-1-59643-670-1 (hardback)
  [1. Cats—Fiction. 2. Pets—Training—Fiction. 3. Humorous stories.] I. Title.
    PZ7.B82832Bao 2012
    [E]—dc23
                                                                    2012015359

Roaring Brook Press books are available for special promotions and premiums.
For details contact: Director of Special Markets, Holtzbrinck Publishers.

First edition 2013
Printed in the United States of America by RR Donnelley & Sons Company,
Harrisonburg, Virginia
1   3   5   7   9   10   8   6   4   2

• CONTENTS •

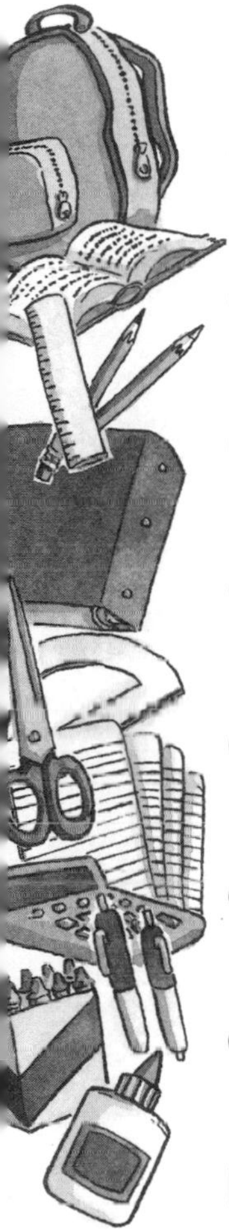

•CHAPTER ONE•

ONE FINE DAY

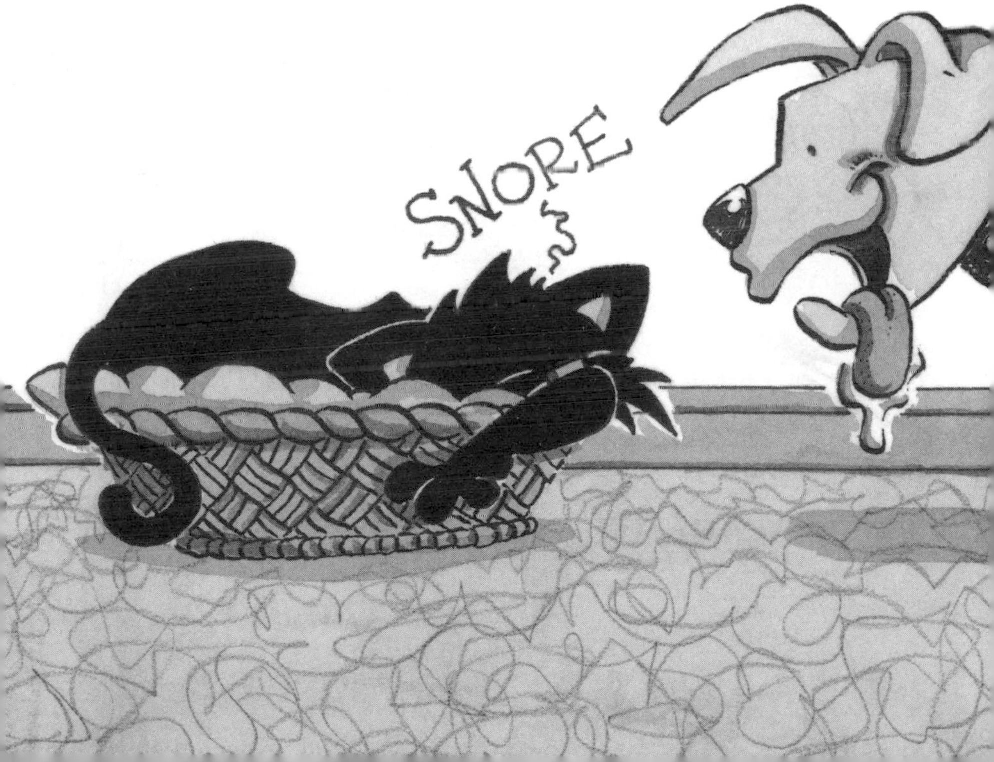
SNORE

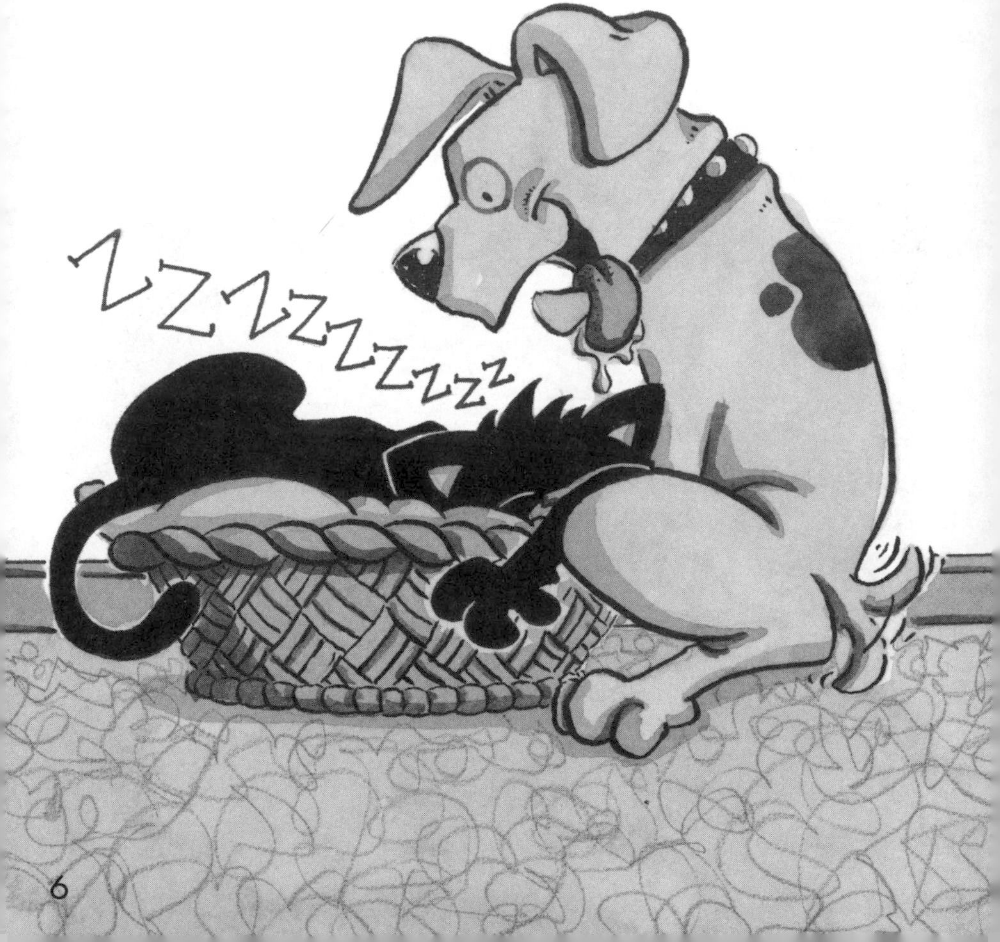
ZZZZZZZZZZ

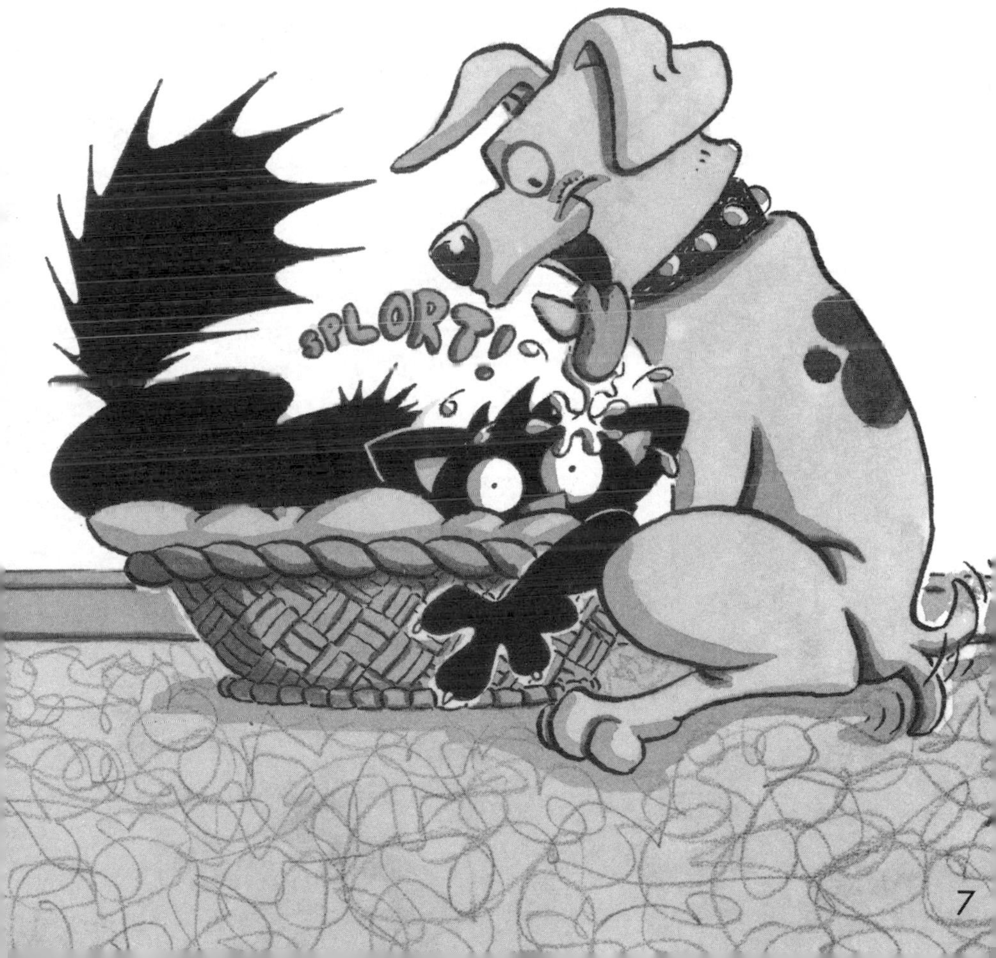
SPLORT!

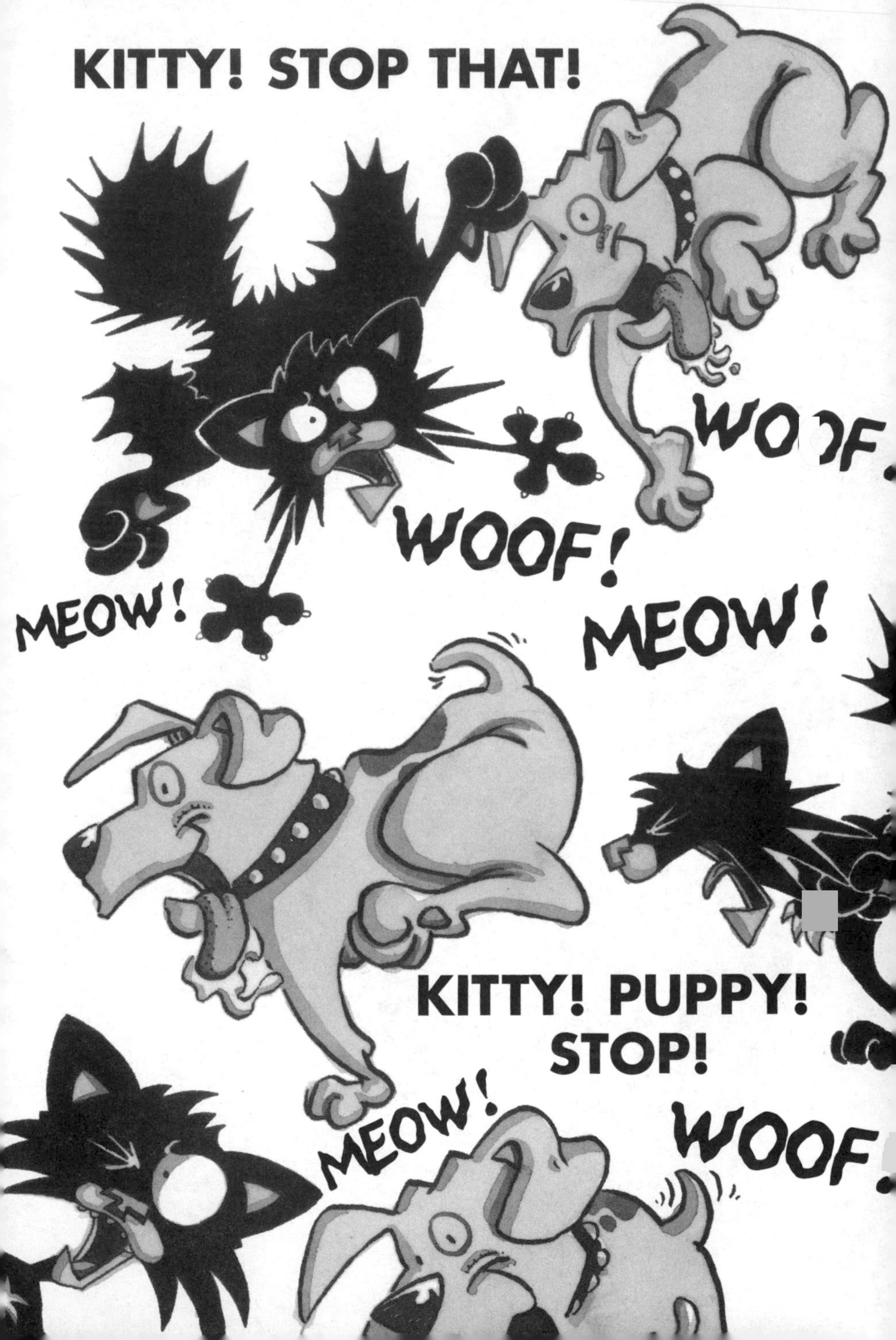

KITTY! STOP THAT!
WOOF!
MEOW!
MEOW!
KITTY! PUPPY! STOP!
MEOW!
WOOF!

BOTH OF YOU, CUT IT OUT!

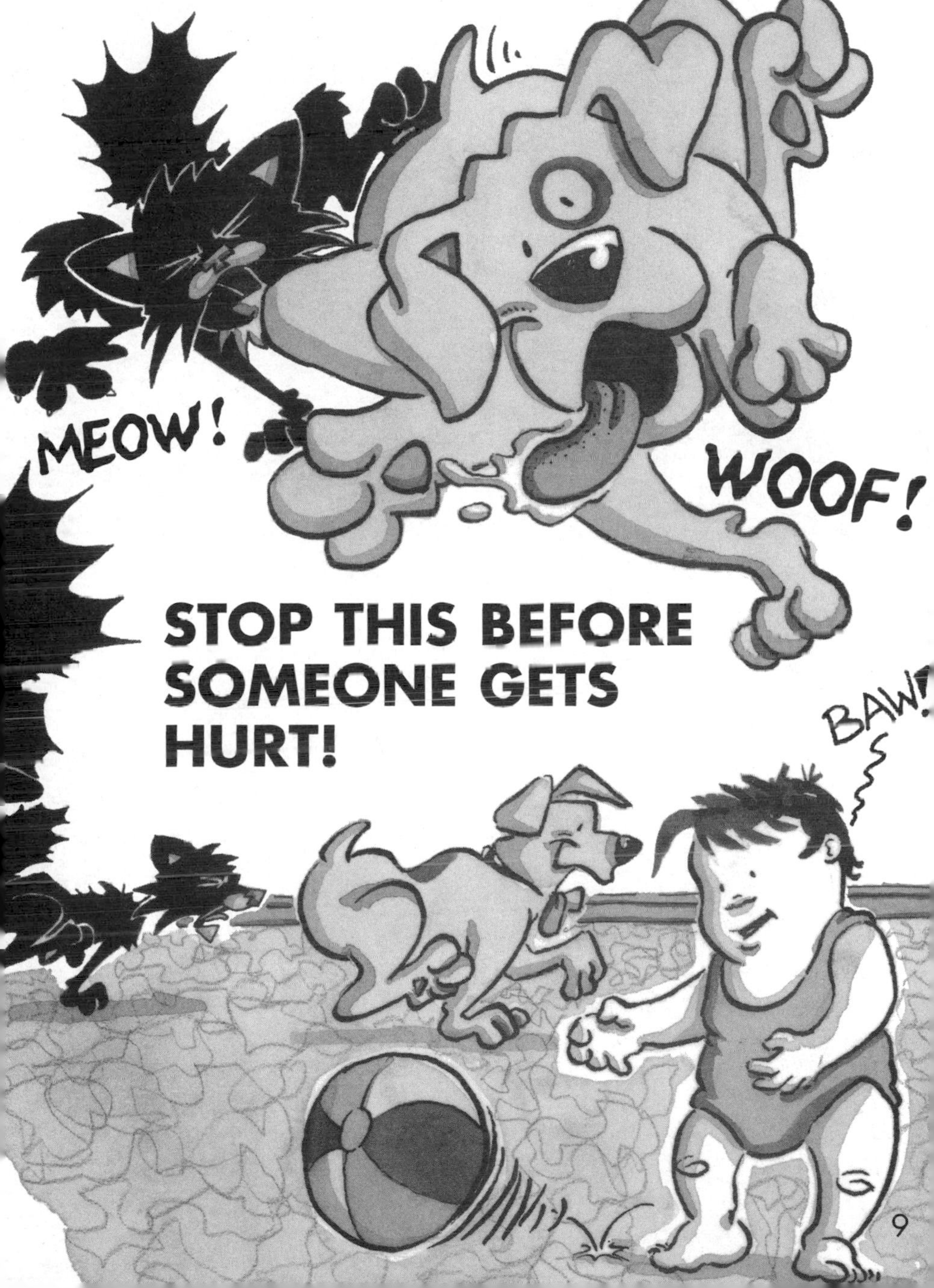
MEOW!
WOOF!
STOP THIS BEFORE SOMEONE GETS HURT!
BAW!

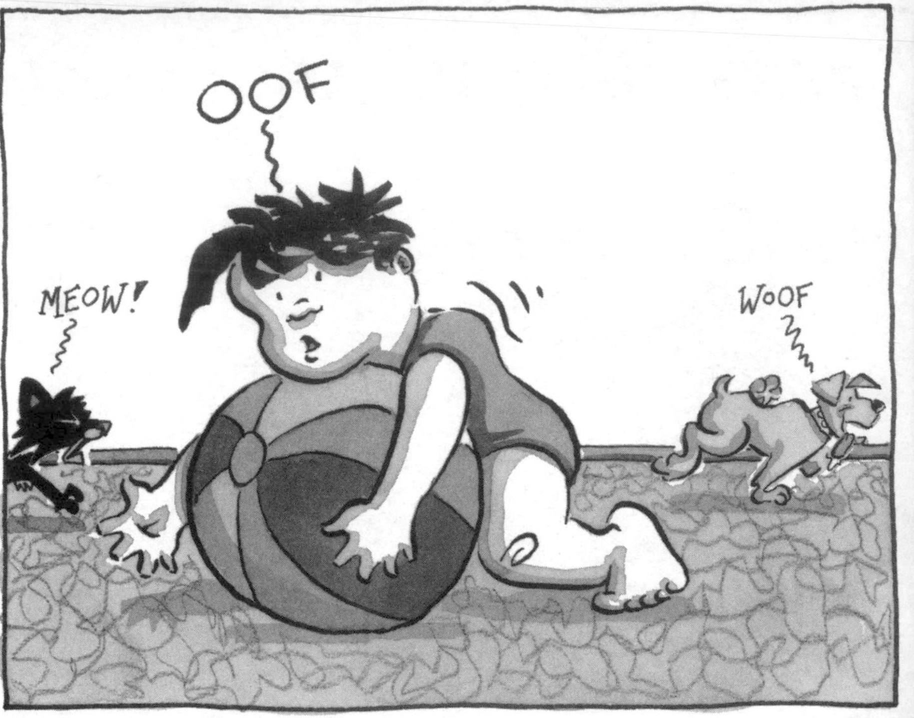
OOF
MEOW!
WOOF

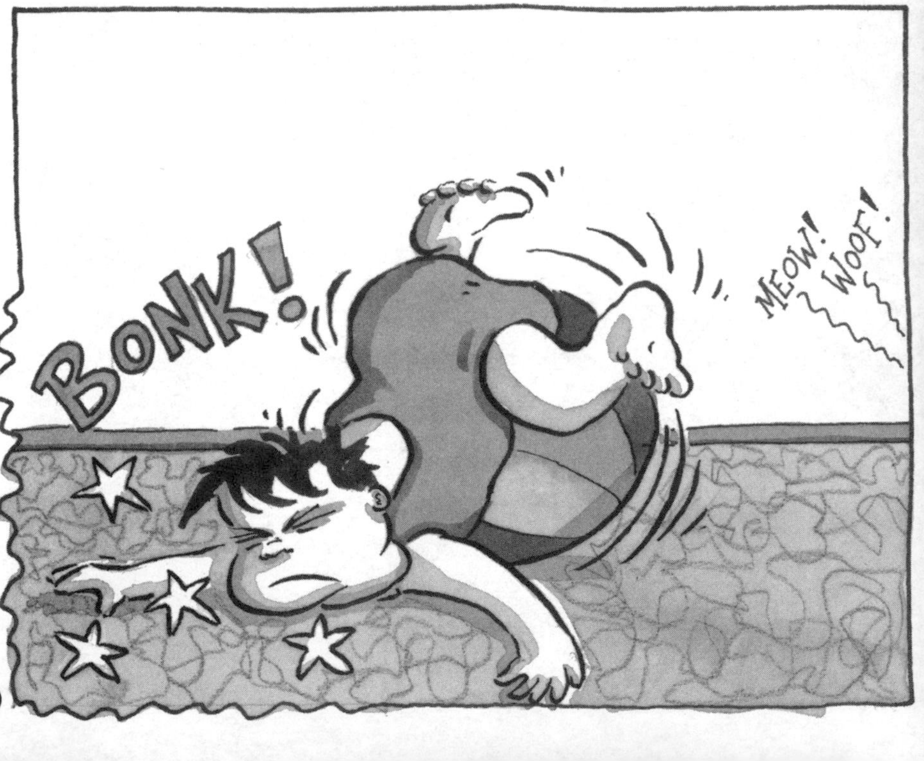
BONK!
MEOW!
WOOF!

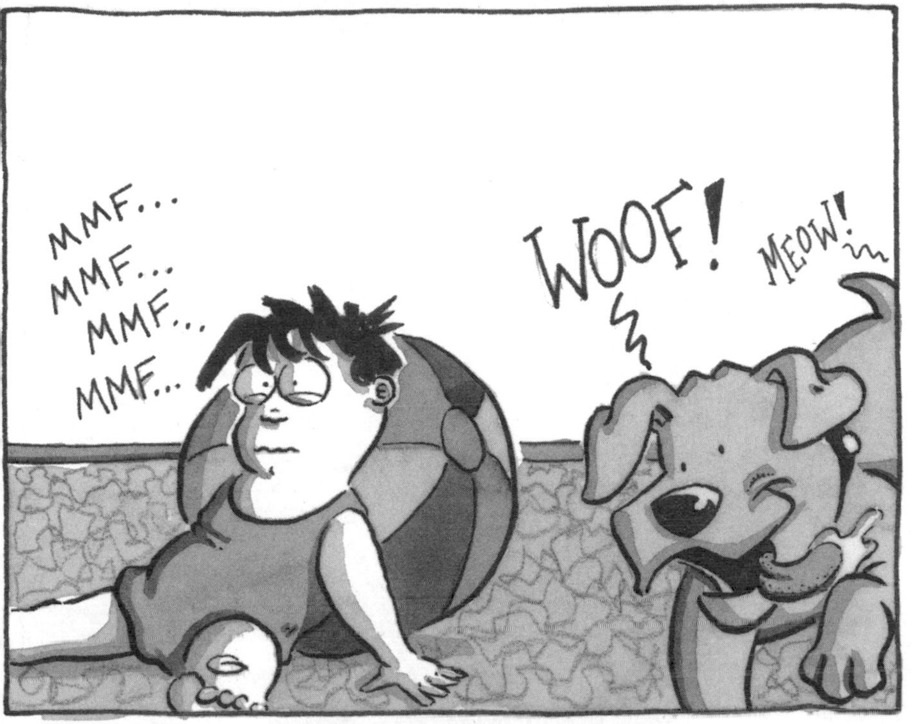
MMF...
MMF...
MMF...
MMF...
WOOF!
MEOW!

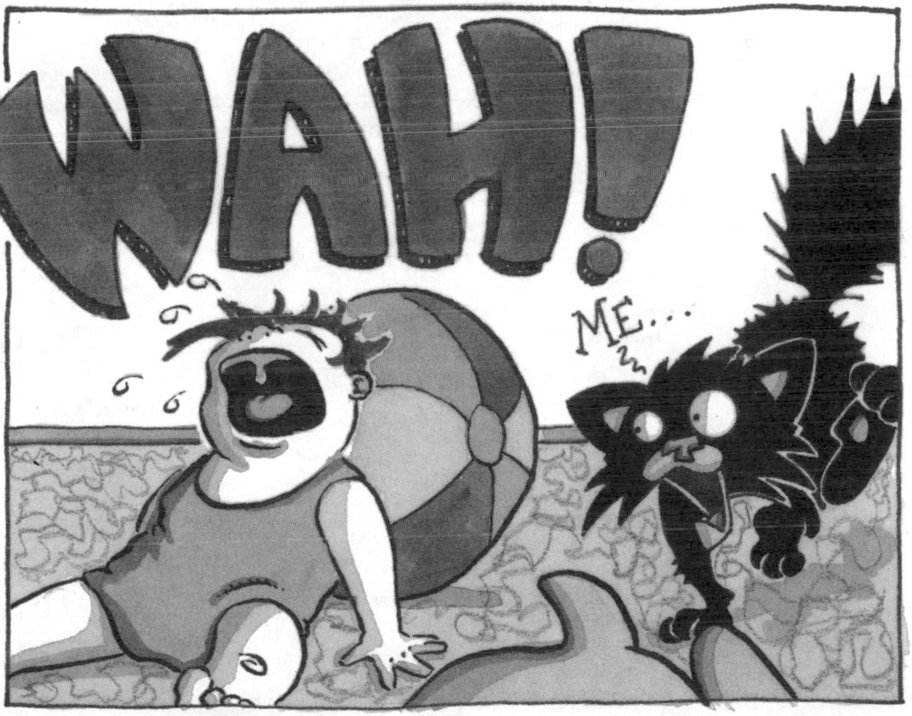
WAH!
ME...

Oh, dear! What happened, Baby? Did you fall down? How did that happen?

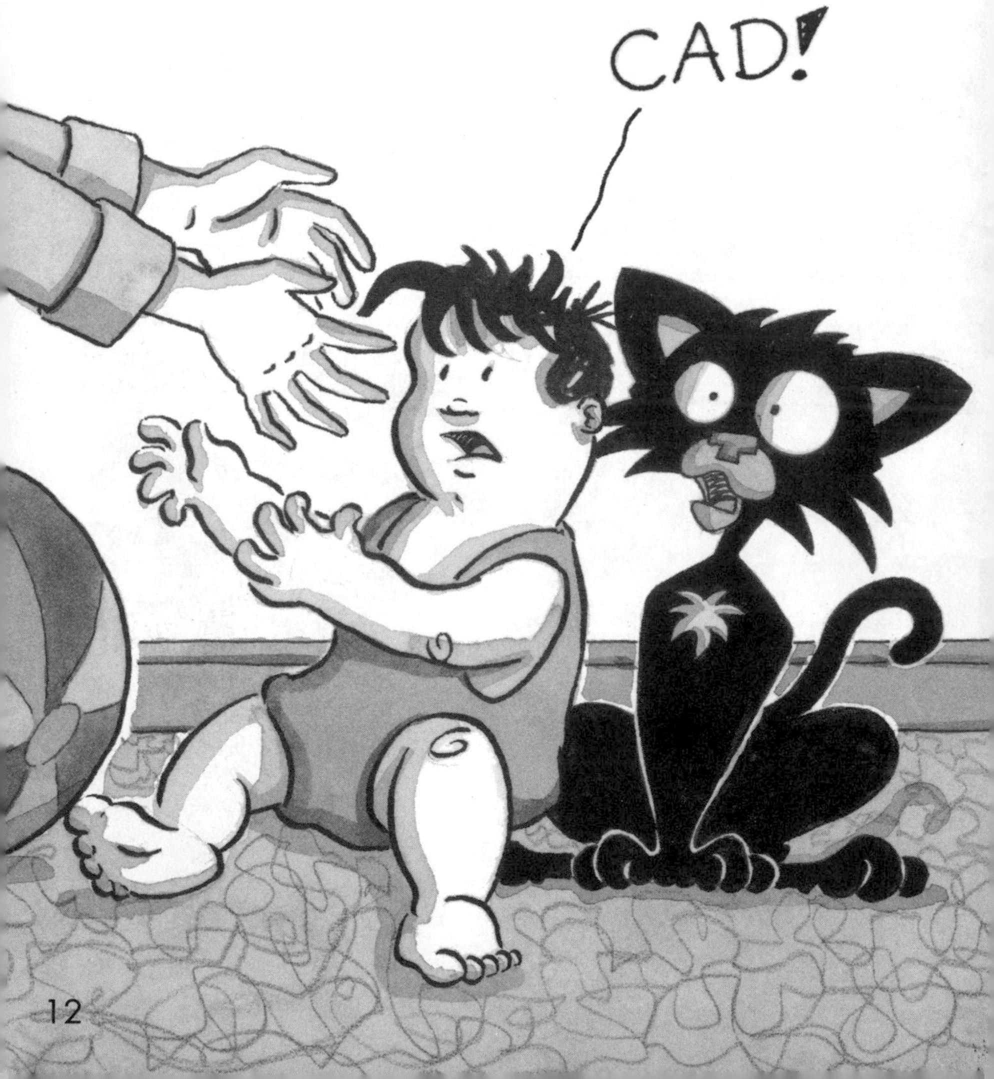
CAD!

The cat did this? Well, I'm not surprised. Tsk, tsk, tsk. The way those two were running and horsing around. But I'm sure it was an accident.

Kitty, it's time for us to have a little talk.

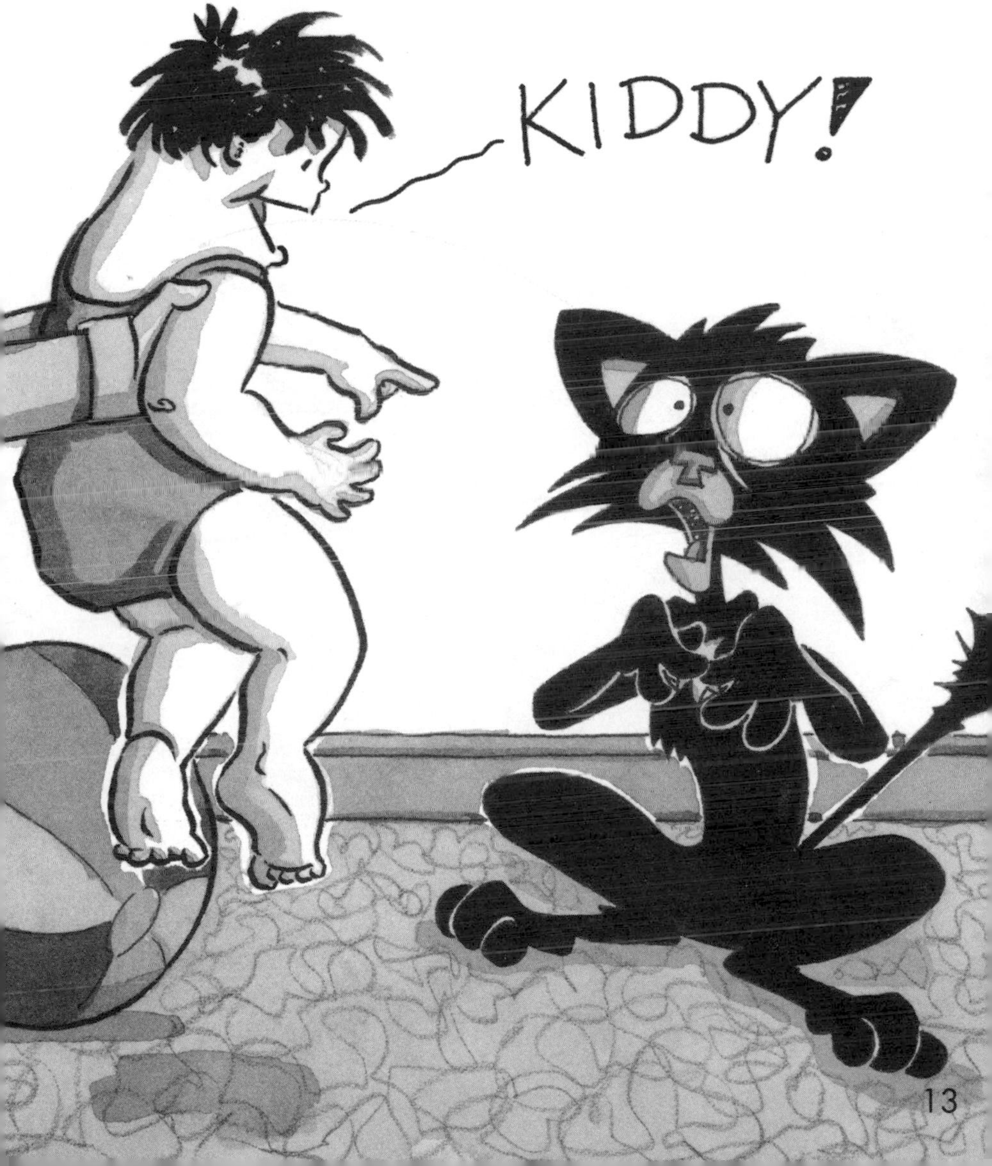
KIDDY!

Kitty, I've had enough of your SCREAMING and HISSING and FIGHTING. It's time we did something about your behavior, your nasty temper, and the fact that you never seem to listen.

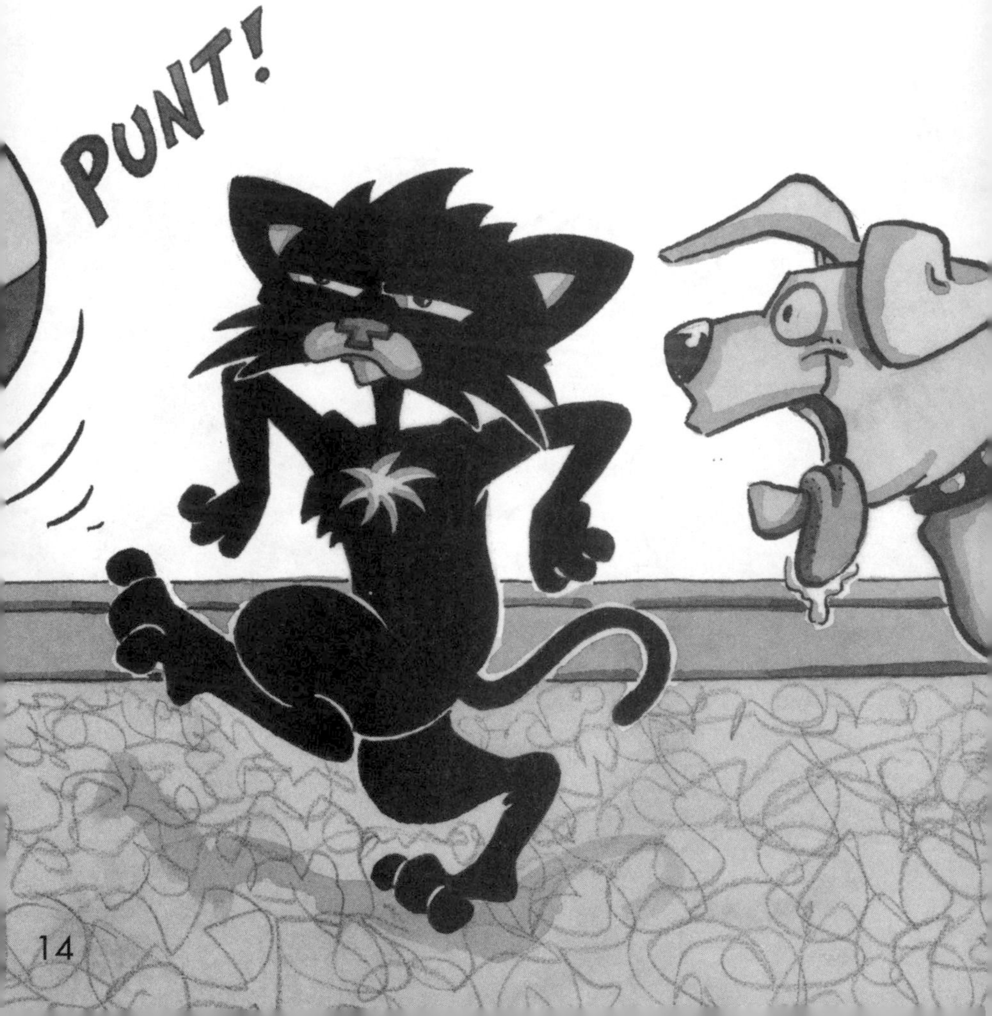
PUNT!

And that goes for you too, Puppy. That drooling problem of yours started all of this.

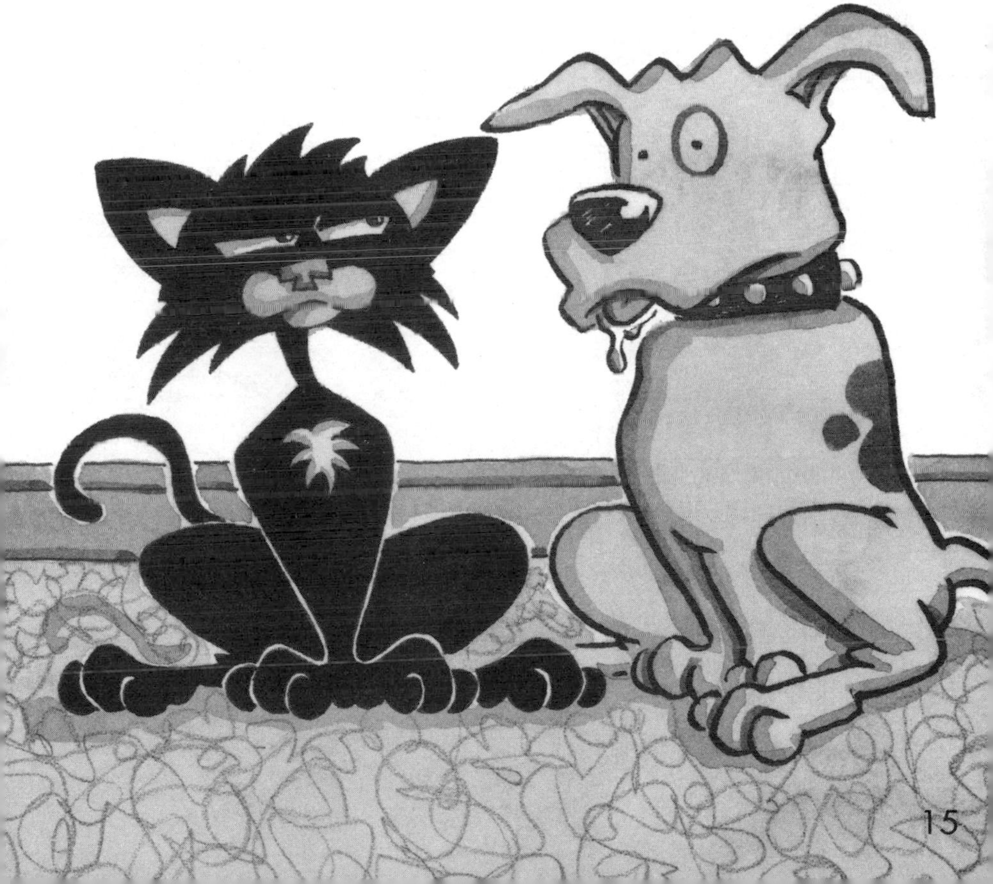

That's why I've decided it's time for both of you to go to . . .

SCHOOL.

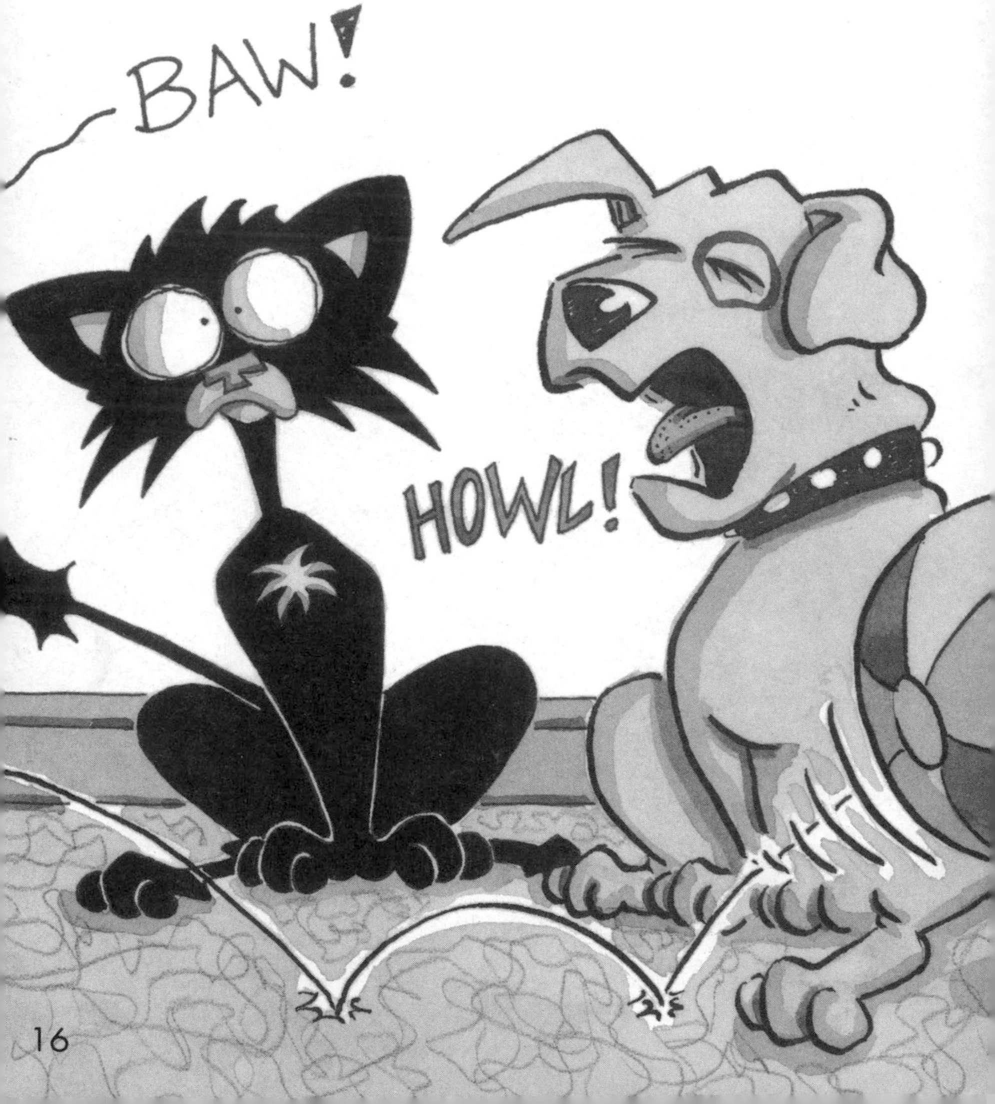
BAW!
HOWL!

•CHAPTER TWO•

THE NEXT FINE DAY

HEY, KITTY! I just got back from the store, and look at all of the super-cool school supplies I bought for you! They all feature your absolute FAVORITE . . .

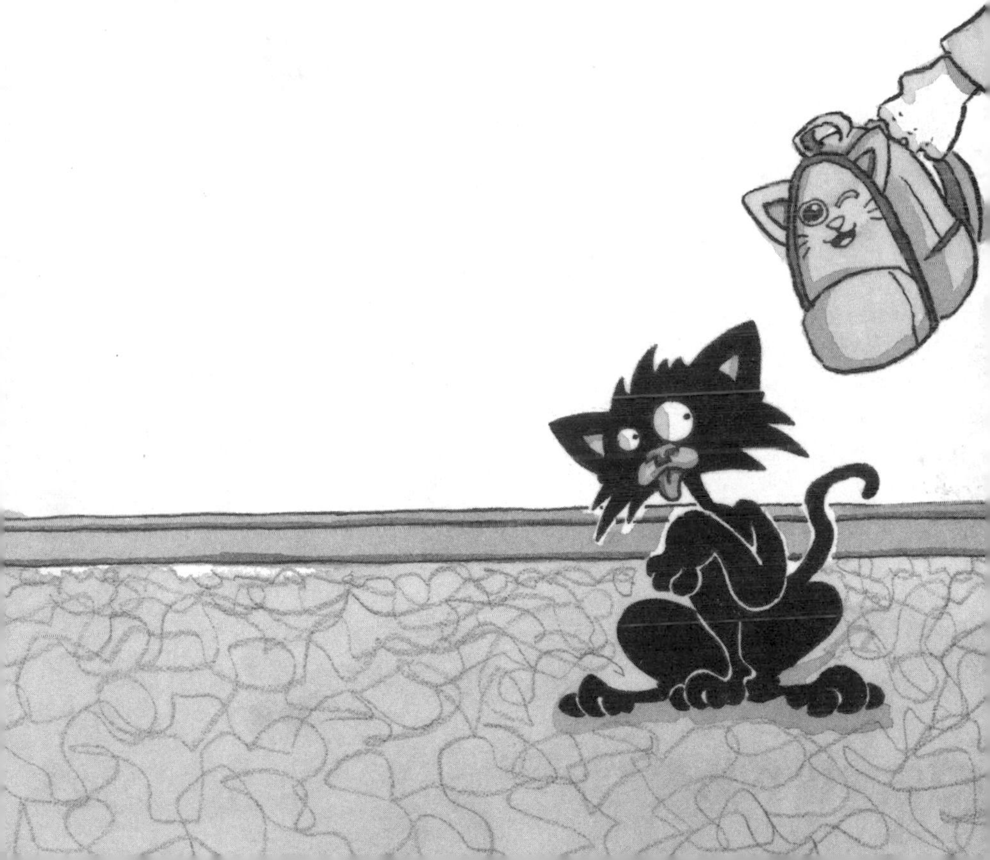

Love Love Angel Kitten

Love Love Angel Kitten
Backpack

Love
Love
Angel
Kitten
Notebook

Love Love Angel Kitten
Eraser

Pinkish
Pink

Reddish
Pink

Deep Pink

Light Pink

Love Love
Angel Kitten
Pencils

Love Love
Angel Kitten
Bowling Ball

Pink

Love Love
Angel Kitten
Crayons

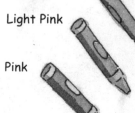

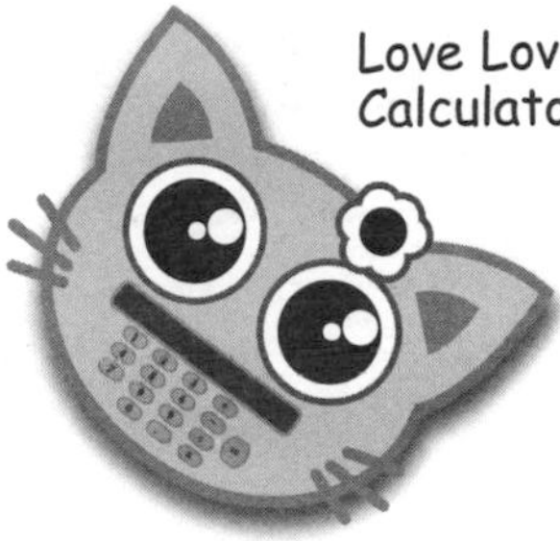

Love Love Angel Kitten
Calculator

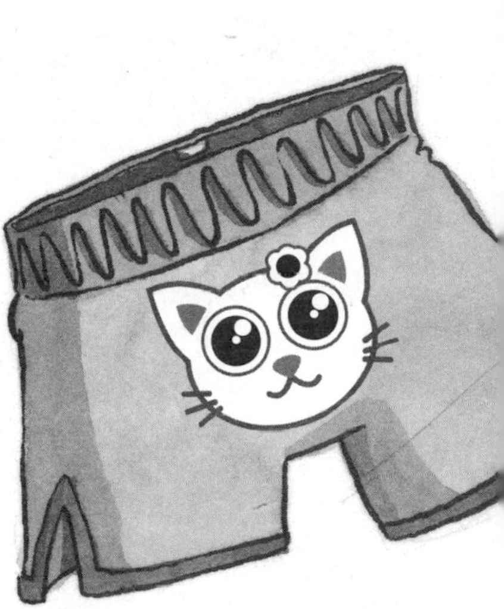

Love Love
Angel
Kitten
Gym Shorts

Love Love
Angel Kitten
Tractor
Tire

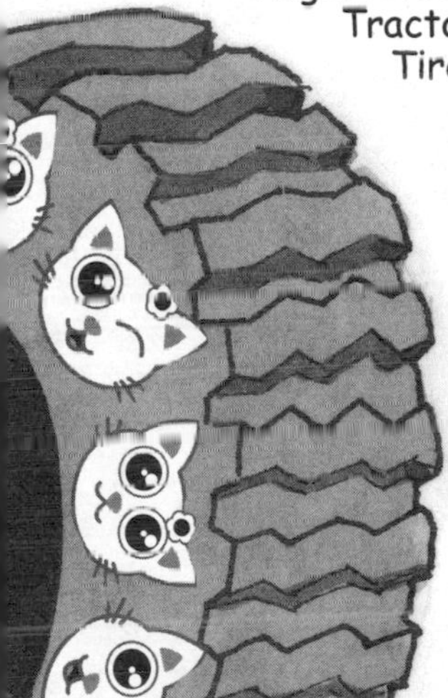

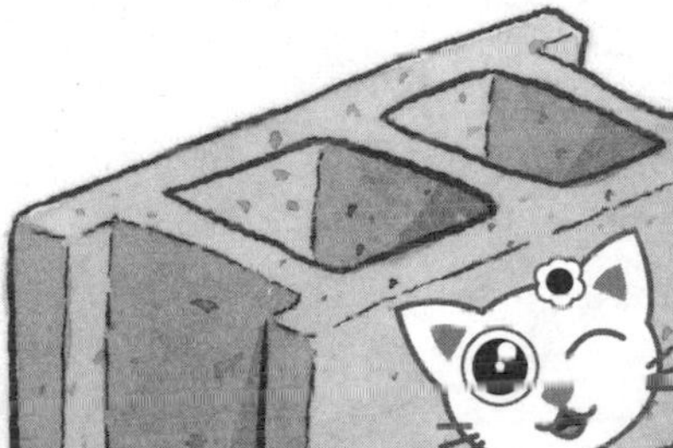

Love Love
Angel Kitten
Cinder Block

Love Love
Angel Kitten
Ruler

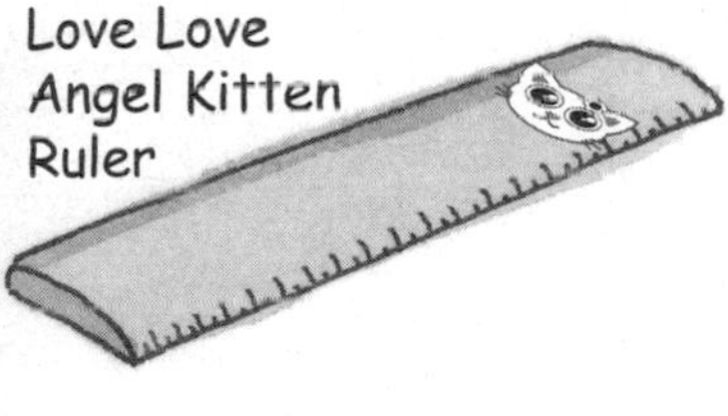

Whew! That's a lot of stuff! Oh well . . . Let's put it all into your backpack.

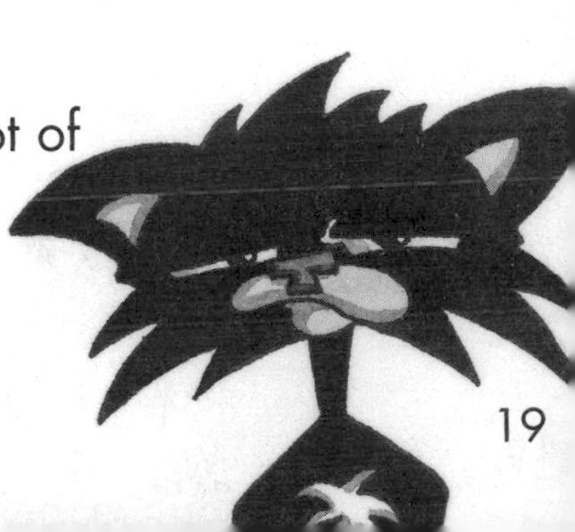

Awww, look at you! All ready for school.

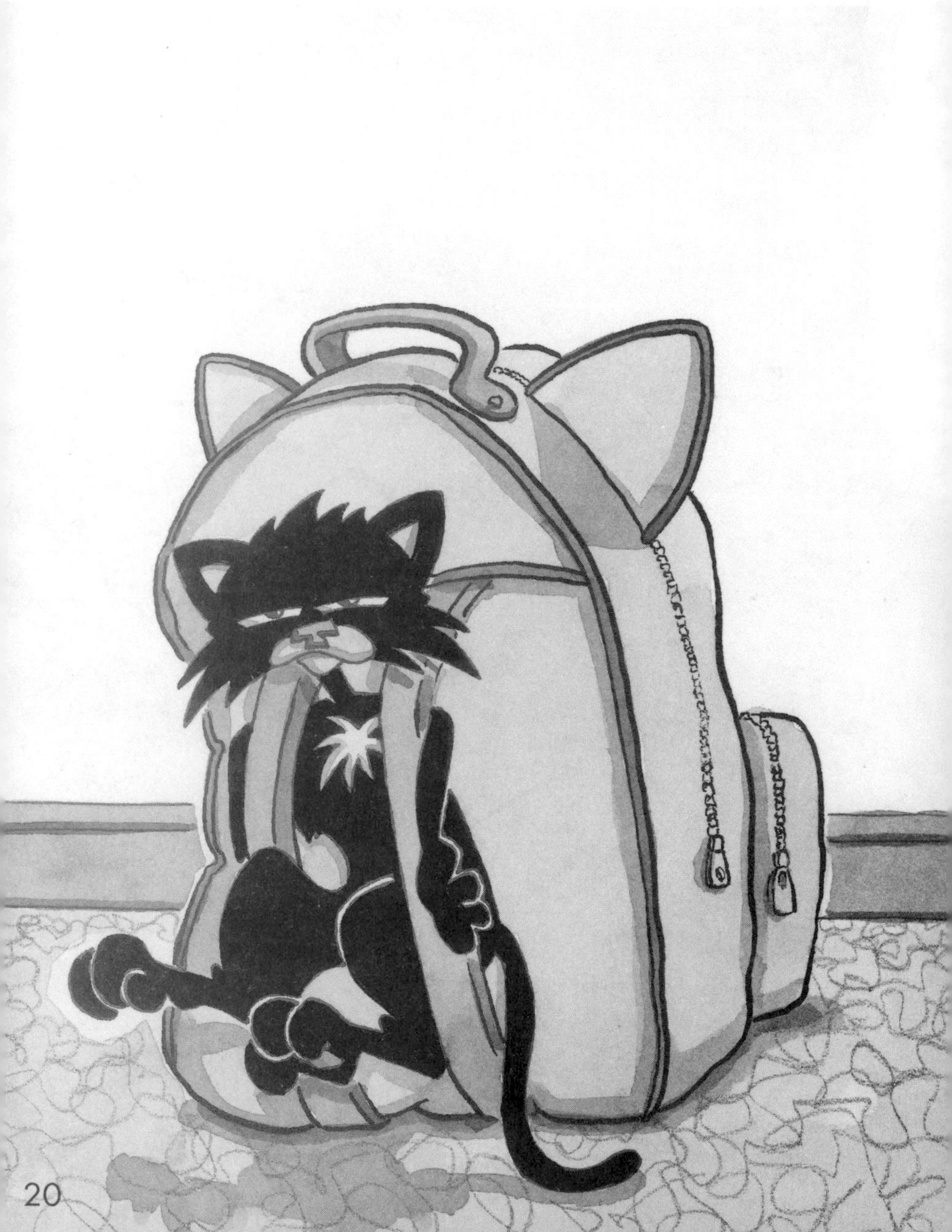

And so is Puppy! Did you pack your bandana, Puppy? I hope so, because you'll need it if you start drooling again.

We better hurry. You guys don't want to be late for the school bus!

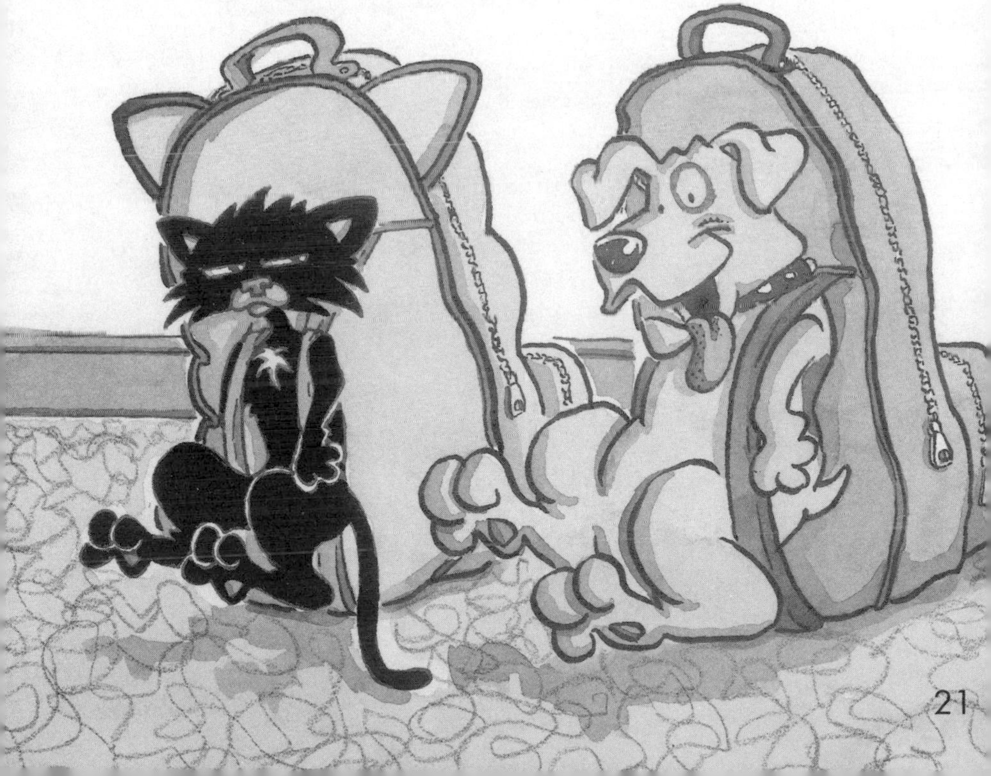

HERE IT COMES!

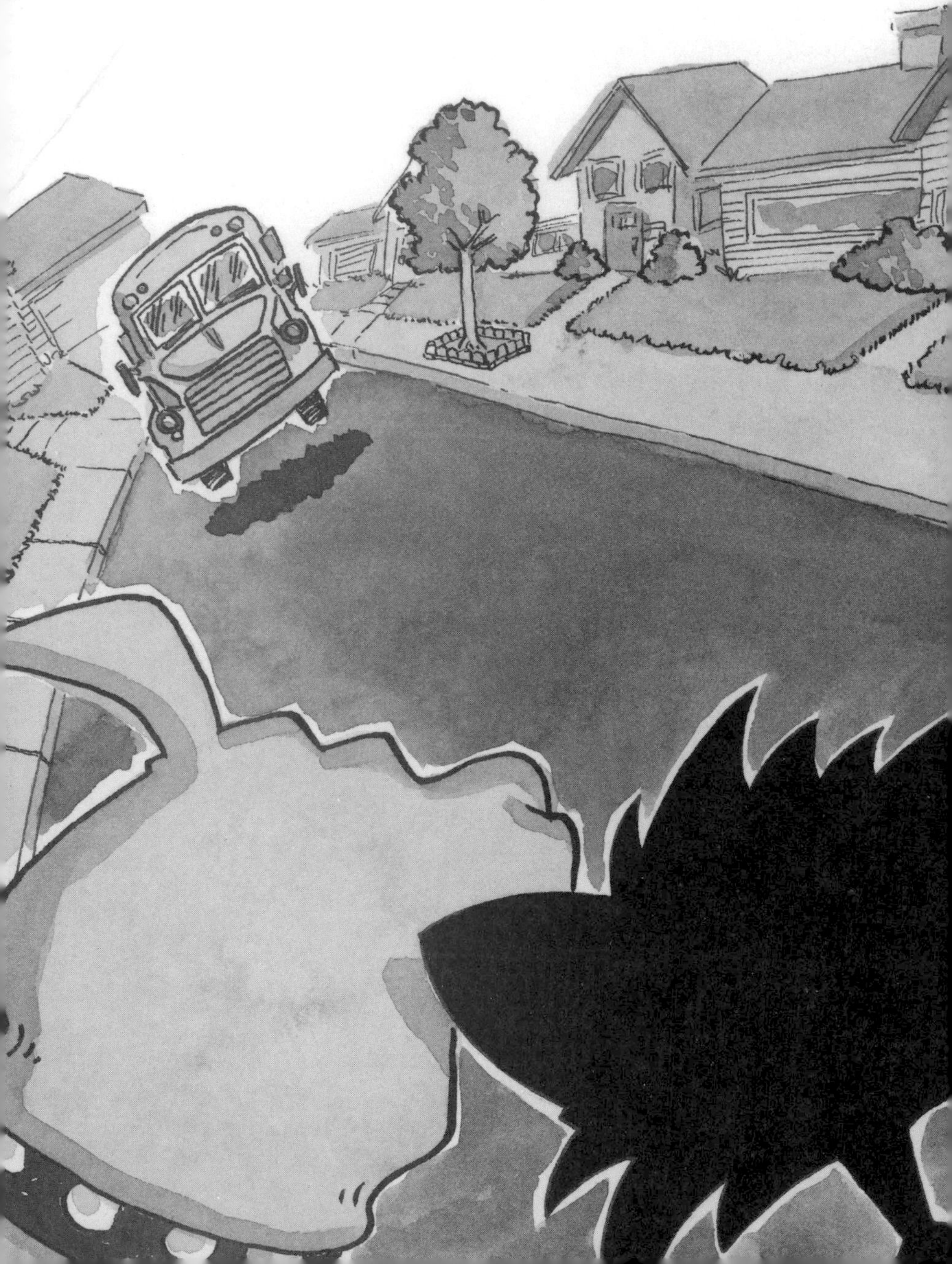

And look who's driving! It's good ol' Uncle Murray!

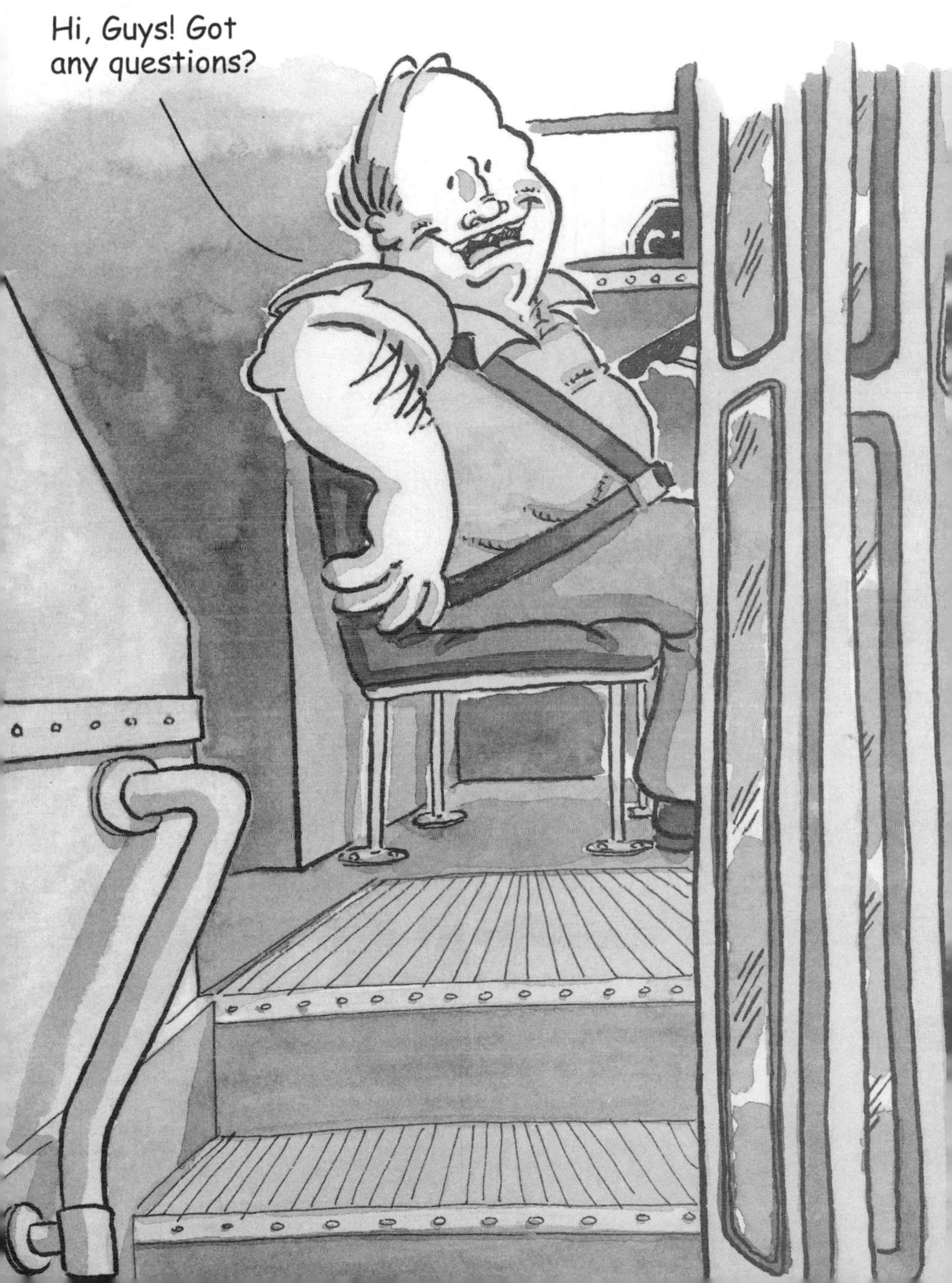
Hi, Guys! Got any questions?

UNCLE MURRAY'S FUN FACTS

WHY DO DOGS CHASE CATS?

Hey, do[n] blame t[h] dog for this!

Dogs don't just chase cats. They chase lots of things, because that's what dogs like to do most.

Herder dogs like border collies are bred to chase sheep and keep the flock together. Hunting dogs like hounds and dachshunds are bred to chase foxes and rats. Police dogs like German shepherds are trained to chase criminals. And dogs chase all of these things not just because they like to do it, but also because

they're so very, very good at it.

When a dog chases a cat, it's not chasing because it's being mean. It's chasing the cat because of instinct. "Instinct" is that part of an animal's brain that controls how an animal is going to act. Birds can fly because their instinct

MEOW*

*Albert Einstein once said that "Peace cannot be kept by force; it can only be achieved by understanding."

24

IS IT FOOD?
IS IT A TOY?
IS IT ANOTHER DOG?
IS IT A SHOE?
SEES OMETHING O CHASE

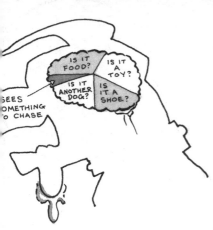

tells them how. Fish can swim because their instinct tells them how. And dogs chase other animals because their instinct tells them it's an important thing to do.

So when a dog sees a strange cat for the first time, his brain tells him that he MUST begin chasing the cat. It doesn't help that dogs are also very territorial, which means that if the cat is anywhere near something the dog thinks he owns, like his bone or his backyard or his house or even YOU, then he will feel compelled to chase that poor cat away.

Cats, by the way, have the same instinct as dogs. Cats are extremely good at chasing other animals, only they chase animals much smaller than they are, like mice and rats. Most dogs are bigger, sometimes MUCH bigger, than cats. So cats do not generally chase dogs.

Dogs, however, do not have the same sense of caution as cats and will often chase things much, much bigger than them. That's why they'll sometimes chase cars.

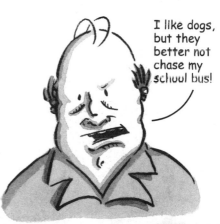

I like dogs, but they better not chase my school bus!

All right, ya goofy cat, move on to the back of the bus and you can meet some of your new classmates!

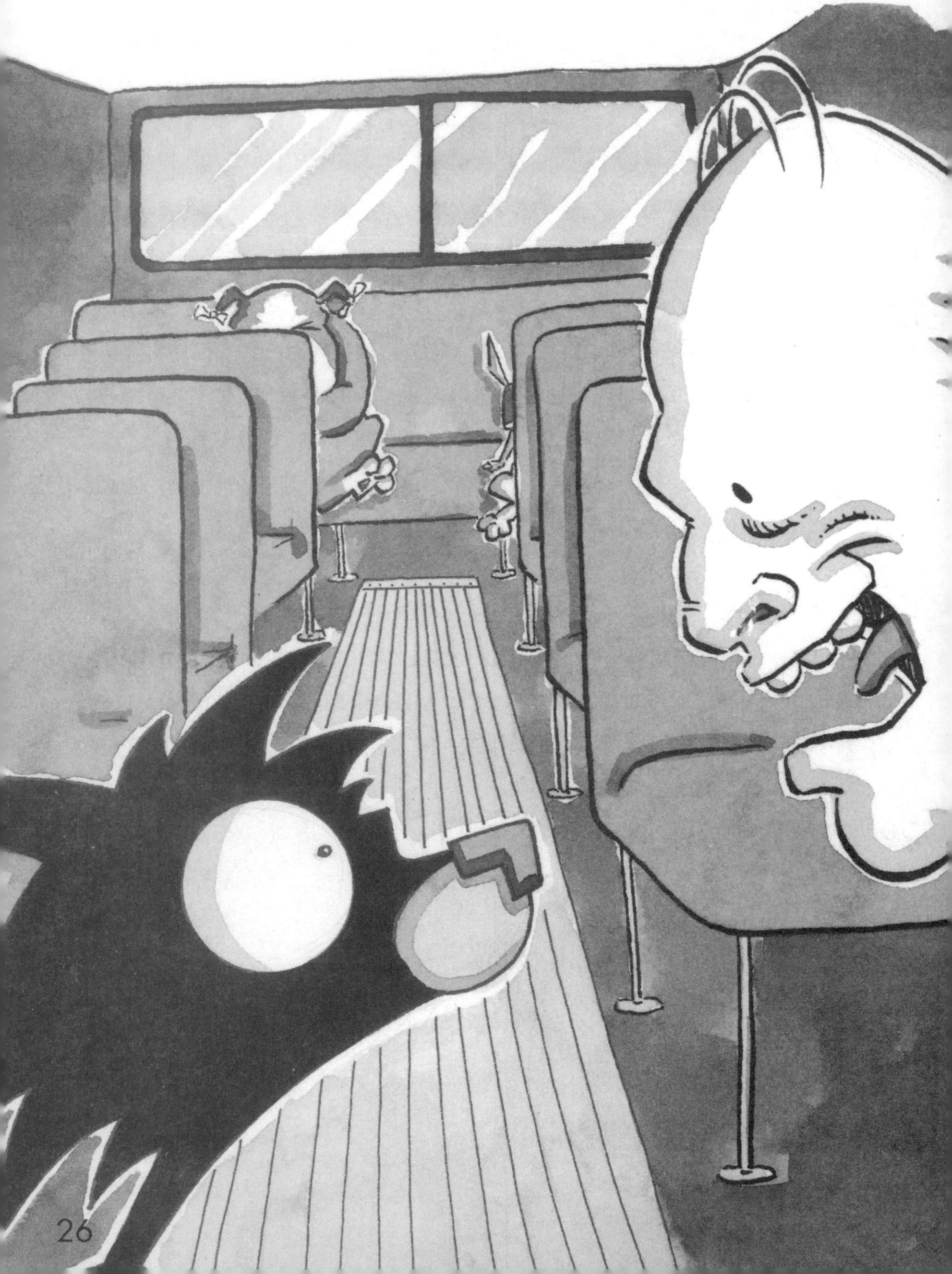

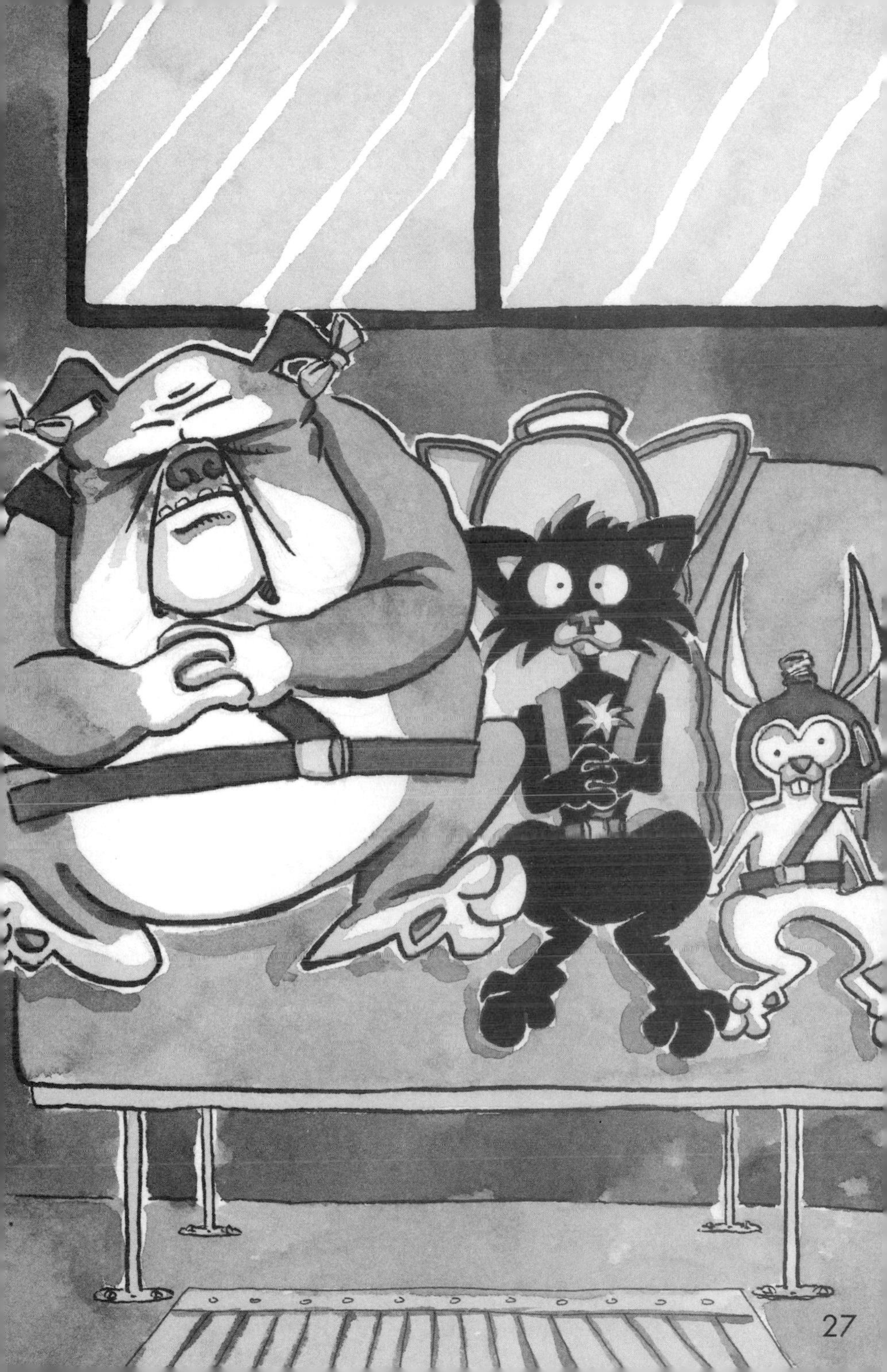

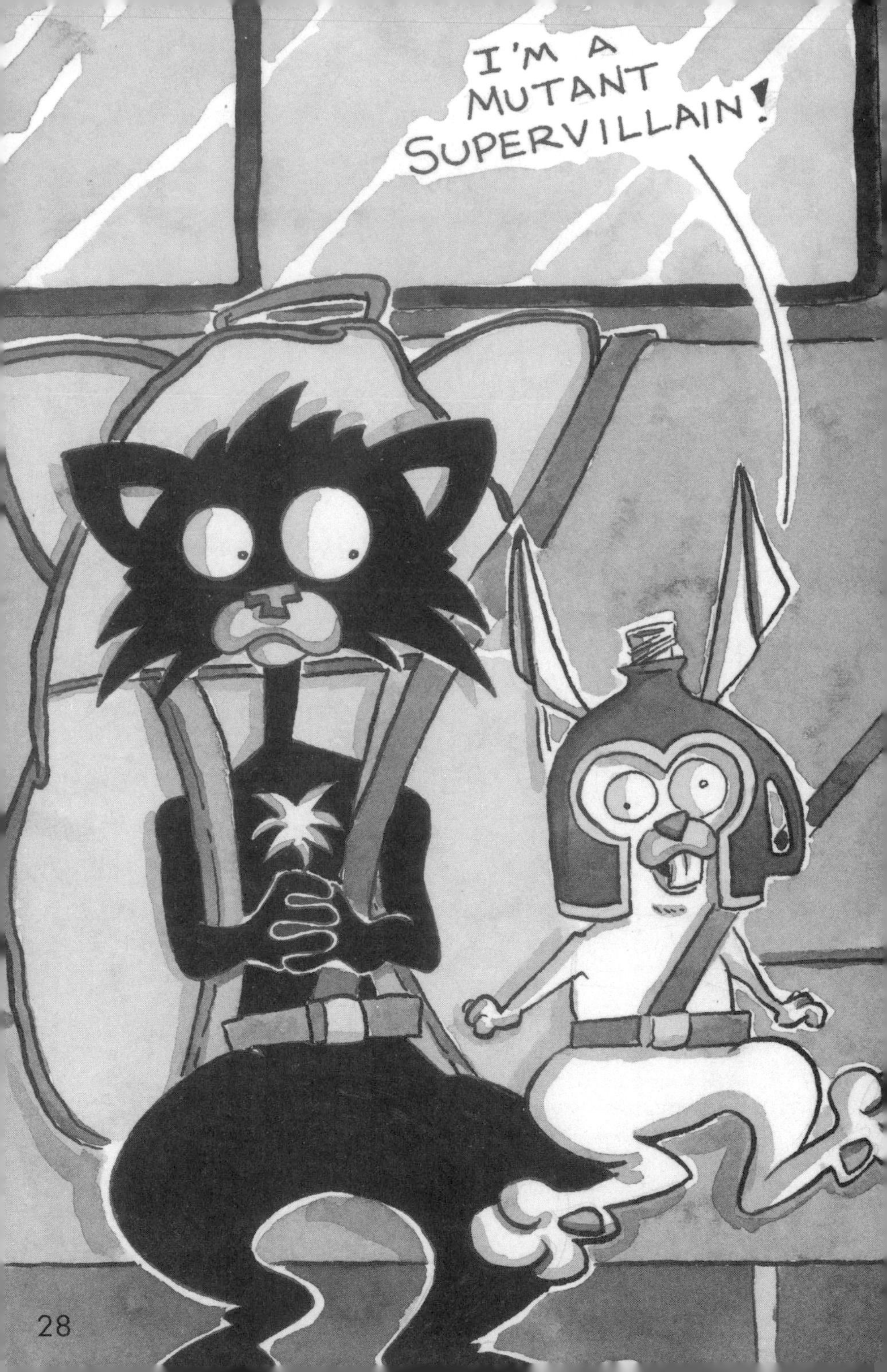
I'M A MUTANT SUPERVILLAIN!

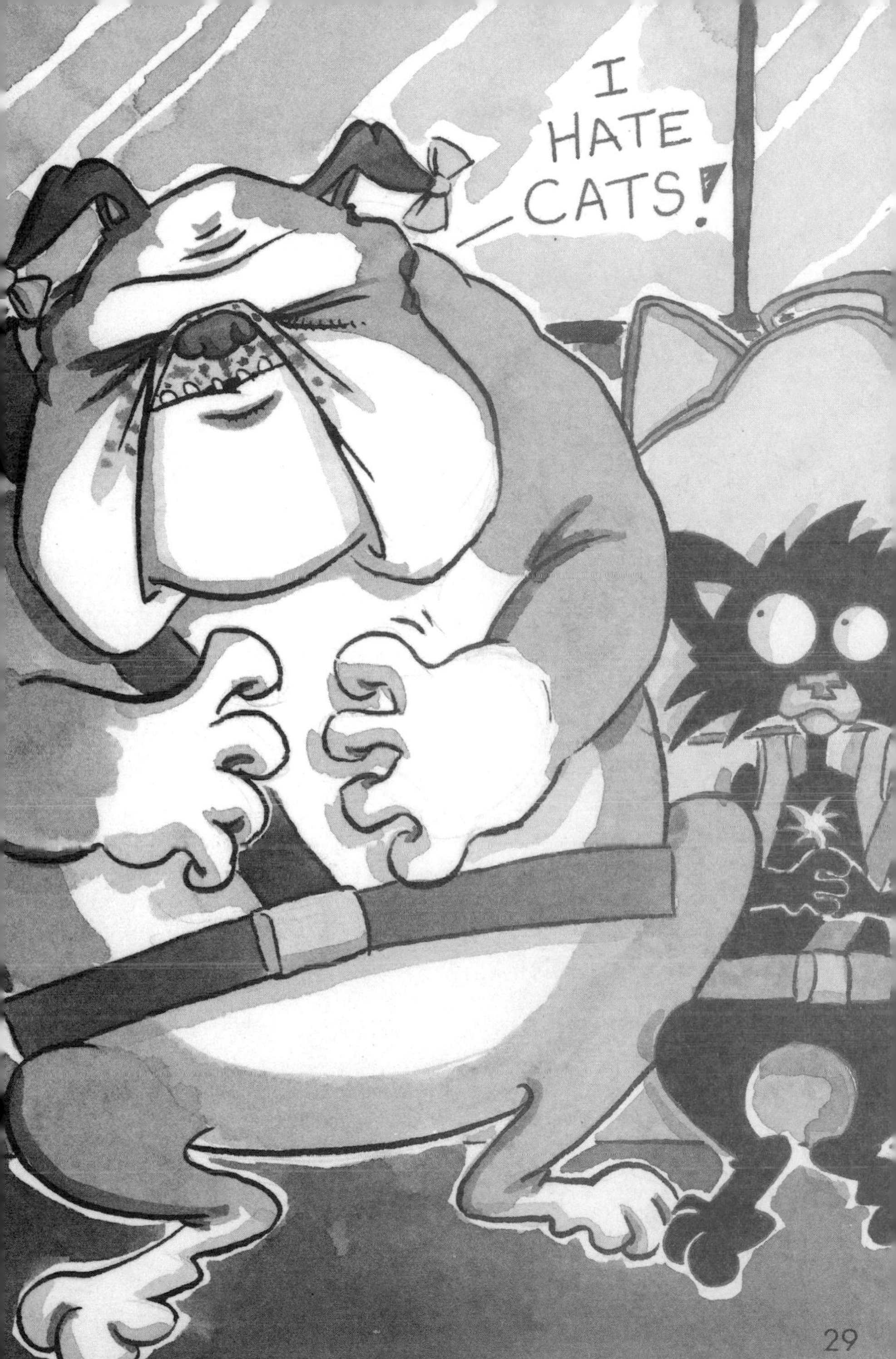
I HATE CATS!

Bye, Kitty! Bye, Puppy! I'll see you at the end of the day!

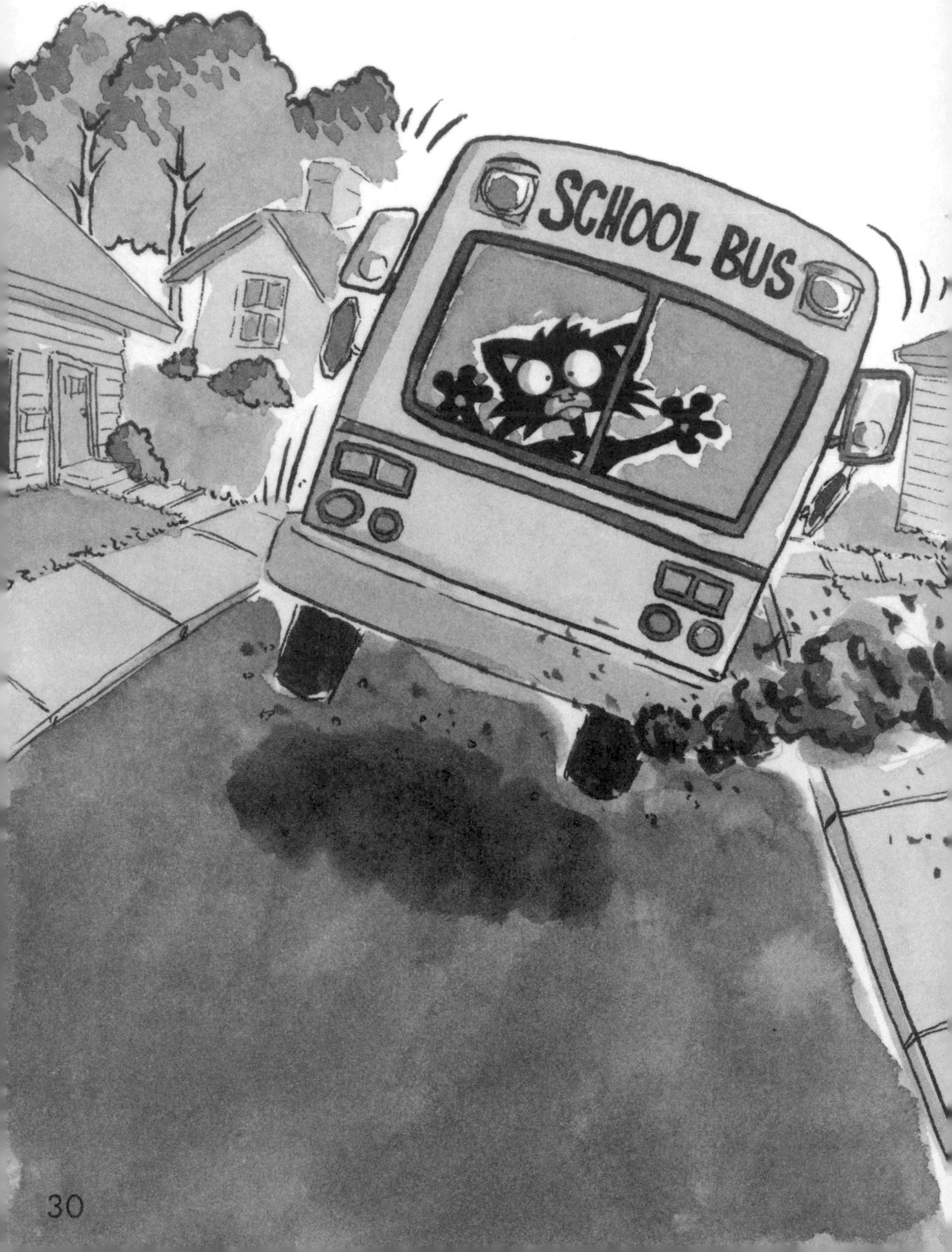
SCHOOL BUS

•CHAPTER THREE•

WELCOME

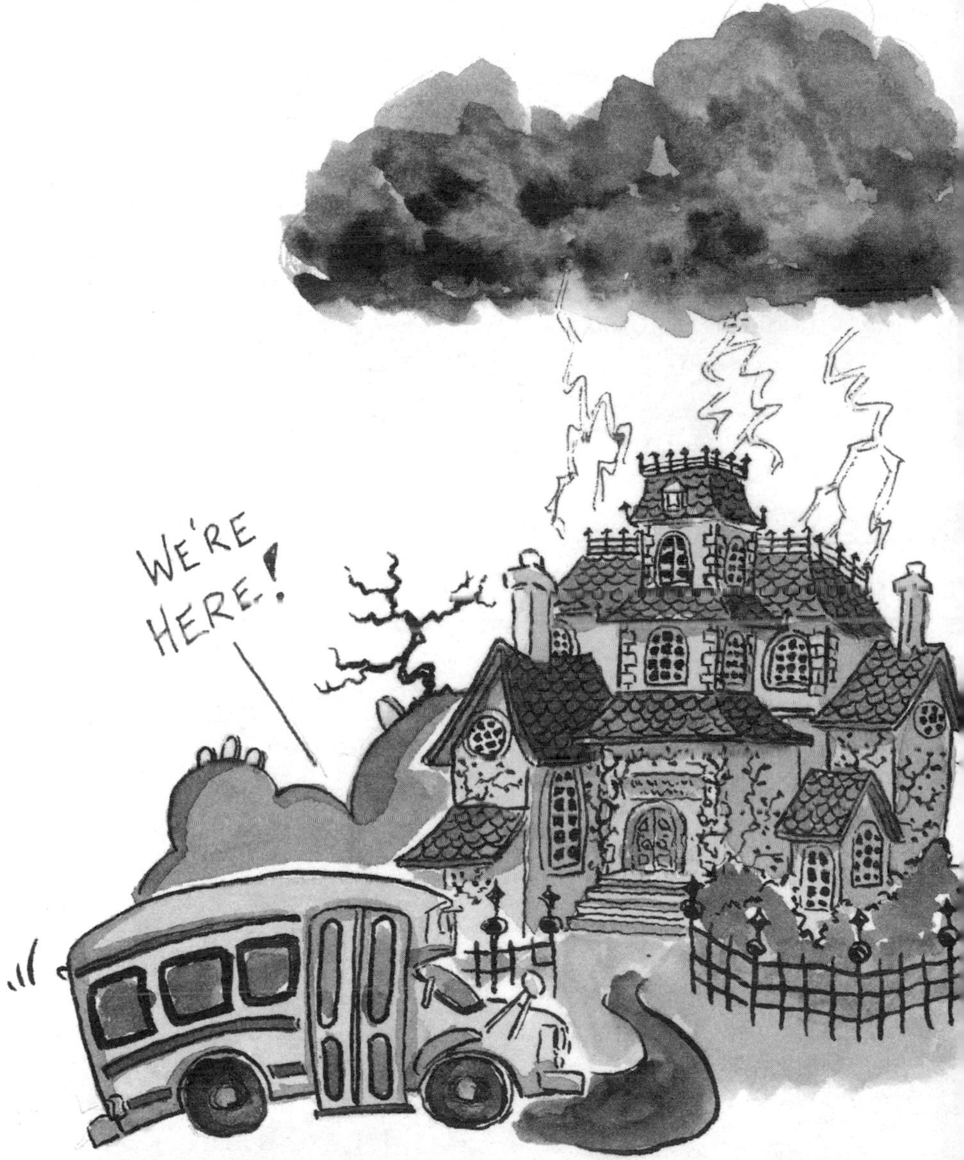
WE'RE HERE!

All right, you guys! Everybody off the bus and welcome to . . .

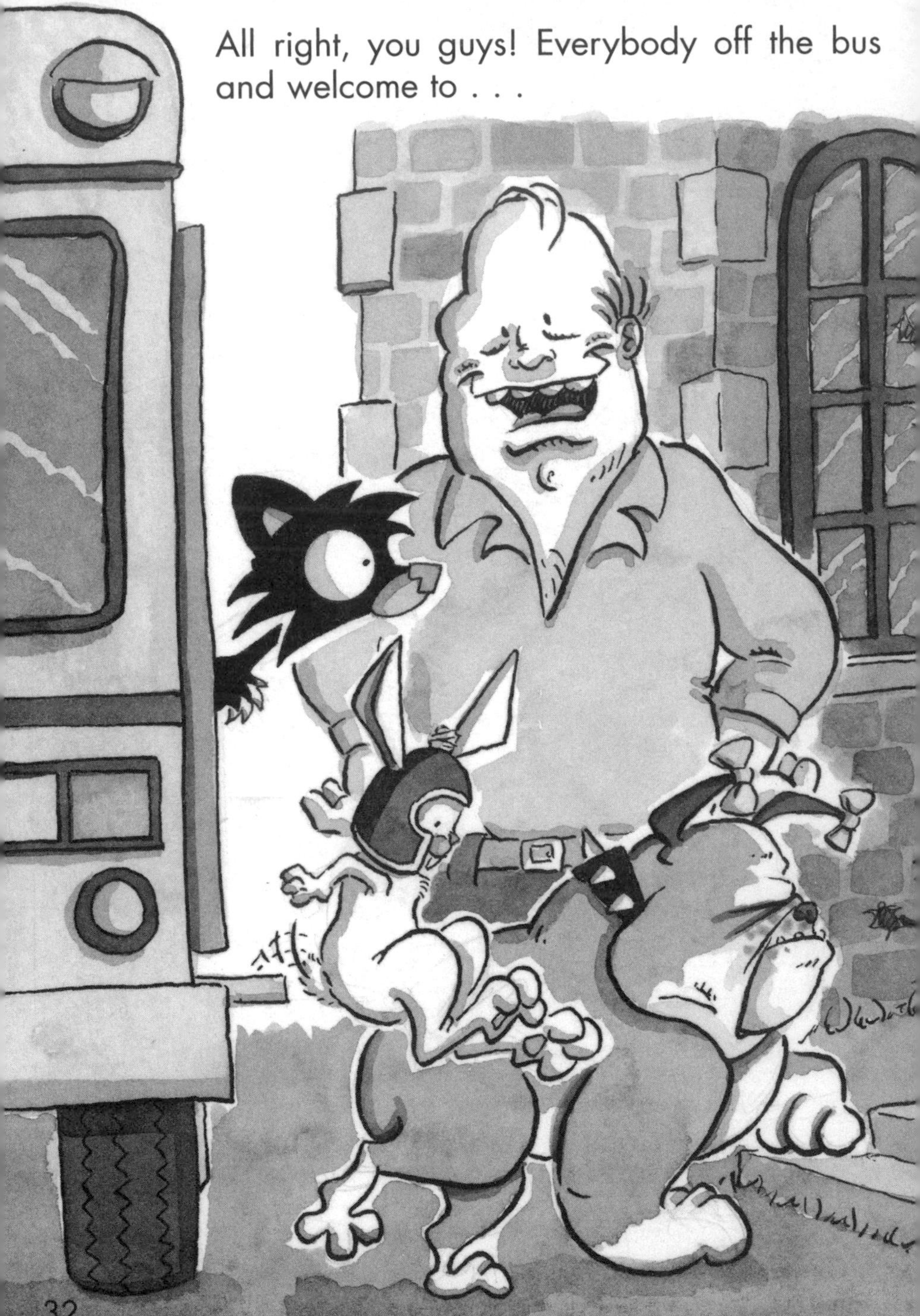

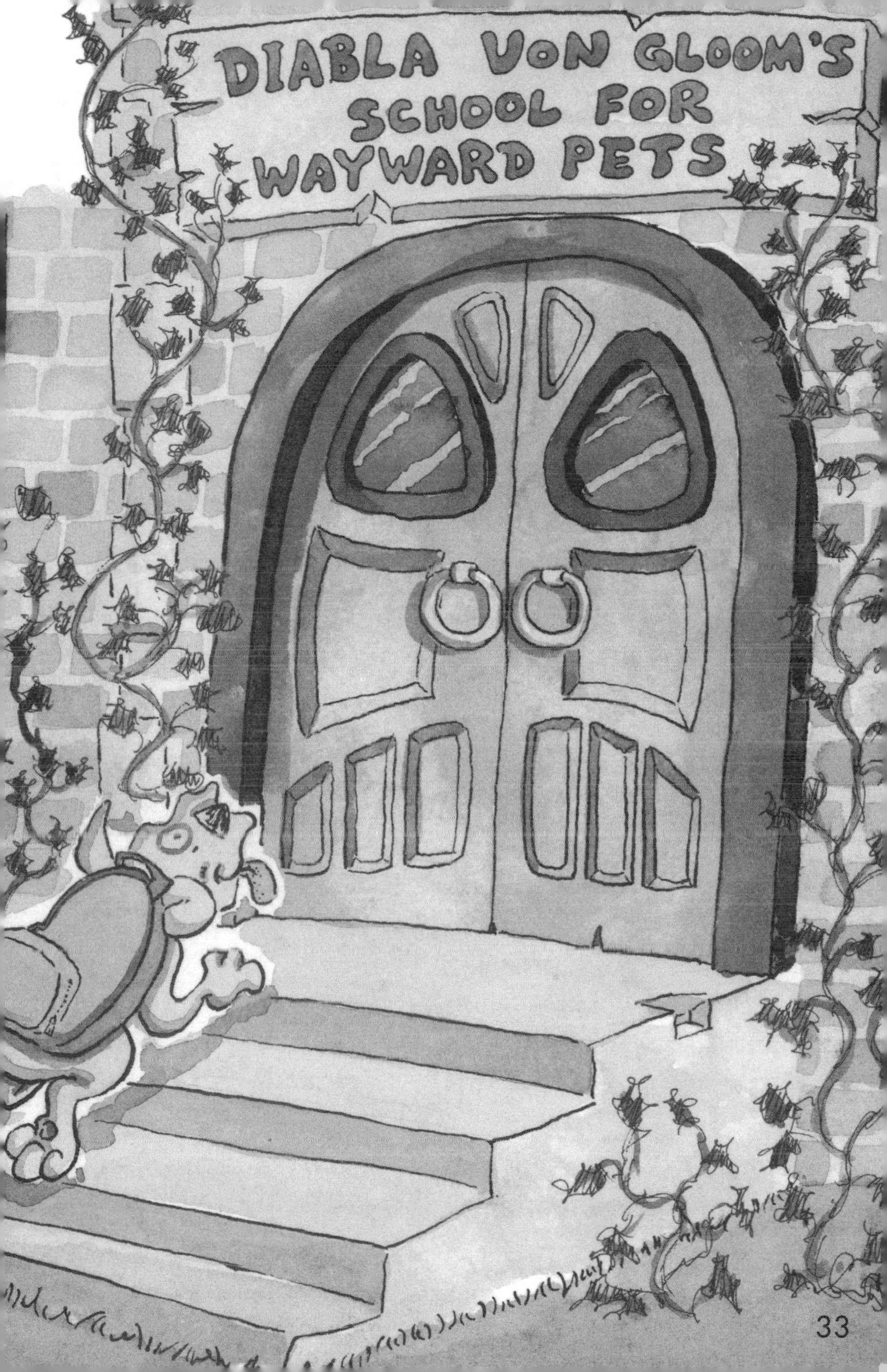
DIABLA VON GLOOM'S
SCHOOL FOR
WAYWARD PETS

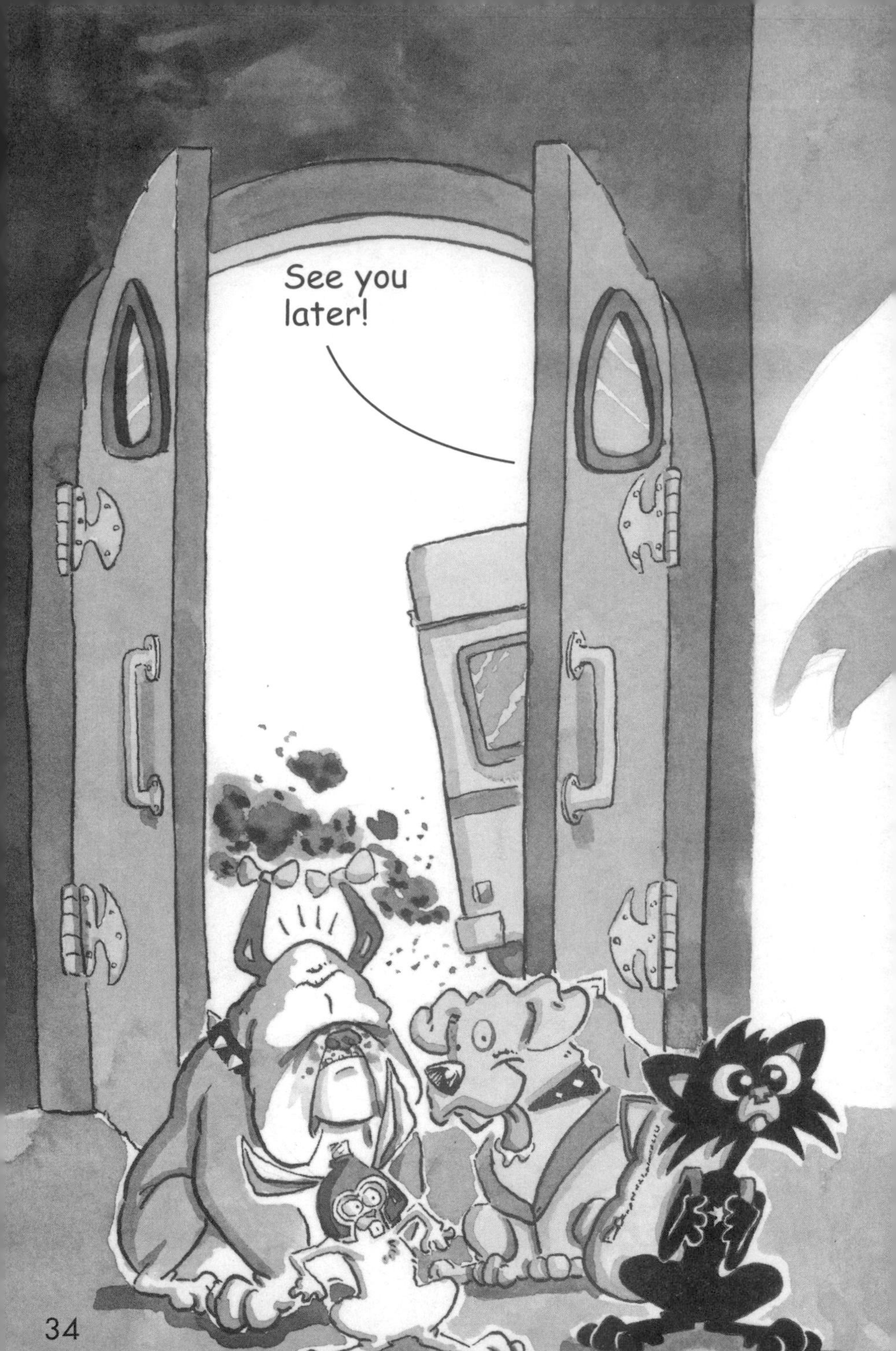
See you later!

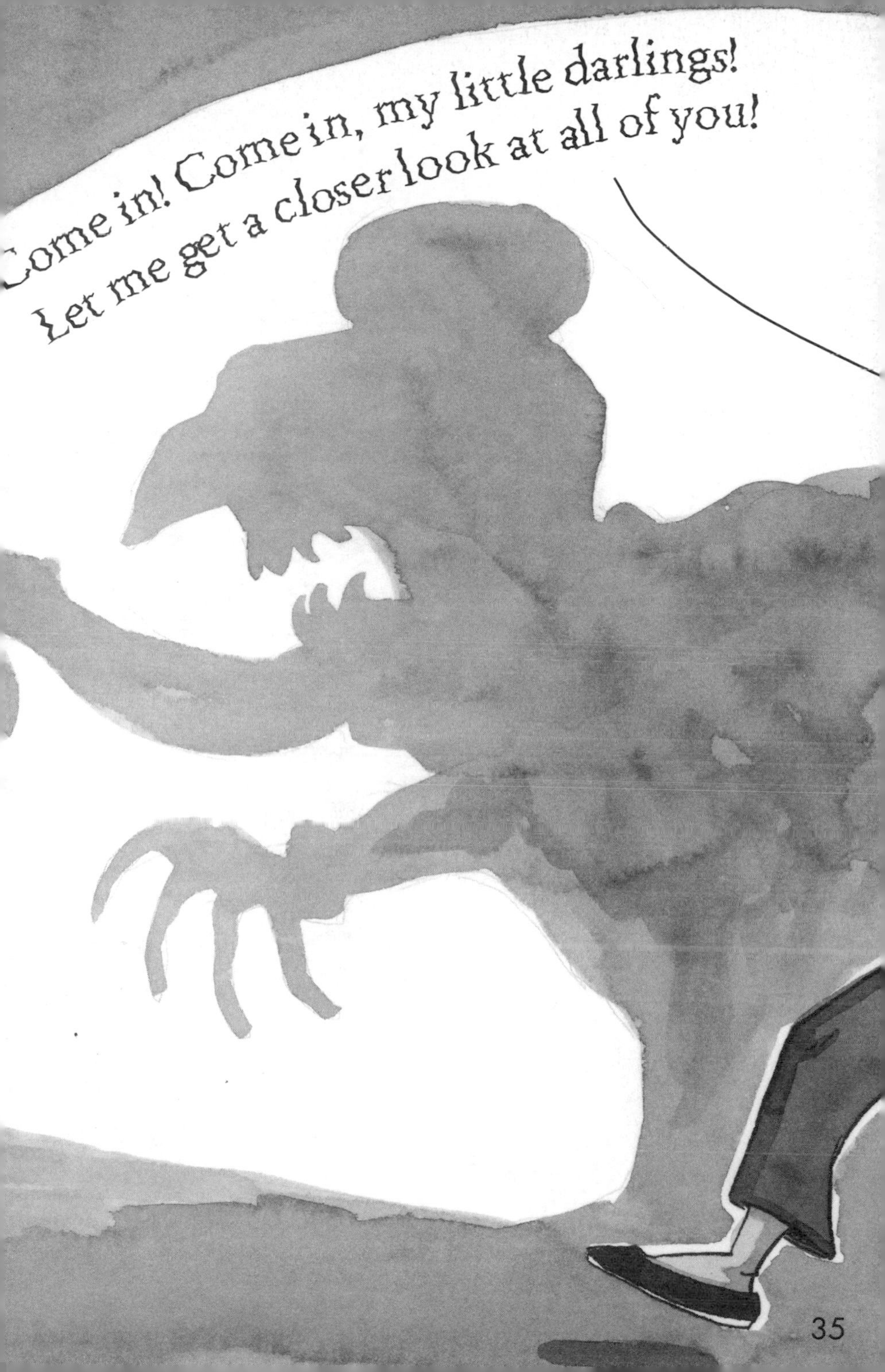
Come in! Come in, my little darlings!
Let me get a closer look at all of you!

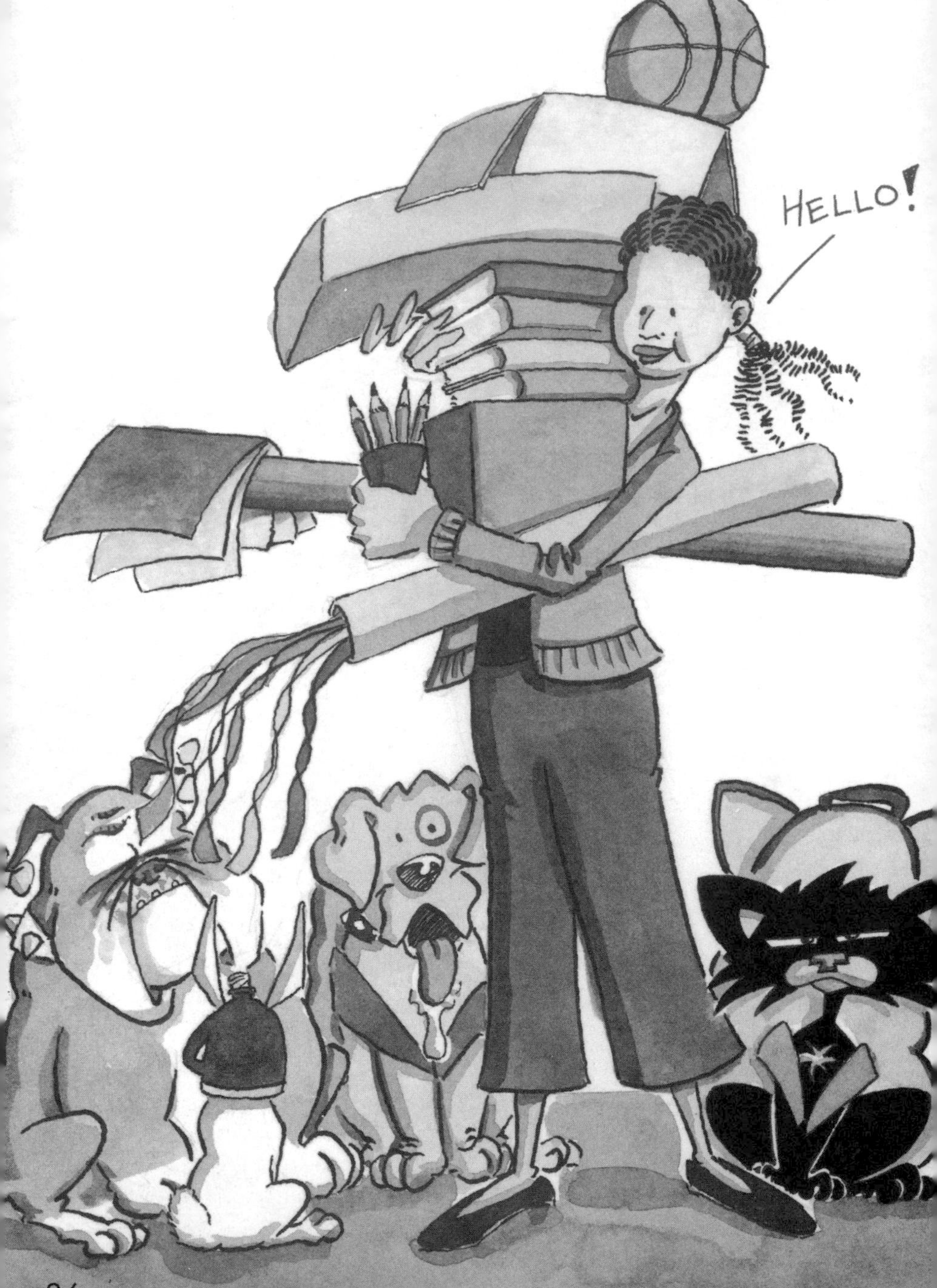
HELLO!

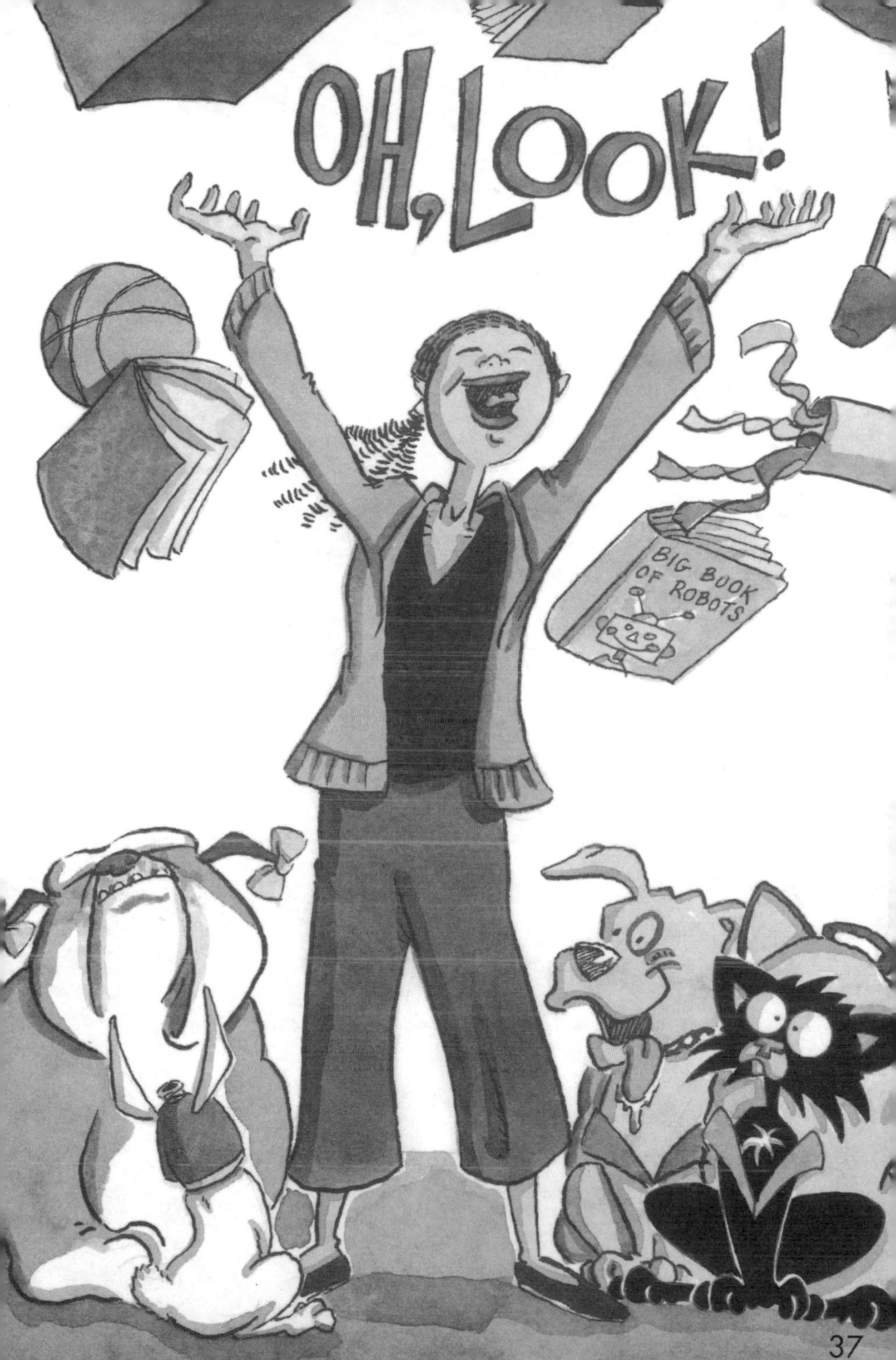
OH, LOOK!
BIG BOOK OF ROBOTS

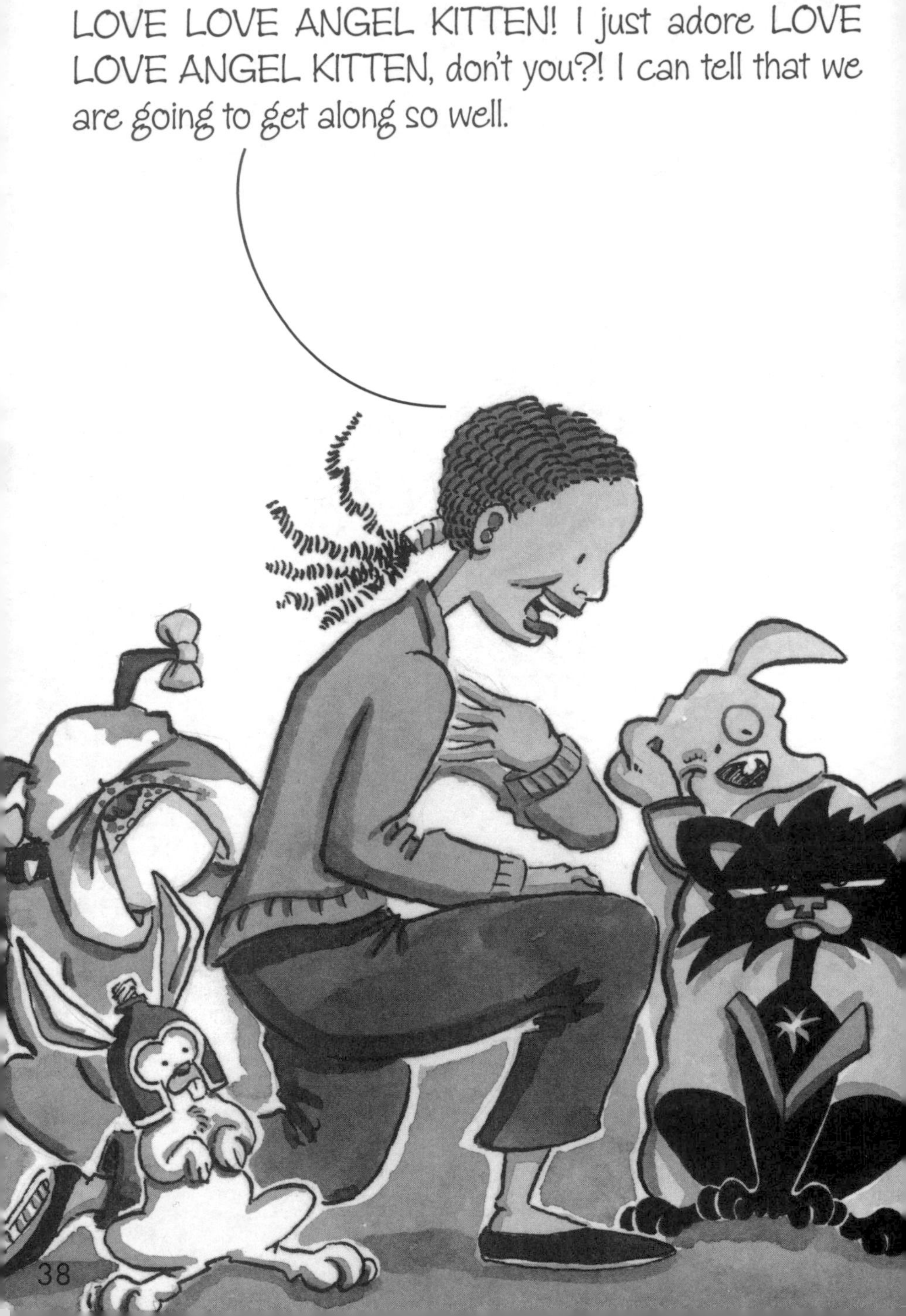
LOVE LOVE ANGEL KITTEN! I just adore LOVE LOVE ANGEL KITTEN, don't you?! I can tell that we are going to get along so well.

Well, pets, my name is Diabla von Gloom. But I want you all to call me Miss Dee. Welcome to my school! School, as you may know, is a place where you go to learn something new. So, I really hope that you all learn something new today.

Let's step into the classroom! And as you all head inside, I want you to understand one thing . . .

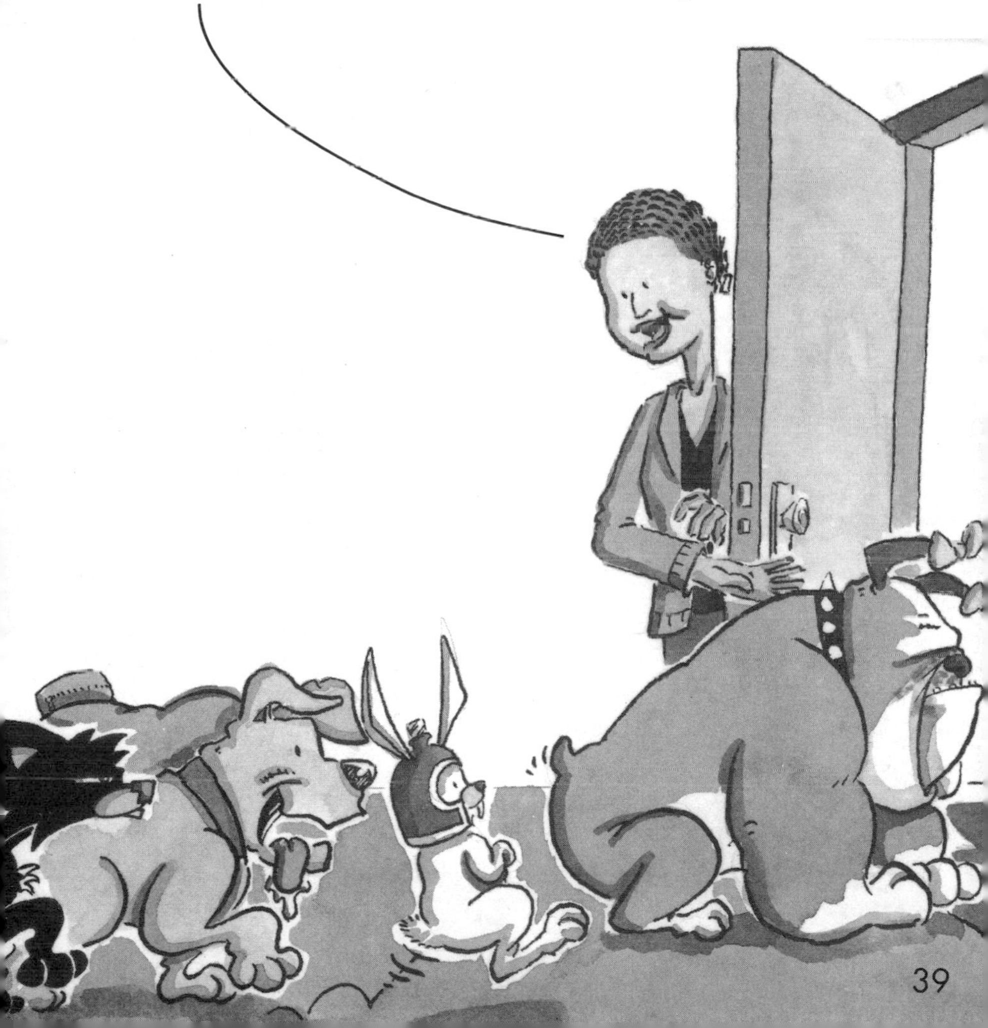

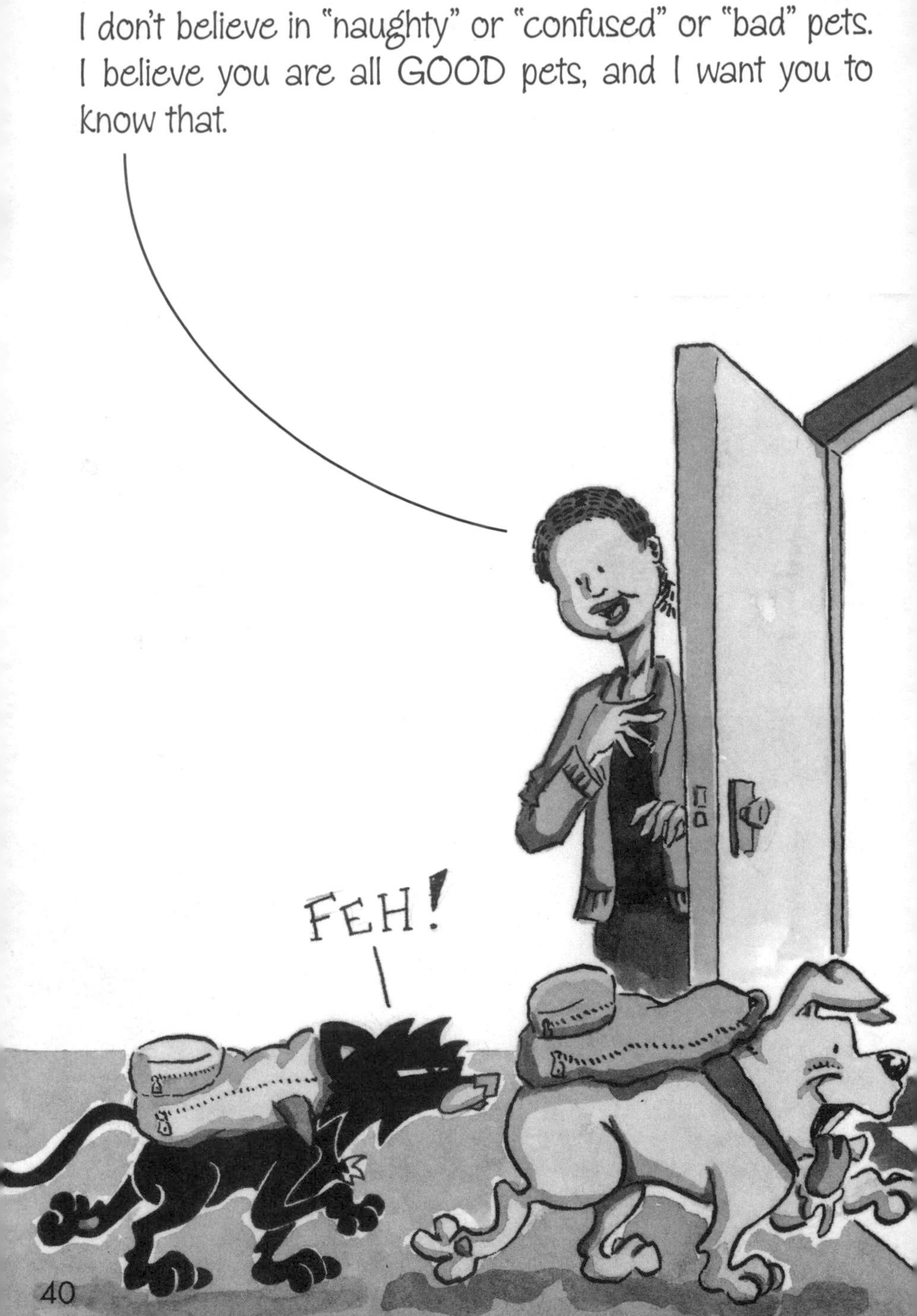
I don't believe in "naughty" or "confused" or "bad" pets. I believe you are all GOOD pets, and I want you to know that.
FEH!

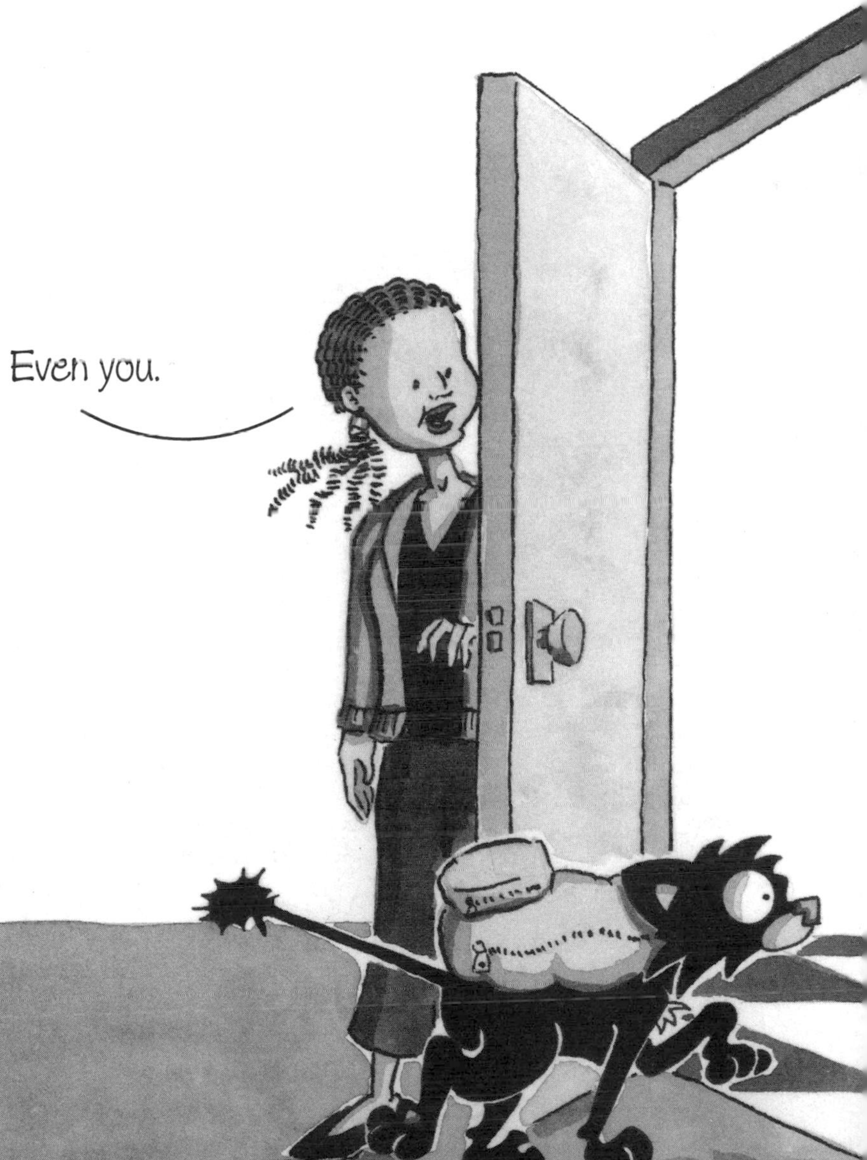
Even you.

•CHAPTER FOUR•

CIRCLE TIME

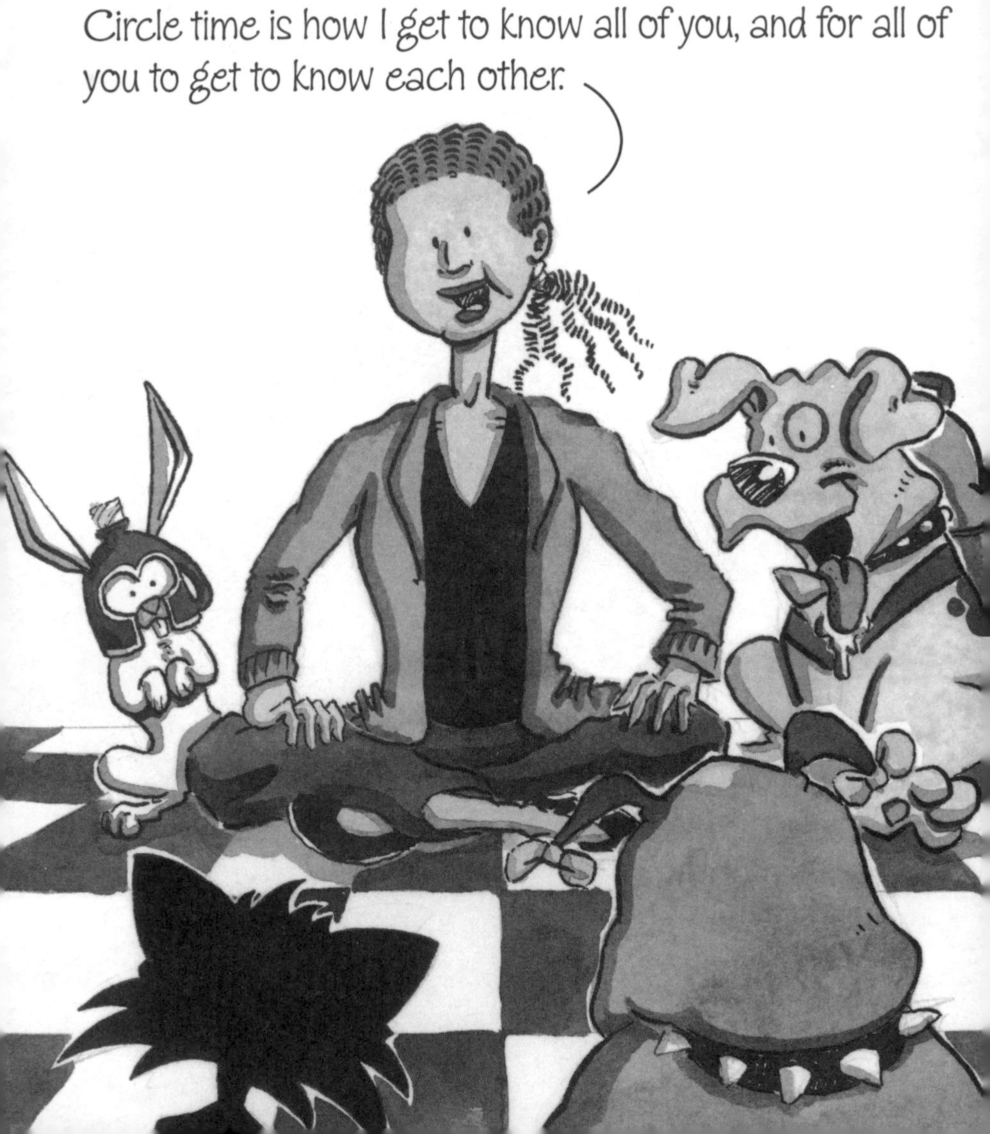
Circle time is how I get to know all of you, and for all of you to get to know each other.

Let's start with you, Petunia. Tell us what's on your mind.

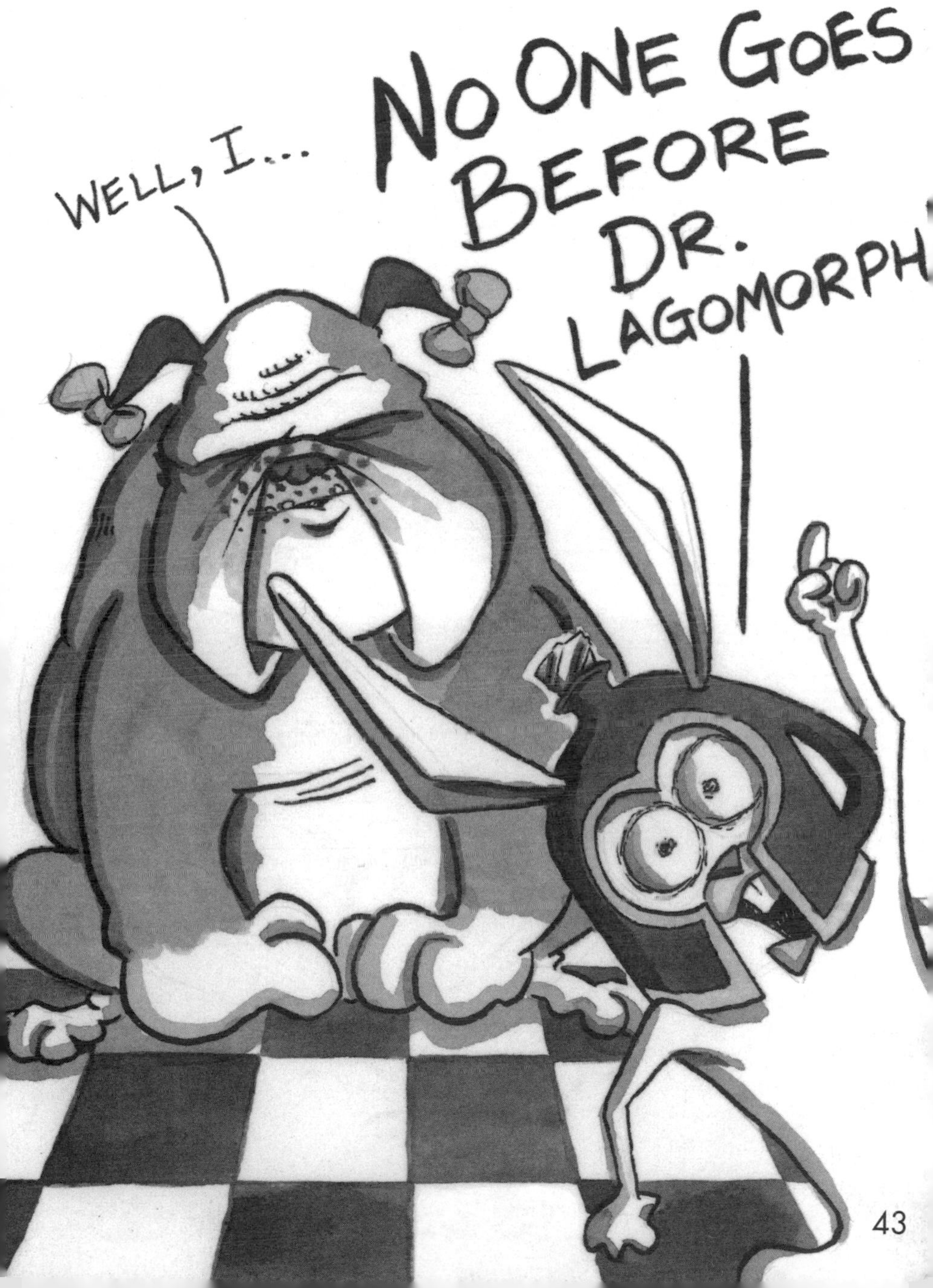
WELL, I...
NO ONE GOES BEFORE DR. LAGOMORPH

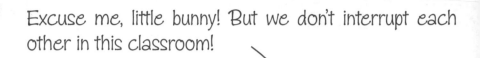

Excuse me, little bunny! But we don't interrupt each other in this classroom!

But I'm Dr. Lagomorph! I'm a diabolical mutant supervillain!

That's no excuse. Sit down, please!

Go ahead, Petunia.

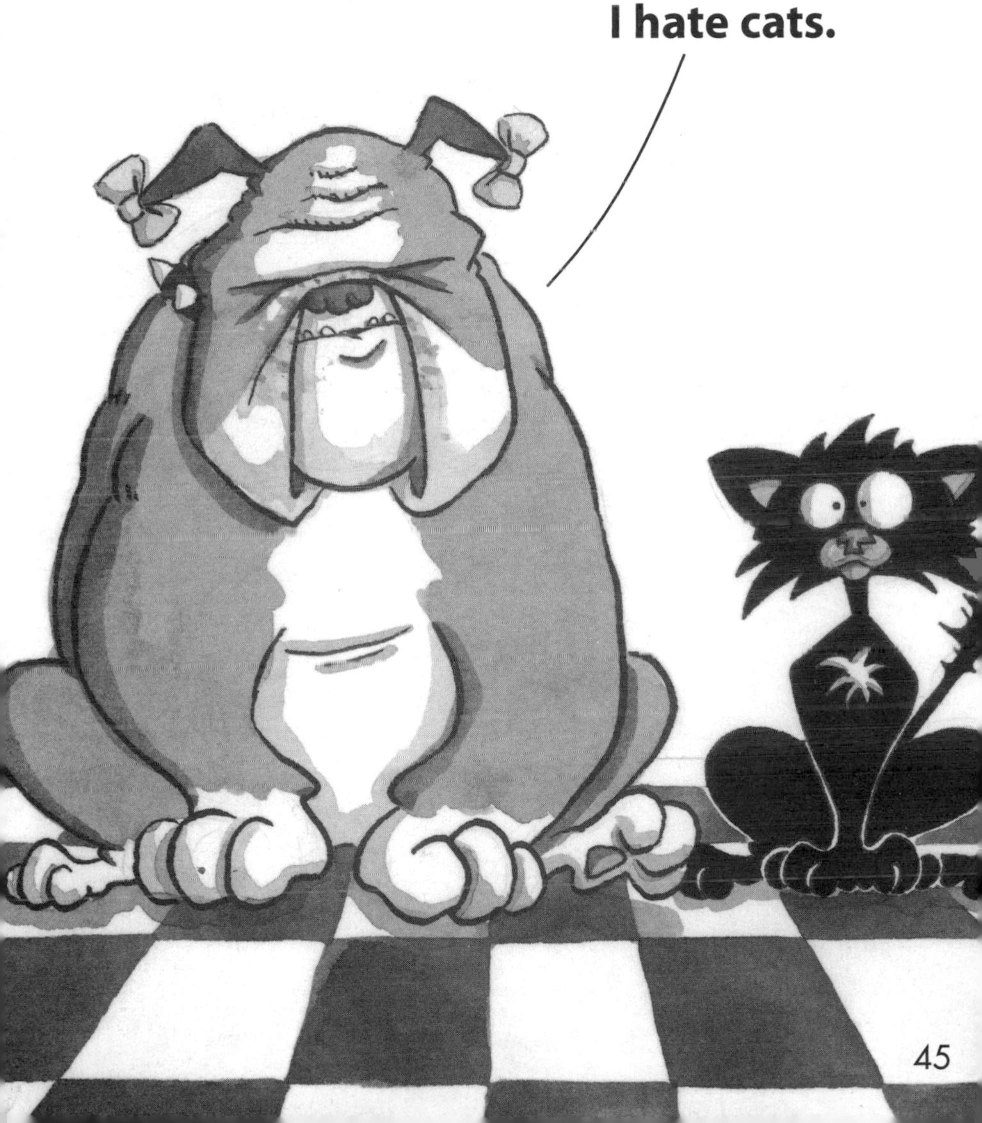
I hate cats.

I just hate them! I hate them so much! I hate their eyes! I hate their noses! I hate their goofy-looking whiskers! When I see them, I just want to punch them!

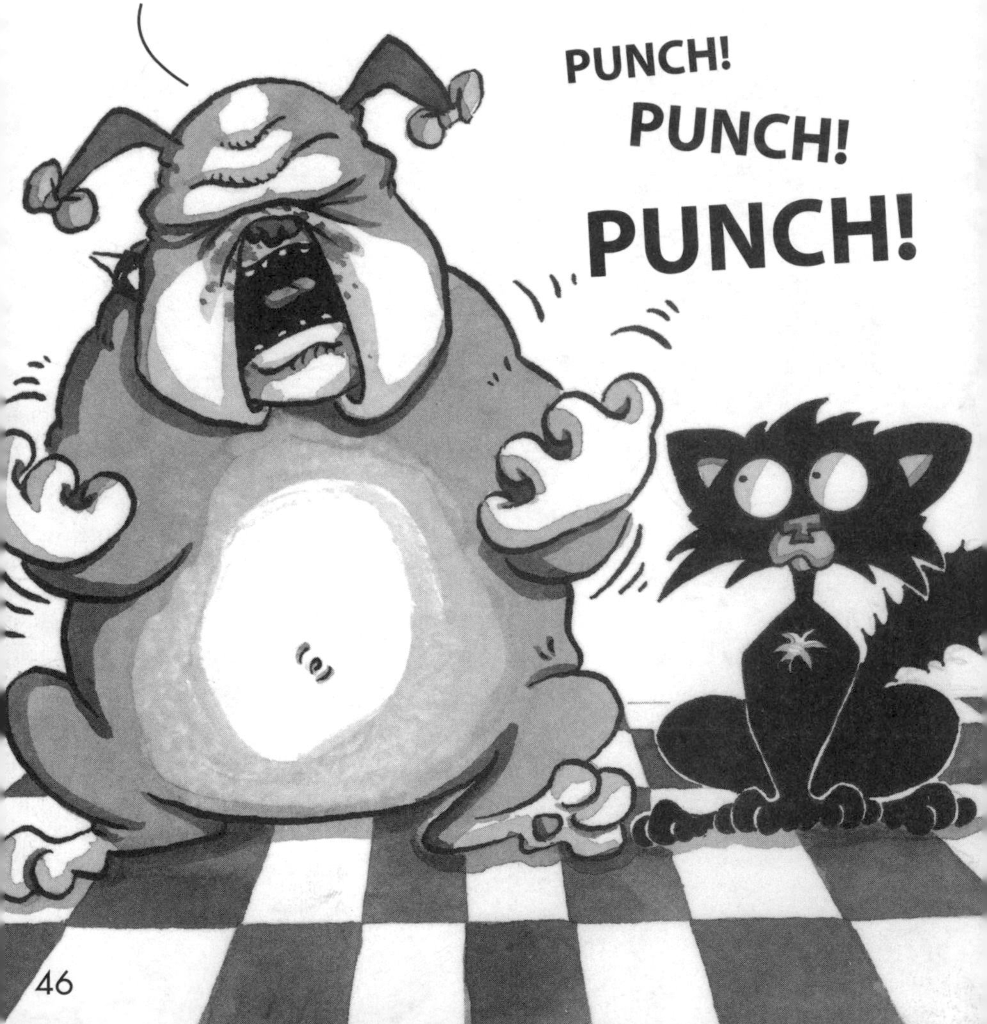
PUNCH!
PUNCH!
PUNCH!

I . . . I . . . just want to bite their heads off and chew their faces like gum! CHEW! CHEW! CHEW! I want to pick them up and throw them all into active volcanos!

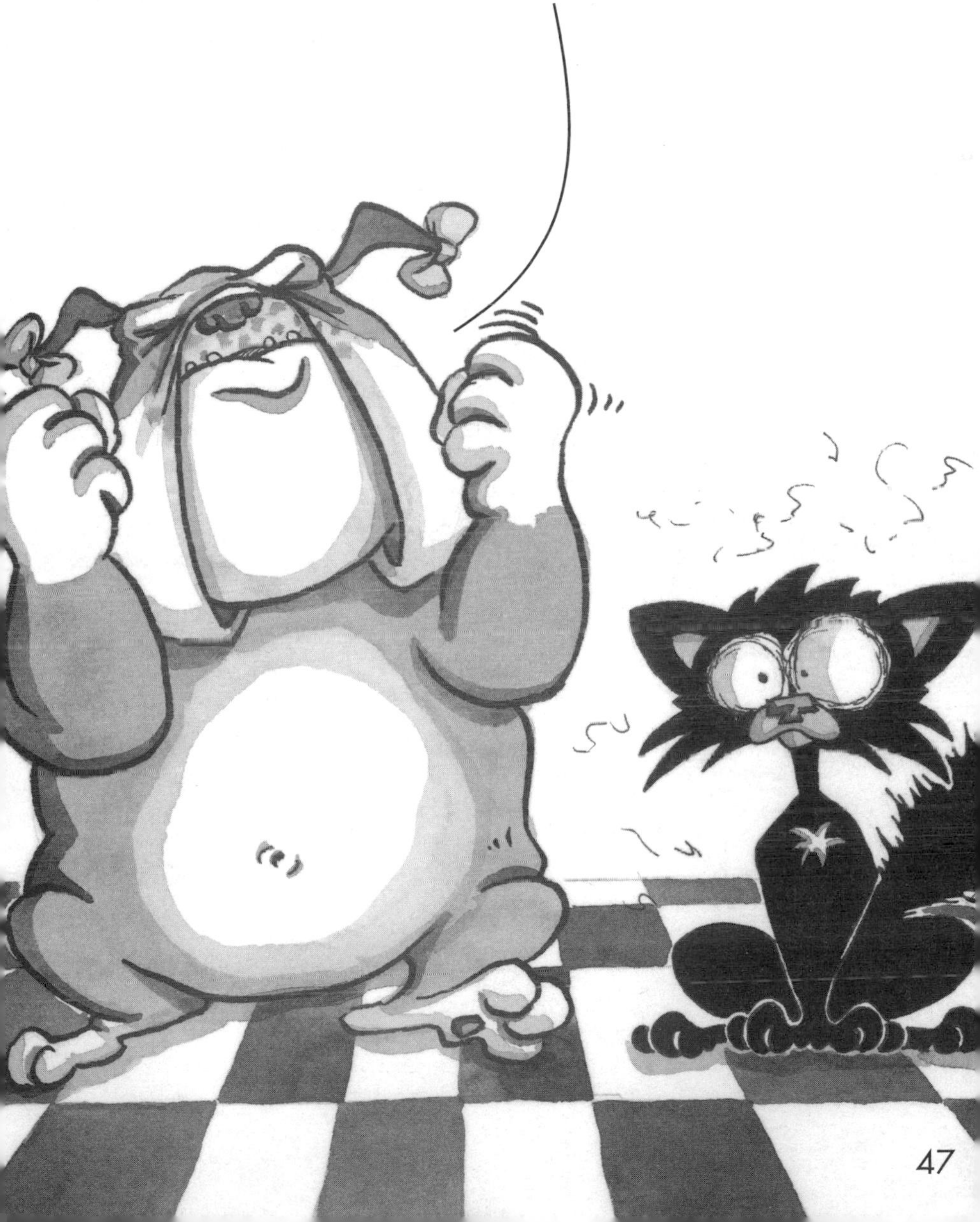

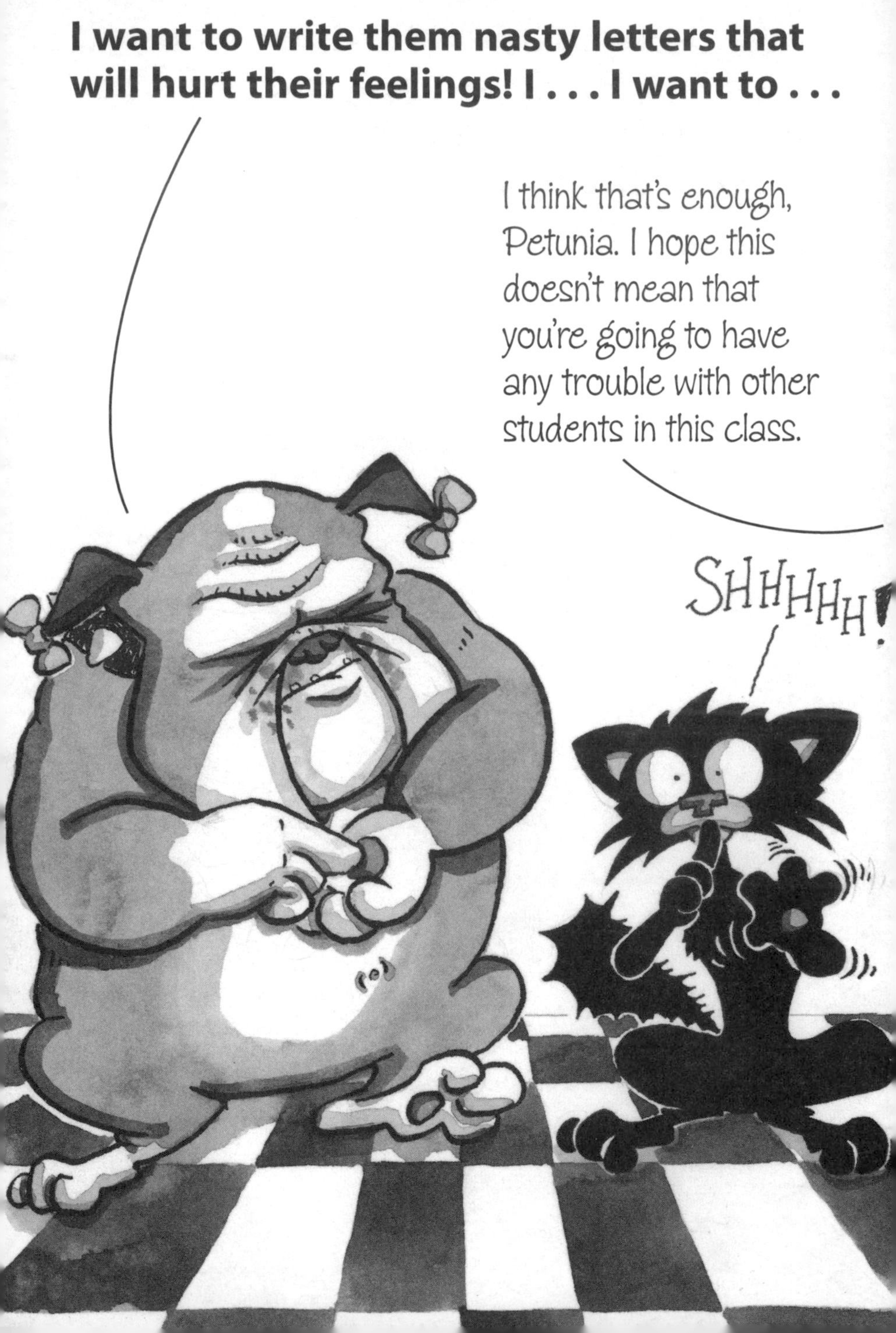
I want to write them nasty letters that will hurt their feelings! I . . . I want to . . .
I think that's enough, Petunia. I hope this doesn't mean that you're going to have any trouble with other students in this class.
SHHHHH!

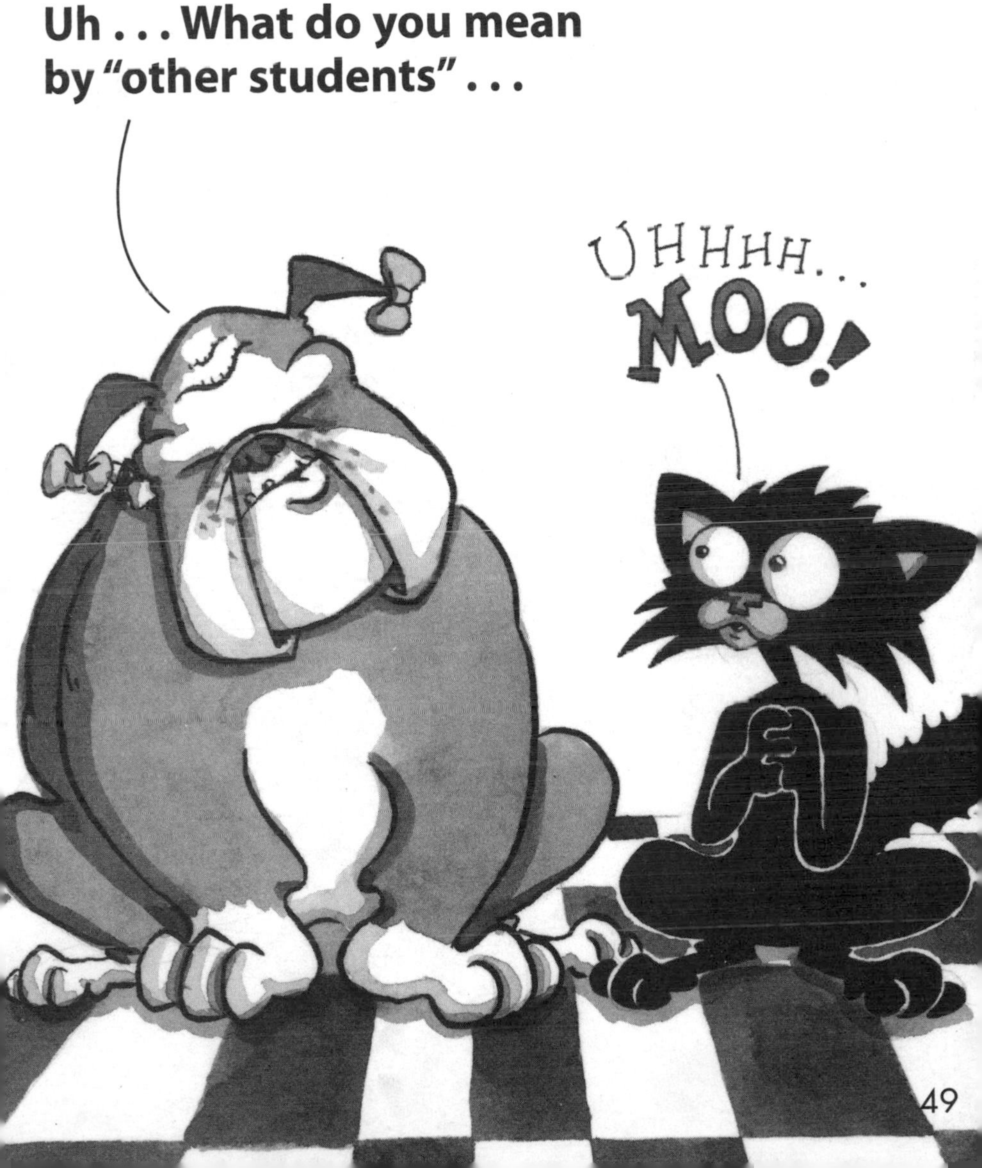
Uh . . . What do you mean
by "other students" . . .
UHHHH. . .
MOO!

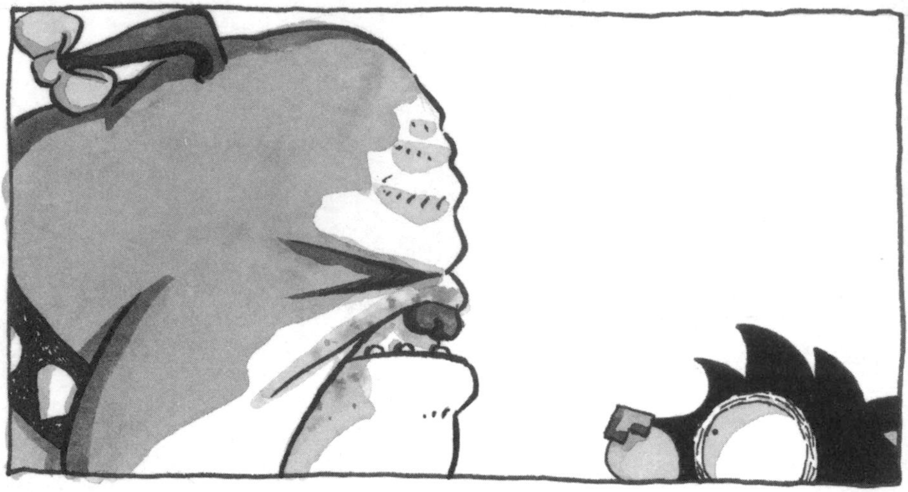

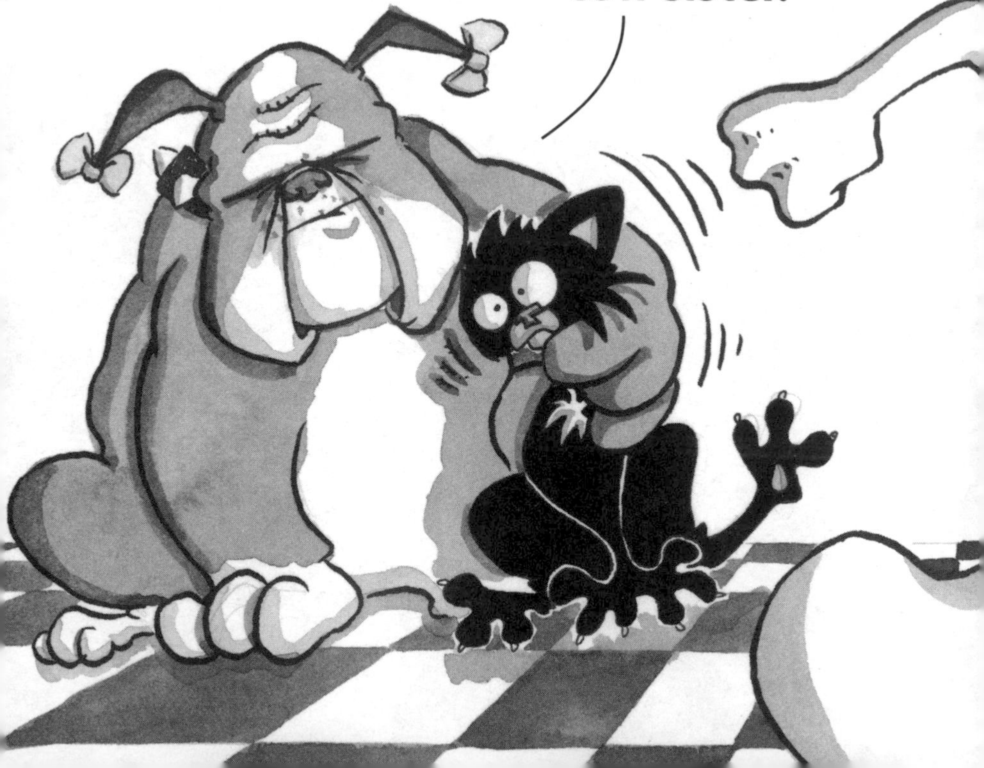
I hear ya,
cow sister.

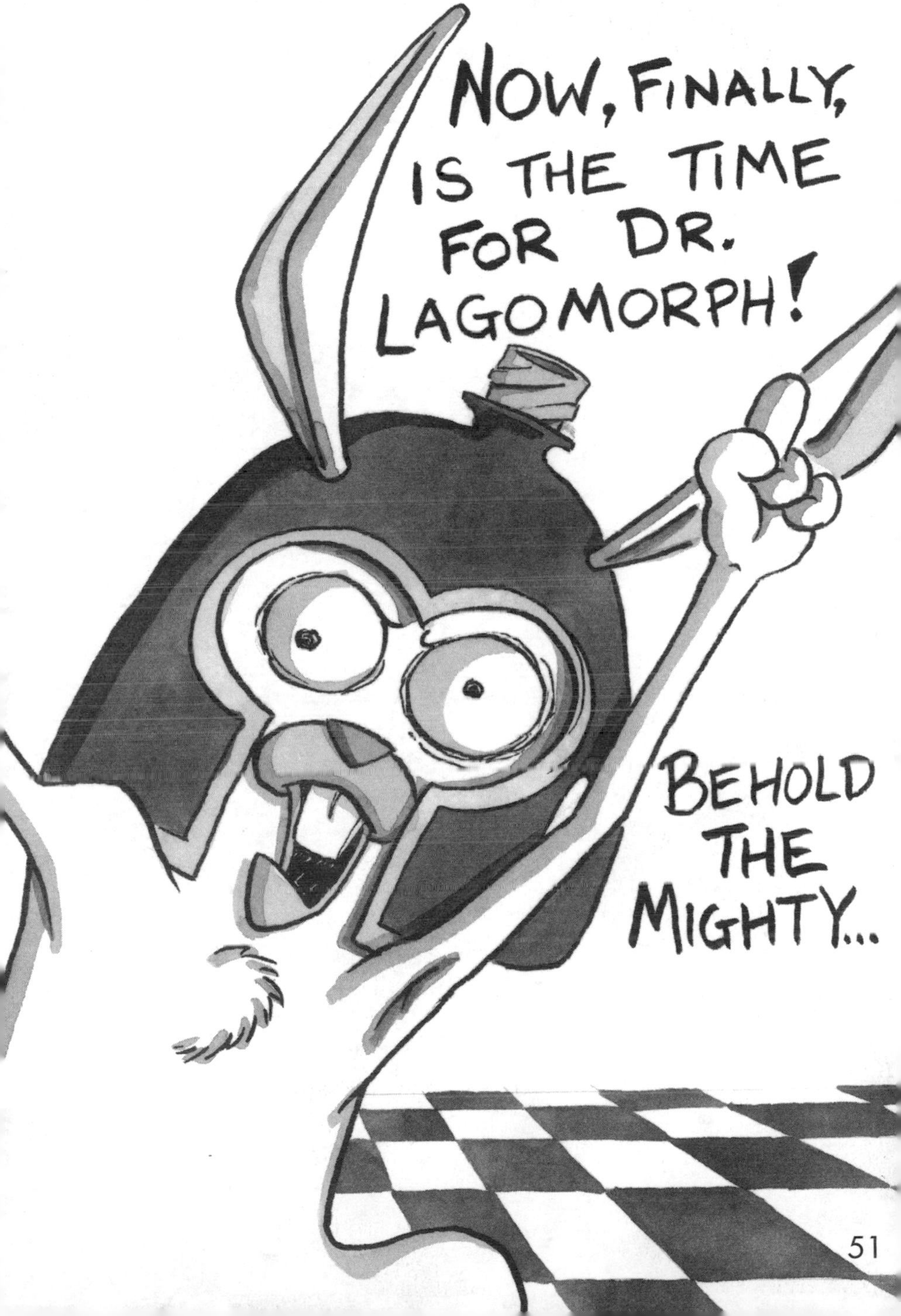
NOW, FINALLY, IS THE TIME FOR DR. LAGOMORPH!
BEHOLD THE MIGHTY...

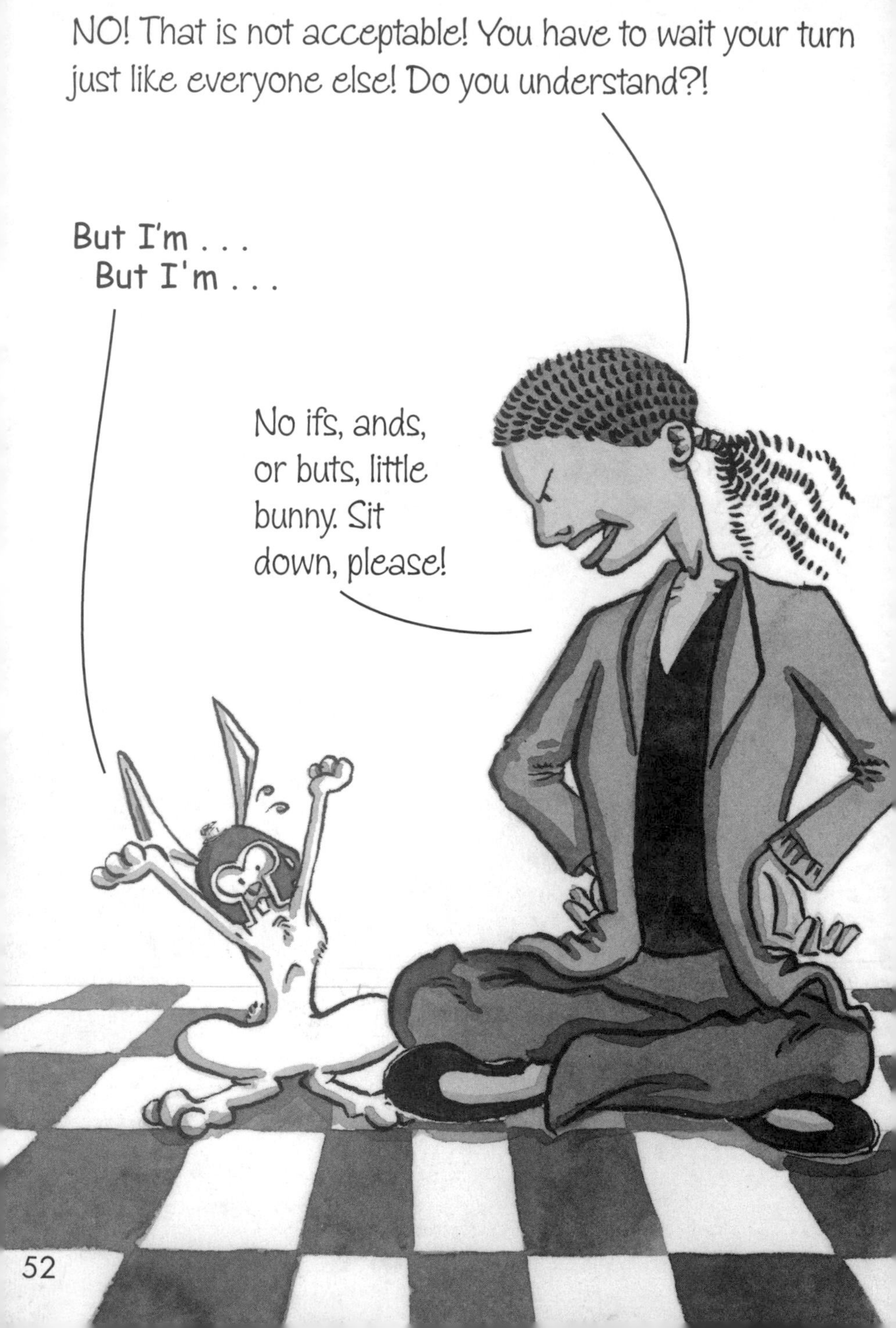
NO! That is not acceptable! You have to wait your turn just like everyone else! Do you understand?!
But I'm . . .
But I'm . . .
No ifs, ands, or buts, little bunny. Sit down, please!

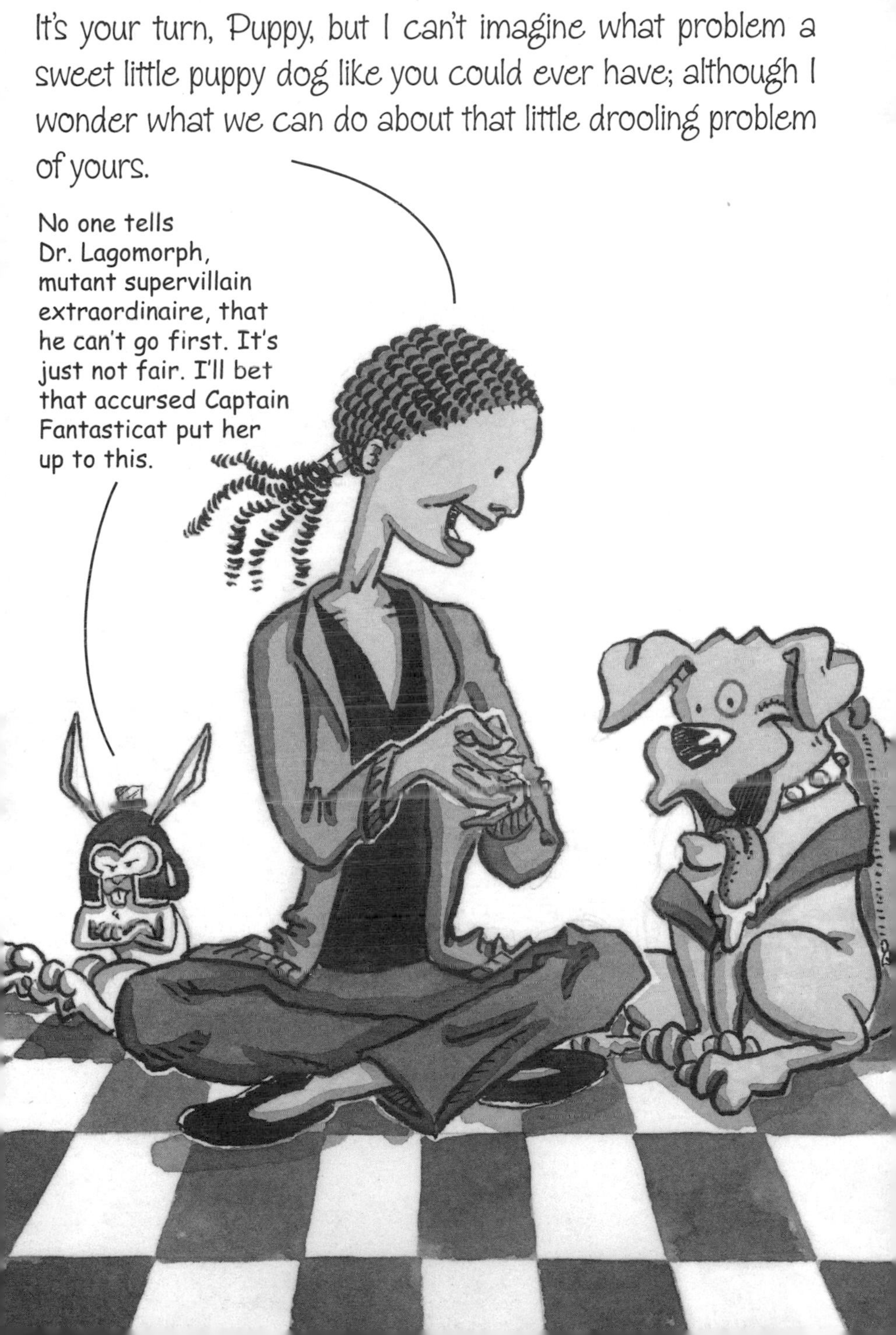
It's your turn, Puppy, but I can't imagine what problem a sweet little puppy dog like you could ever have; although I wonder what we can do about that little drooling problem of yours.
No one tells Dr. Lagomorph, mutant supervillain extraordinaire, that he can't go first. It's just not fair. I'll bet that accursed Captain Fantasticat put her up to this.

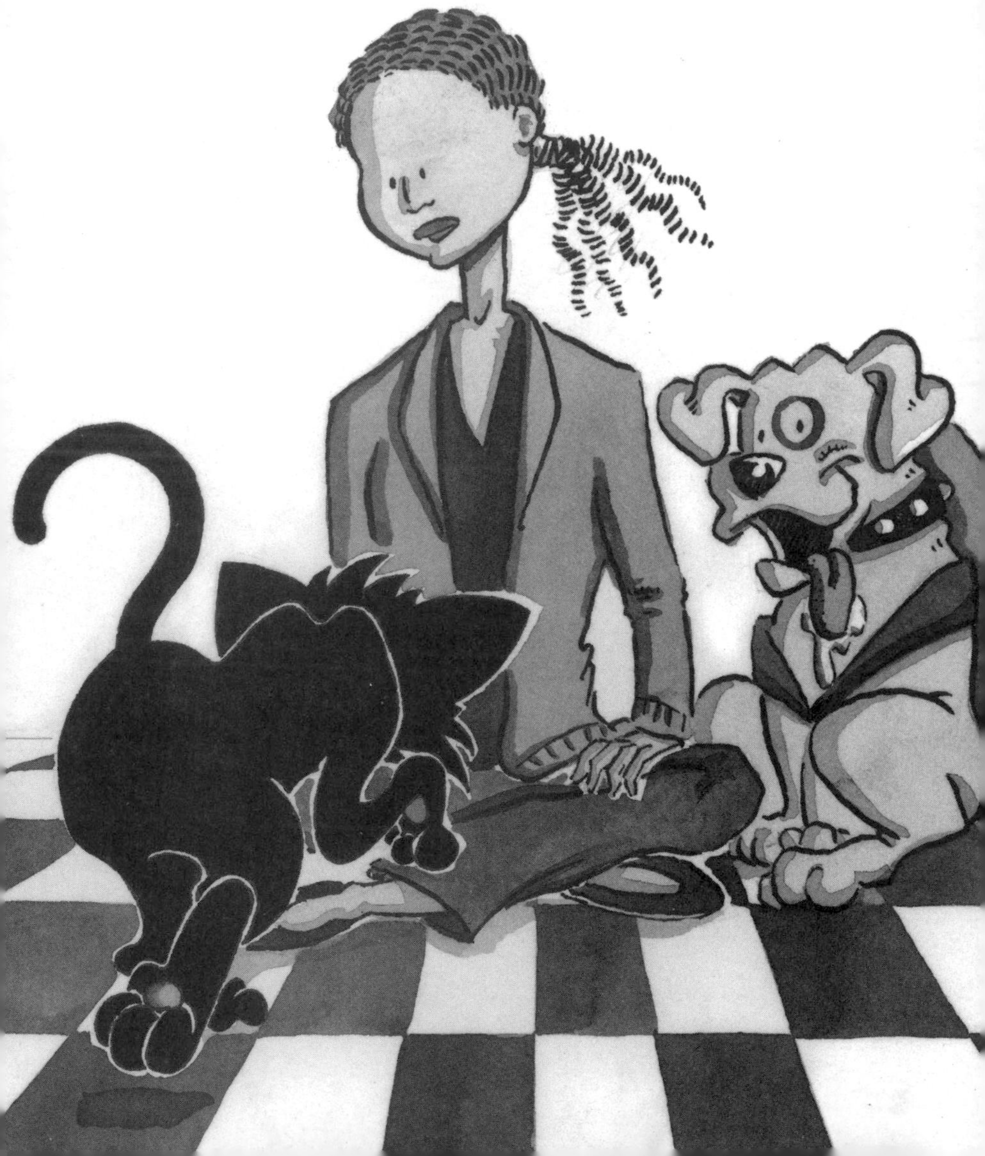

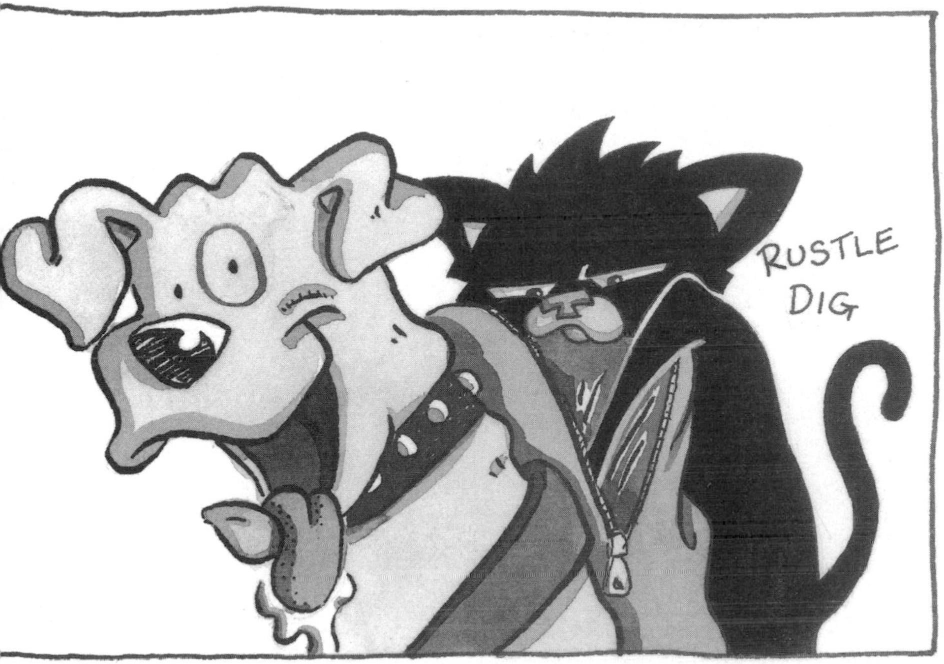
RUSTLE
DIG

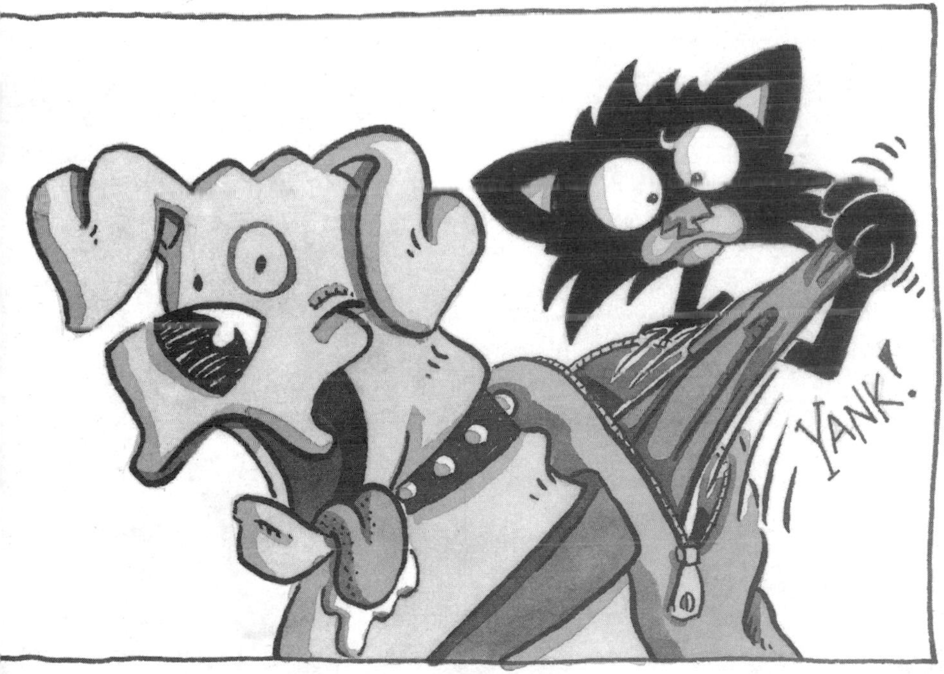
YANK!

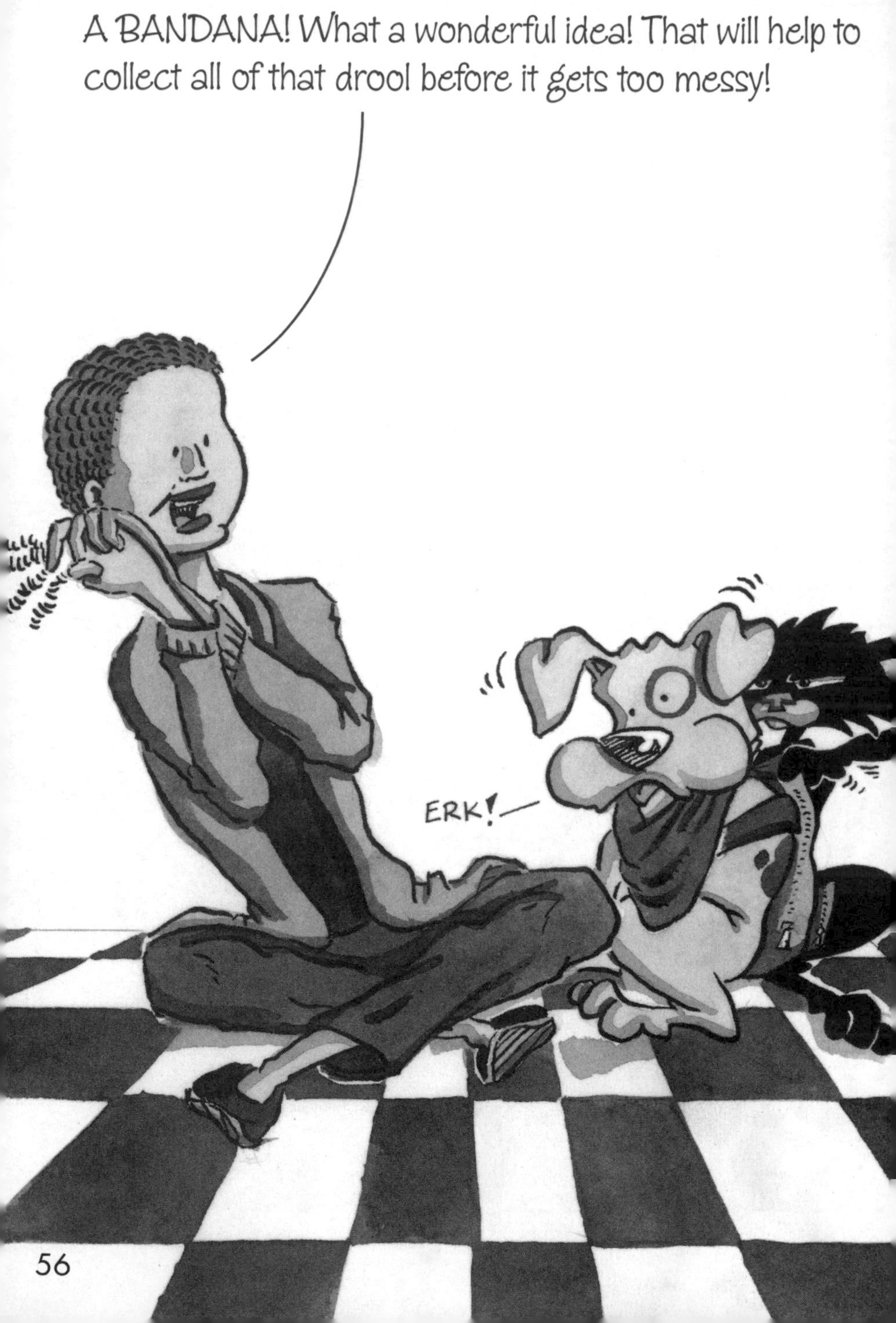
A BANDANA! What a wonderful idea! That will help to collect all of that drool before it gets too messy!
ERK!

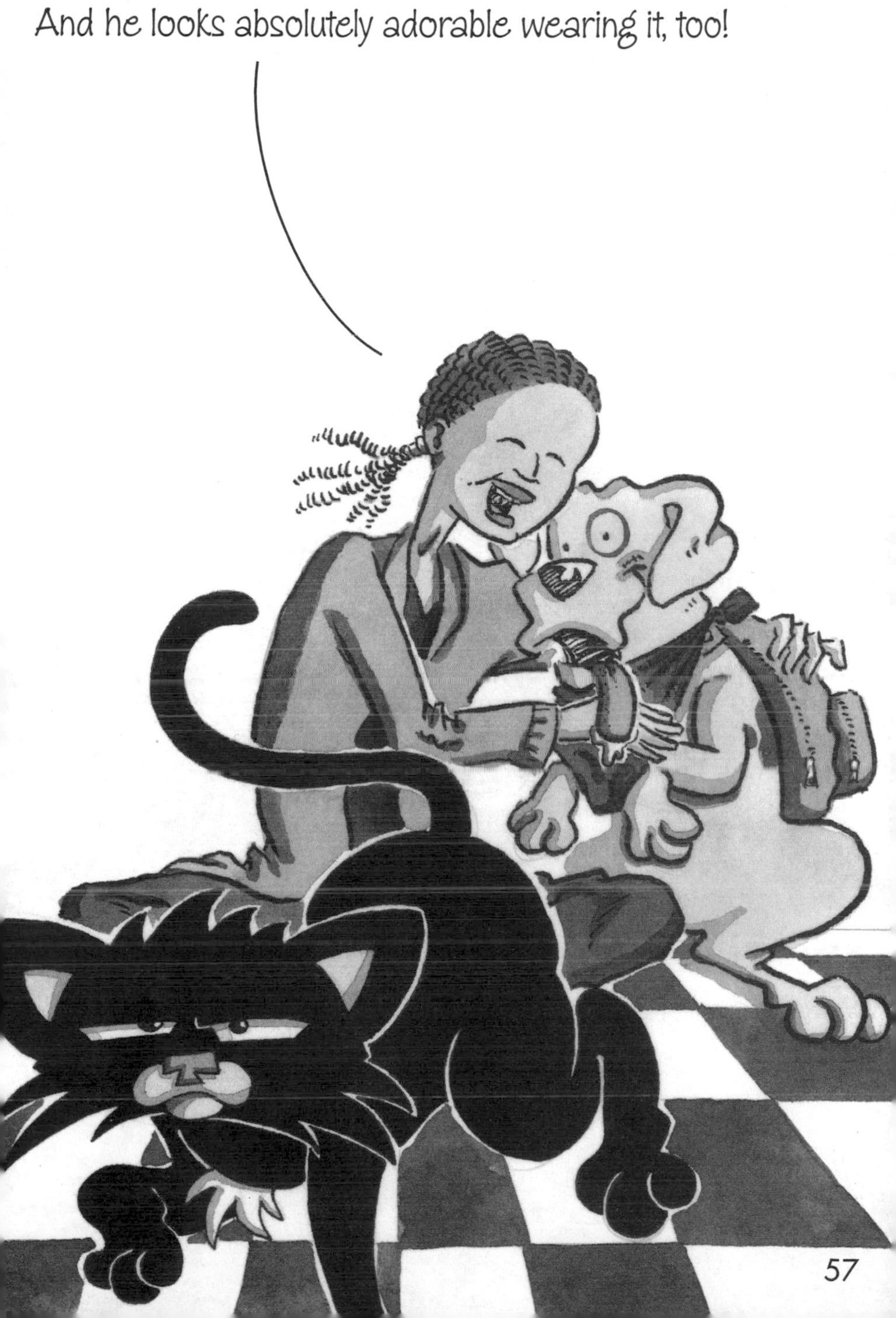
And he looks absolutely adorable wearing it, too!

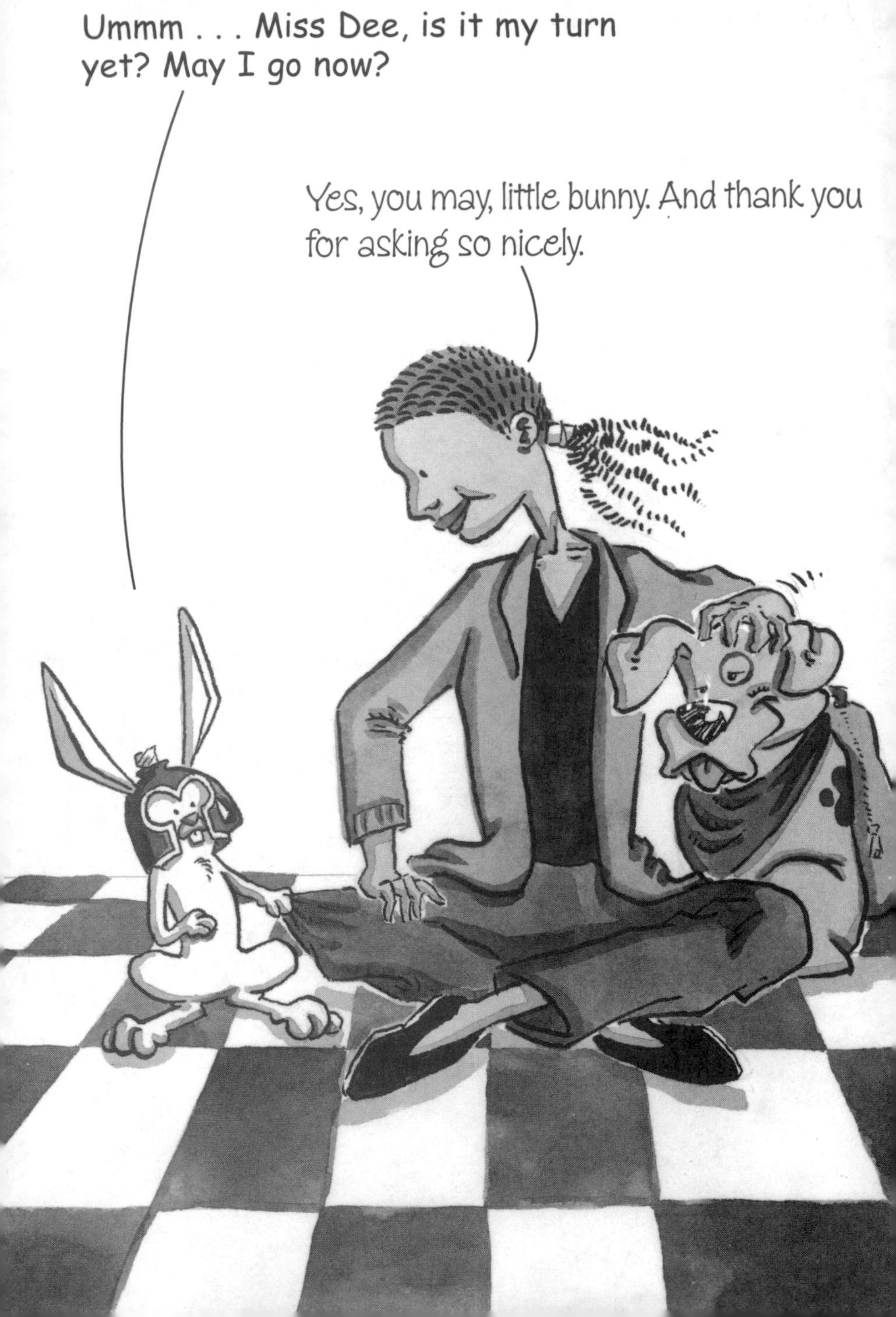
Ummm . . . Miss Dee, is it my turn yet? May I go now?
Yes, you may, little bunny. And thank you for asking so nicely.

NOW IS THE TIME FOR DR. LAGOMORPH! BEHOLD THE MIGHTY POWER OF THE WORLD'S MOST AWESOME MUTANT SUPER-VILLAIN! TREMBLE BEFORE MY DREADFUL AUTHORITY! COWER BEFORE MY FIERCE SUPREMACY! CRINGE BEFORE MY FORMIDABLE EFFICACY! FOR I AM DR. LAGO-MORPH!

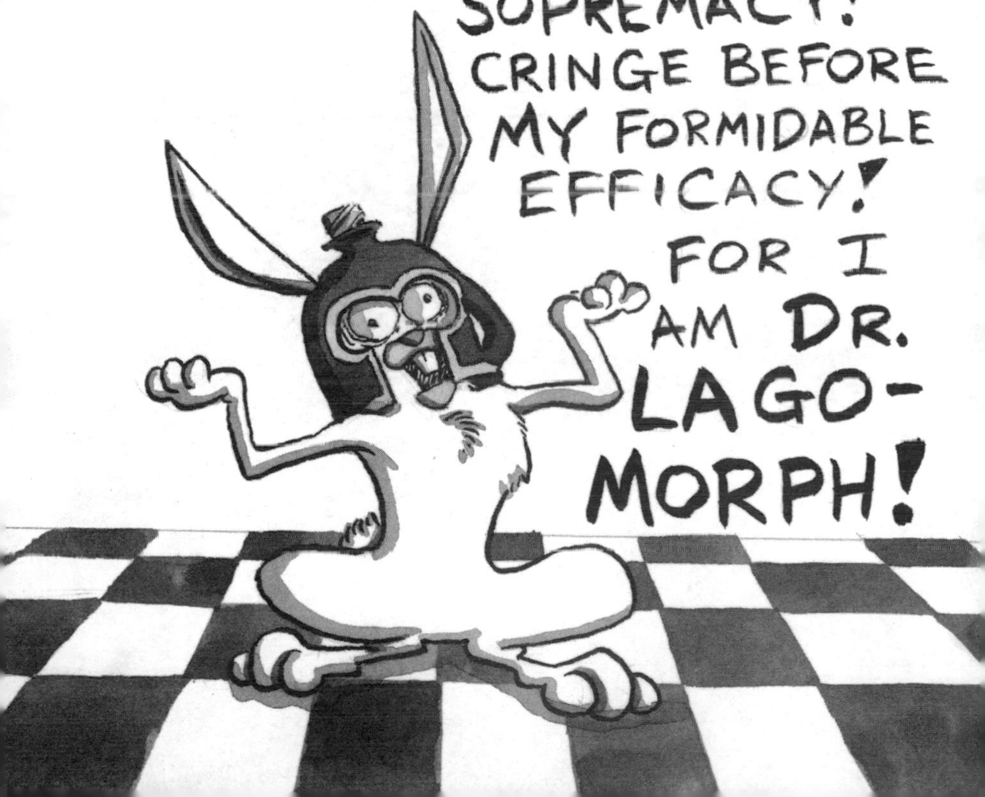

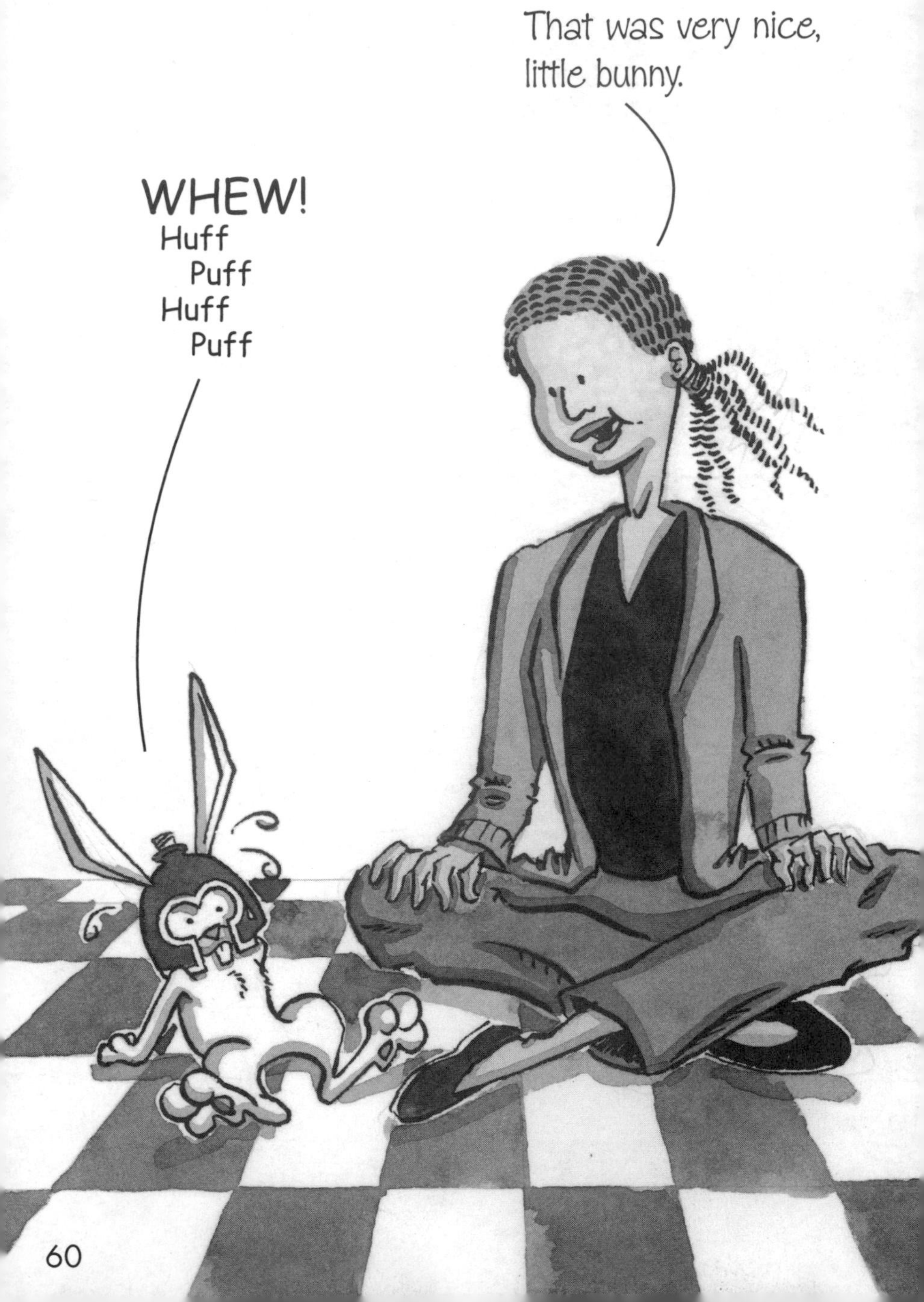
That was very nice, little bunny.
WHEW!
Huff
Puff
Huff
Puff

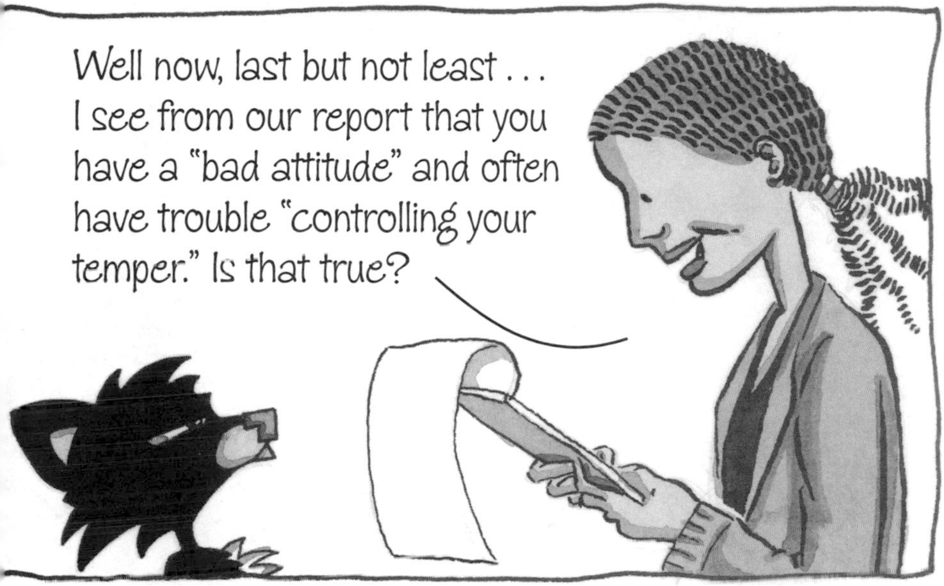
Well now, last but not least . . .
I see from our report that you have a "bad attitude" and often have trouble "controlling your temper." Is that true?

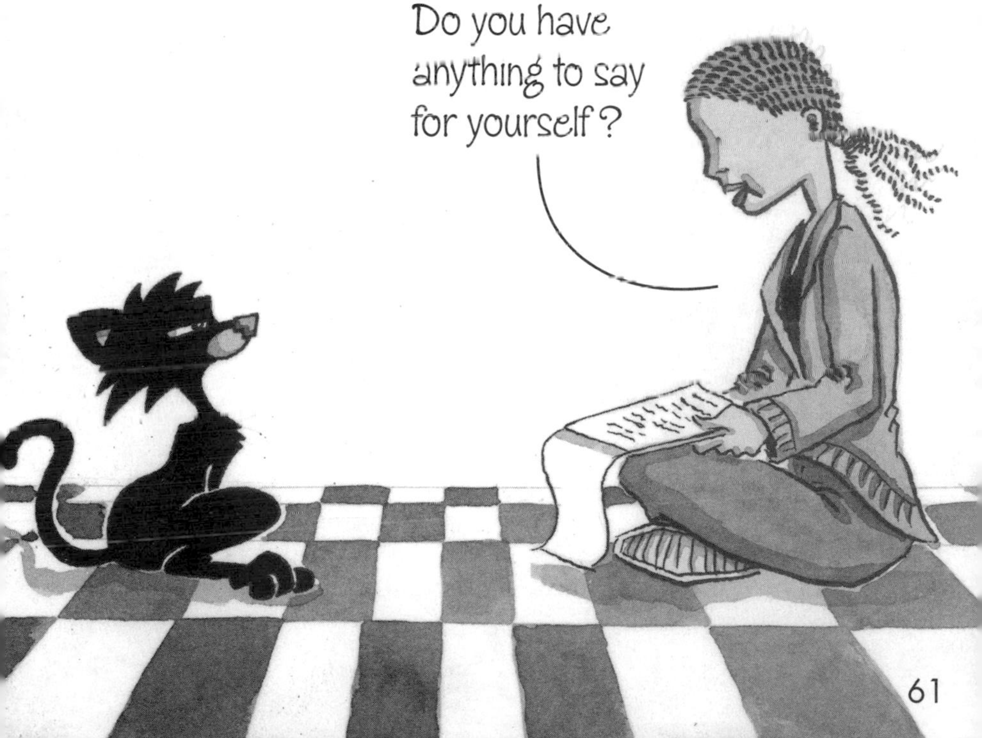
Do you have anything to say for yourself?

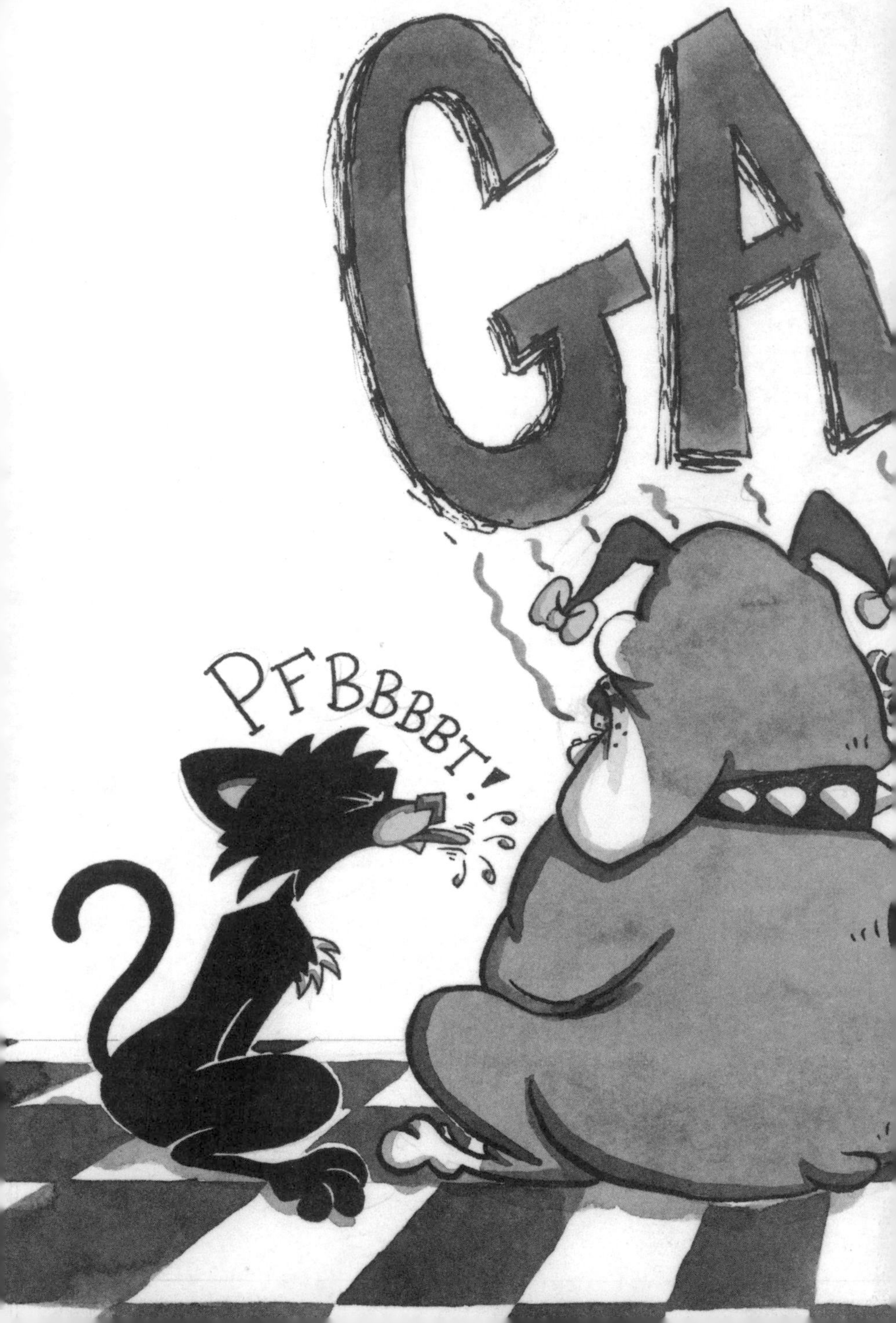
GA
PFBBBBT!

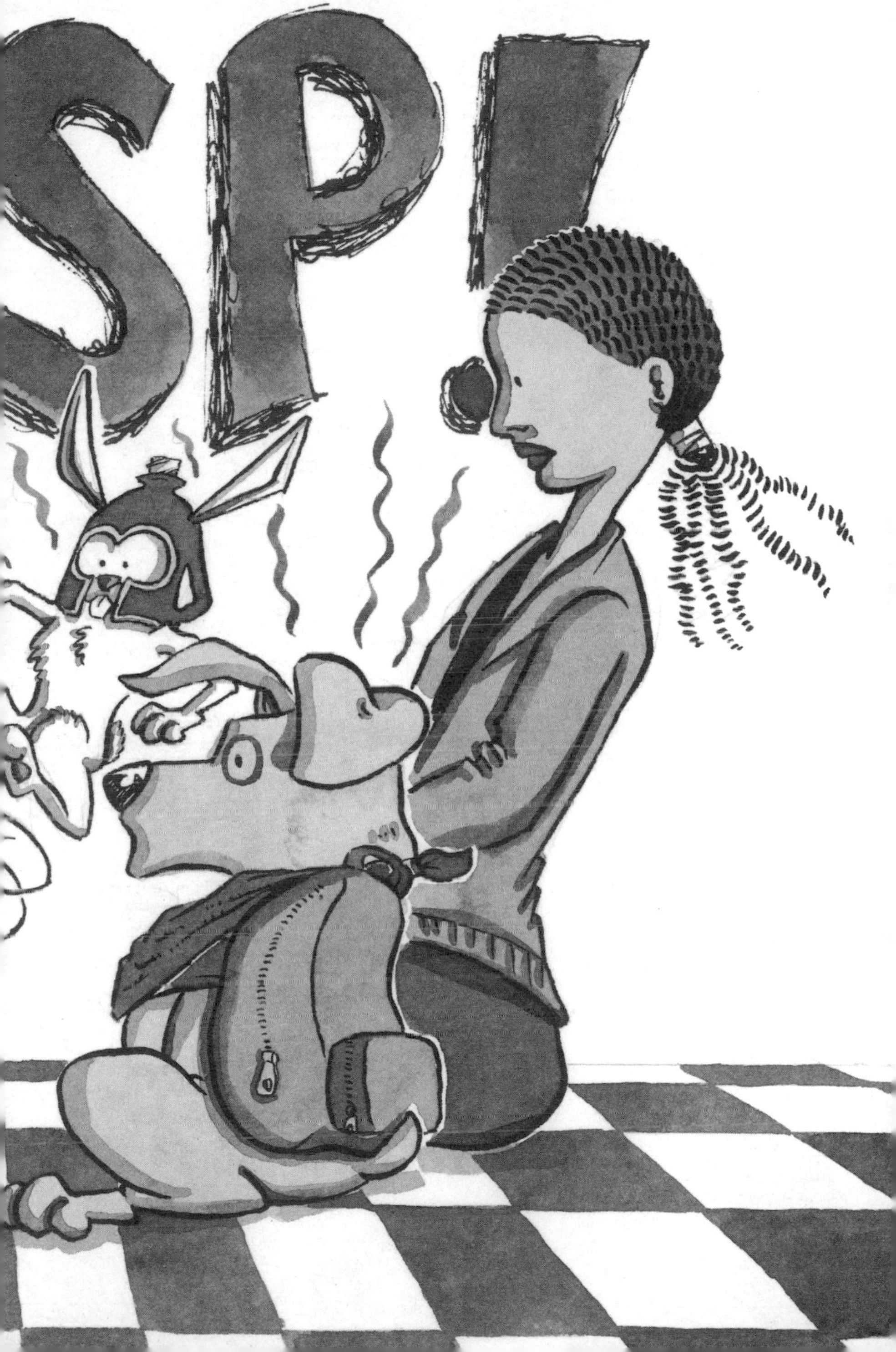
SPL

Okay, then. You don't have to answer the question if you don't want to, but that does not give you the right to be rude to me.

When you're ready to tell me why you're so angry, I'll be listening.

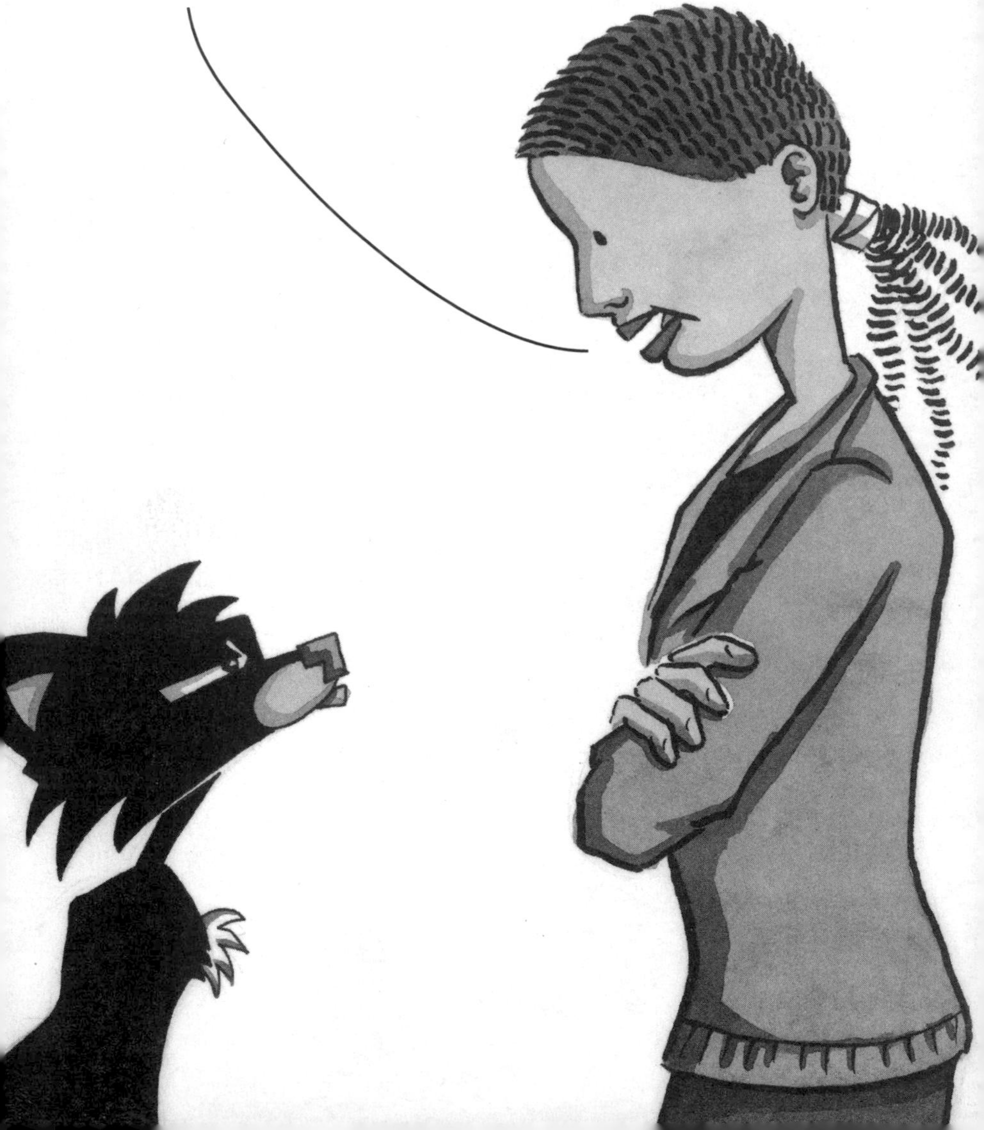

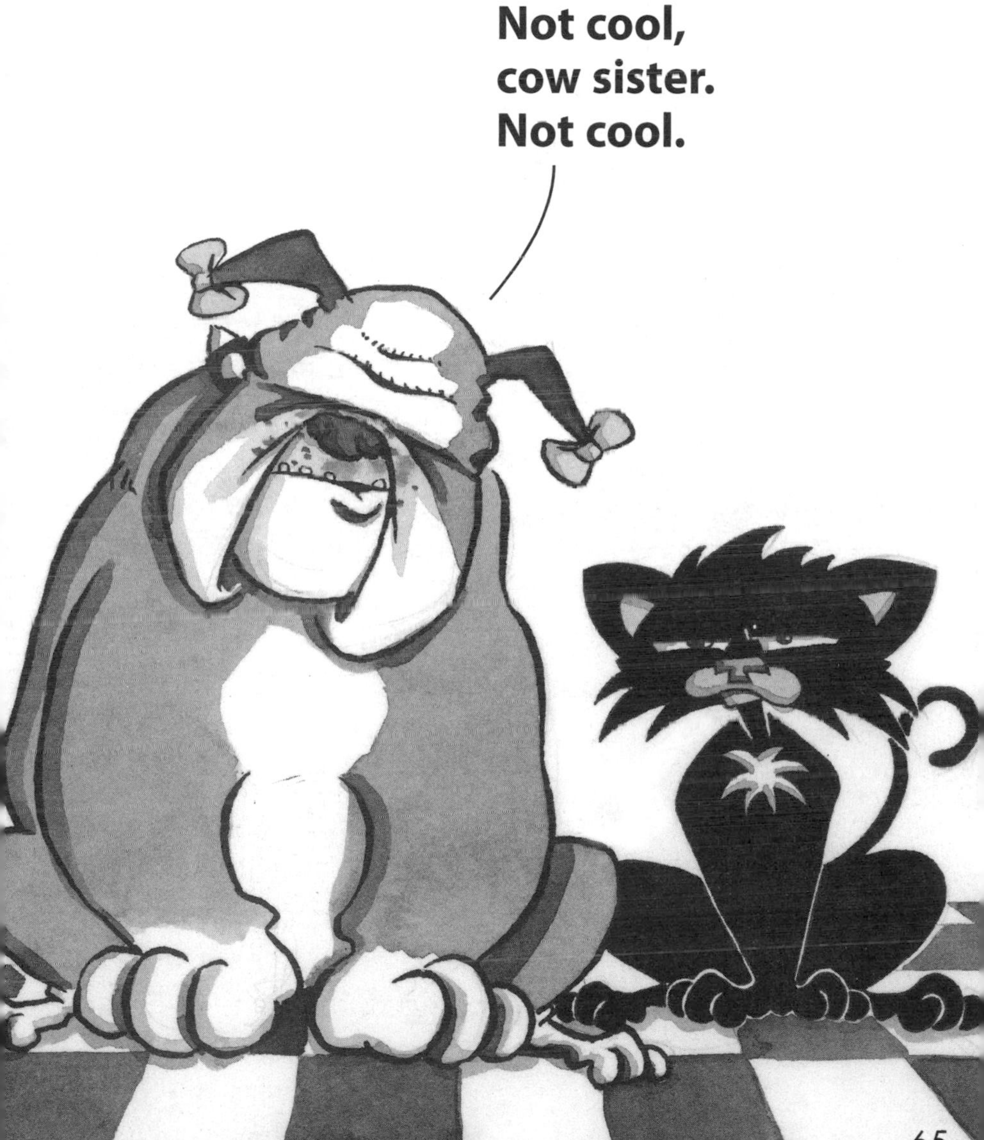
Not cool,
cow sister.
Not cool.

UNCLE MURRAY'S FUN FACTS

WHY DO DOGS AND CATS HATE EACH OTHER?

Stop blamin' dogs! This is all the fault of goofy cats!

The problem between dogs and cats isn't so much that they hate each other . . . they just don't understand each other. Let's think about how dogs and cats are different from each other.

NOSE—SNIFFS EVERYTHING

TONGUE— LICKS YOU BECAUSE HE LIKES YOU

TAIL—WAGS WHEN HAPPY

Dogs are very social. They live in packs and usually enjoy the company of other dogs. Dogs like to play by wrestling and biting. When a dog first meets you, he likes to sniff you (especially in places where you may not like to be sniffed). When a dog likes you, he expresses it by licking you. When a dog is happy, he wags his tail.

Cats, on the other hand, are not social animals. They lead independent lives and usually do not seek the company of other cats. Except for when they're young, cats do not play with each other and especially not by wrestling or biting. Cats don't sniff things nearly as much as dogs. Cats generally only lick themselves, and then only to clean themselves. And cats only shake their tails when they're feeling nervous or angry.

TAIL— SHAKES WHEN NERVOUS

NOSE—USUALLY ONLY SNIFFS TO SENSE DANGER OR SAFETY

TONGUE— ONLY LICKS HERSELF

Now imagine what happens when a strange dog and cat meet for the first time. The dog runs up to the cat with its tail wagging, expecting to sniff her, lick her, and play with her. But the cat meanwhile sees the dog's running as an attack. She sees the wagging tail as a sign of anger. And the last thing the cat wants is to be sniffed (especially in a place where she doesn't want to be sniffed), licked, and played with. So the cat either runs away or attacks, neither of which the dog expected.

Okay, so maybe the dogs are just kinda sorta partly to blame.

So now the dog has a perception that cats just *aren't* friendly. This isn't going to encourage the dog to be friendly with any cats in the future. And so begins a cycle of misunderstanding that can sometimes lead to a real mess.

•CHAPTER FIVE•

ARTS + CRAFTS

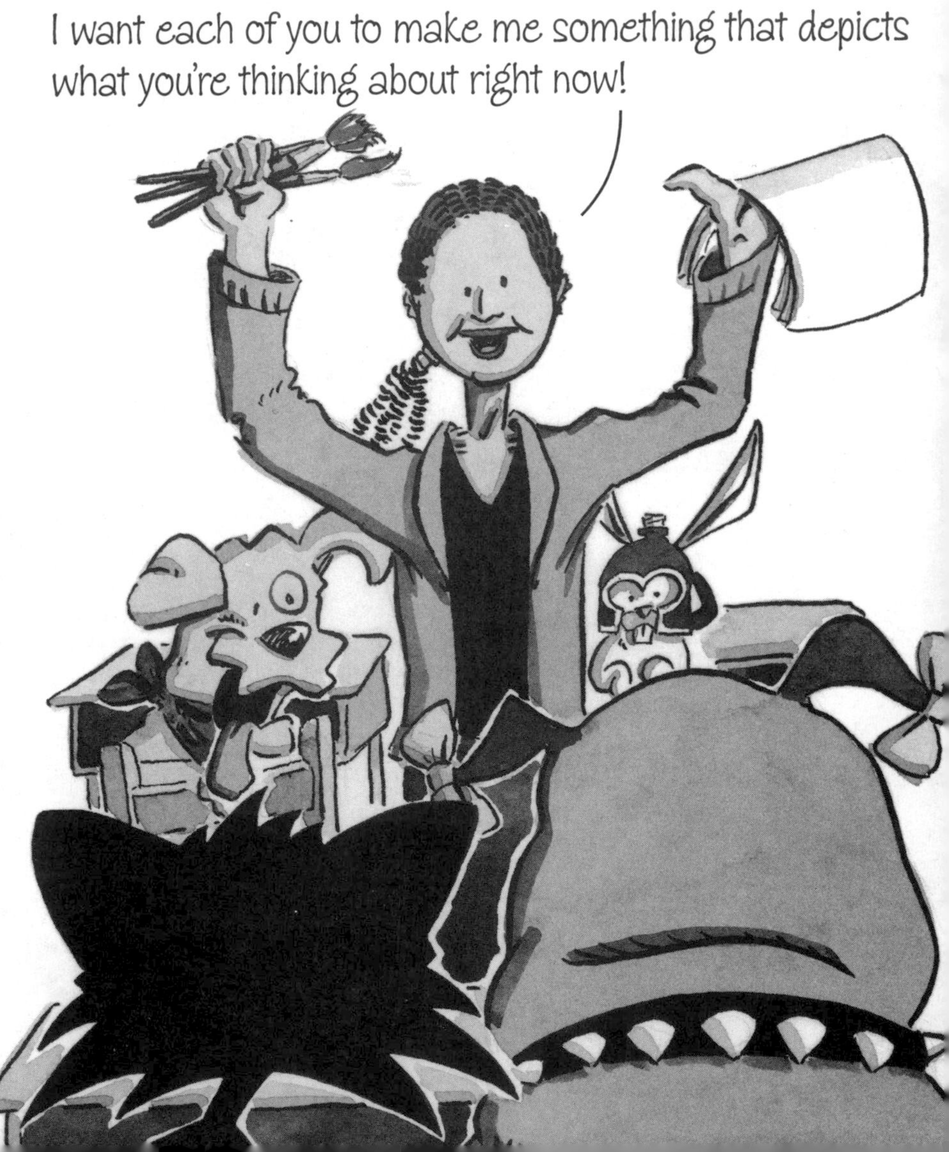
I want each of you to make me something that depicts what you're thinking about right now!

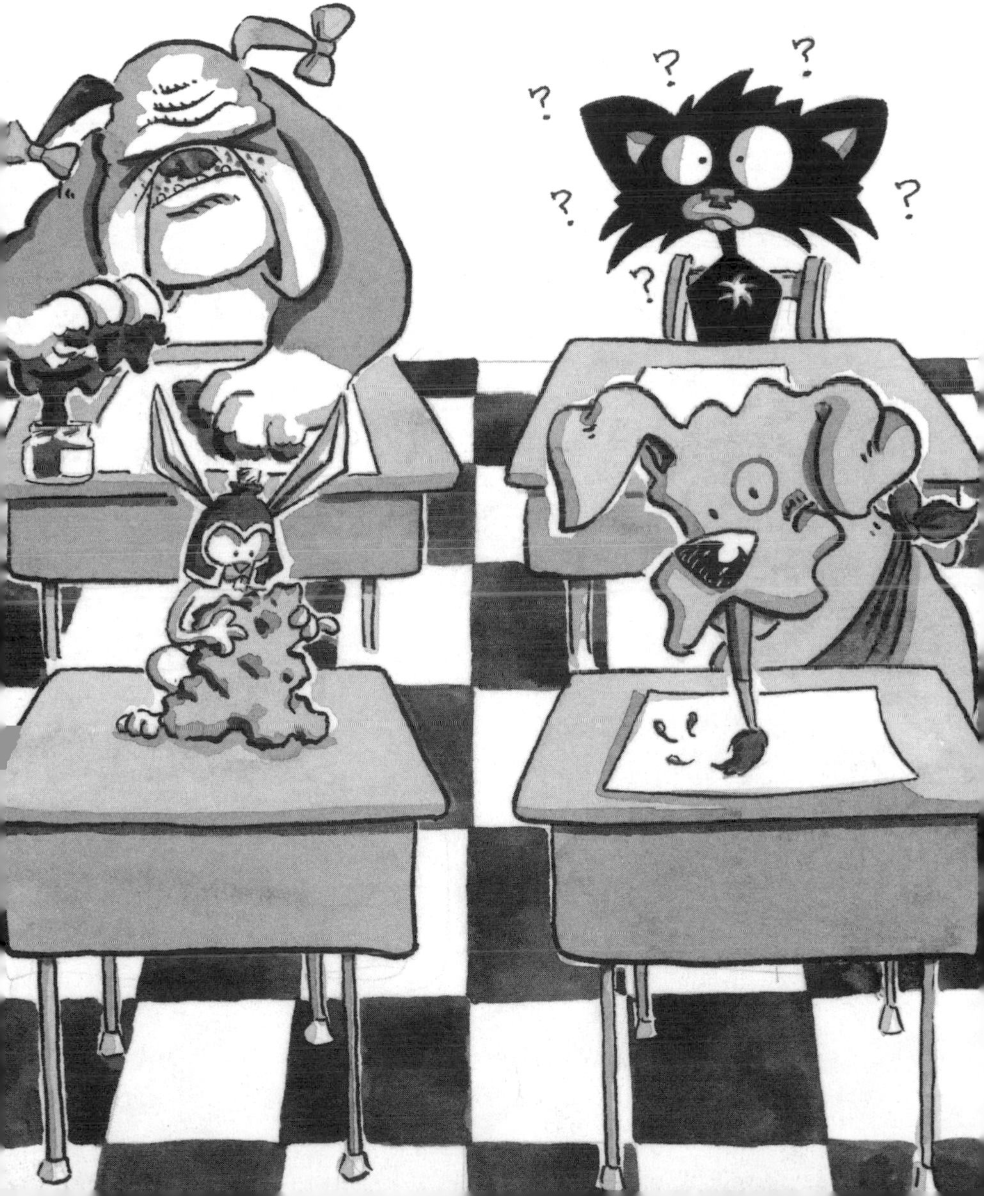
? ? ? ? ? ?

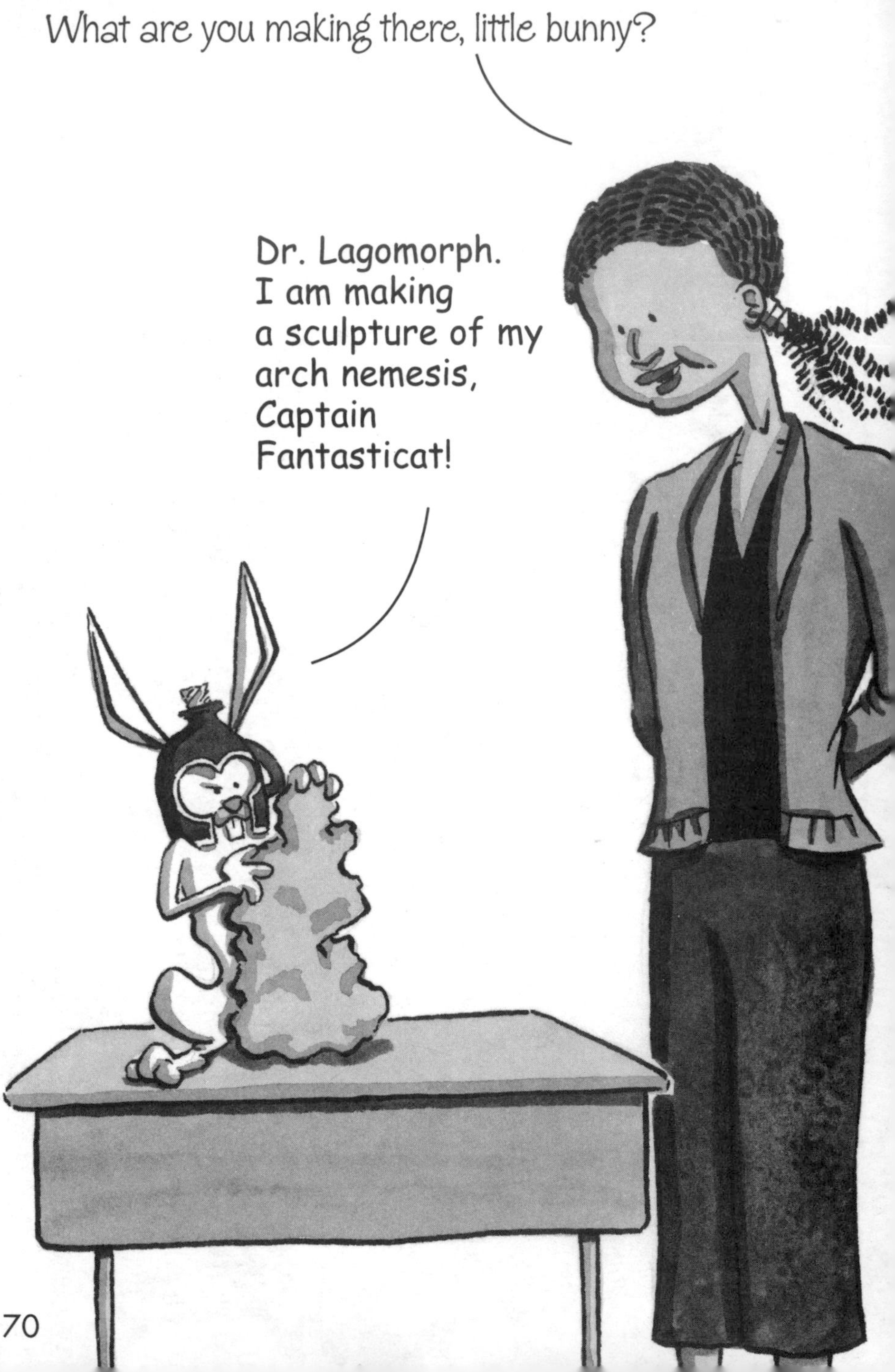
What are you making there, little bunny?
Dr. Lagomorph. I am making a sculpture of my arch nemesis, Captain Fantasticat!

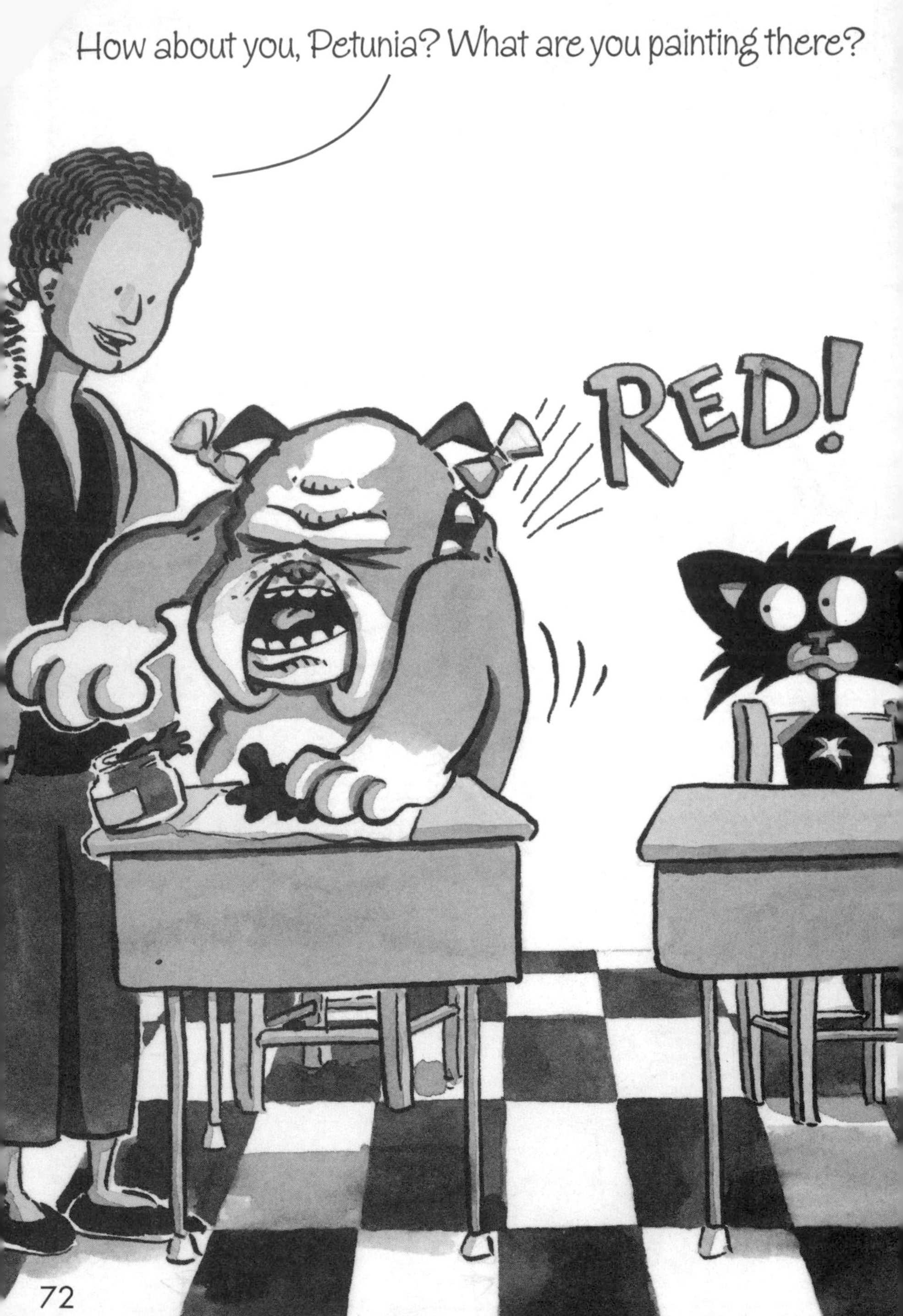
How about you, Petunia? What are you painting there?
RED!

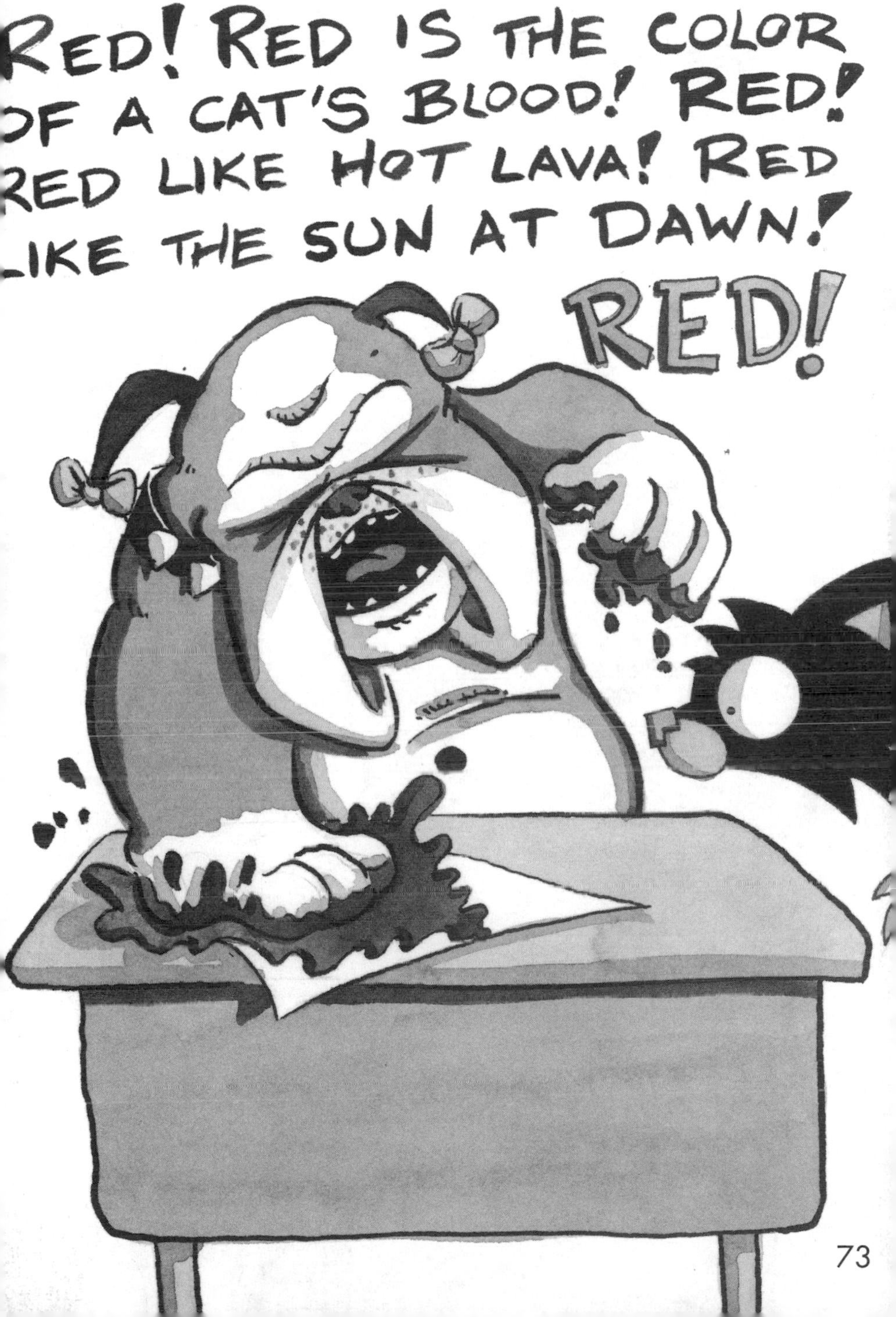

RED! RED IS THE COLOR OF A CAT'S BLOOD! RED! RED LIKE HOT LAVA! RED LIKE THE SUN AT DAWN!
RED!

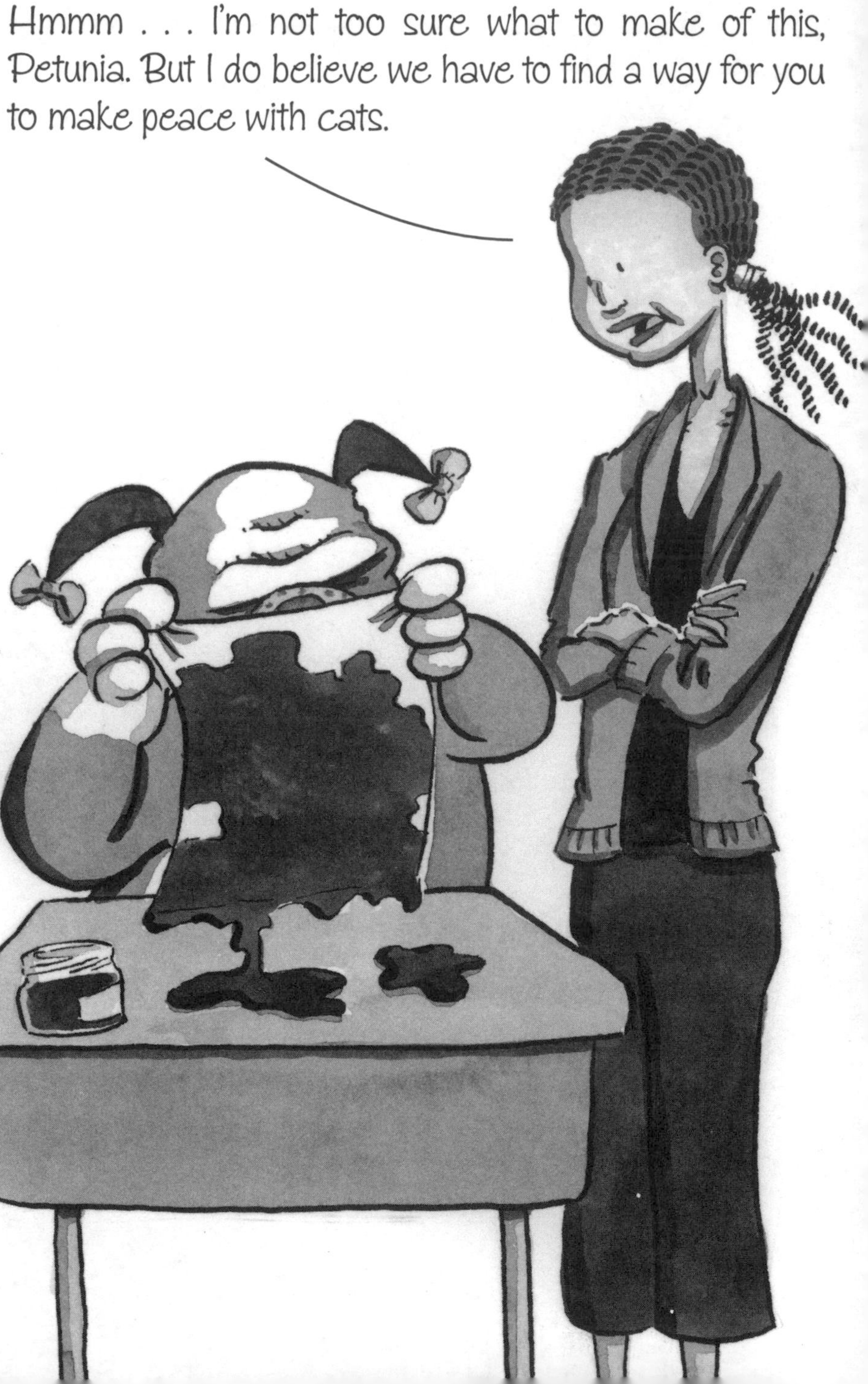
Hmmm . . . I'm not too sure what to make of this, Petunia. But I do believe we have to find a way for you to make peace with cats.

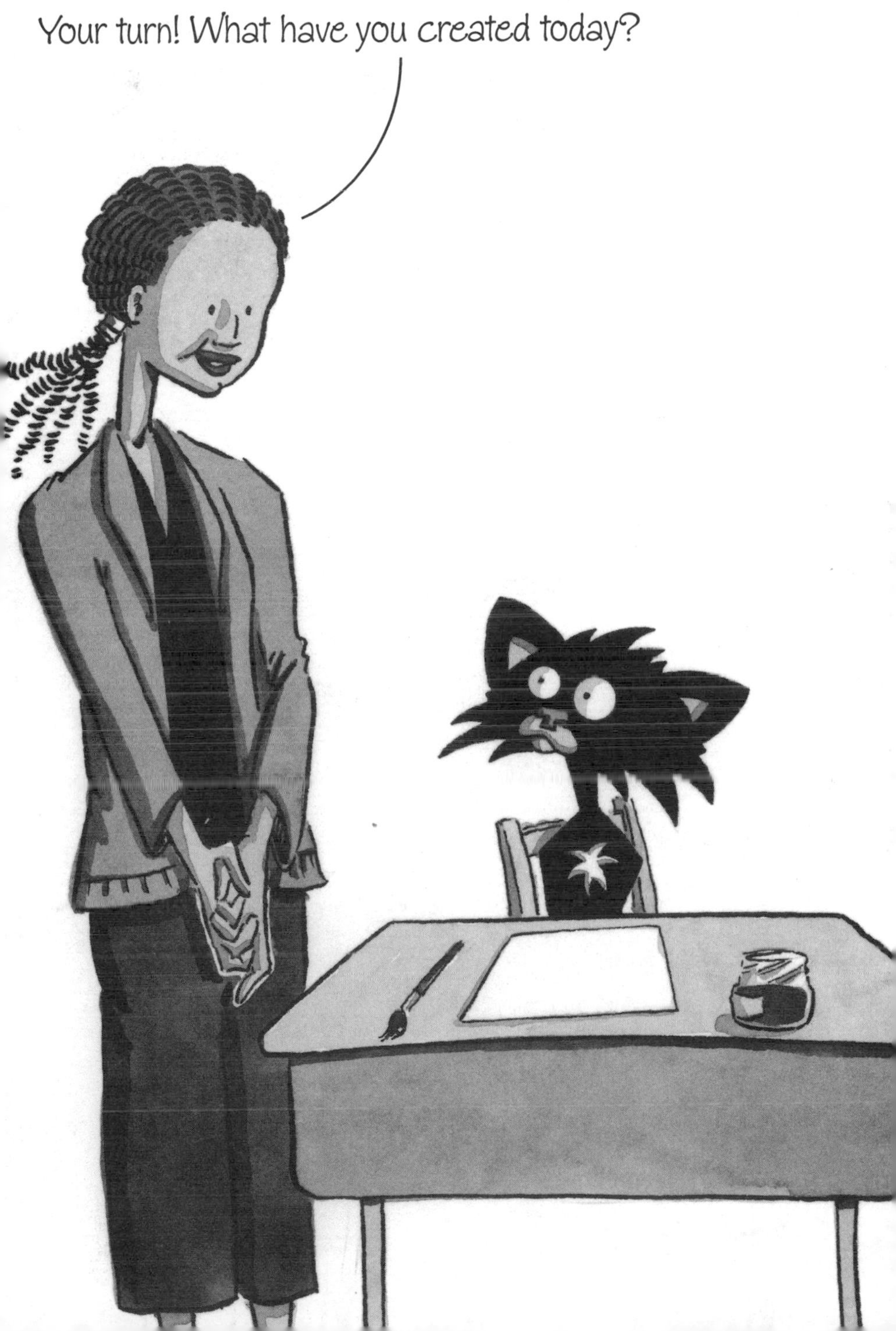
Your turn! What have you created today?

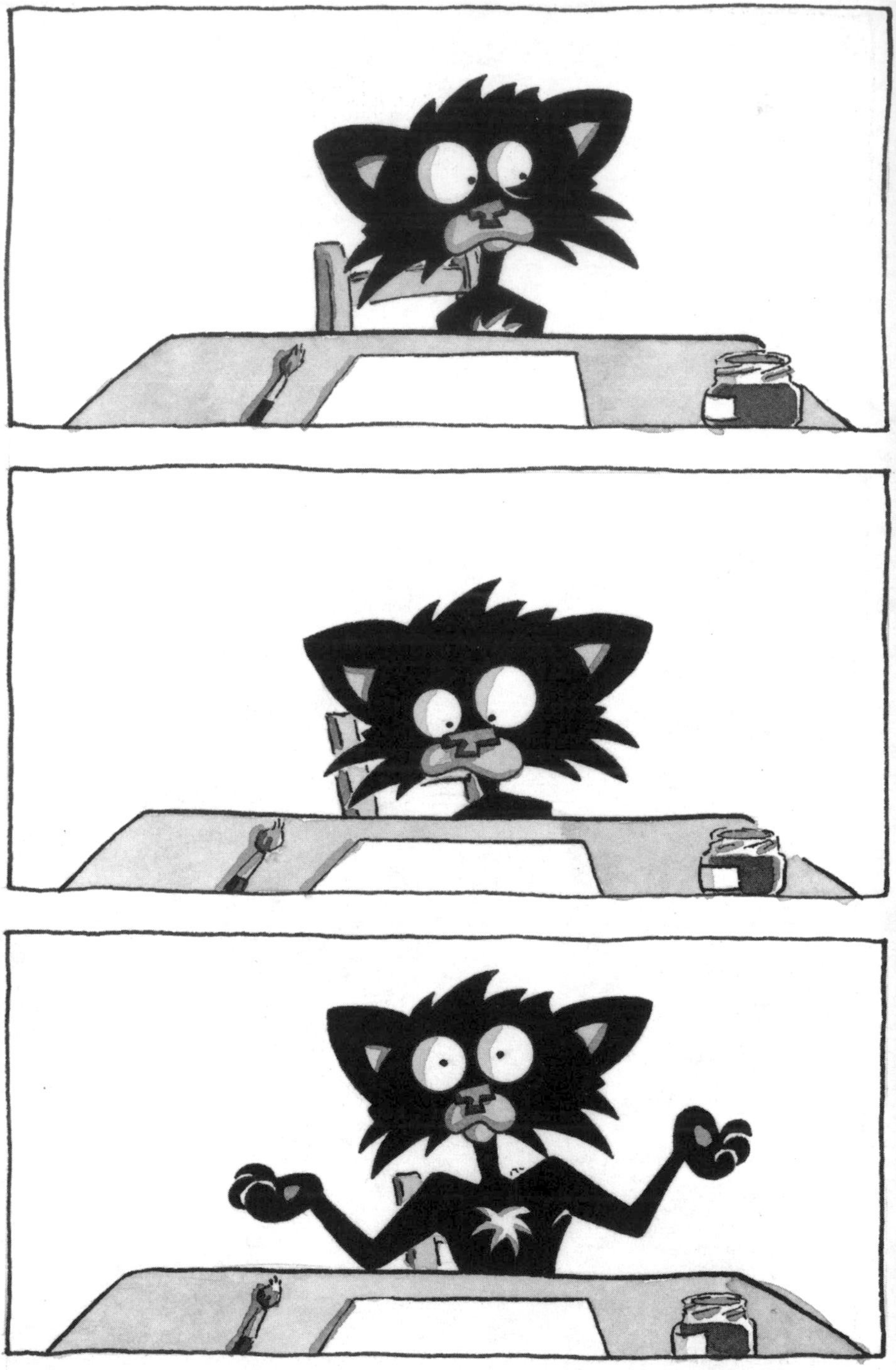

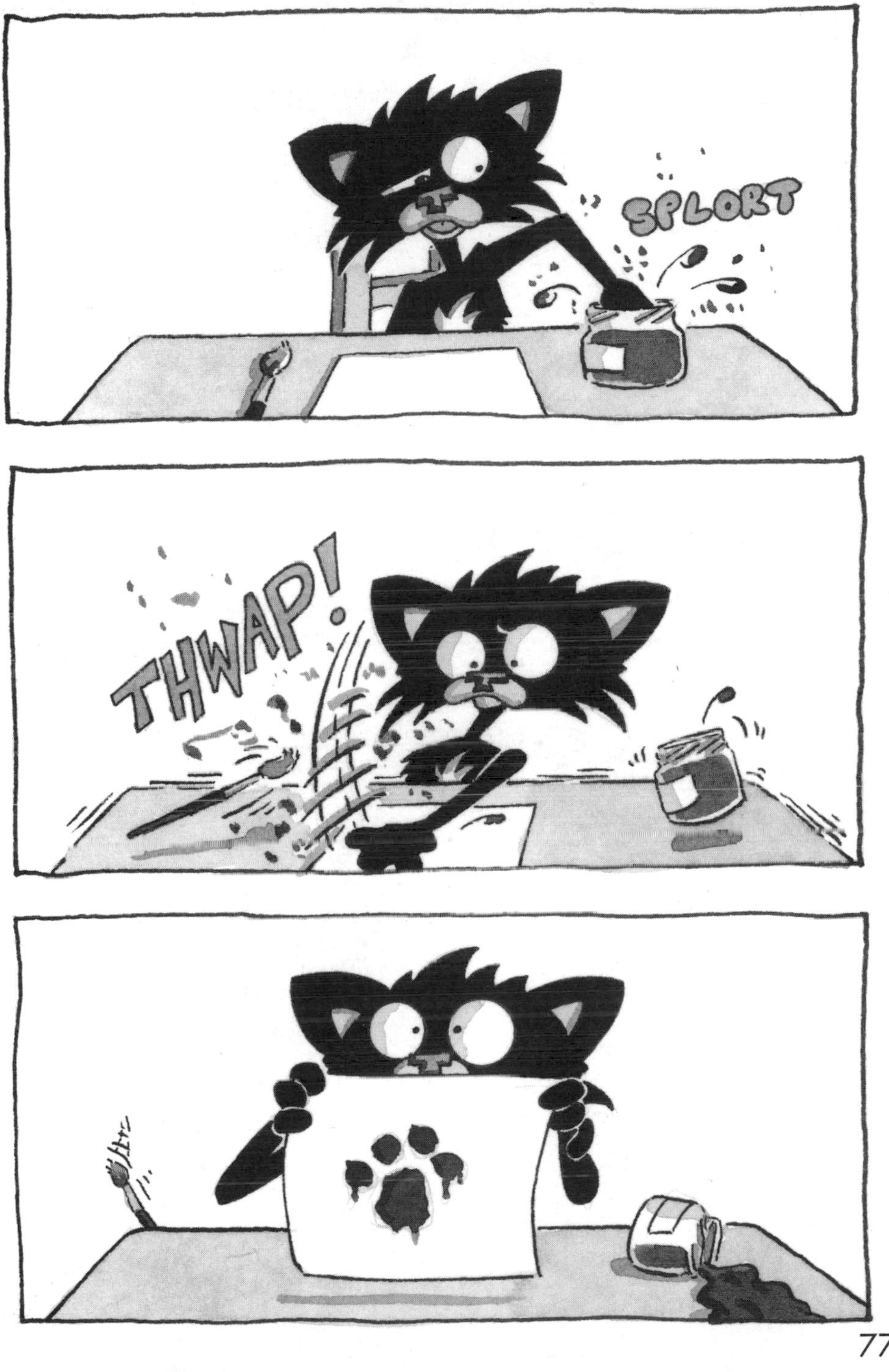
SPLORT
THWAP!

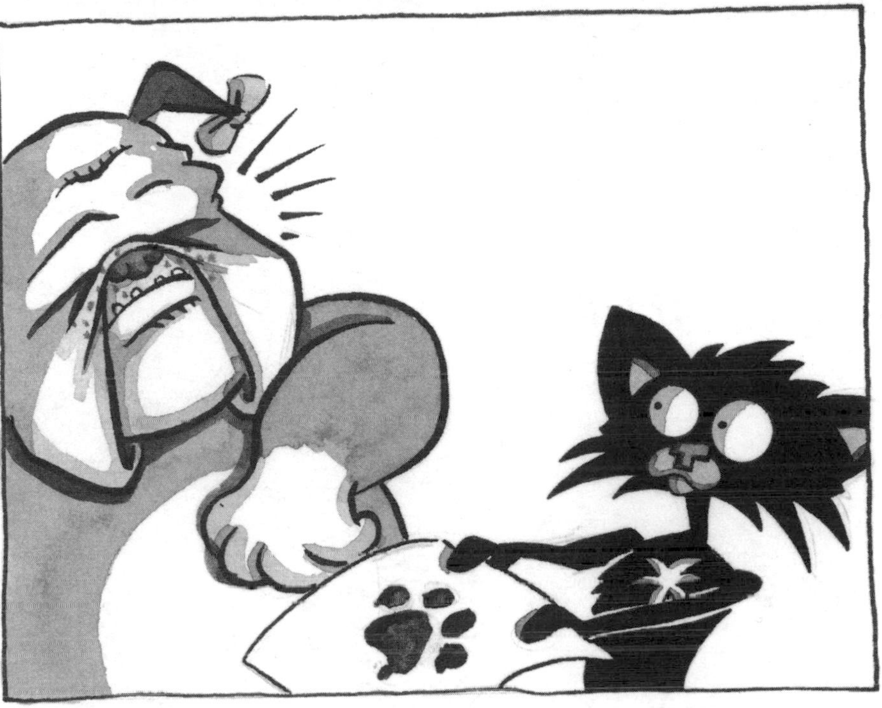

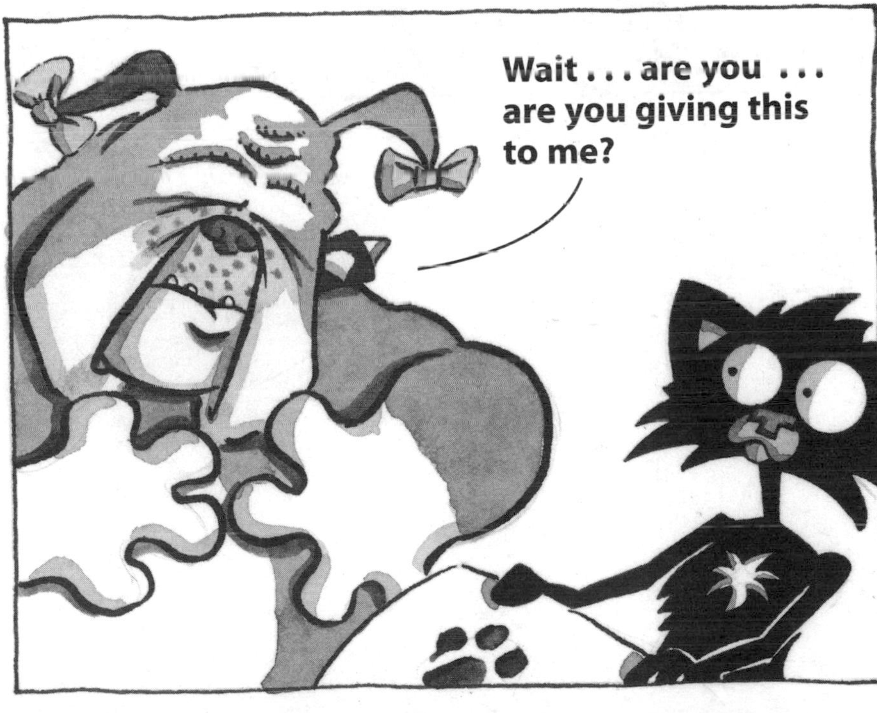
Wait . . . are you . . . are you giving this to me?

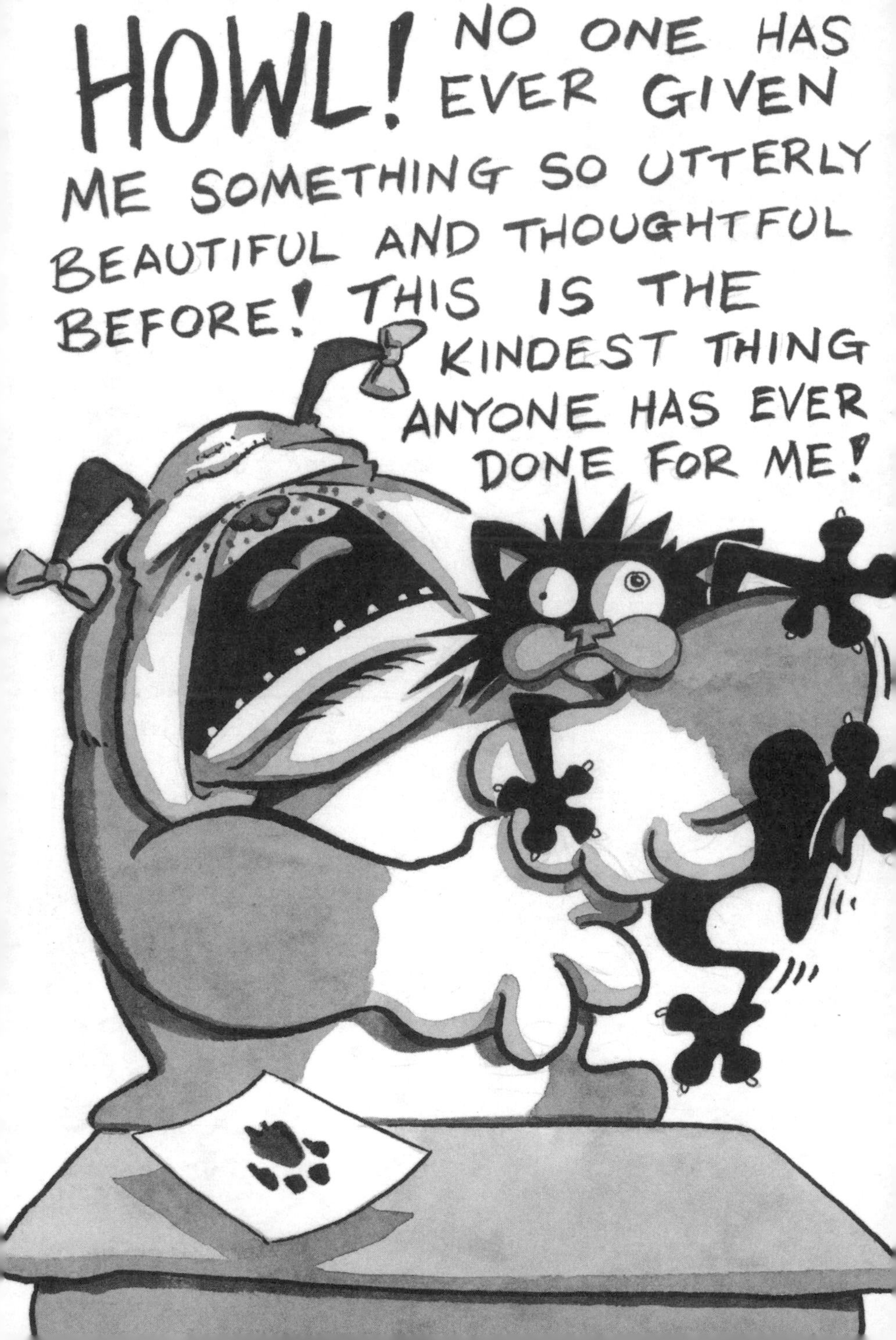
HOWL! NO ONE HAS EVER GIVEN ME SOMETHING SO UTTERLY BEAUTIFUL AND THOUGHTFUL BEFORE! THIS IS THE KINDEST THING ANYONE HAS EVER DONE FOR ME!

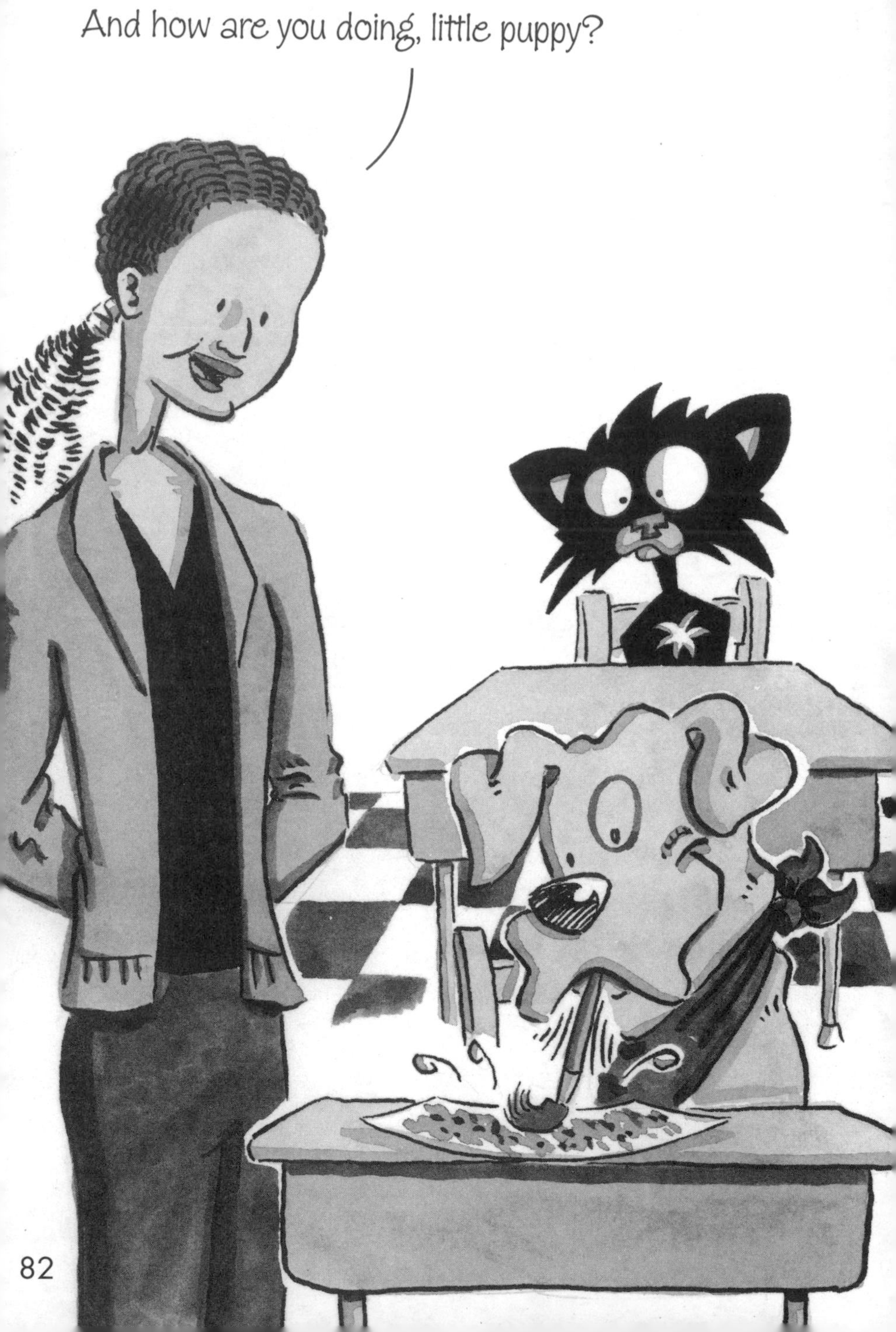
And how are you doing, little puppy?

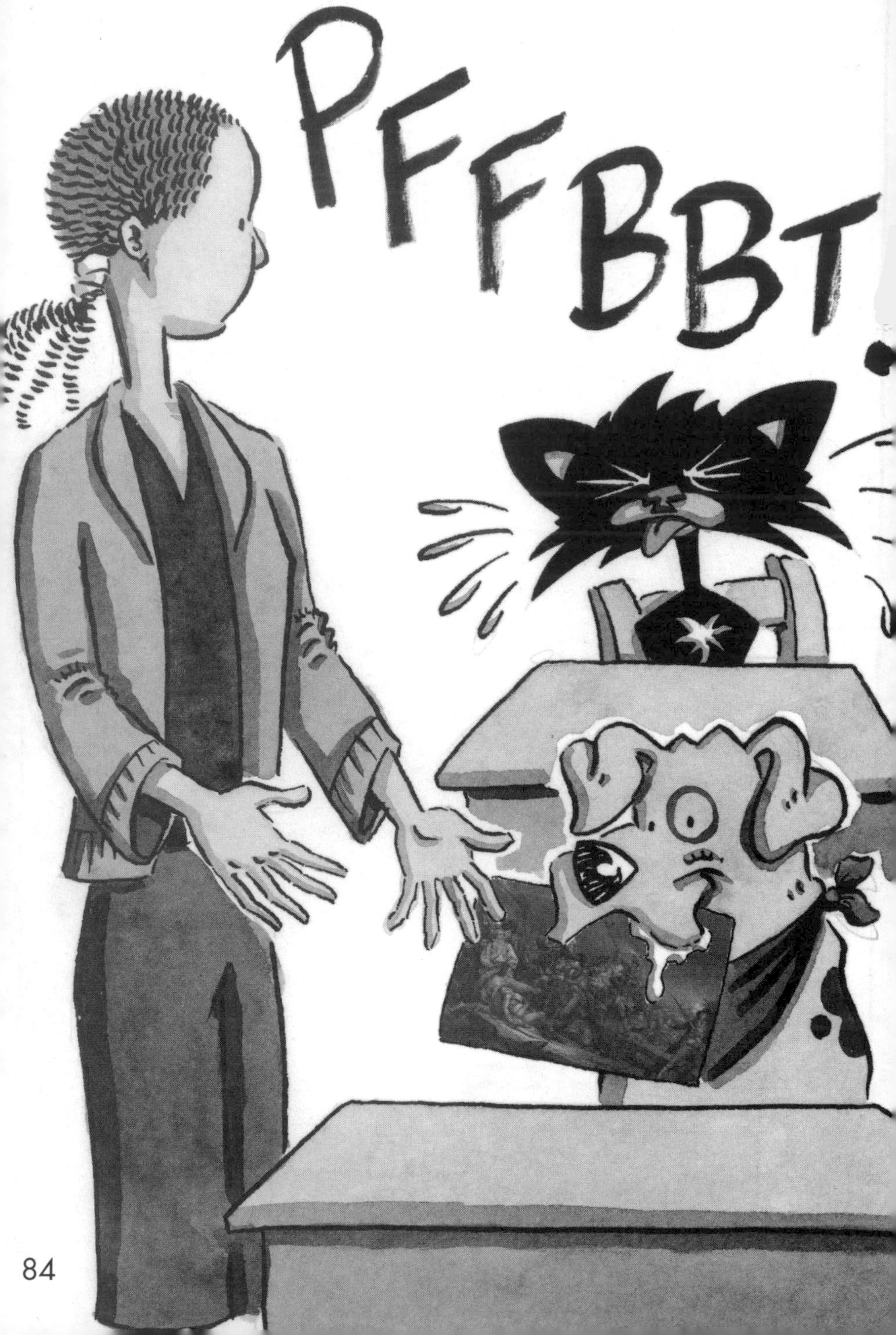
PFFBBT!

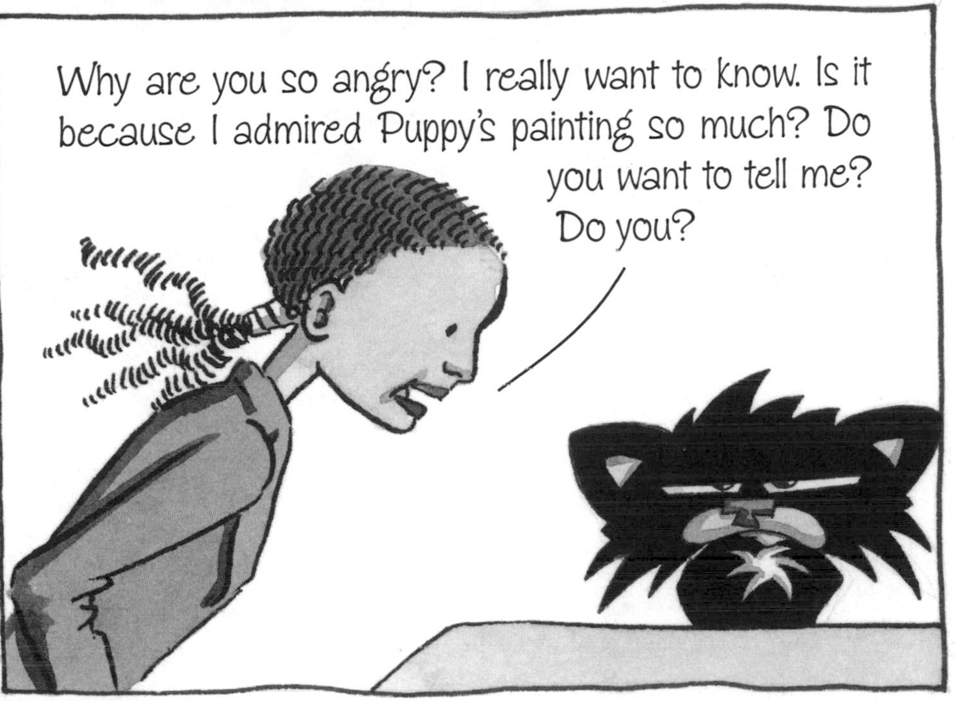
Why are you so angry? I really want to know. Is it because I admired Puppy's painting so much? Do you want to tell me? Do you?

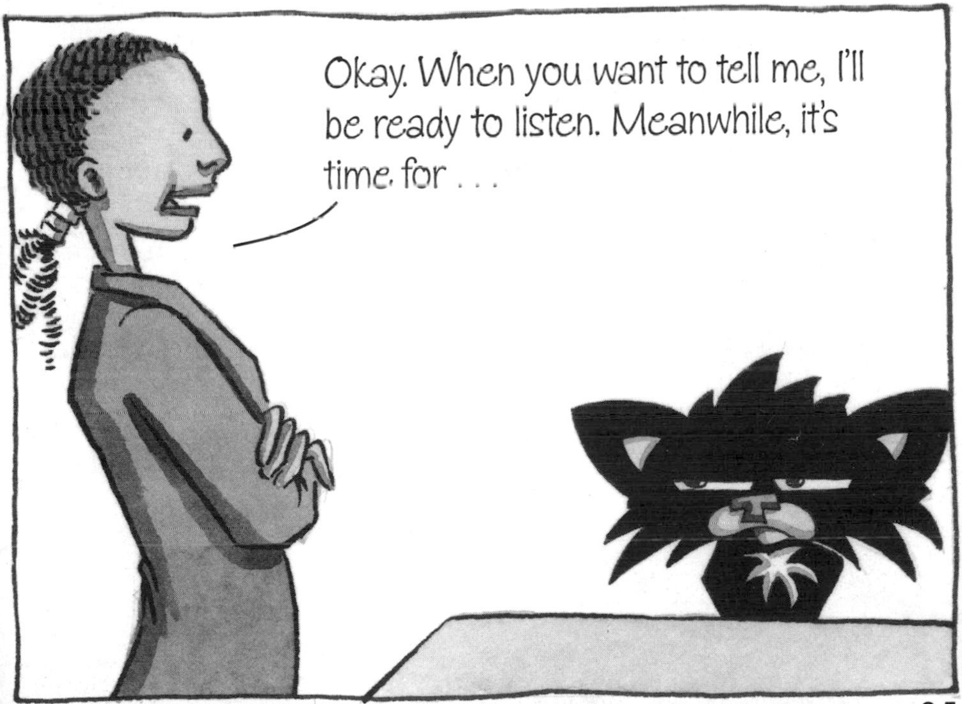
Okay. When you want to tell me, I'll be ready to listen. Meanwhile, it's time for . . .

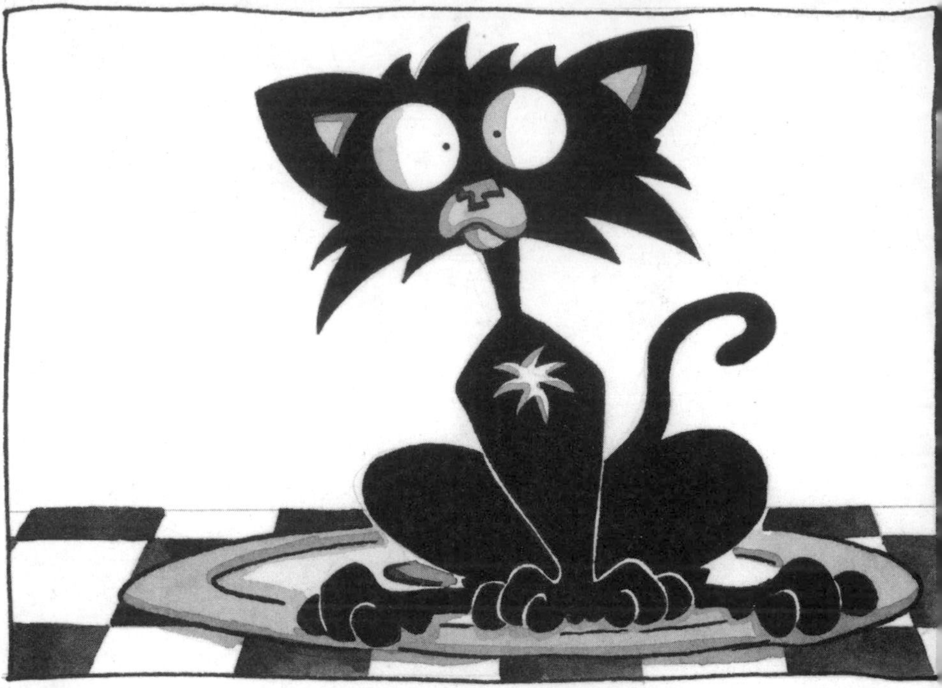

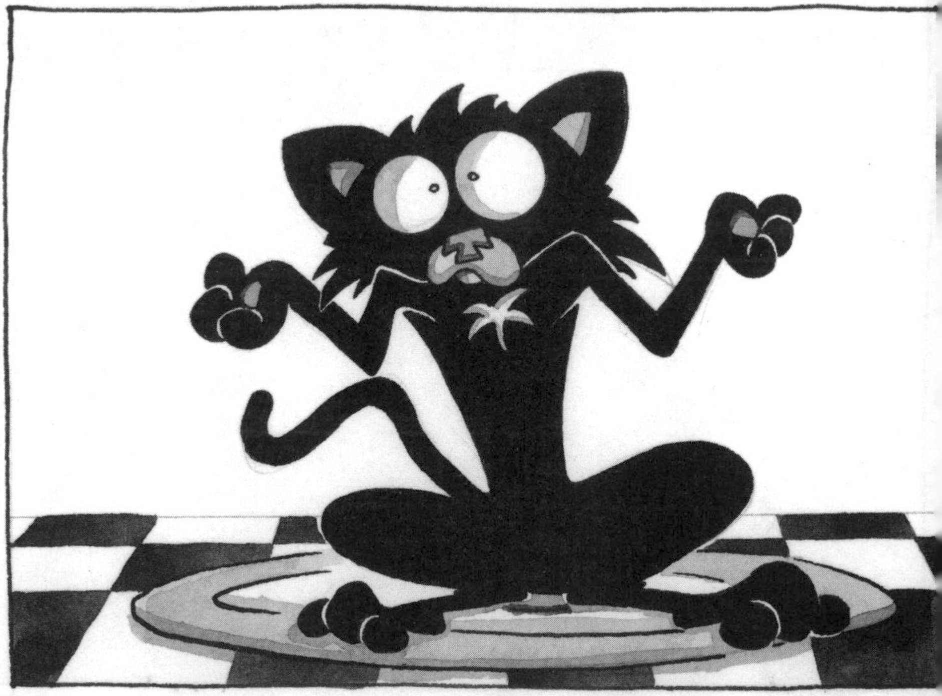

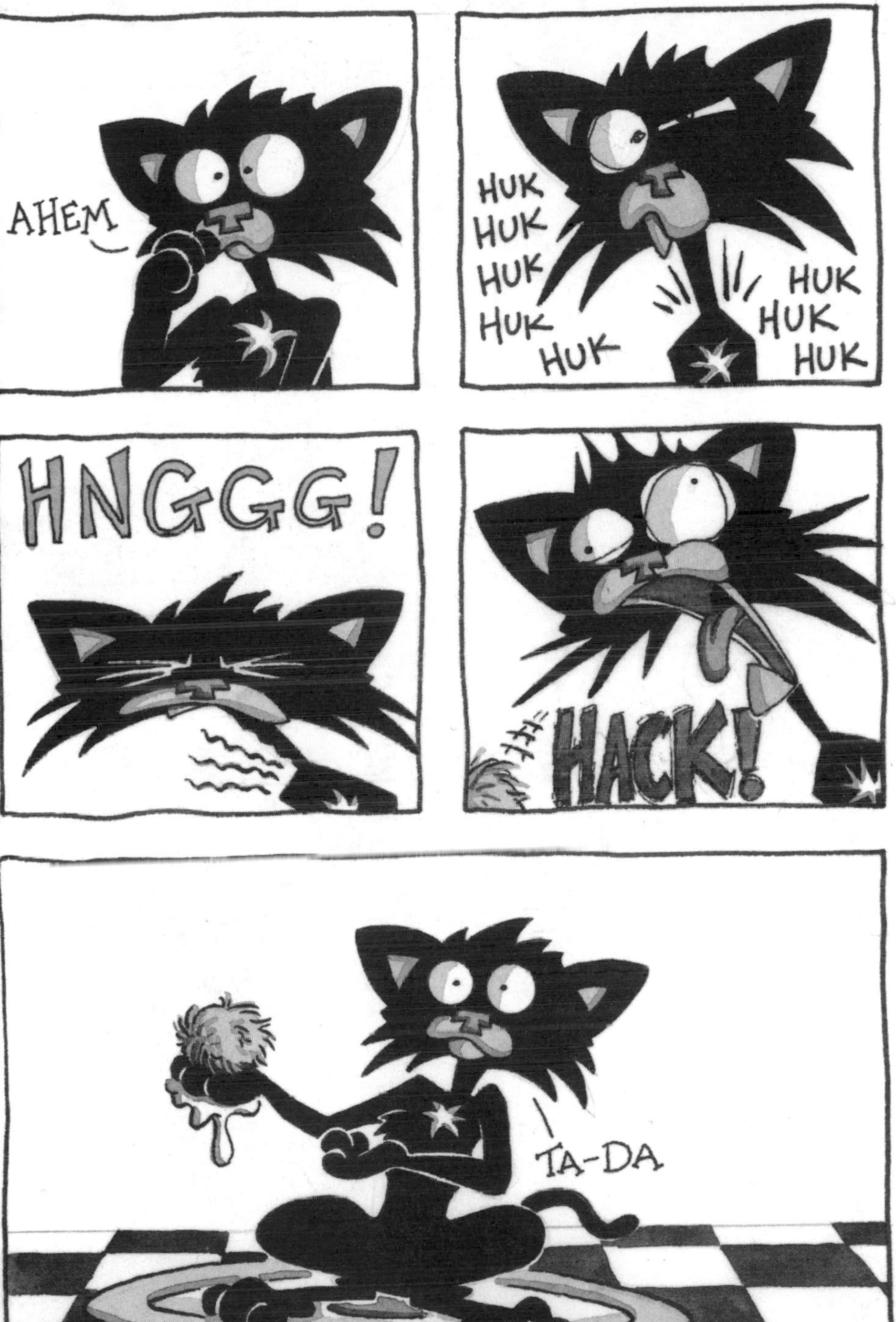
AHEM
HUK
HUK
HUK
HUK
HUK
HUK
HUK
HUK
HNGGG!
HACK!
TA-DA

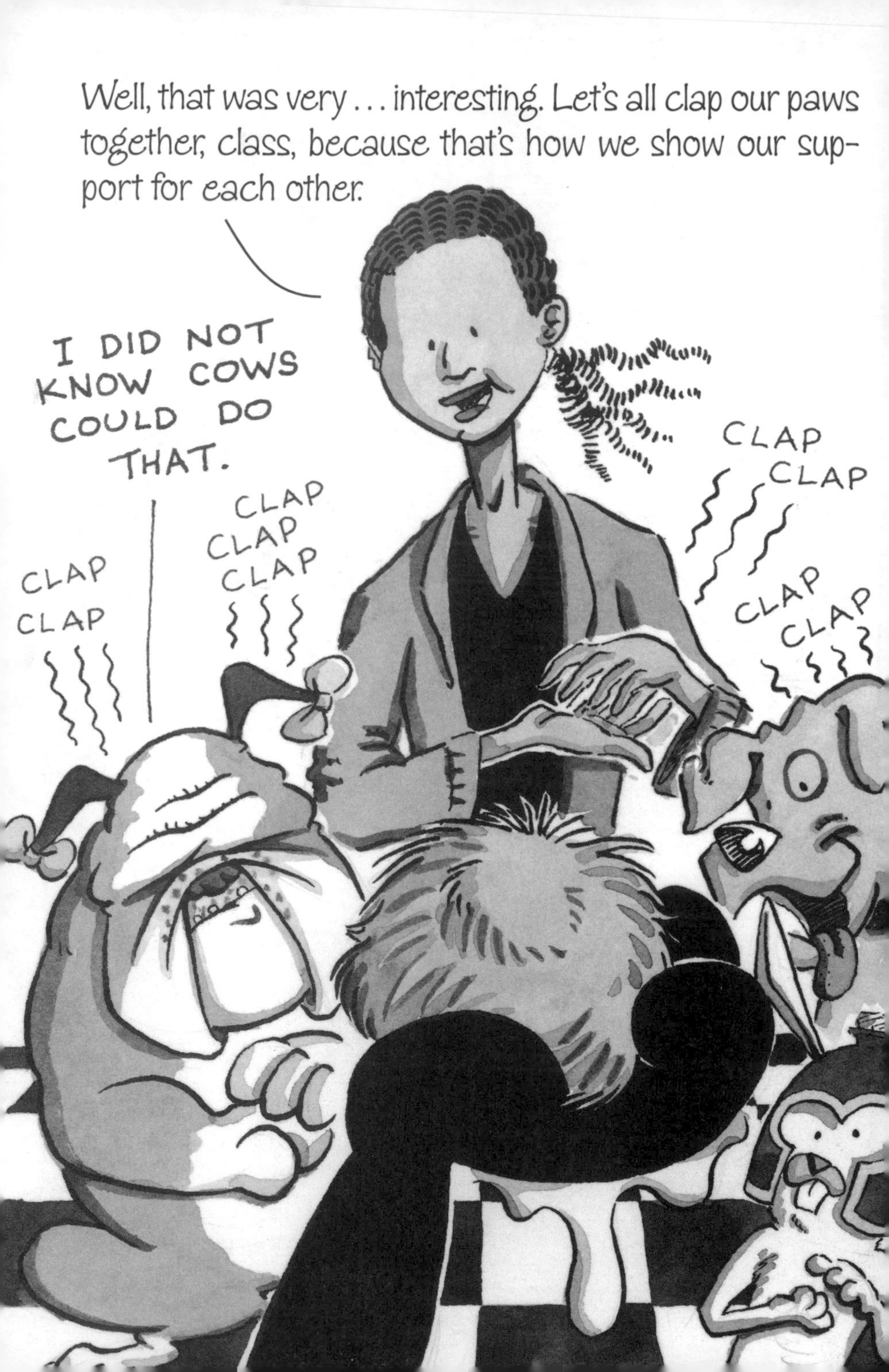
Well, that was very . . . interesting. Let's all clap our paws together, class, because that's how we show our support for each other.
I DID NOT KNOW COWS COULD DO THAT.
CLAP CLAP
CLAP CLAP CLAP
CLAP CLAP
CLAP CLAP

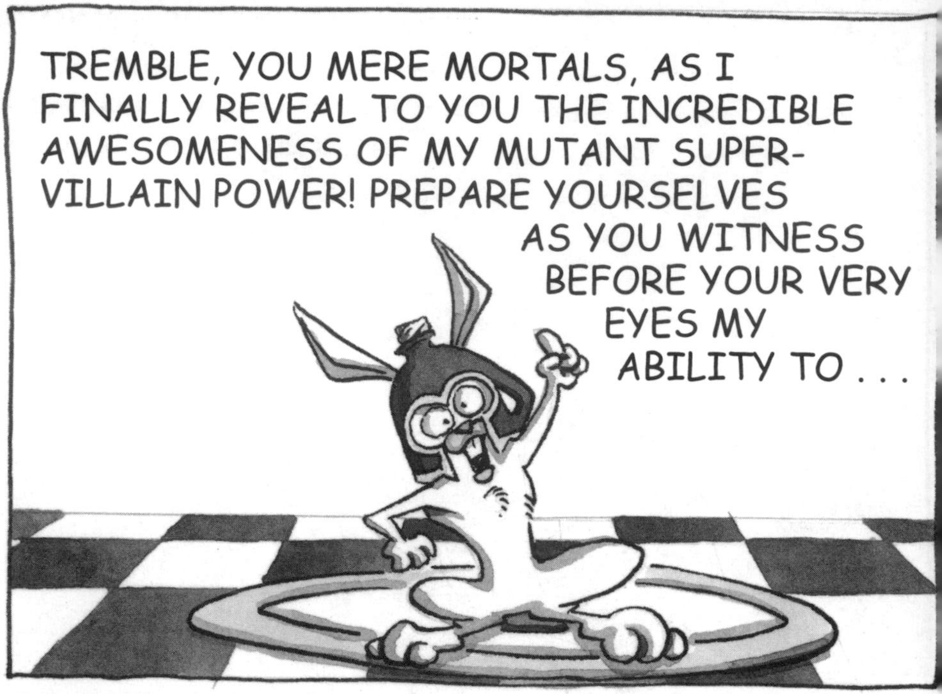
TREMBLE, YOU MERE MORTALS, AS I FINALLY REVEAL TO YOU THE INCREDIBLE AWESOMENESS OF MY MUTANT SUPER-VILLAIN POWER! PREPARE YOURSELVES AS YOU WITNESS BEFORE YOUR VERY EYES MY ABILITY TO . . .

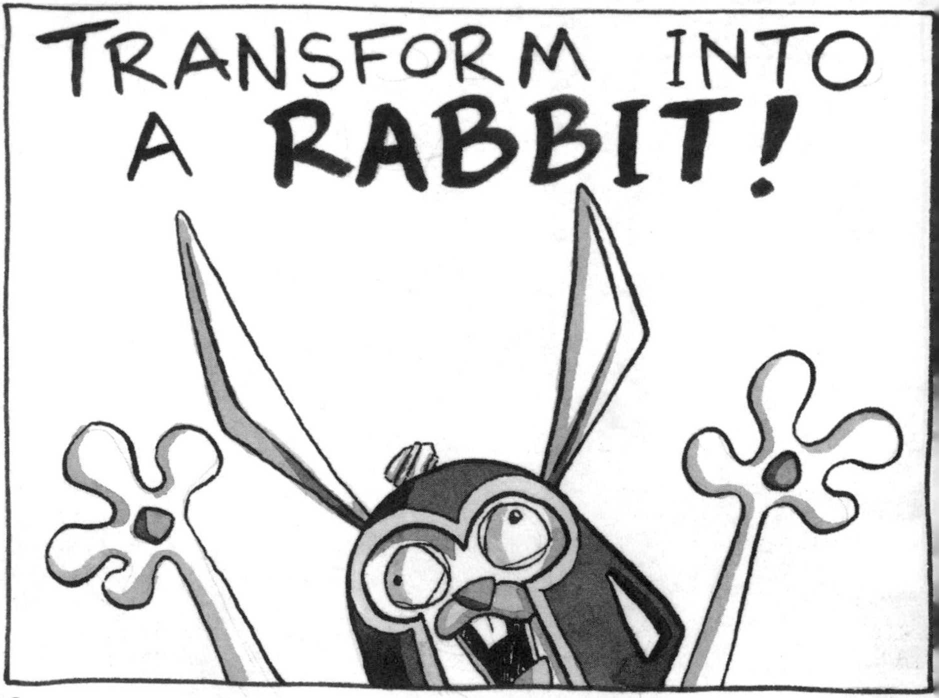
TRANSFORM INTO A RABBIT!

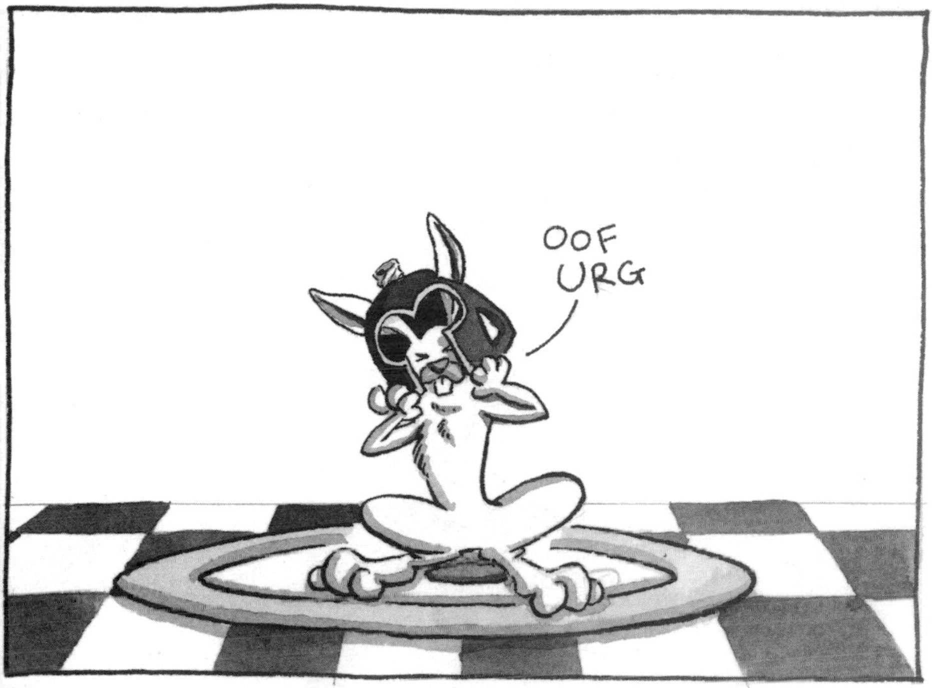
OOF
URG

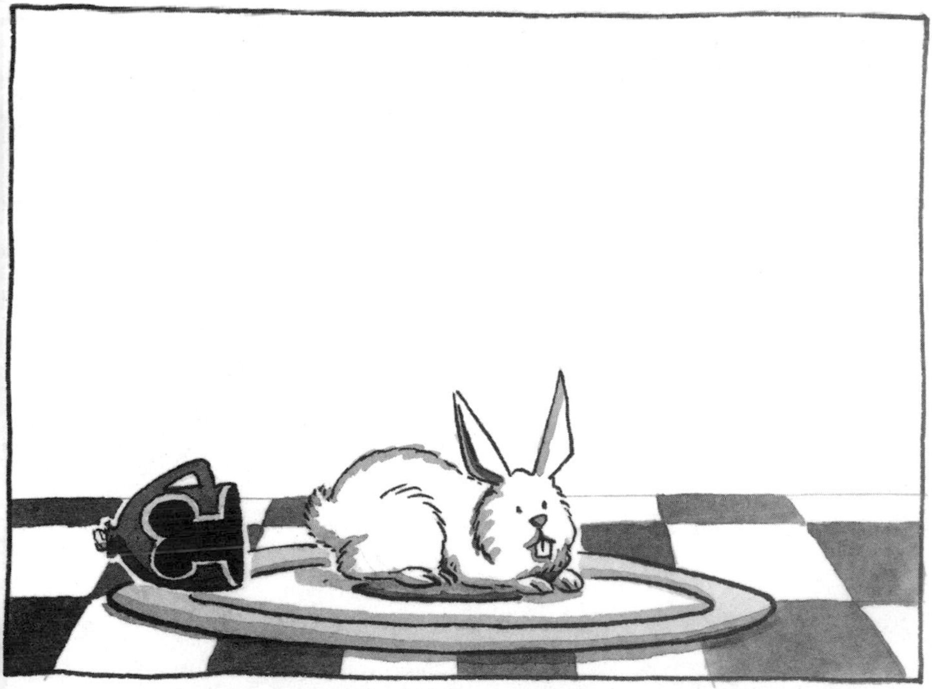

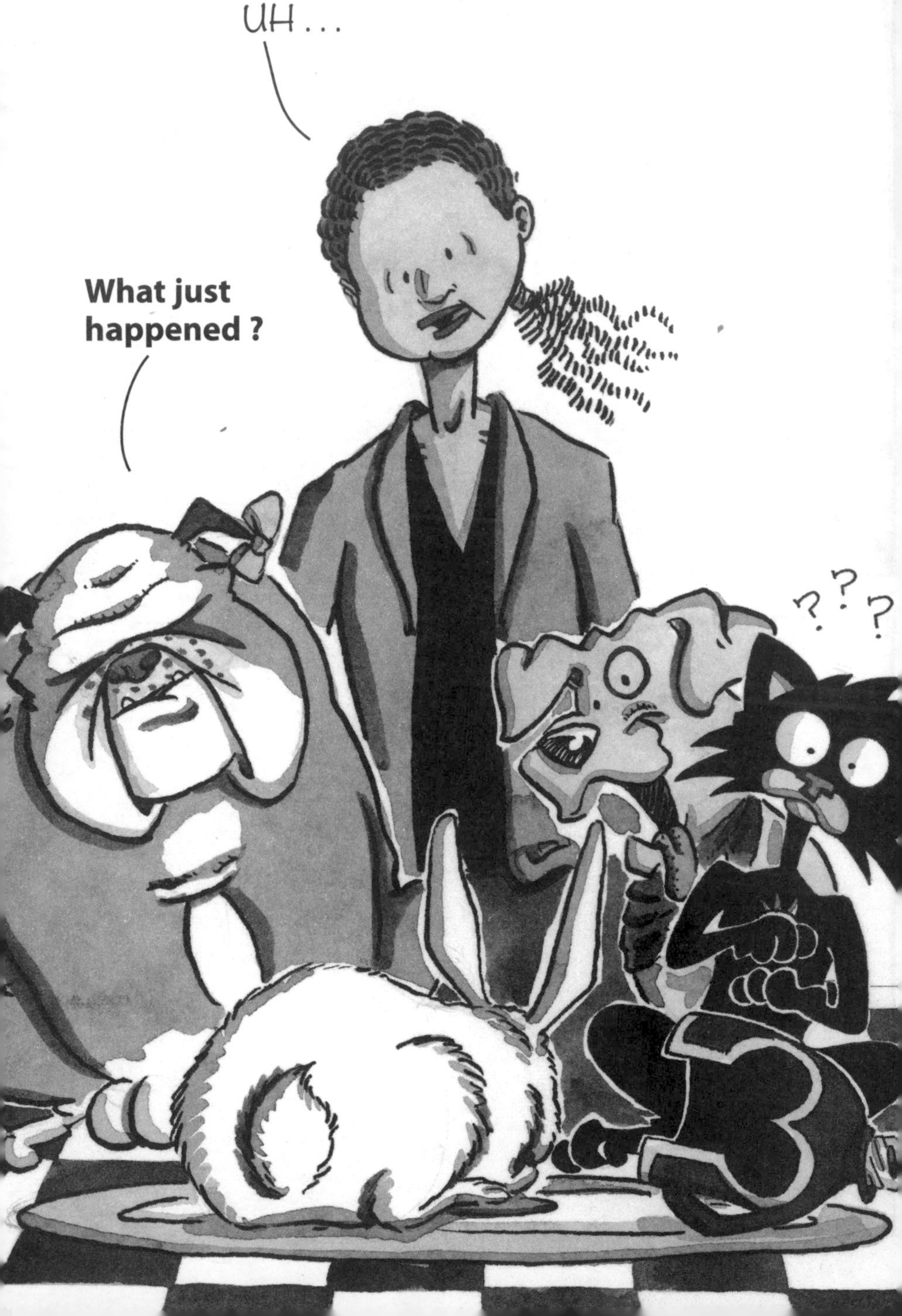
UH...
What just happened?
???

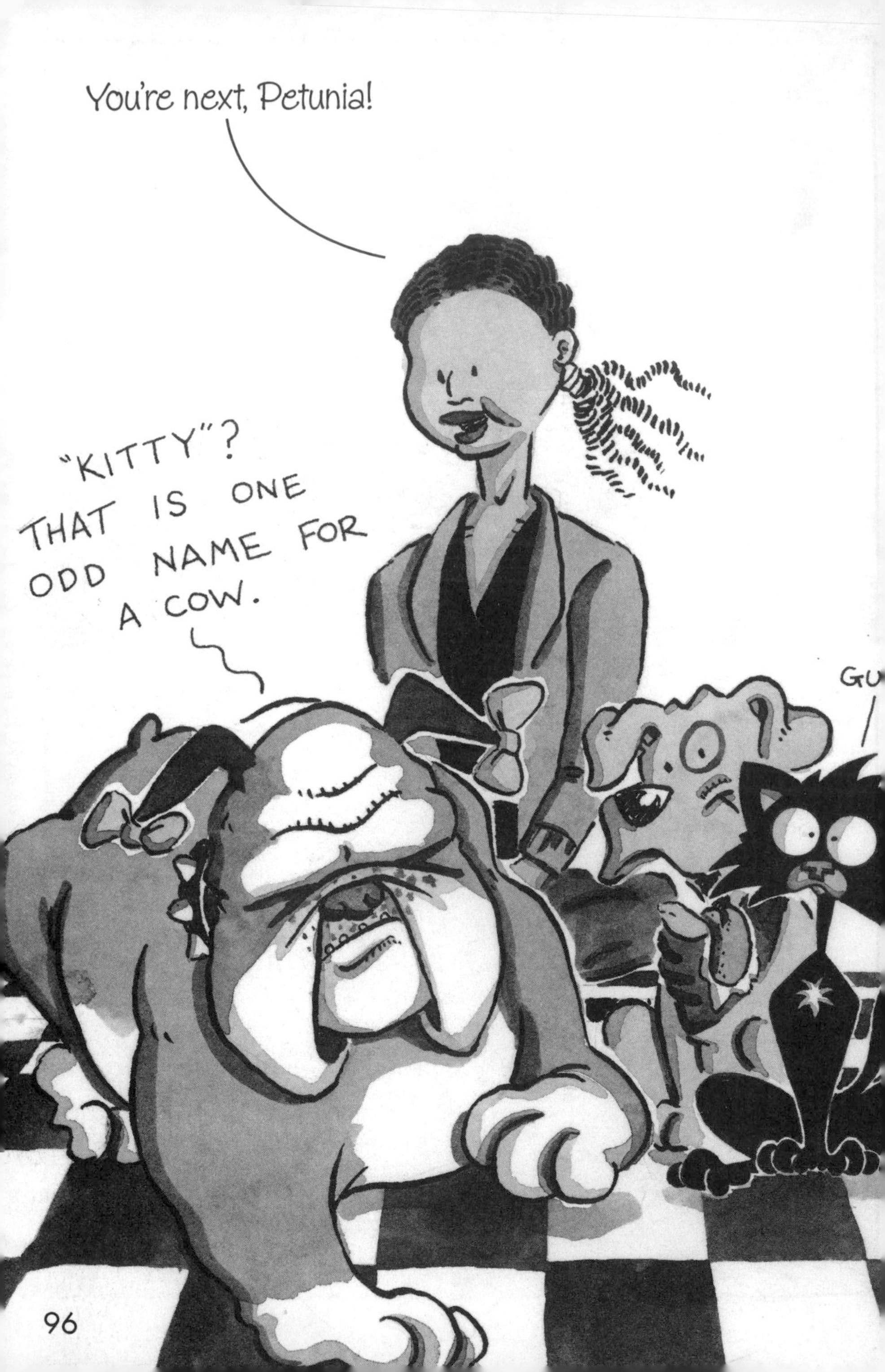
You're next, Petunia!
"KITTY"? THAT IS ONE ODD NAME FOR A COW.
GU

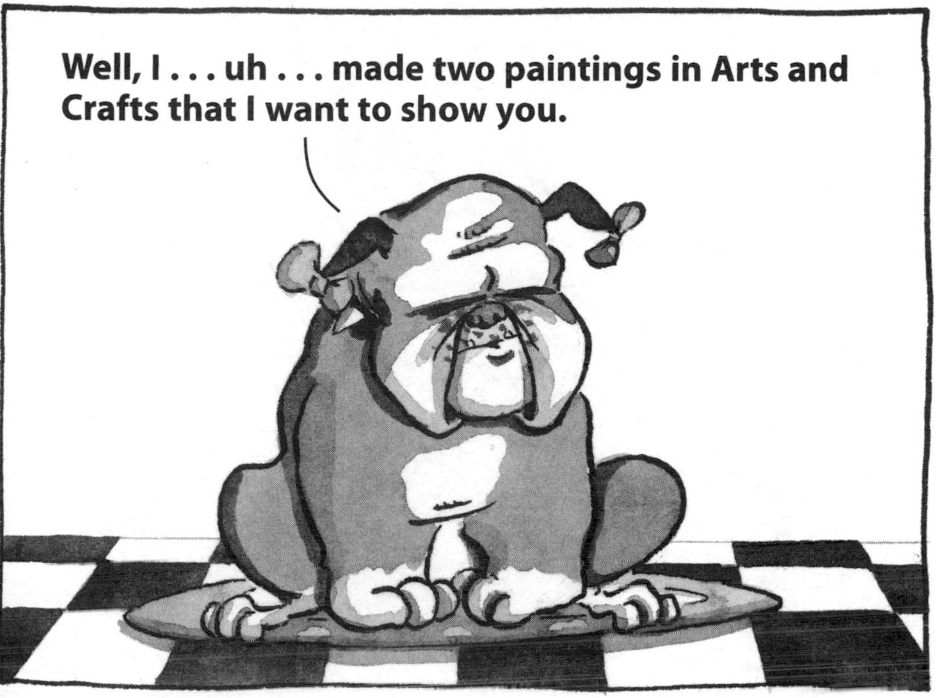
Well, I . . . uh . . . made two paintings in Arts and Crafts that I want to show you.

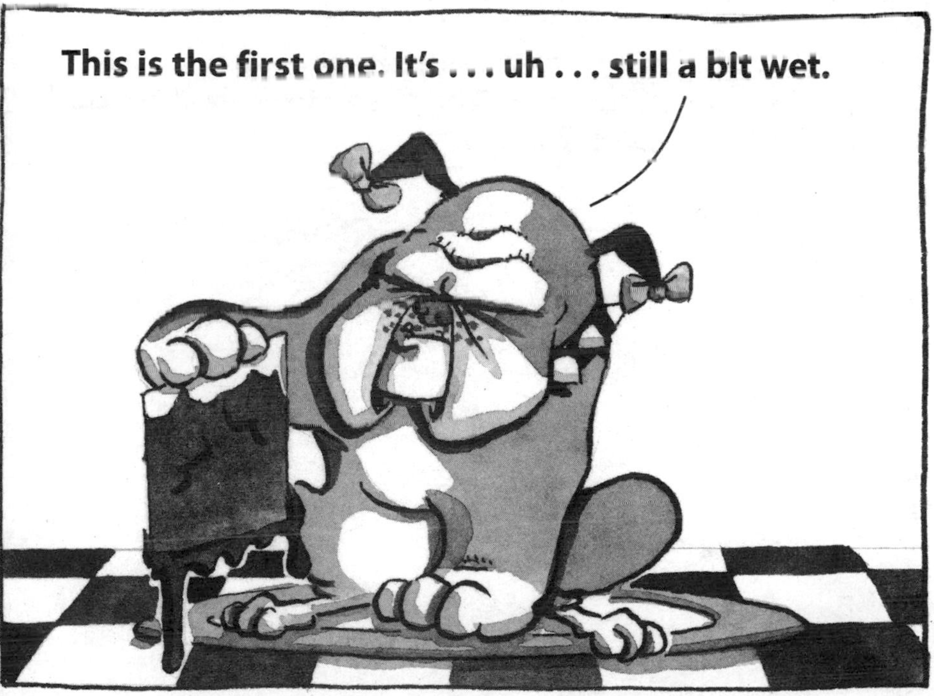
This is the first one. It's . . . uh . . . still a bit wet.

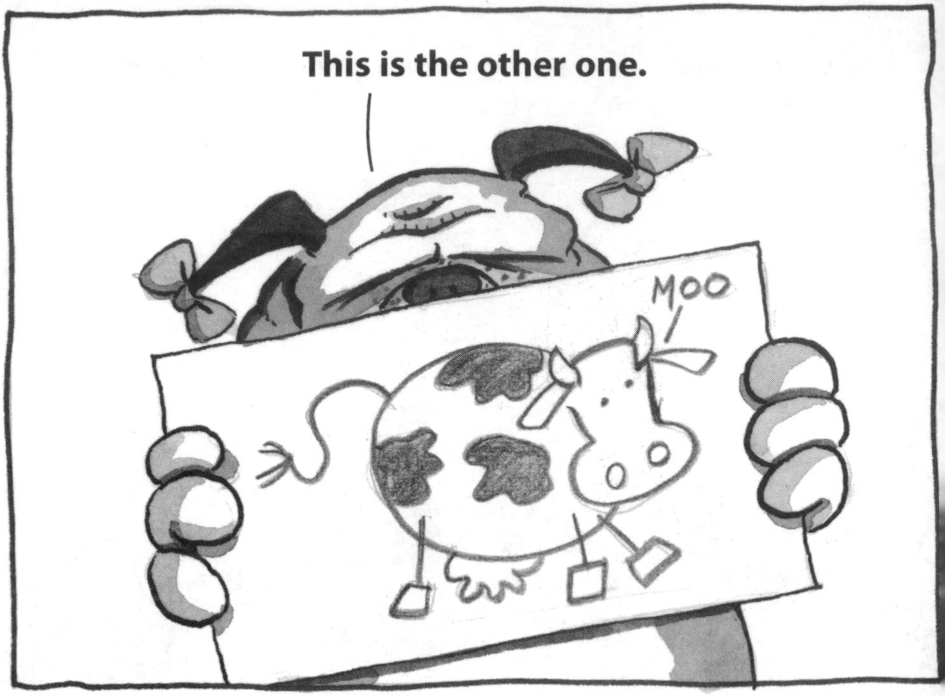
This is the other one.
MOO

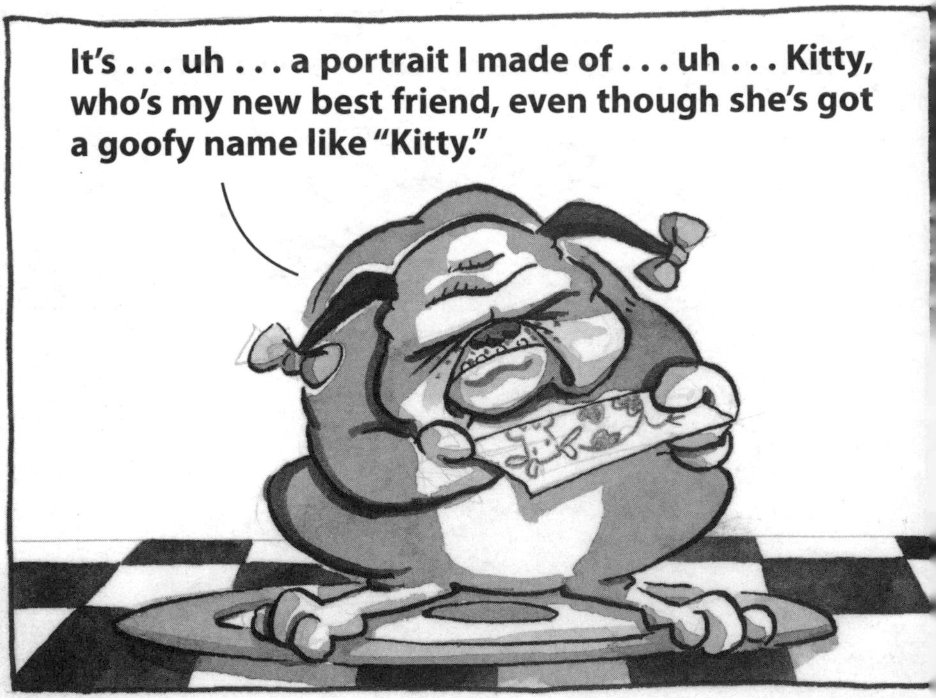
It's . . . uh . . . a portrait I made of . . . uh . . . Kitty, who's my new best friend, even though she's got a goofy name like "Kitty."

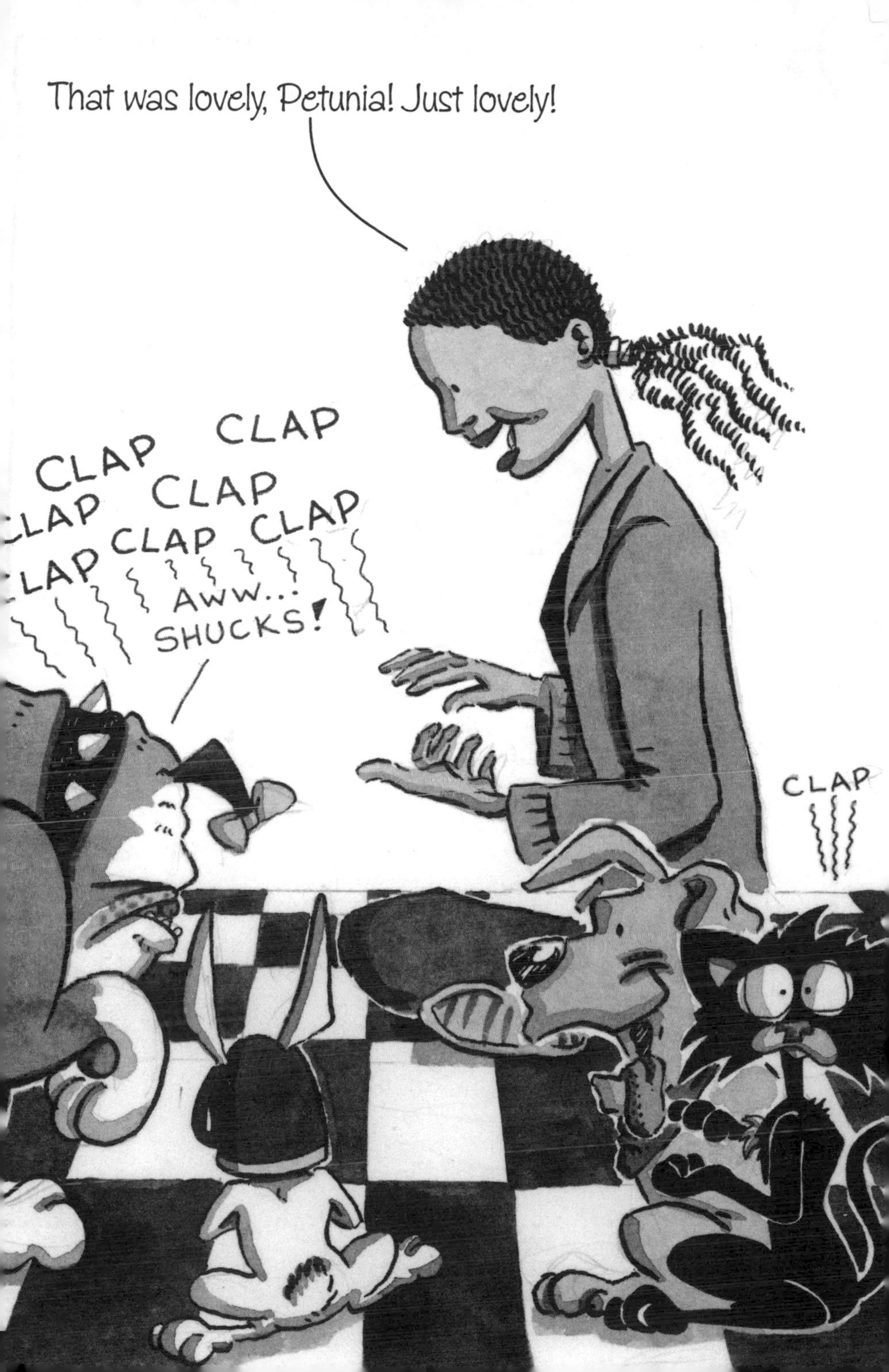
That was lovely, Petunia! Just lovely!
CLAP CLAP
CLAP CLAP
CLAP
CLAP CLAP CLAP
AWW... SHUCKS!
CLAP

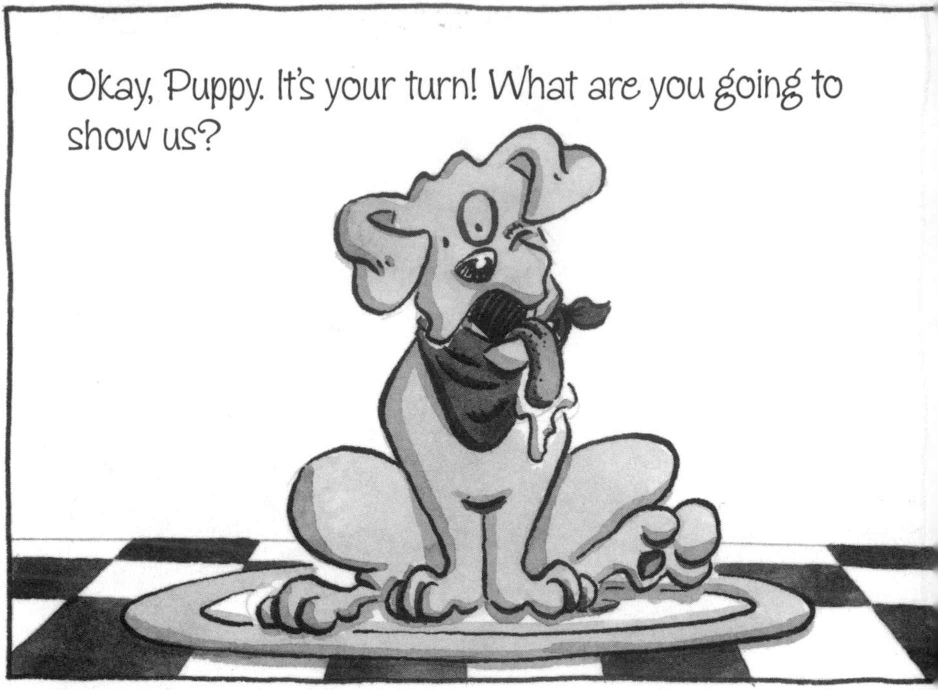
Okay, Puppy. It's your turn! What are you going to show us?

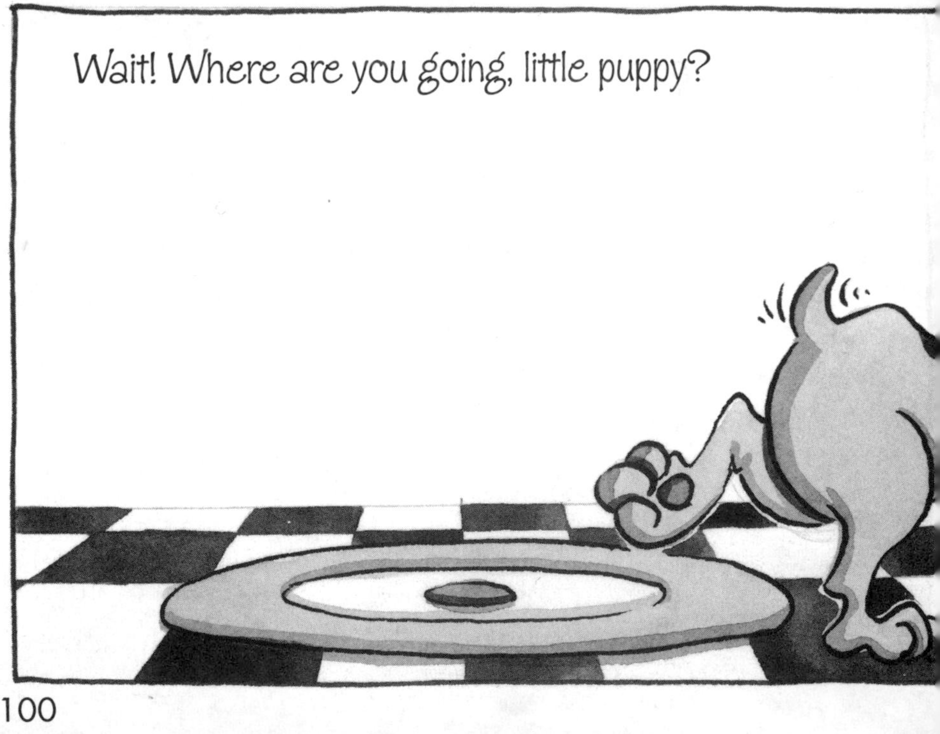
Wait! Where are you going, little puppy?

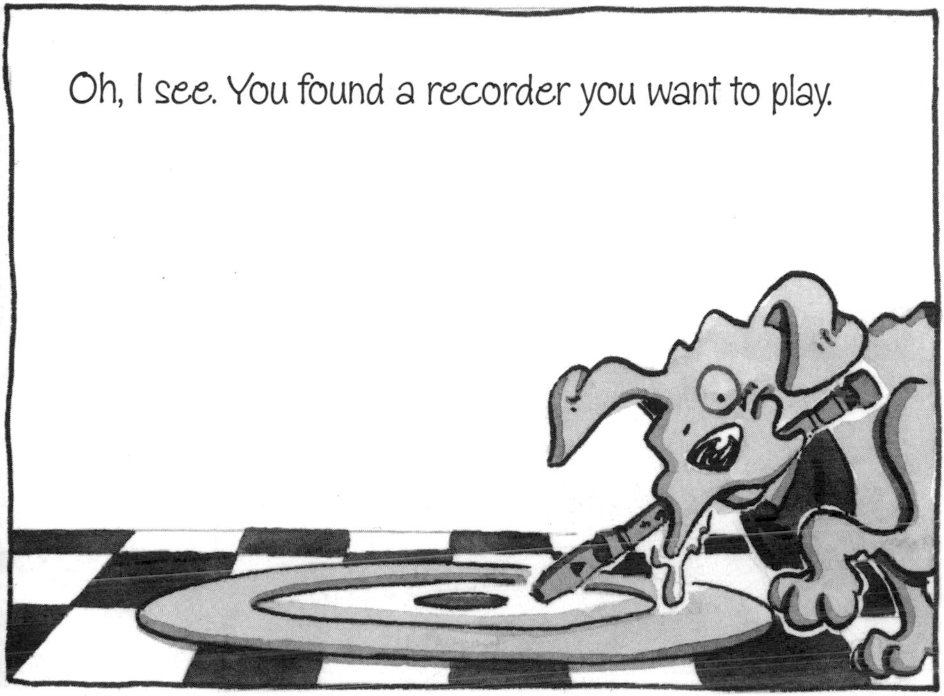
Oh, I see. You found a recorder you want to play.

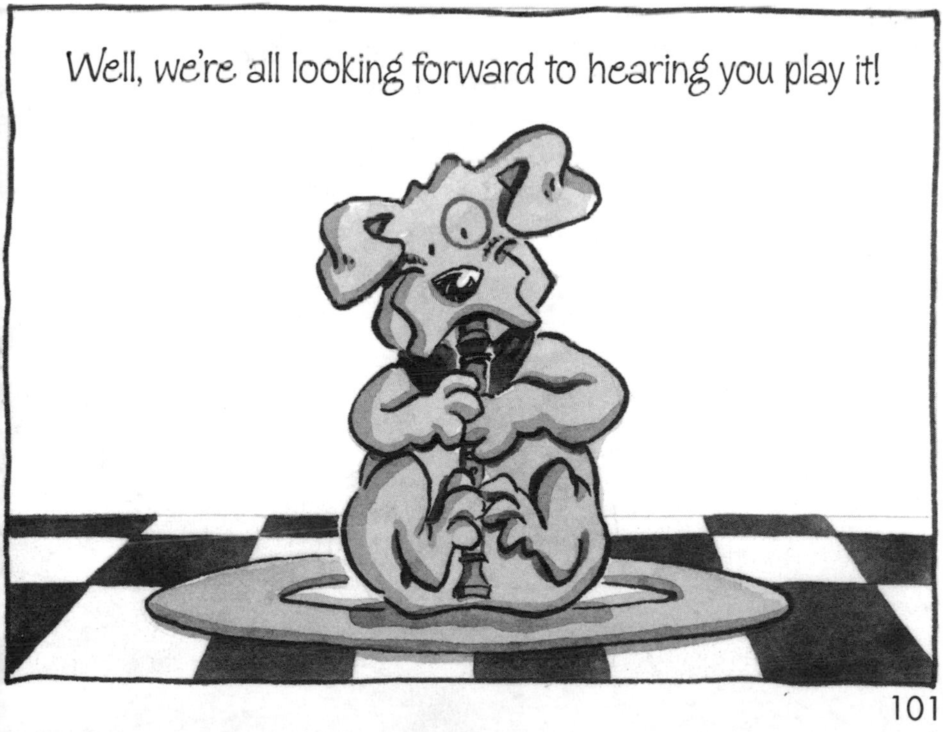
Well, we're all looking forward to hearing you play it!

Partita in a minor

for Solo Flute

J. S. Bach
BWV 1013

Allemande

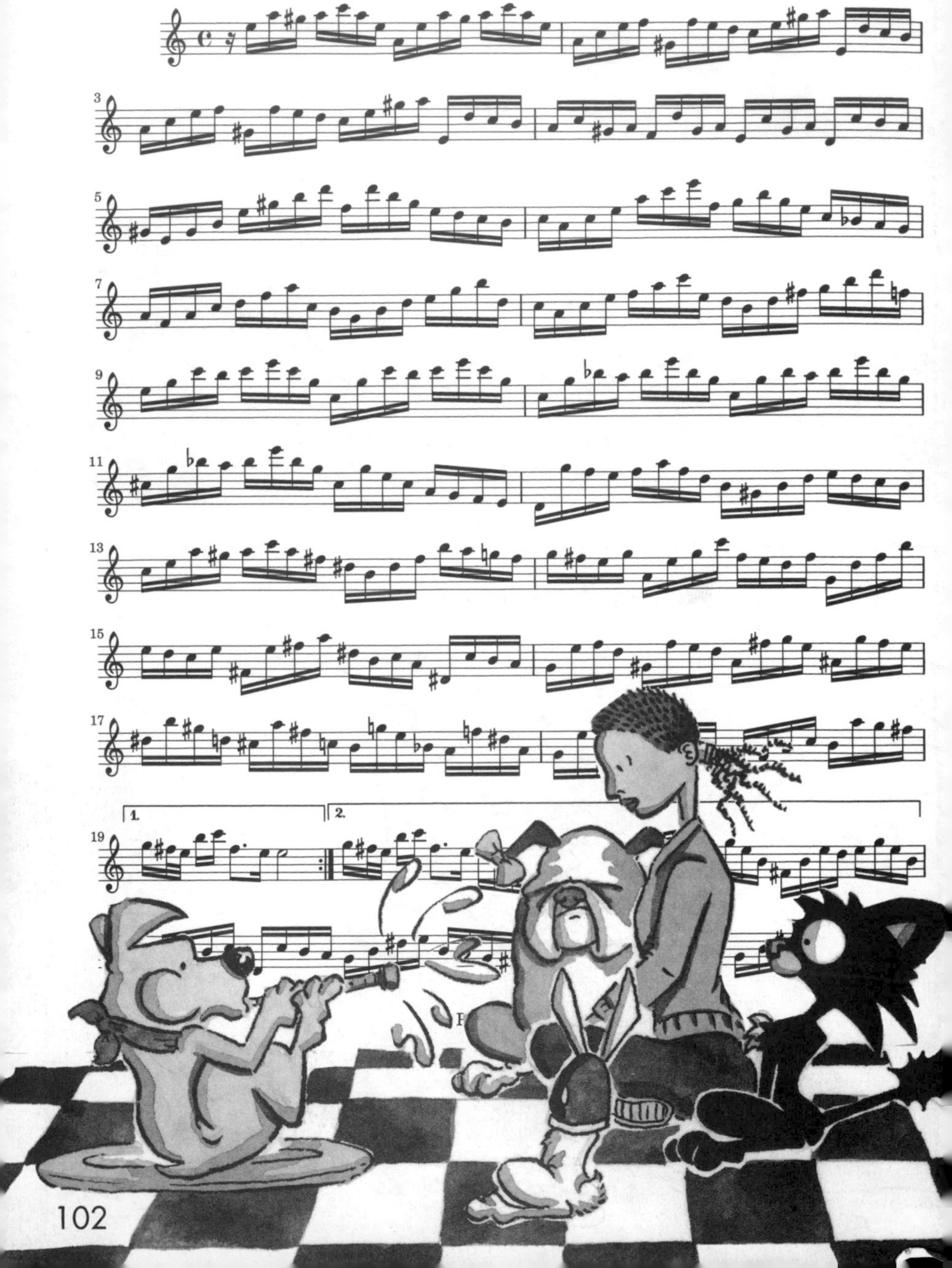

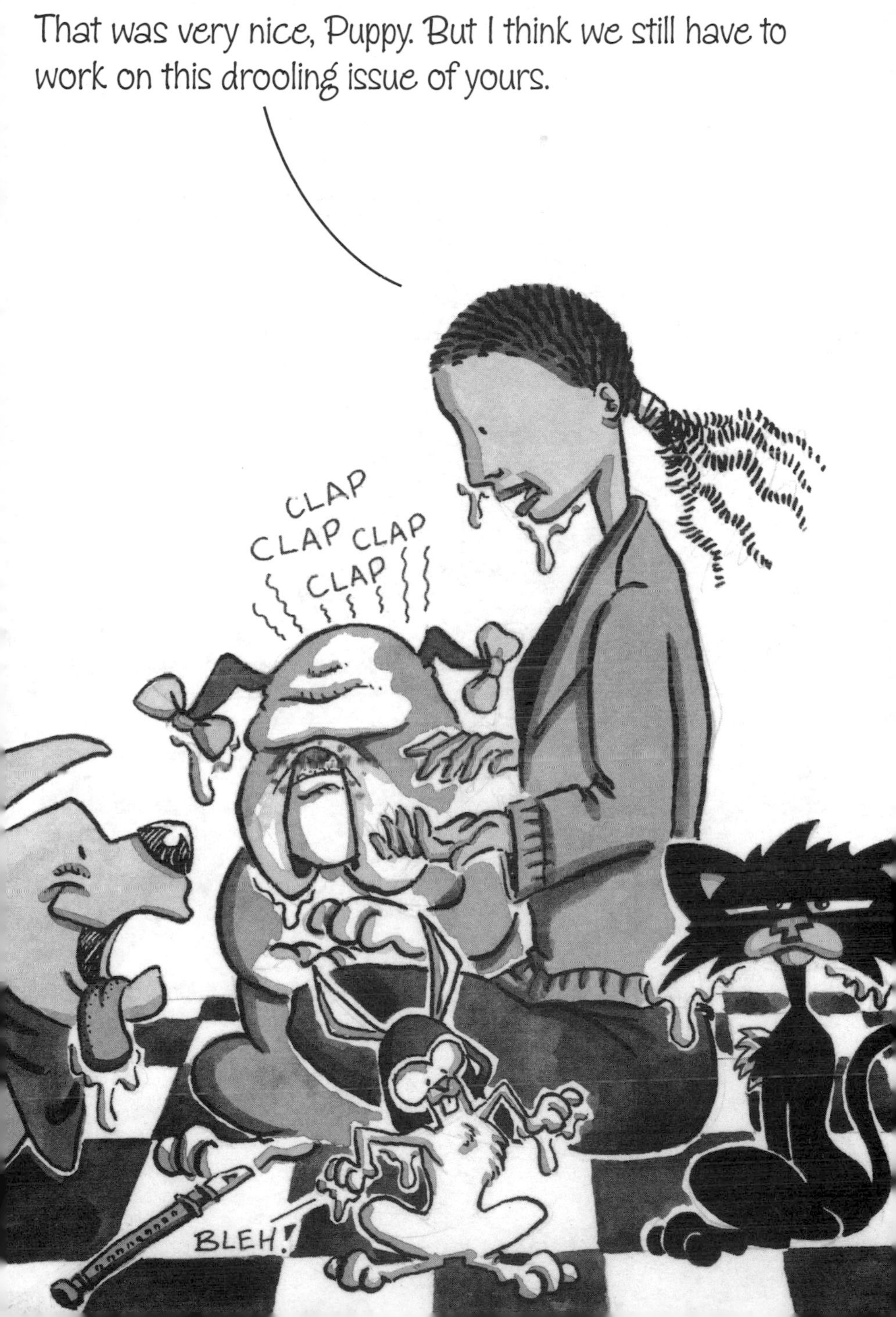
That was very nice, Puppy. But I think we still have to work on this drooling issue of yours.
CLAP
CLAP CLAP
CLAP
BLEH!

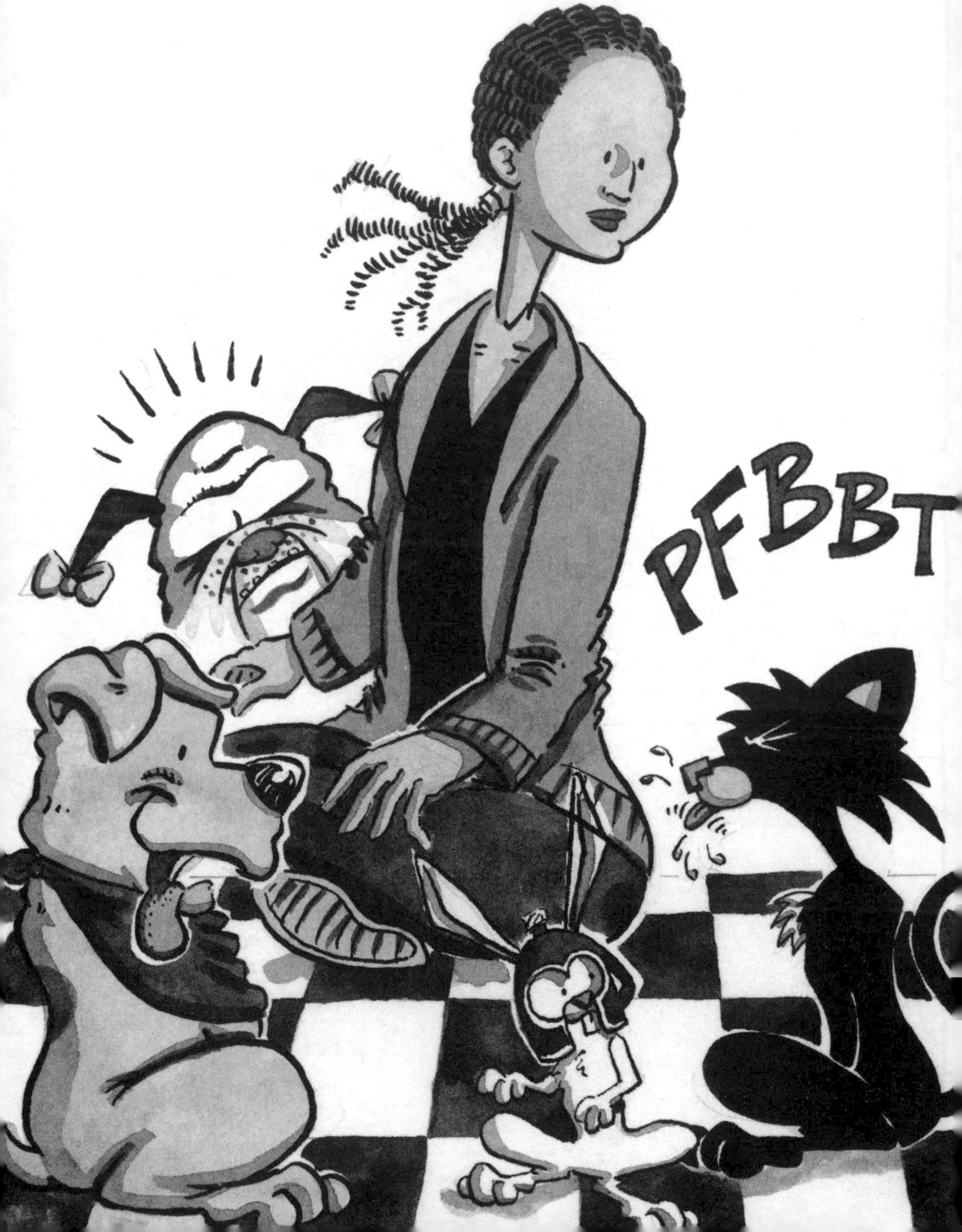
PFBBT

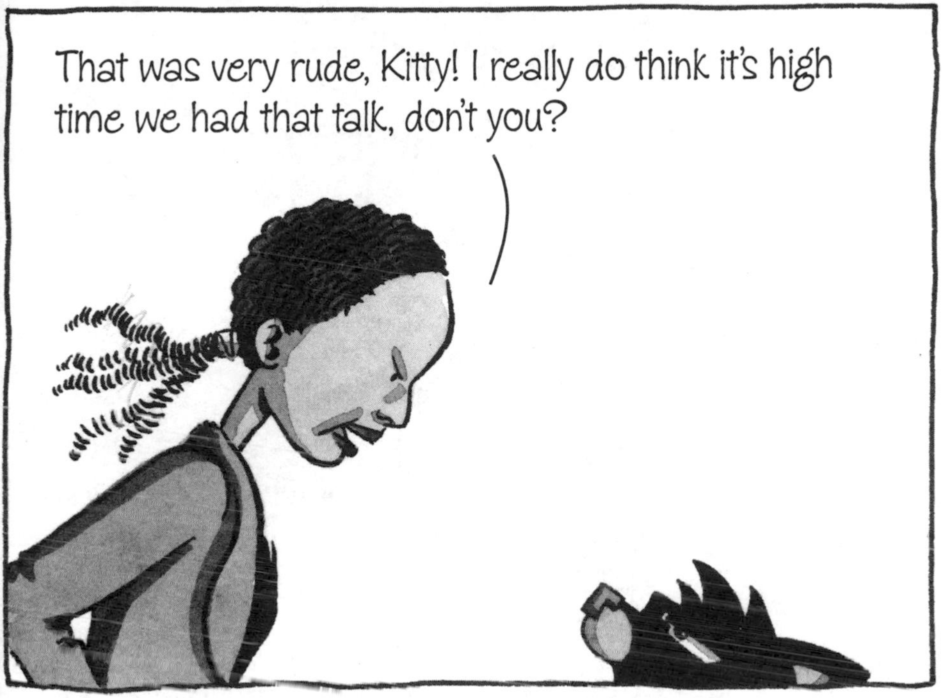
That was very rude, Kitty! I really do think it's high time we had that talk, don't you?

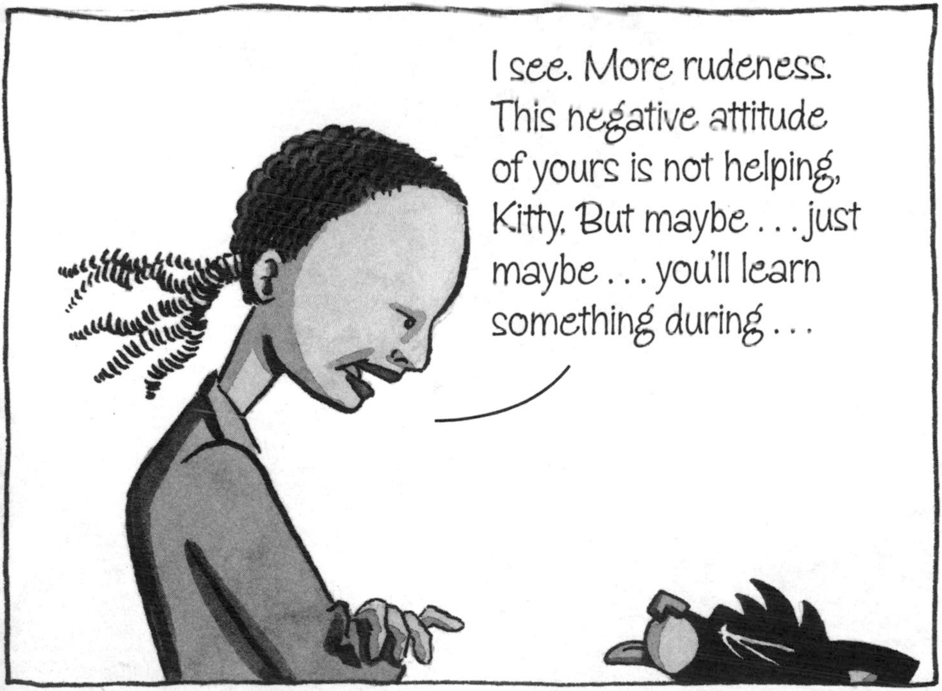
I see. More rudeness. This negative attitude of yours is not helping, Kitty. But maybe . . . just maybe . . . you'll learn something during . . .

•CHAPTER SEVEN•

STORYTIME

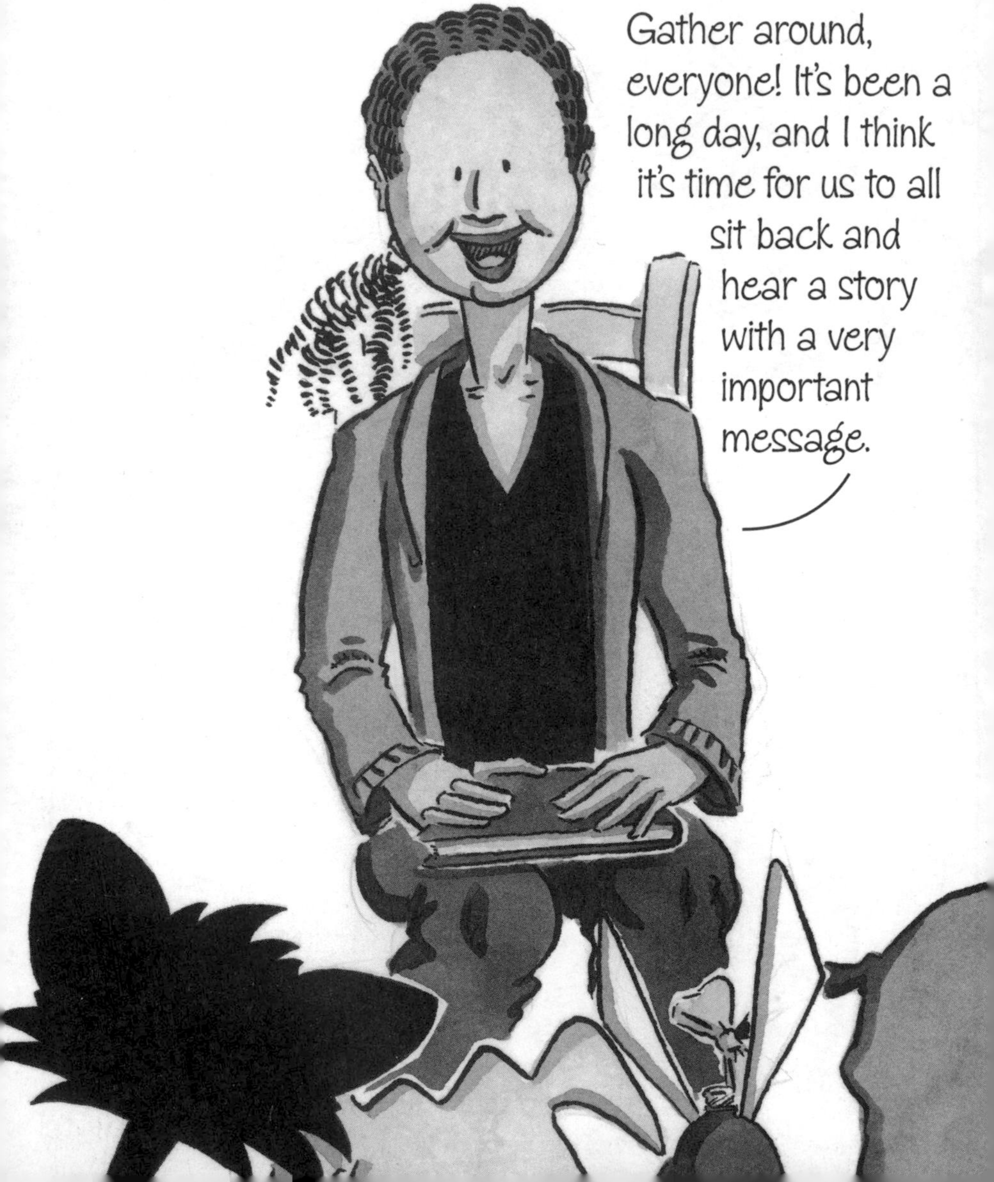
Gather around, everyone! It's been a long day, and I think it's time for us to all sit back and hear a story with a very important message.

Today's story is "Love Love Angel Kitten and Her Friends on the Farm."

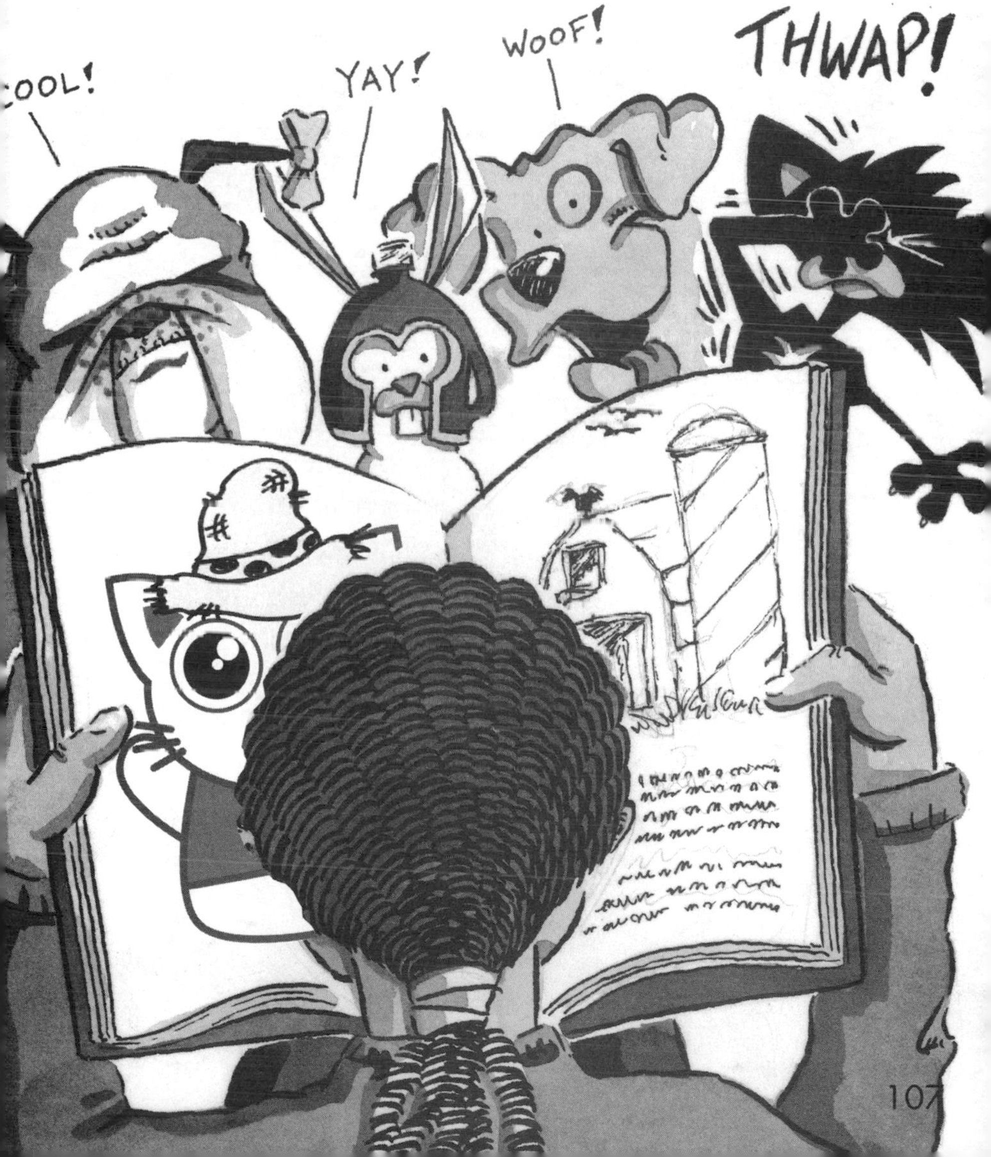
OOL!
YAY!
WOOF!
THWAP!

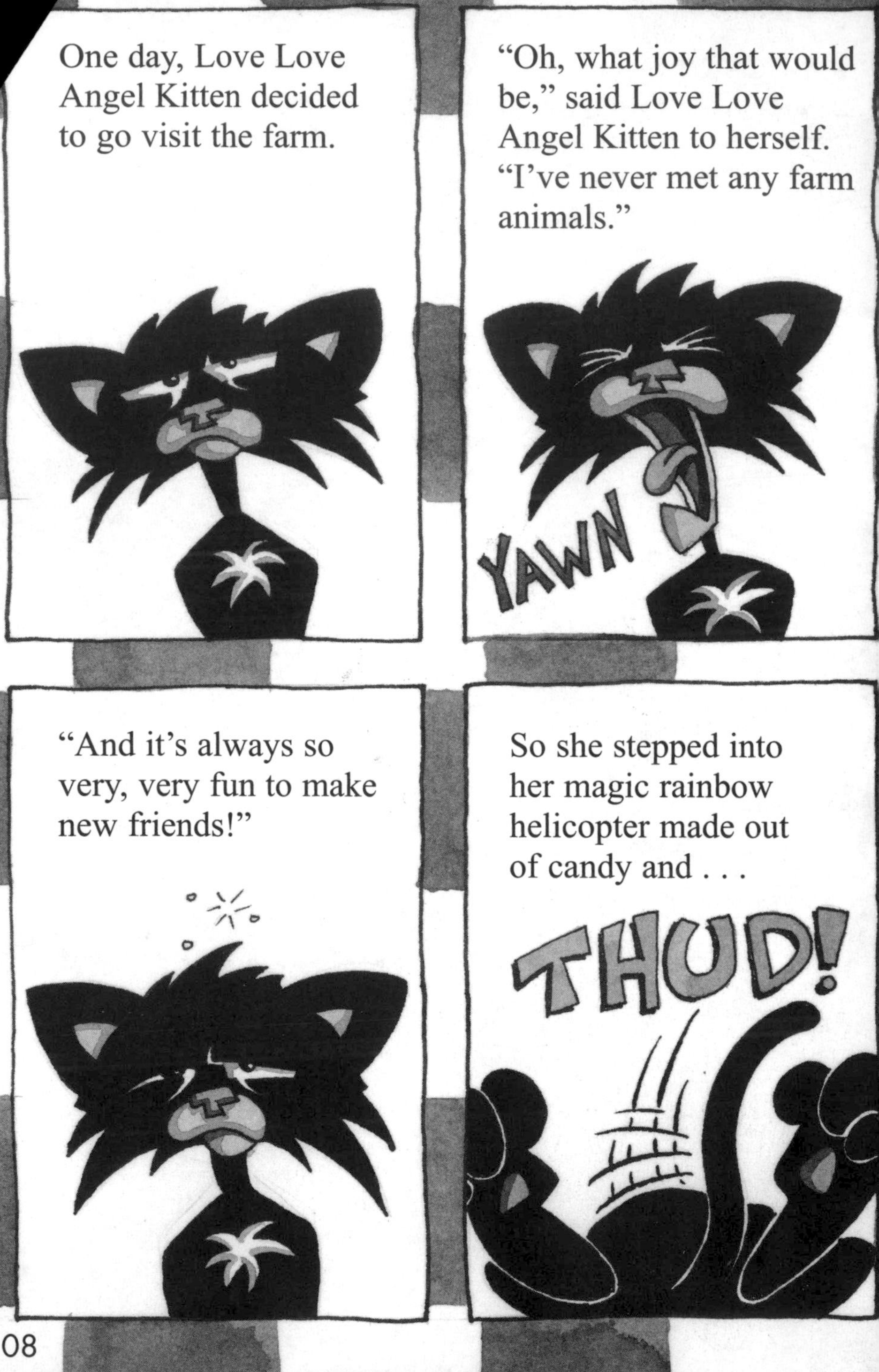
One day, Love Love Angel Kitten decided to go visit the farm.
"Oh, what joy that would be," said Love Love Angel Kitten to herself. "I've never met any farm animals."
YAWN
"And it's always so very, very fun to make new friends!"
So she stepped into her magic rainbow helicopter made out of candy and . . .
THUD!

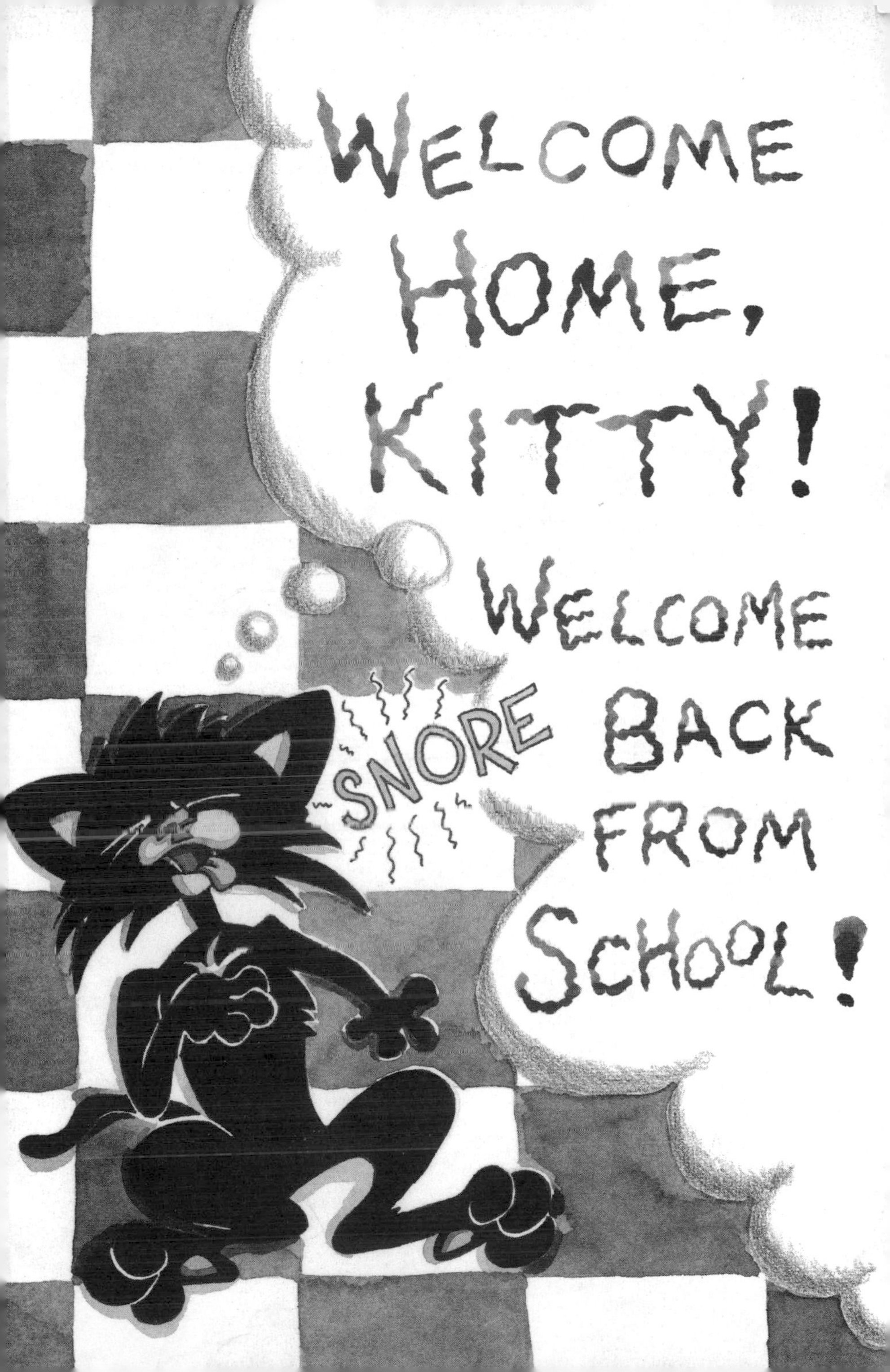
WELCOME HOME, KITTY!
WELCOME BACK FROM SCHOOL!
SNORE

But you're not just plain ol' Kitty anymore, are you? No, now you're . . .

LOVE LOVE ANGEL KITTY!

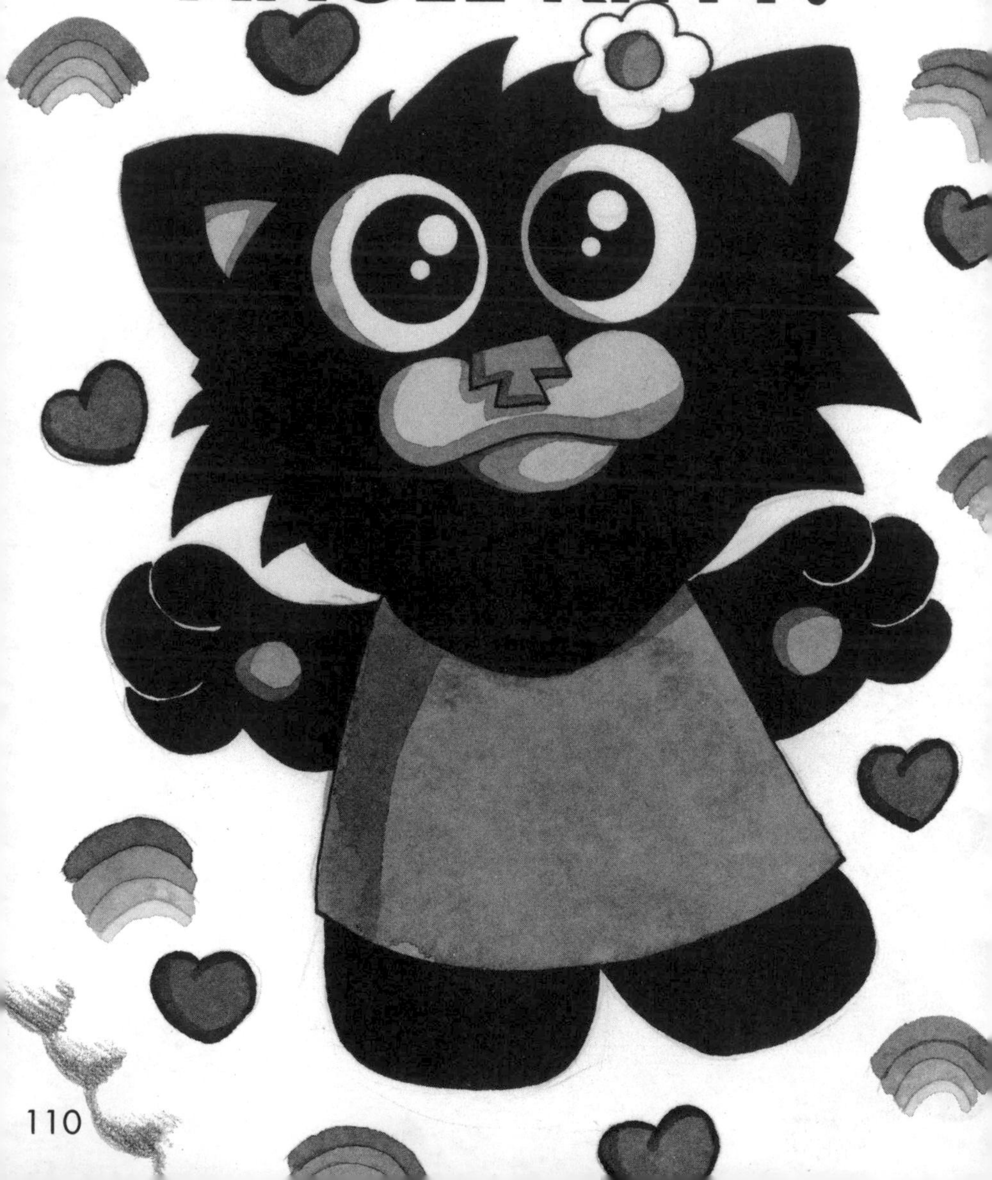

HEY, EVERYBODY! Look at Love Love Angel Kitty!

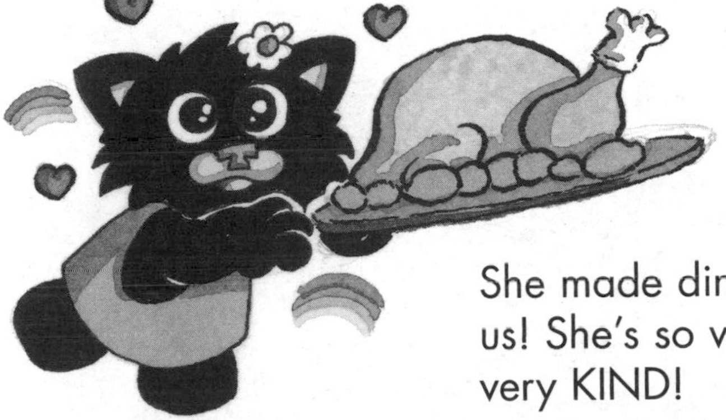

She made dinner for us! She's so very, very KIND!

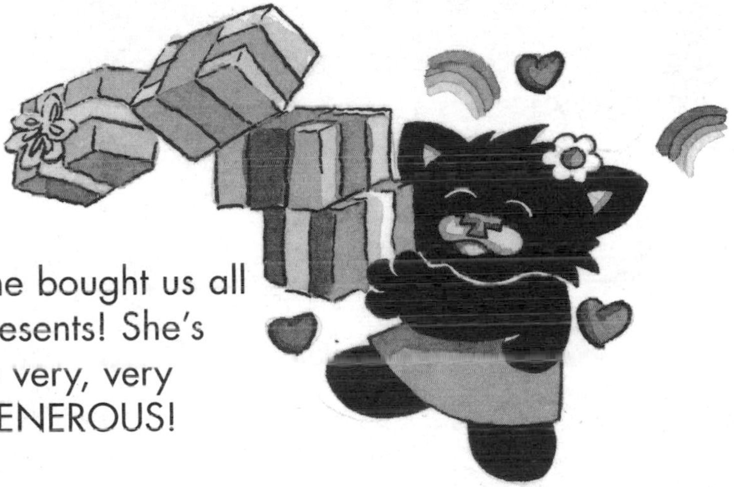

She bought us all presents! She's so very, very GENEROUS!

She cleaned her own litterbox! She's so very, very HELPFUL!

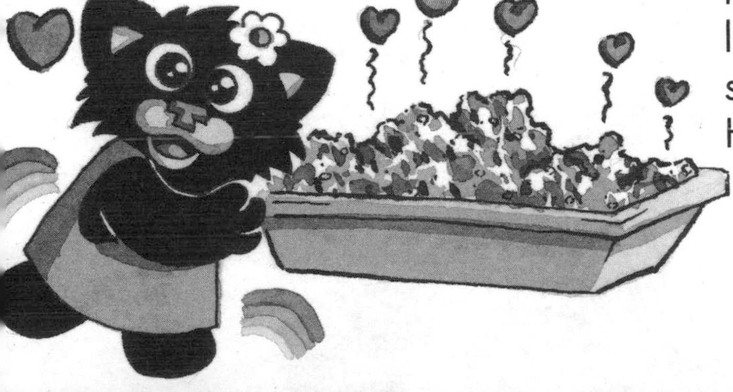

Love Love Angel Kitty is such a very, very, good, good, GOOD Kitty! Look at how much she loves Baby!

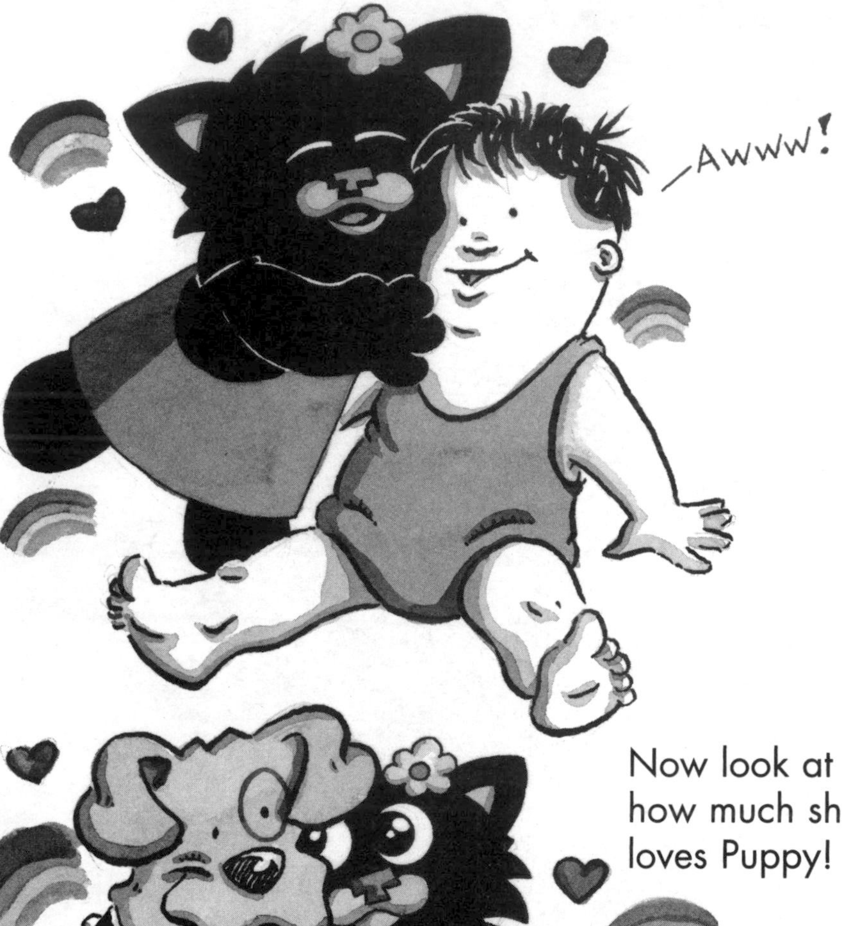
AWWW!

Now look at how much she loves Puppy!

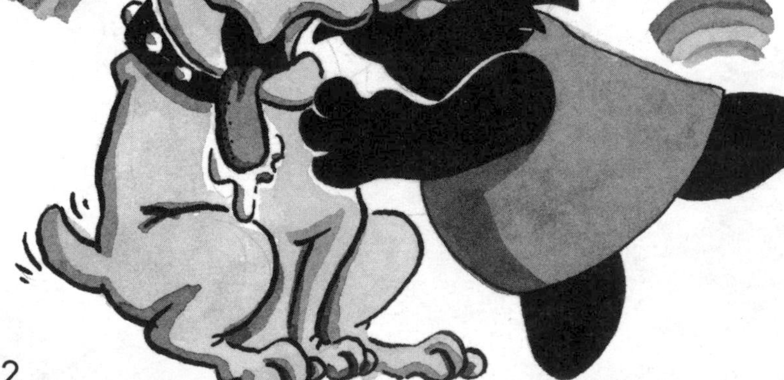

Finally, there is peace in our home. Where once there were screaming temper tantrums, now there are only kisses. Where once there were fights and shrieks and howls, now there are only hugs. Where once there was only mayhem, now there is only love. Sweet, wonderful LOVE.

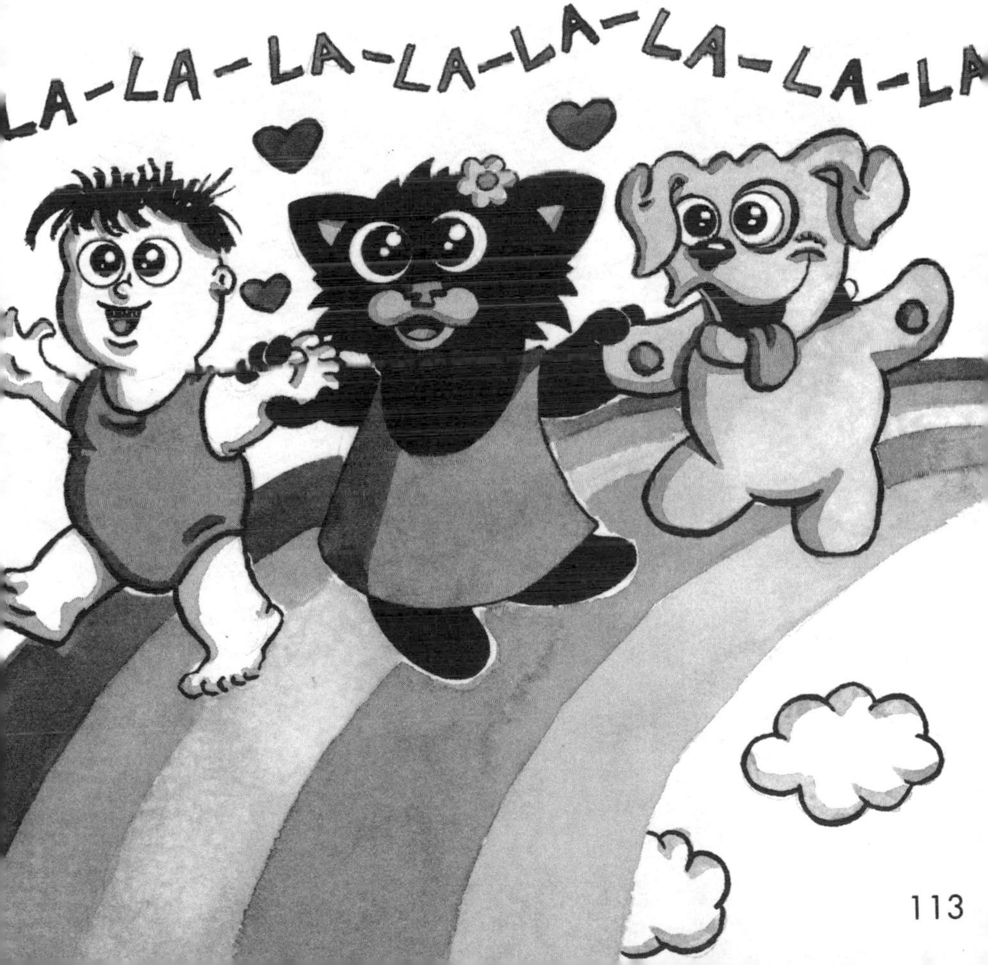
LA-LA-LA-LA-LA-LA-LA-LA

And it's all thanks to

SCHOOL
SCHOOL
SCHOOL
SCHOOL
SCHOOL
SCHOOL

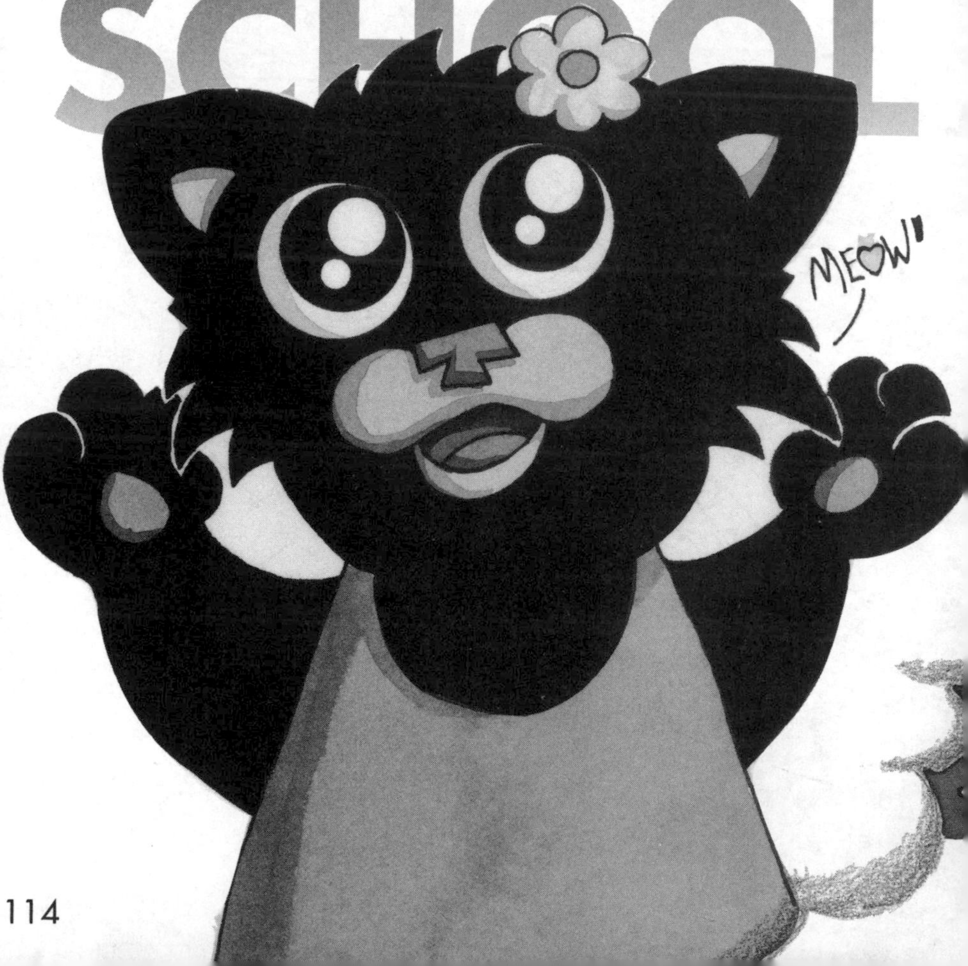
MEOW!

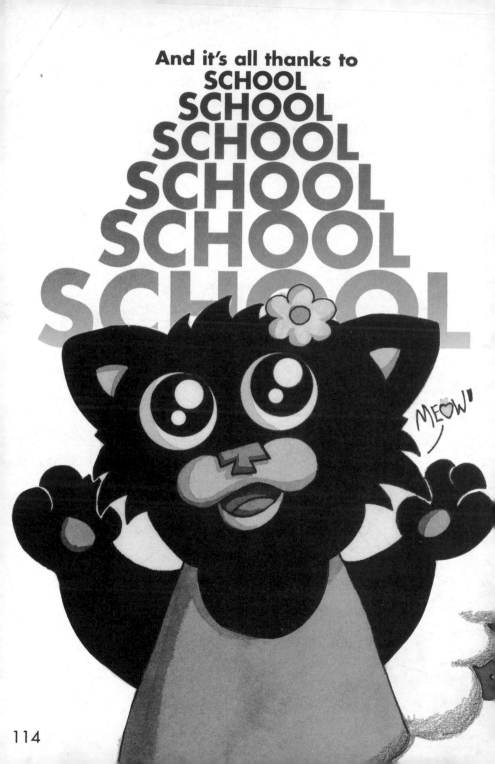

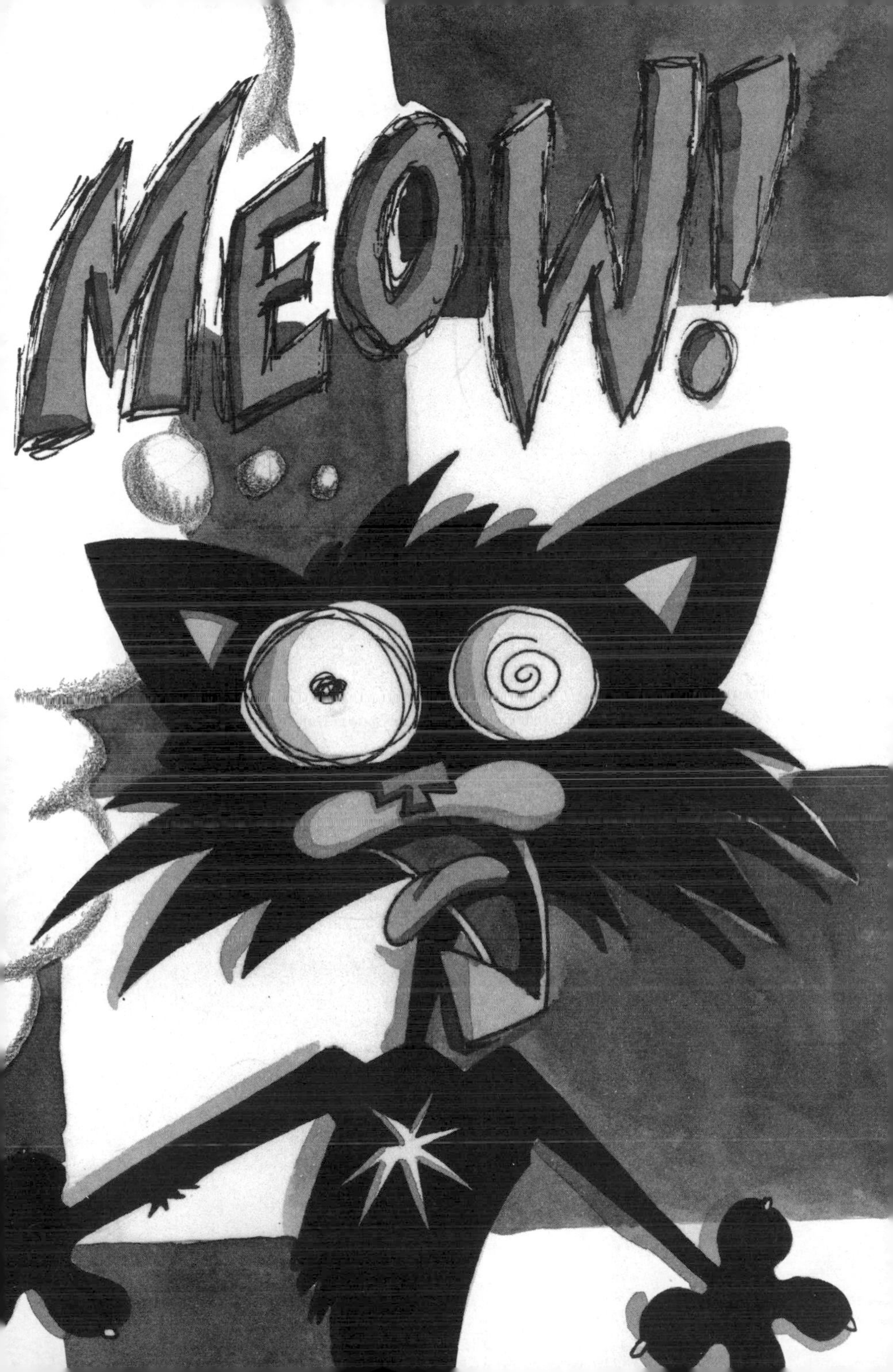
MEOW!

Are you all right, Kitty? Did something upset you? Were you frightened by the part where Love Love Angel Kitten tried to hug the disobedient chicken?

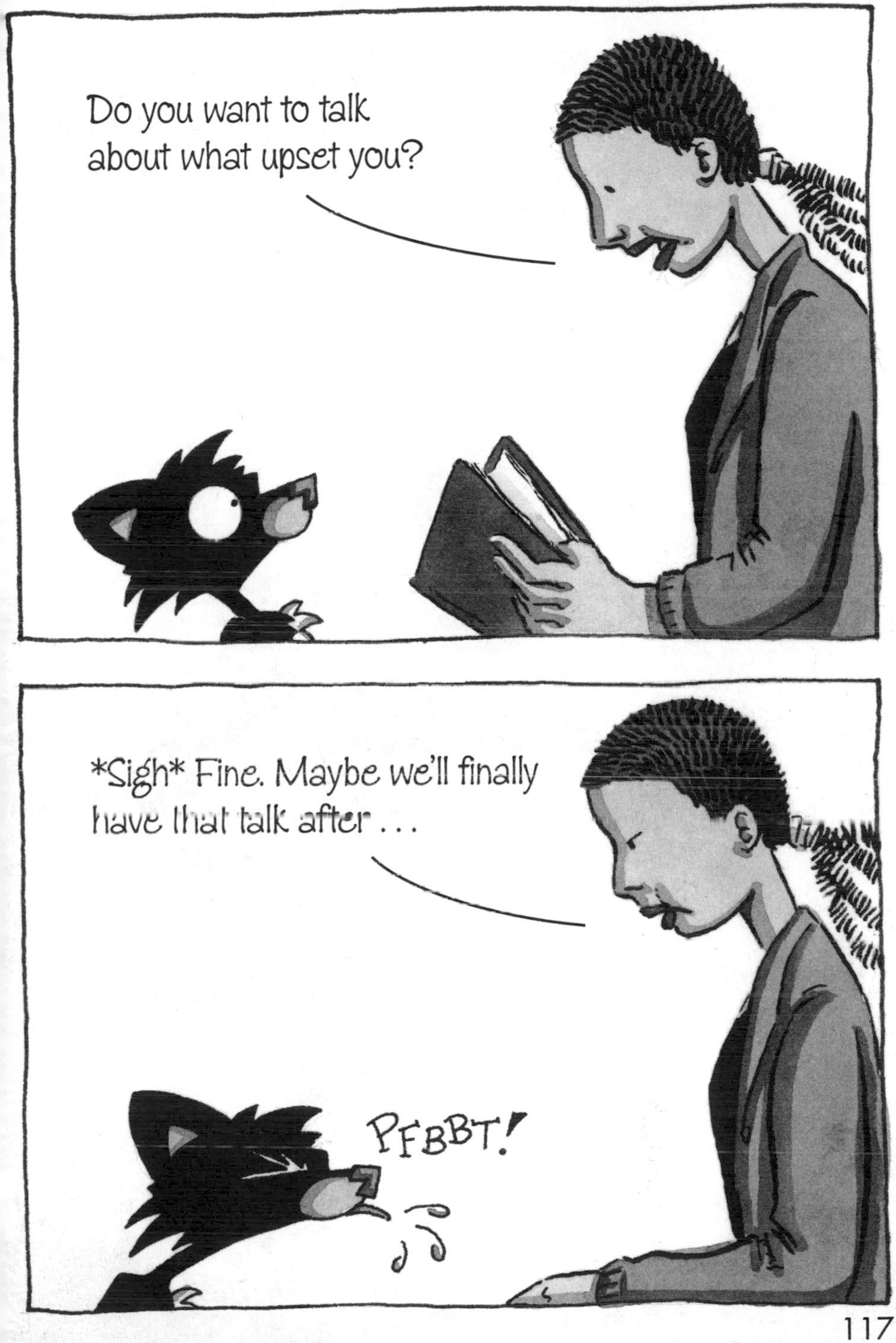
Do you want to talk about what upset you?
Sigh Fine. Maybe we'll finally have that talk after . . .
PFBBT!

•CHAPTER EIGHT•

GRADUATION

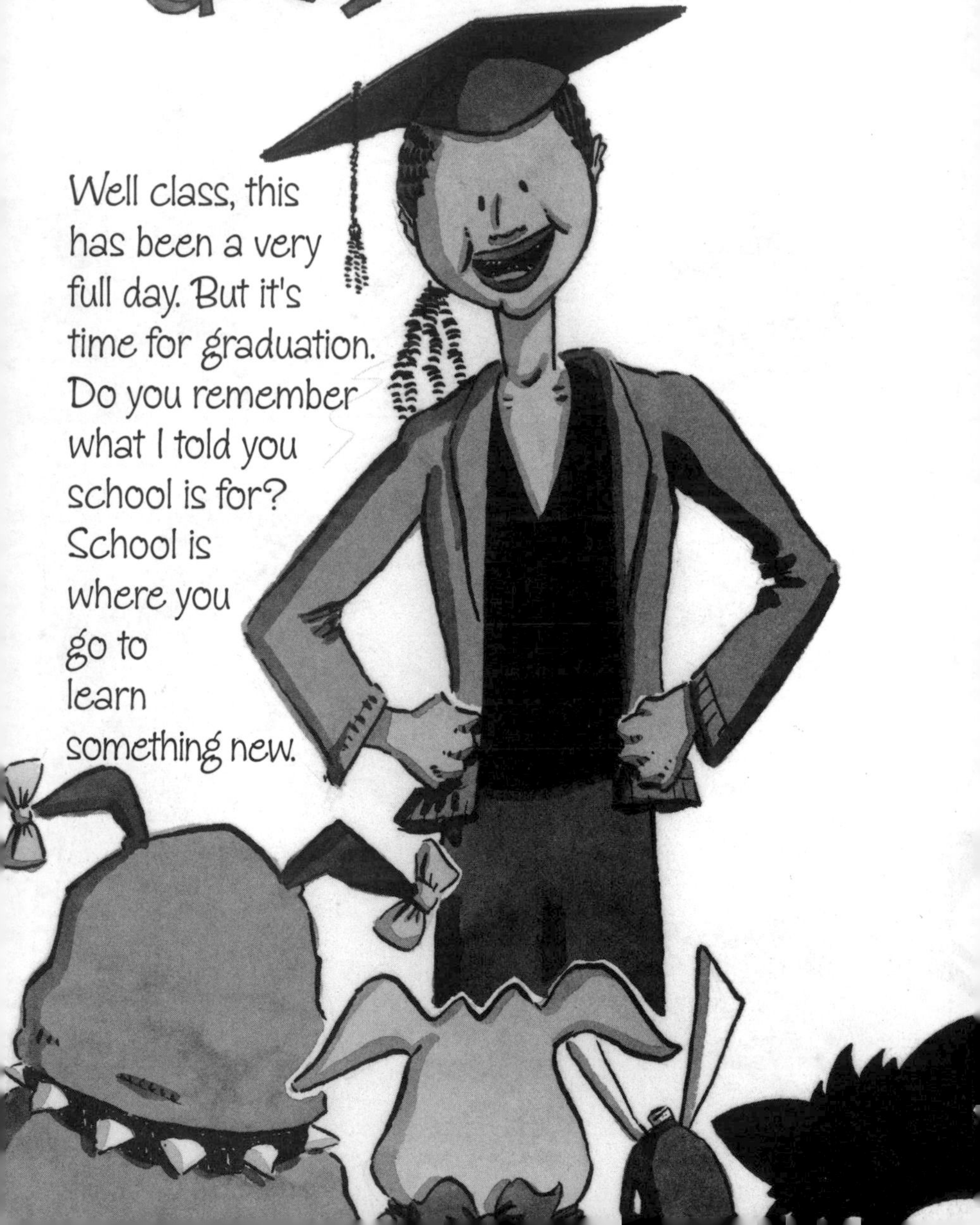
Well class, this has been a very full day. But it's time for graduation. Do you remember what I told you school is for? School is where you go to learn something new.

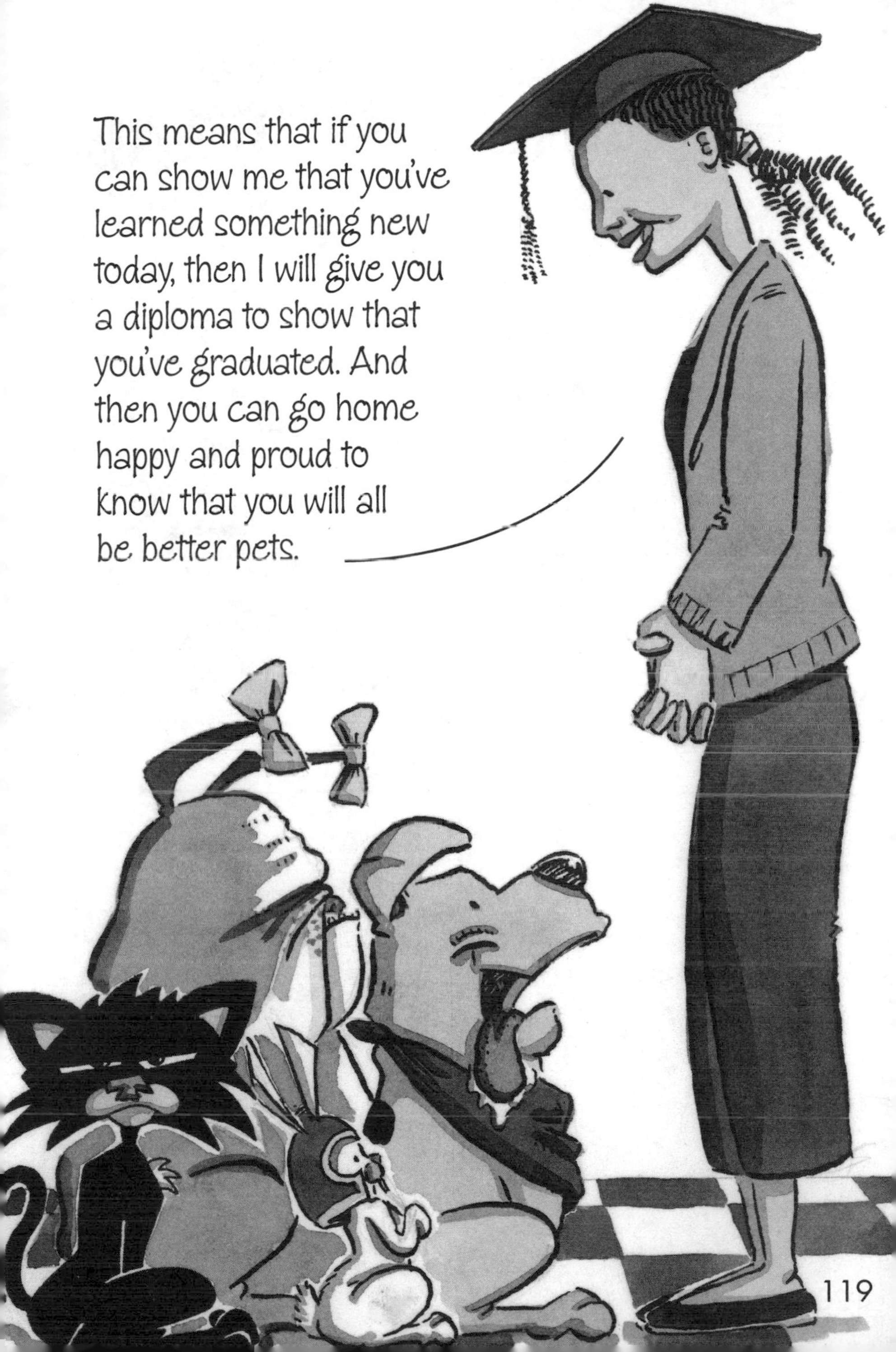
This means that if you can show me that you've learned something new today, then I will give you a diploma to show that you've graduated. And then you can go home happy and proud to know that you will all be better pets.

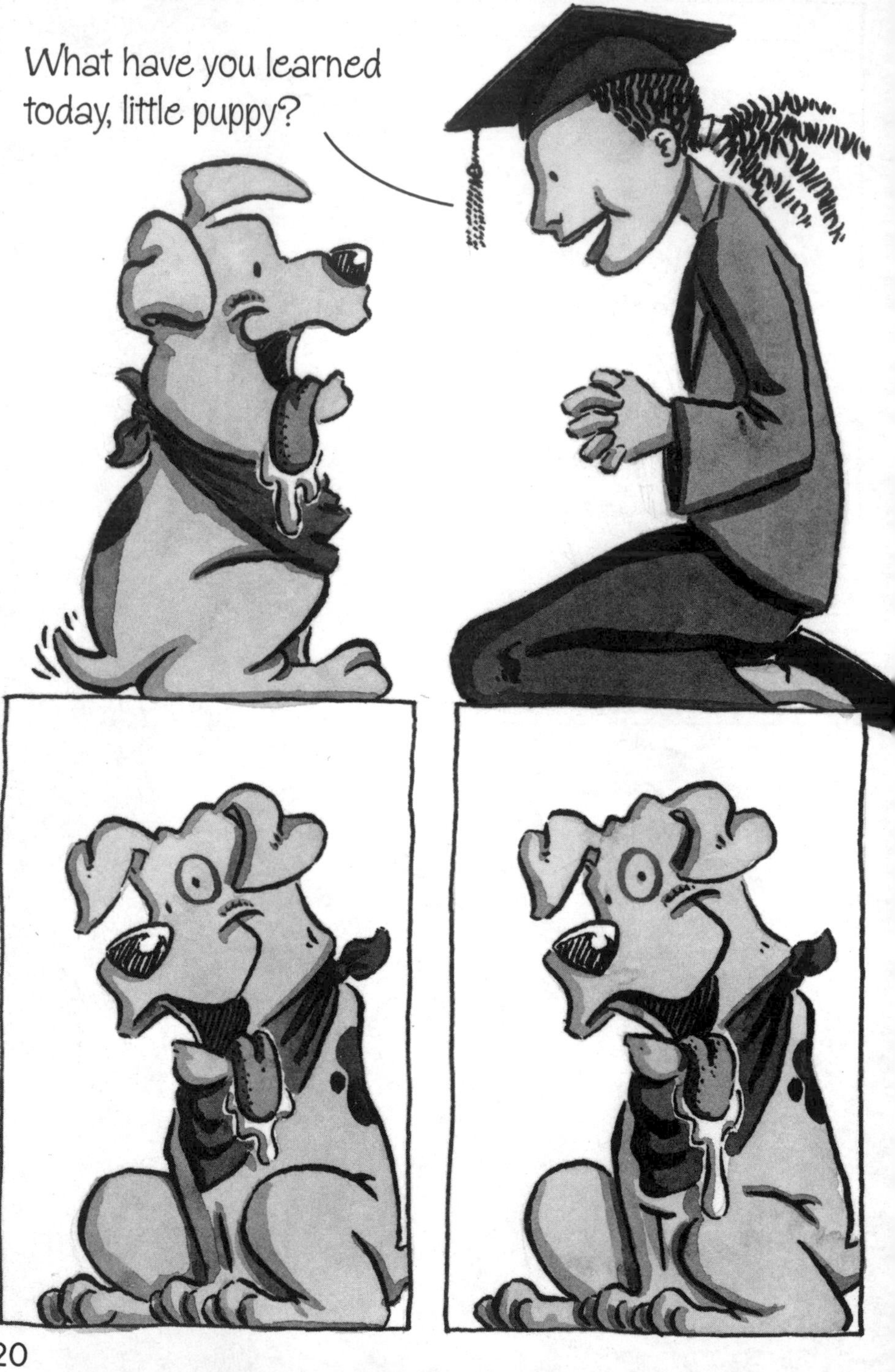
What have you learned today, little puppy?

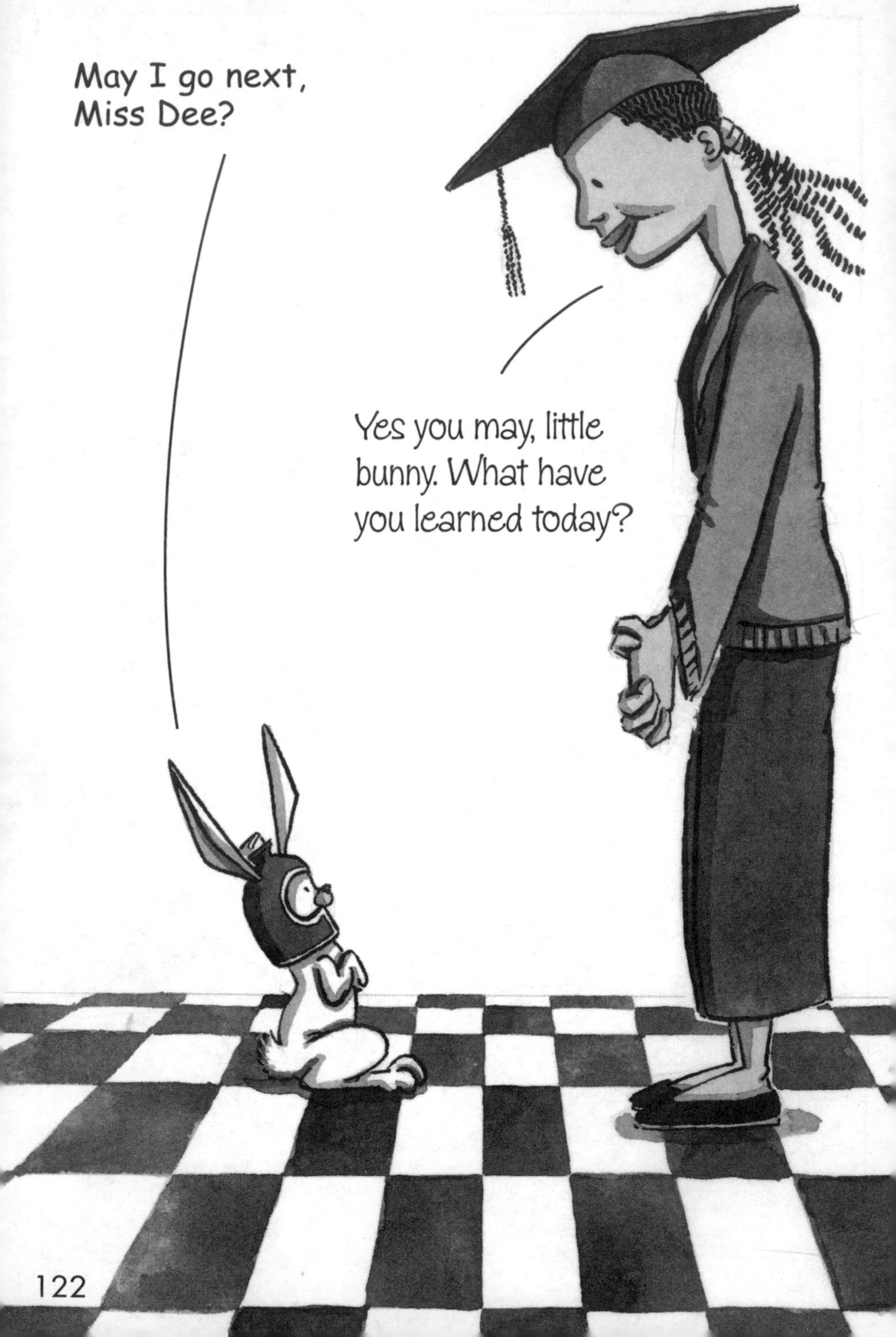
May I go next, Miss Dee?
Yes you may, little bunny. What have you learned today?

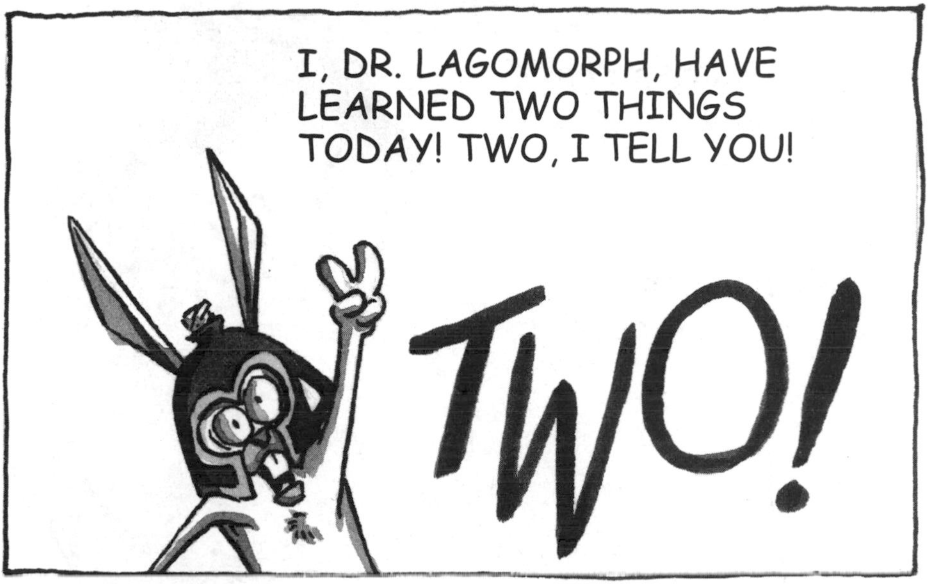
I, DR. LAGOMORPH, HAVE LEARNED TWO THINGS TODAY! TWO, I TELL YOU!
TWO!

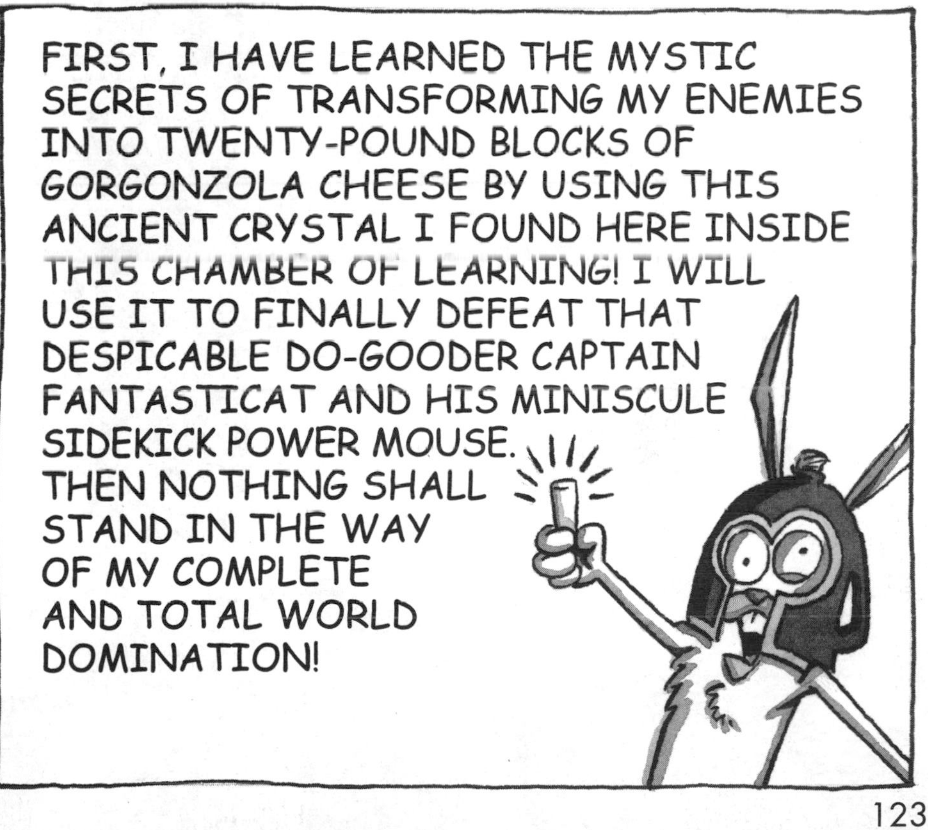
FIRST, I HAVE LEARNED THE MYSTIC SECRETS OF TRANSFORMING MY ENEMIES INTO TWENTY-POUND BLOCKS OF GORGONZOLA CHEESE BY USING THIS ANCIENT CRYSTAL I FOUND HERE INSIDE THIS CHAMBER OF LEARNING! I WILL USE IT TO FINALLY DEFEAT THAT DESPICABLE DO-GOODER CAPTAIN FANTASTICAT AND HIS MINISCULE SIDEKICK POWER MOUSE.
THEN NOTHING SHALL STAND IN THE WAY OF MY COMPLETE AND TOTAL WORLD DOMINATION!

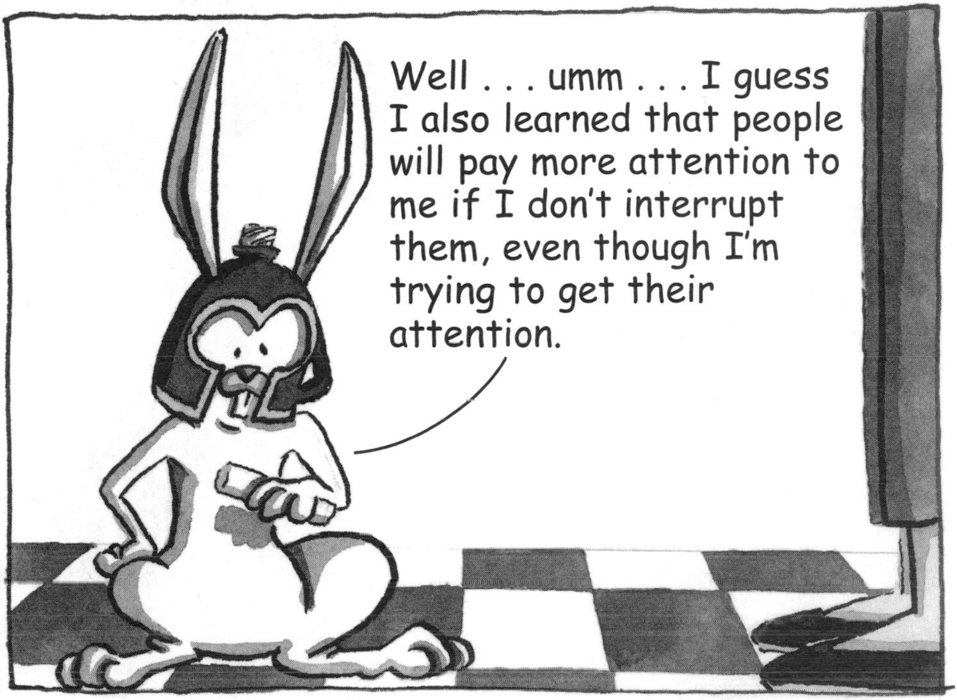
Well . . . umm . . . I guess I also learned that people will pay more attention to me if I don't interrupt them, even though I'm trying to get their attention.

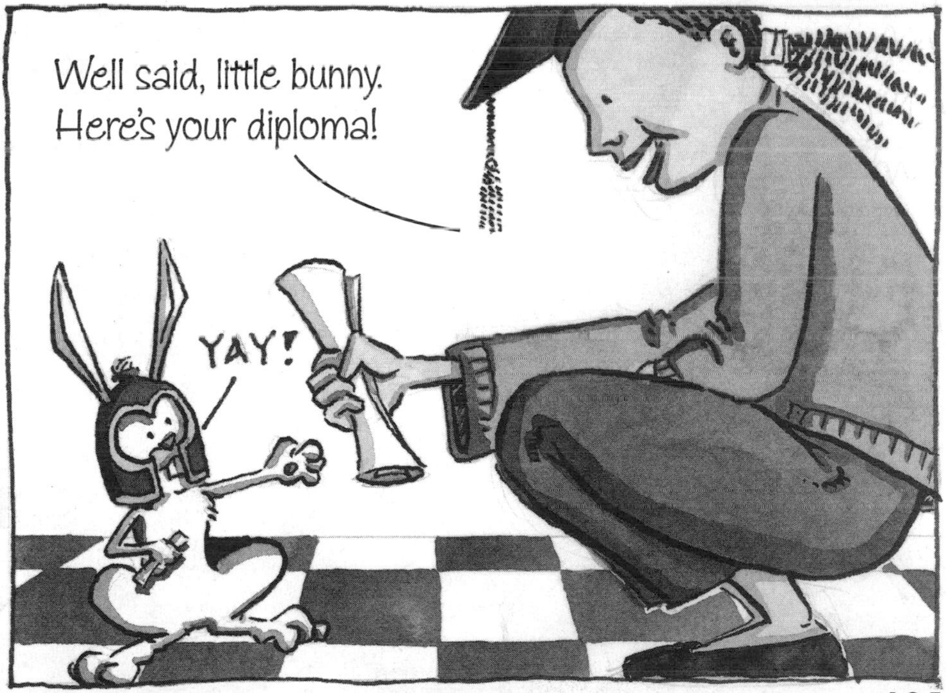
Well said, little bunny. Here's your diploma!
YAY!

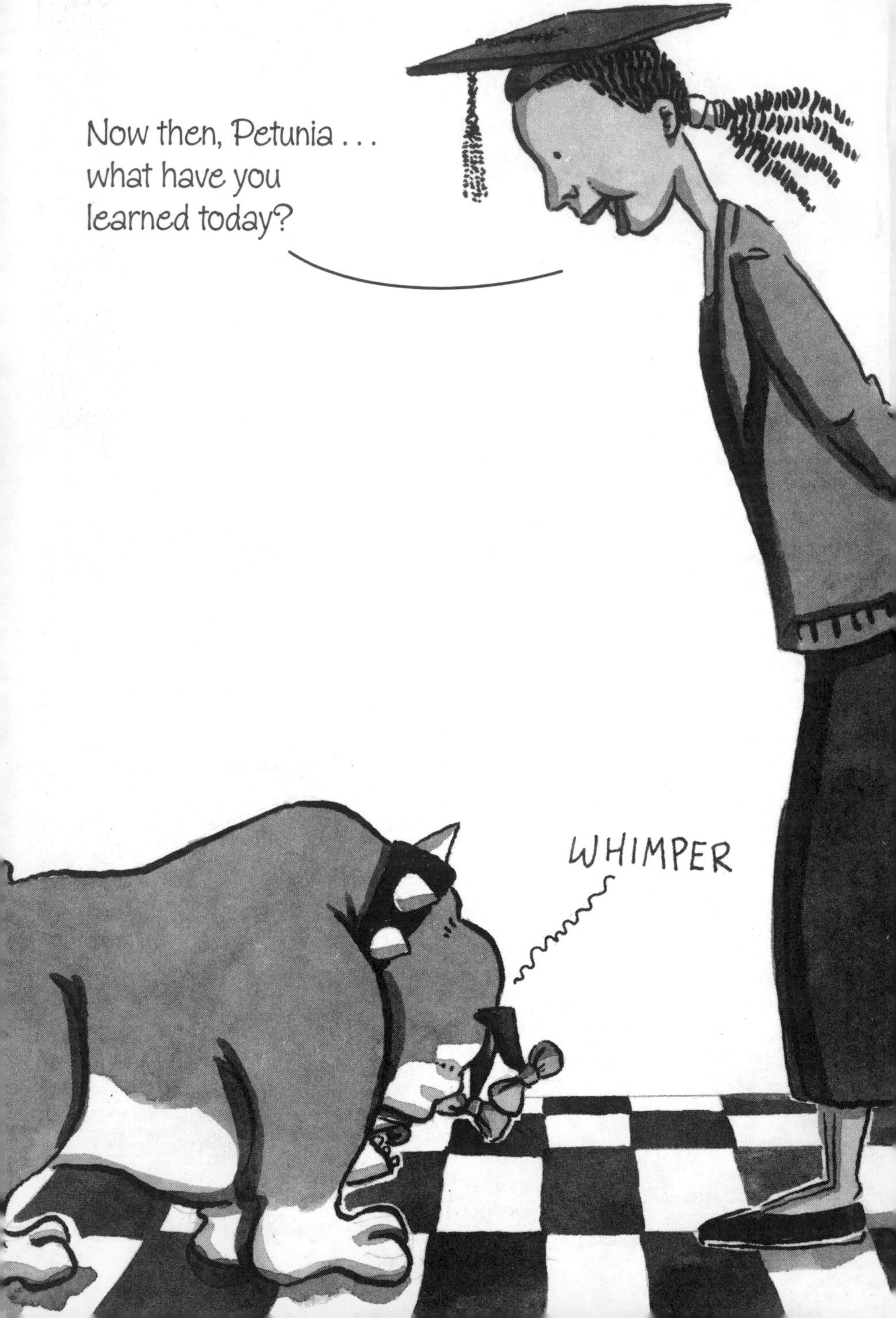
Now then, Petunia . . .
what have you
learned today?
WHIMPER

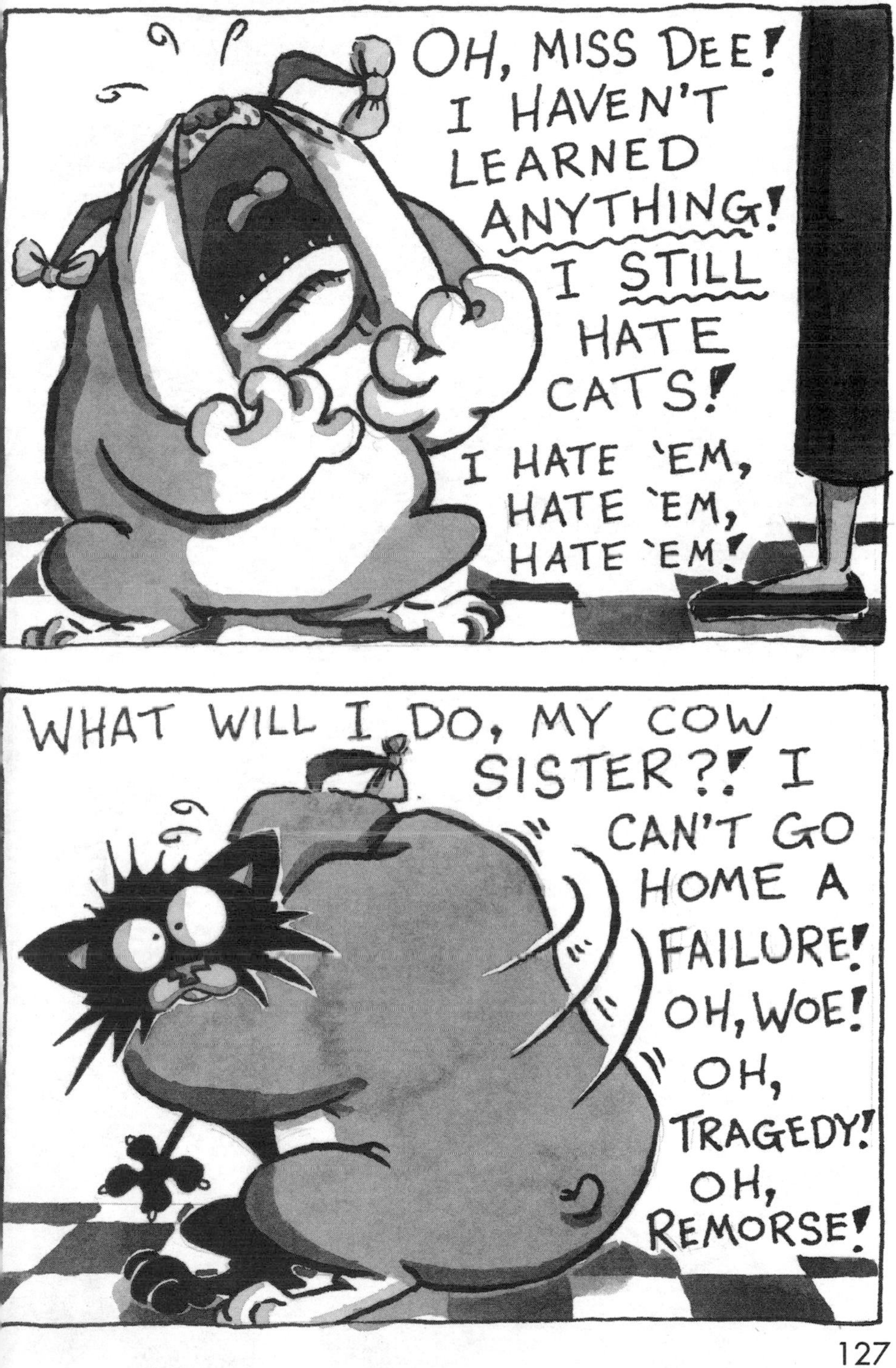
OH, MISS DEE! I HAVEN'T LEARNED ANYTHING! I STILL HATE CATS!
I HATE 'EM, HATE 'EM, HATE 'EM!
WHAT WILL I DO, MY COW SISTER?! I CAN'T GO HOME A FAILURE! OH, WOE! OH, TRAGEDY! OH, REMORSE!

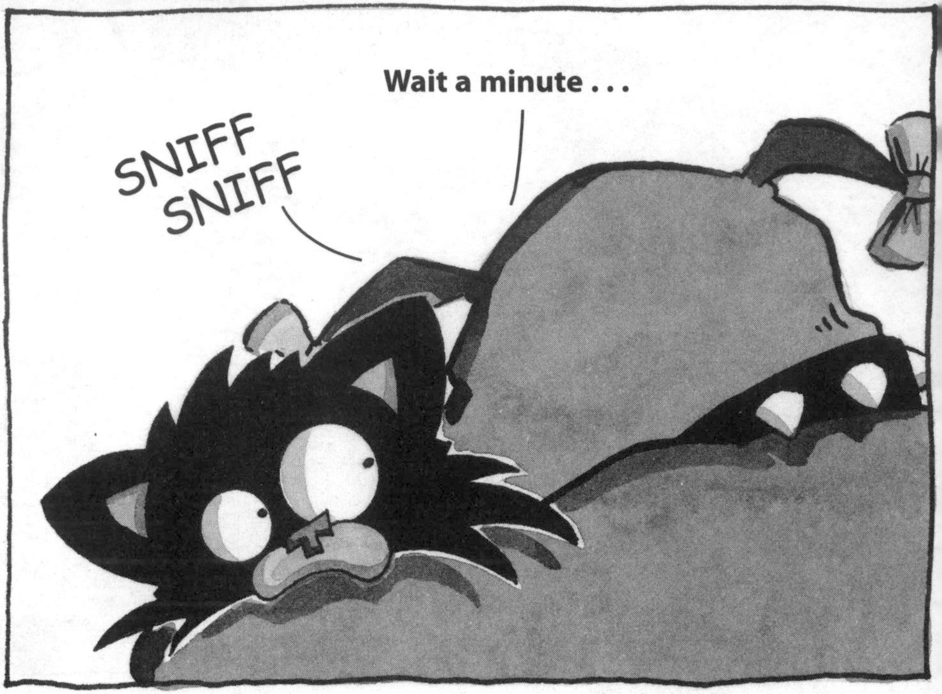
Wait a minute . . .
SNIFF SNIFF

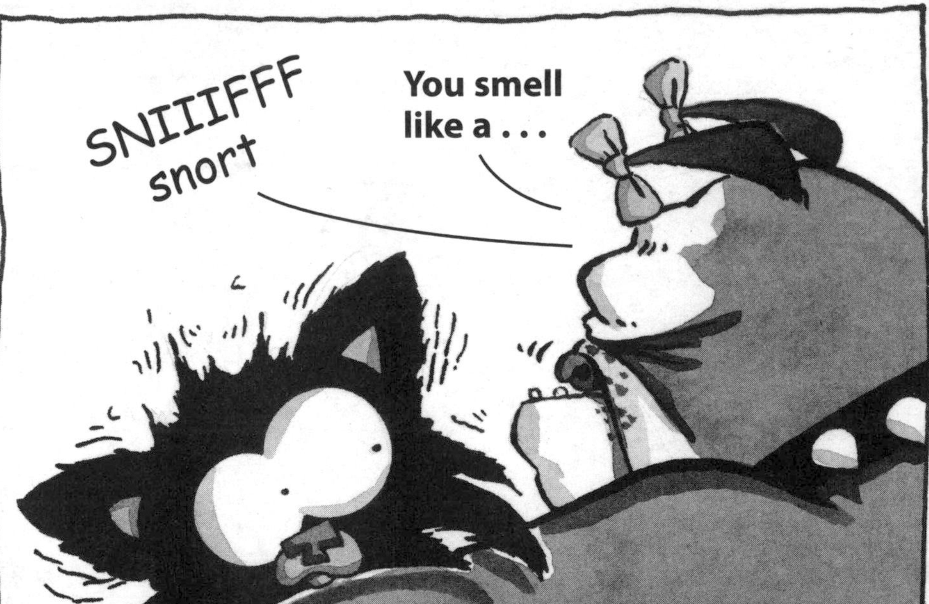
You smell like a . . .
SNIIIFFF snort

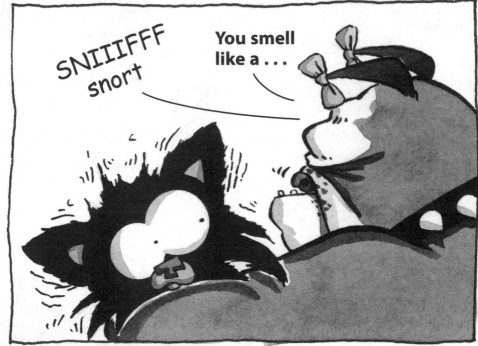

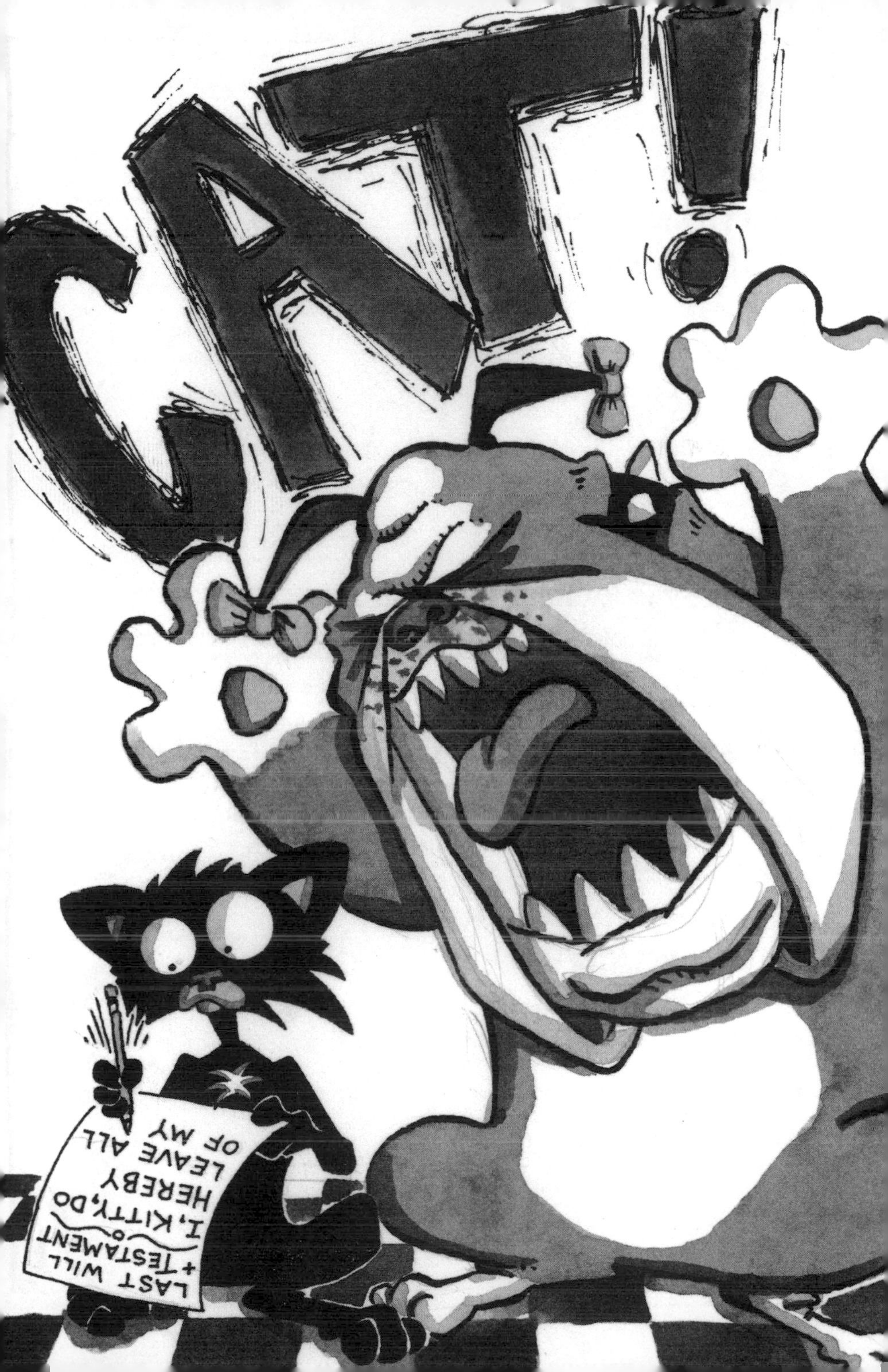
CAT!
LAST WILL + TESTAMENT
I, KITTY, DO HEREBY LEAVE ALL OF MY

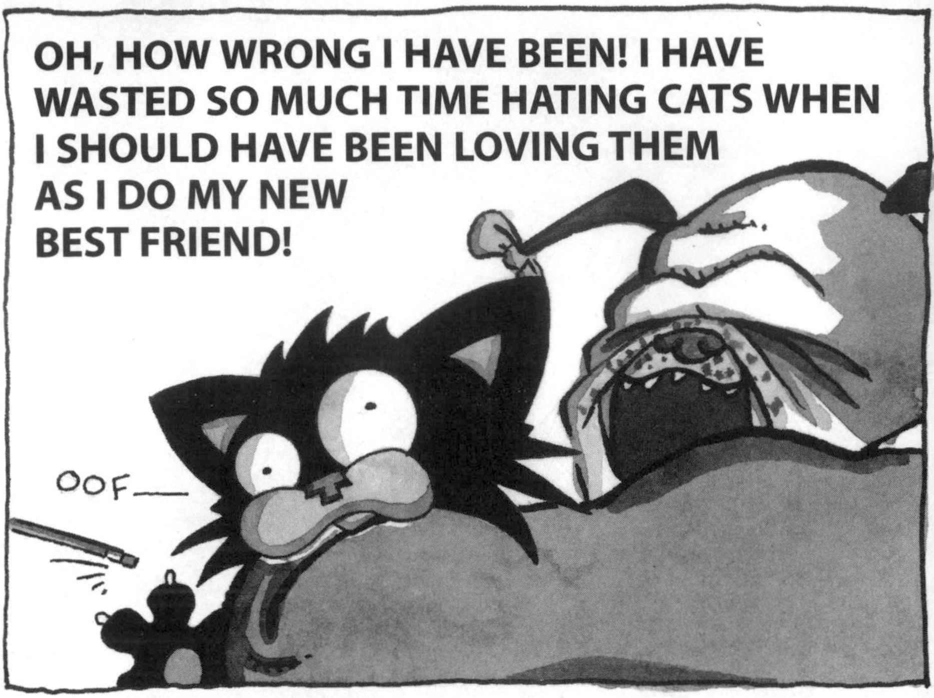
OH, HOW WRONG I HAVE BEEN! I HAVE WASTED SO MUCH TIME HATING CATS WHEN I SHOULD HAVE BEEN LOVING THEM AS I DO MY NEW BEST FRIEND!
OOF—

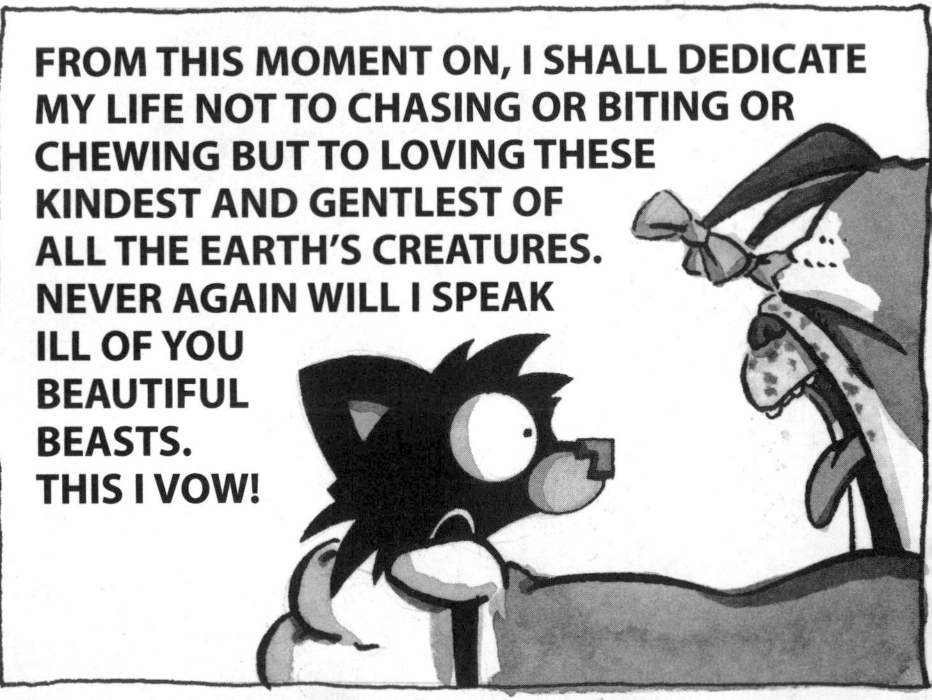
FROM THIS MOMENT ON, I SHALL DEDICATE MY LIFE NOT TO CHASING OR BITING OR CHEWING BUT TO LOVING THESE KINDEST AND GENTLEST OF ALL THE EARTH'S CREATURES. NEVER AGAIN WILL I SPEAK ILL OF YOU BEAUTIFUL BEASTS. THIS I VOW!

I watched you help your puppy friend with his drooling problem.

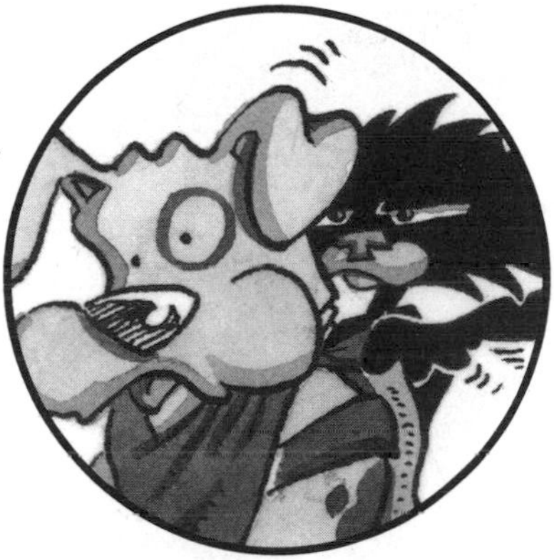

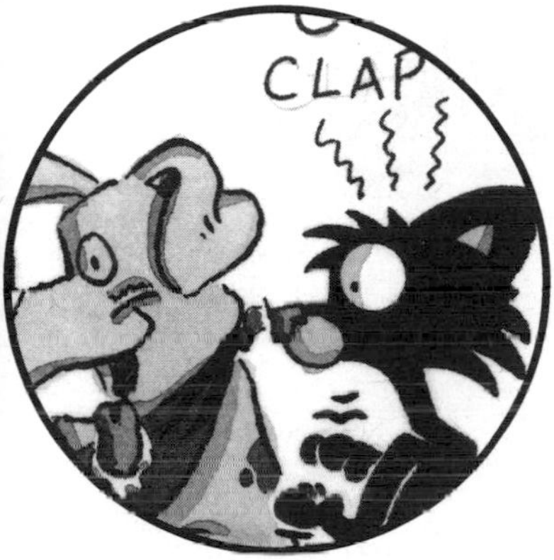
CLAP

I watched you be the first to support the little bunny with your applause.

I watched you give Petunia your painting and make a new friend.

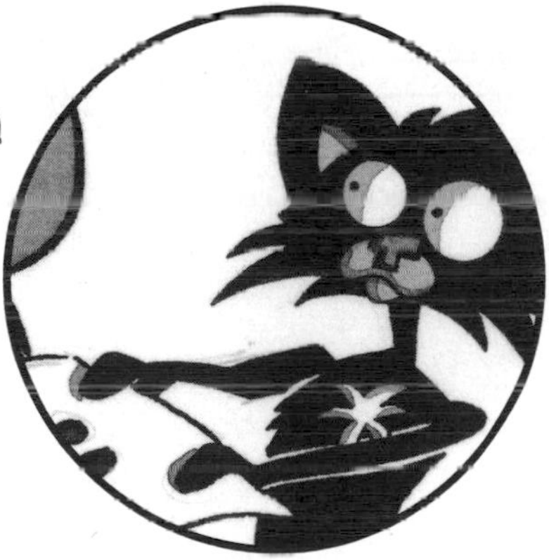

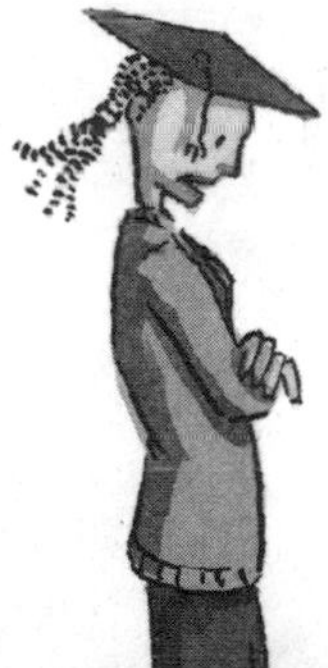

Do you want to know what I learned about you today, Kitty?

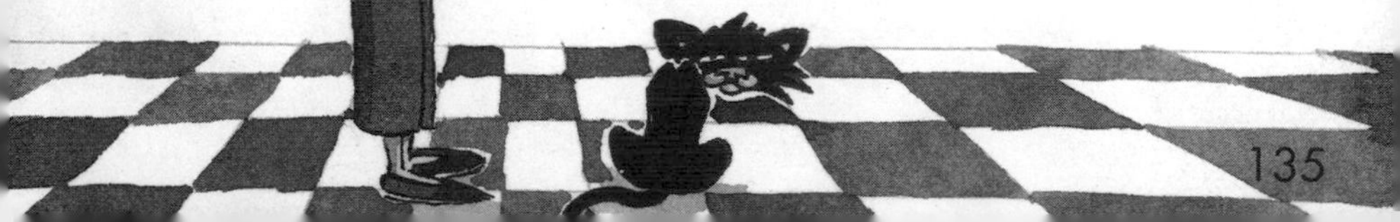

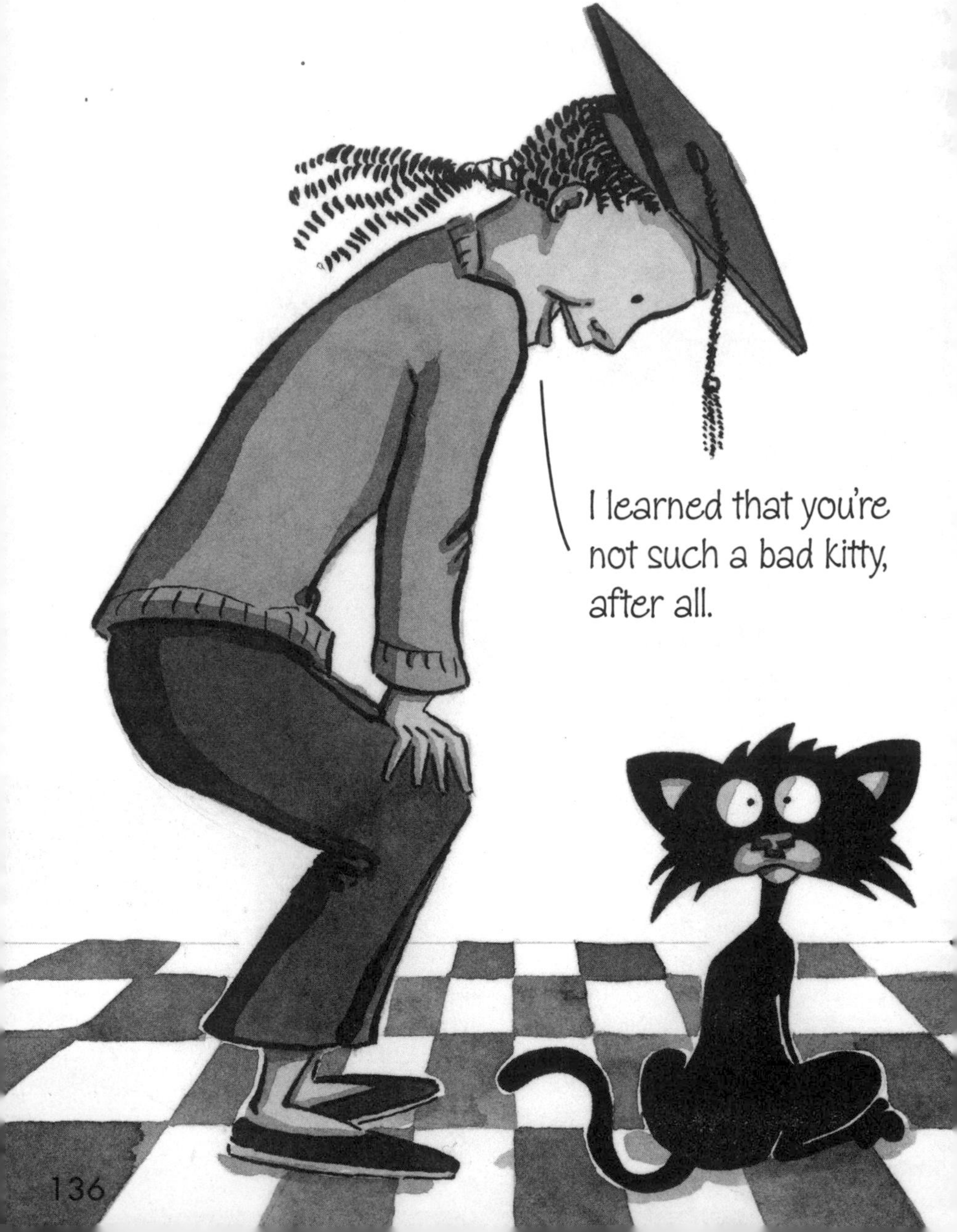
I learned that you're not such a bad kitty, after all.

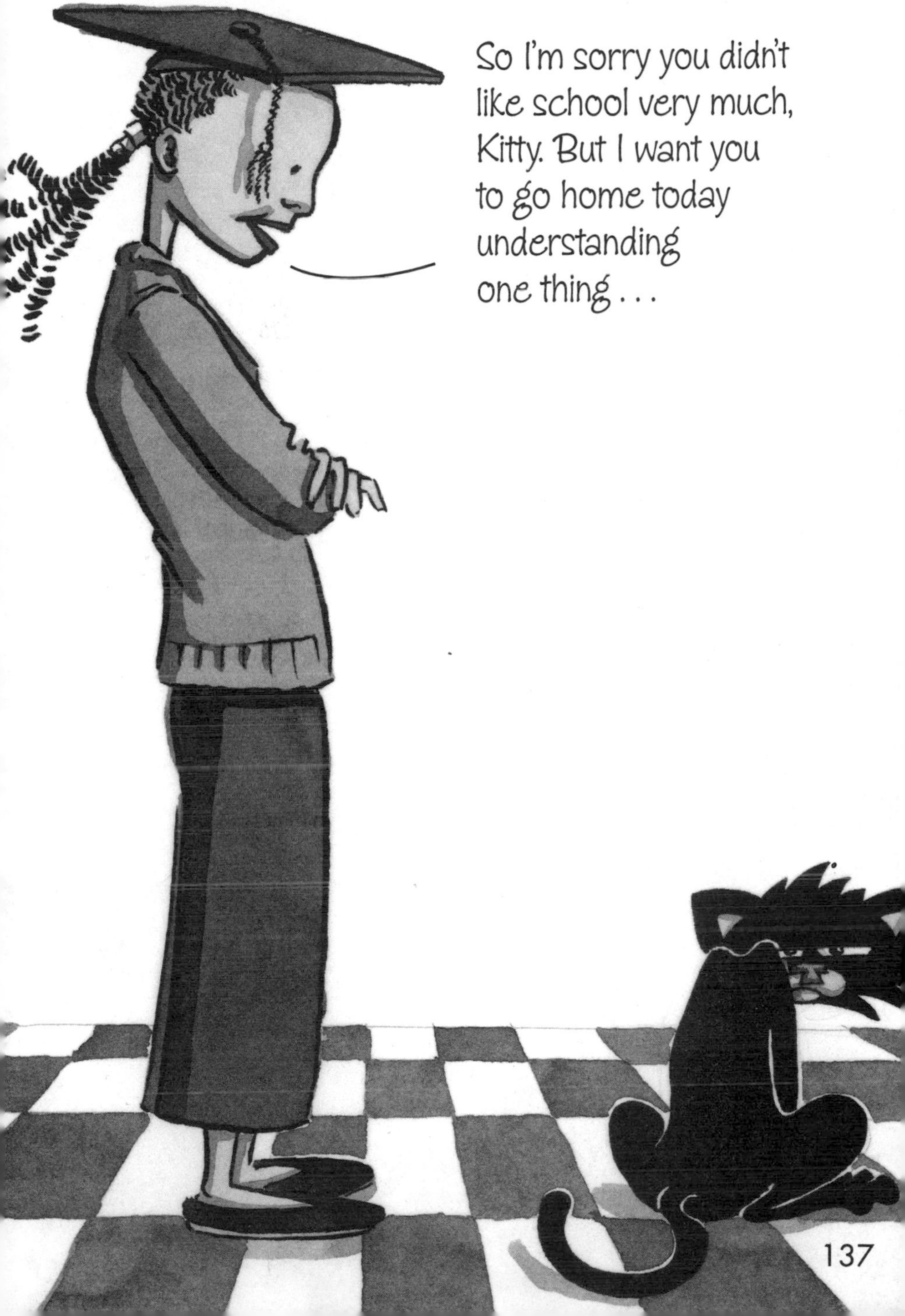
So I'm sorry you didn't like school very much, Kitty. But I want you to go home today understanding one thing . . .

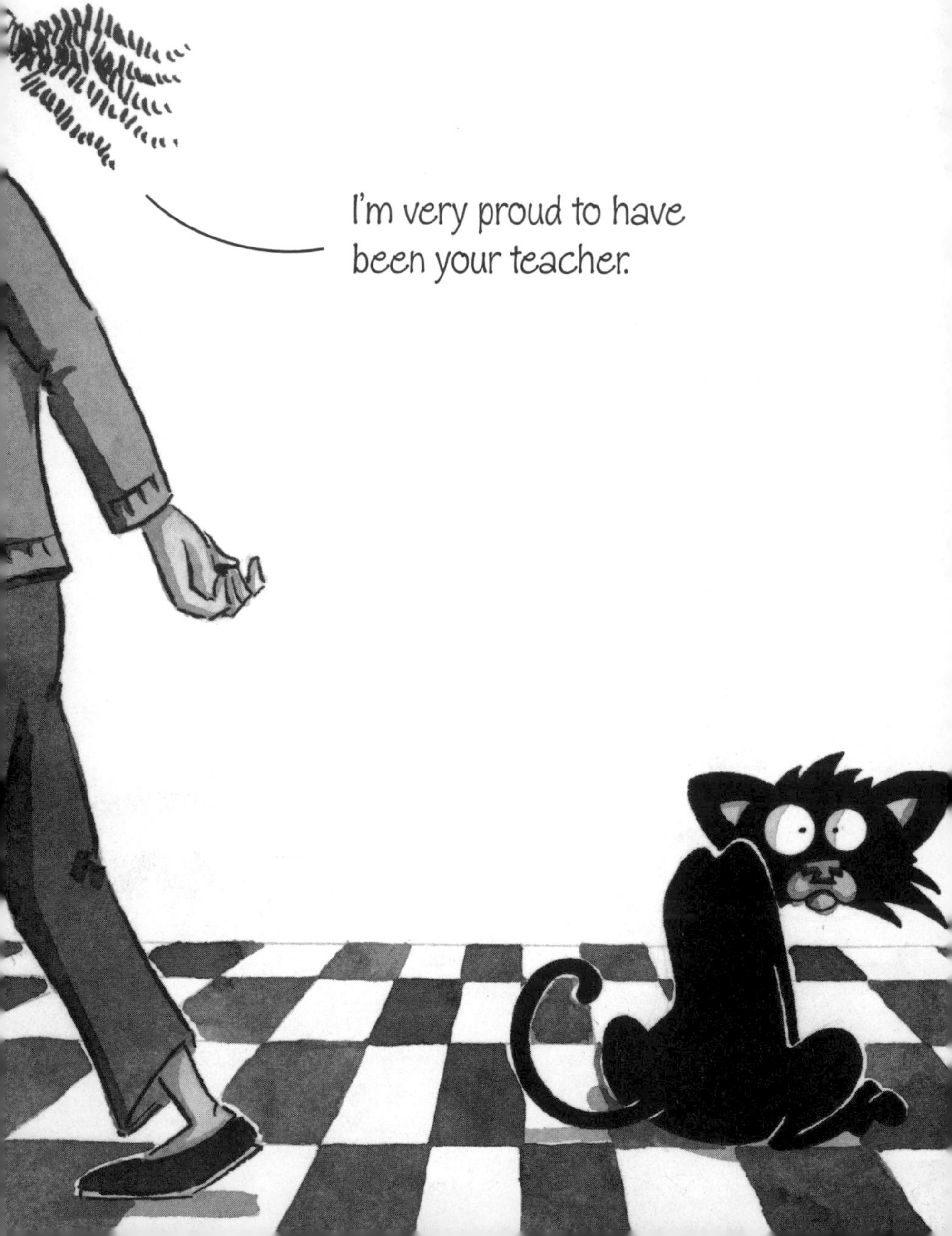
I'm very proud to have
been your teacher.

139

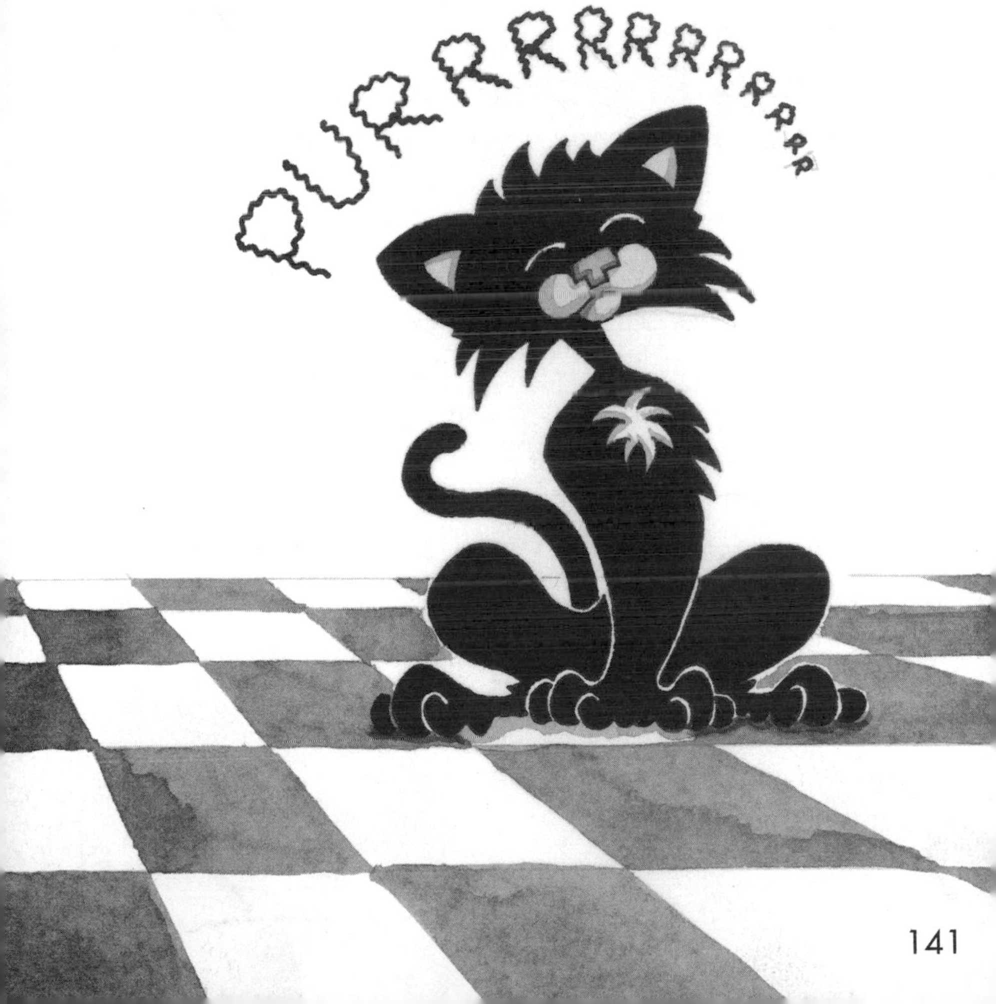
QURRRRRRRRRRR

Never!

CAN DOGS AND CATS EVER BECOME FRIENDS?

Dogs and cats can and will become friends, but they can't do this by themselves. They'll need your

MEOW?

help. The key is PATIENCE. Helping your pets to get along could take a long time and will require a lot of your attention.

First, take a few precautions. Trim the claws on your cat. Put the dog on a leash. Make sure the cat has a place to hide or escape if things get out of hand. And keep some treats on hand . . . you'll see why in a moment.

If you're bringing a cat into the home, keep her in her carrier and let the dog sniff the cat through the air holes. If the dog is calm, give him some treats as a reward. If he barks or is excitable, pull on the leash and tell him "NO" until he calms down.

ARF?

If you're bringing a dog into the home, also keep the dog in a cage if you can, at first. Bring the cat into the room by carrying her and petting her to let her know it's okay. If your cat gets wiggly or runs, don't punish her for being understandably anxious. Just pet her and console her.

Another tactic you might try is to keep both animals inside their respective carriers and place them

both in the same room with their doors facing each other. You should stay in the room, too, if only to give them both treats when they are calm. If either of your pets continues to be anxious about the situation, you should be prepared to keep them separate from each other the best you can and repeat this process each day for as long as it takes.

In time, you should be able to train each pet to think of the other as another member of the family . . . an annoying member, perhaps, but part of the family nonetheless.

SIGH—I already have a lot of annoying members of my family.

•EPILOGUE•

Well, Kitty, I'm pretty disappointed with you that you didn't graduate. I can't help but think that maybe you just didn't try hard enough.

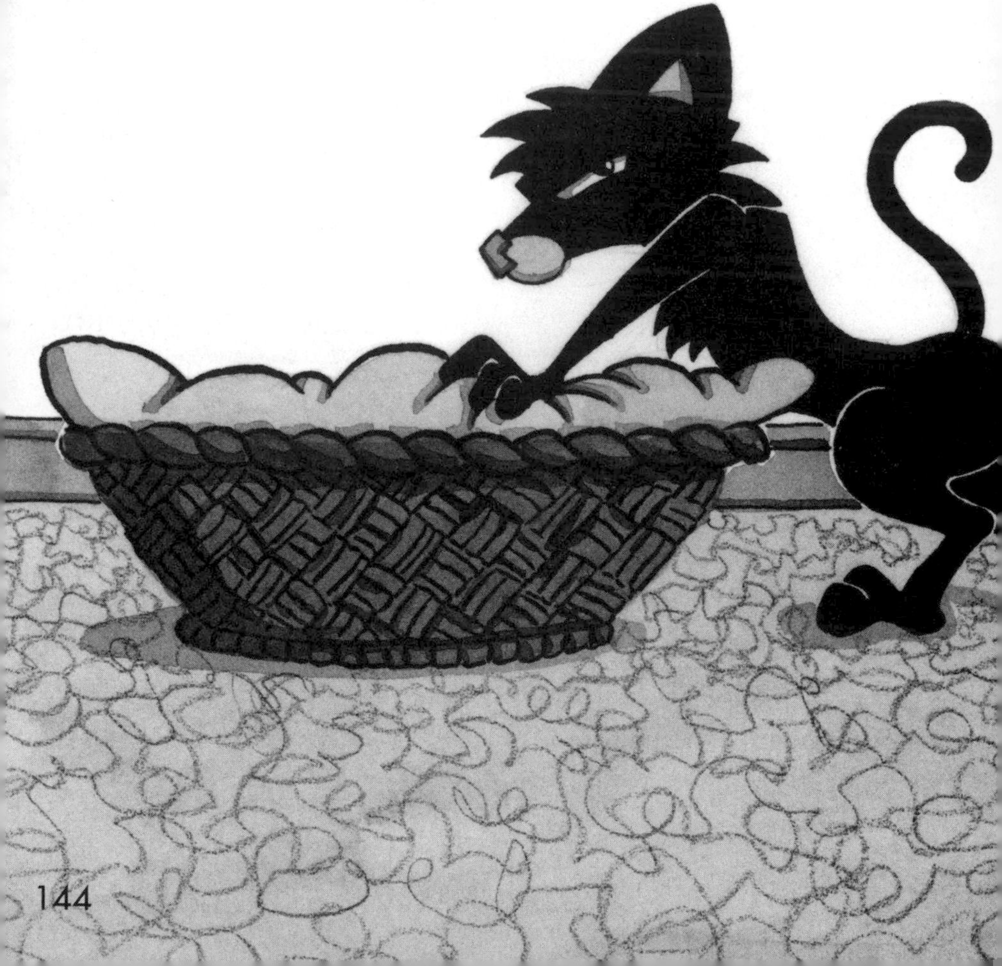

SIGH And I guess this means that you're the same old, cranky, ornery, disagreeable Kitty you've always been.

Your teacher Miss Dee kept telling me how much she likes you and how much she hopes that you'll be able to go back to school for another chance. She seemed to really like you, Kitty. But I don't know. I just don't see any reason to send you back to that school . . .

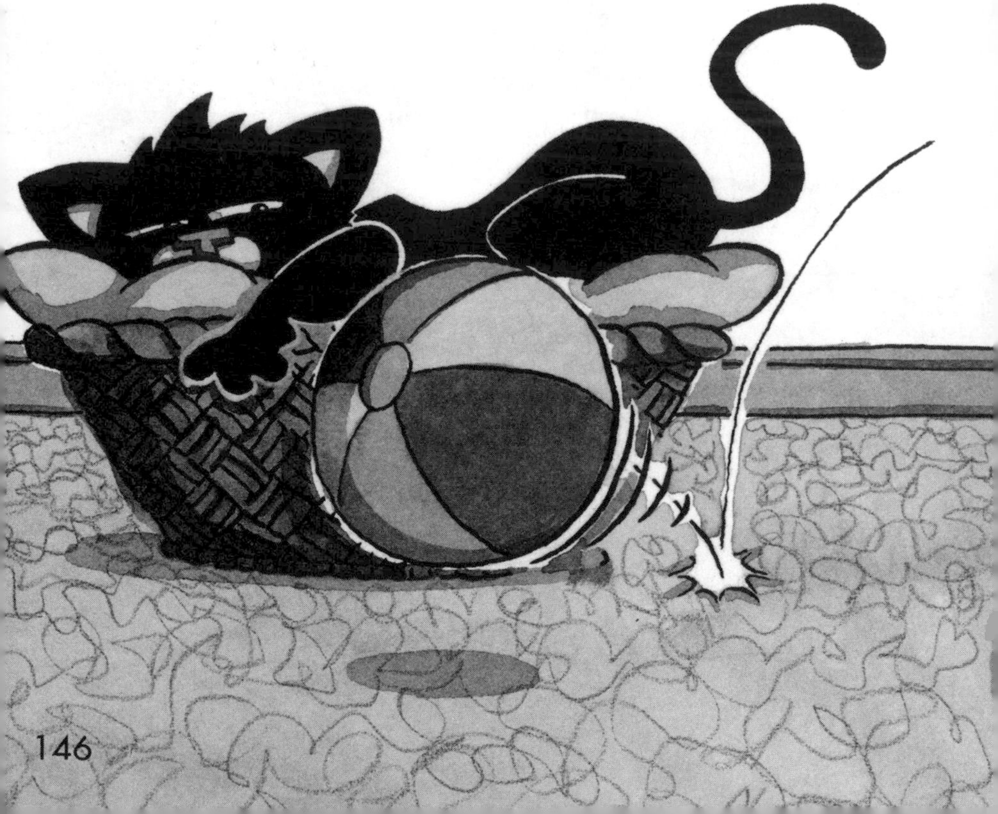

unless we really, really, REALLY have to.

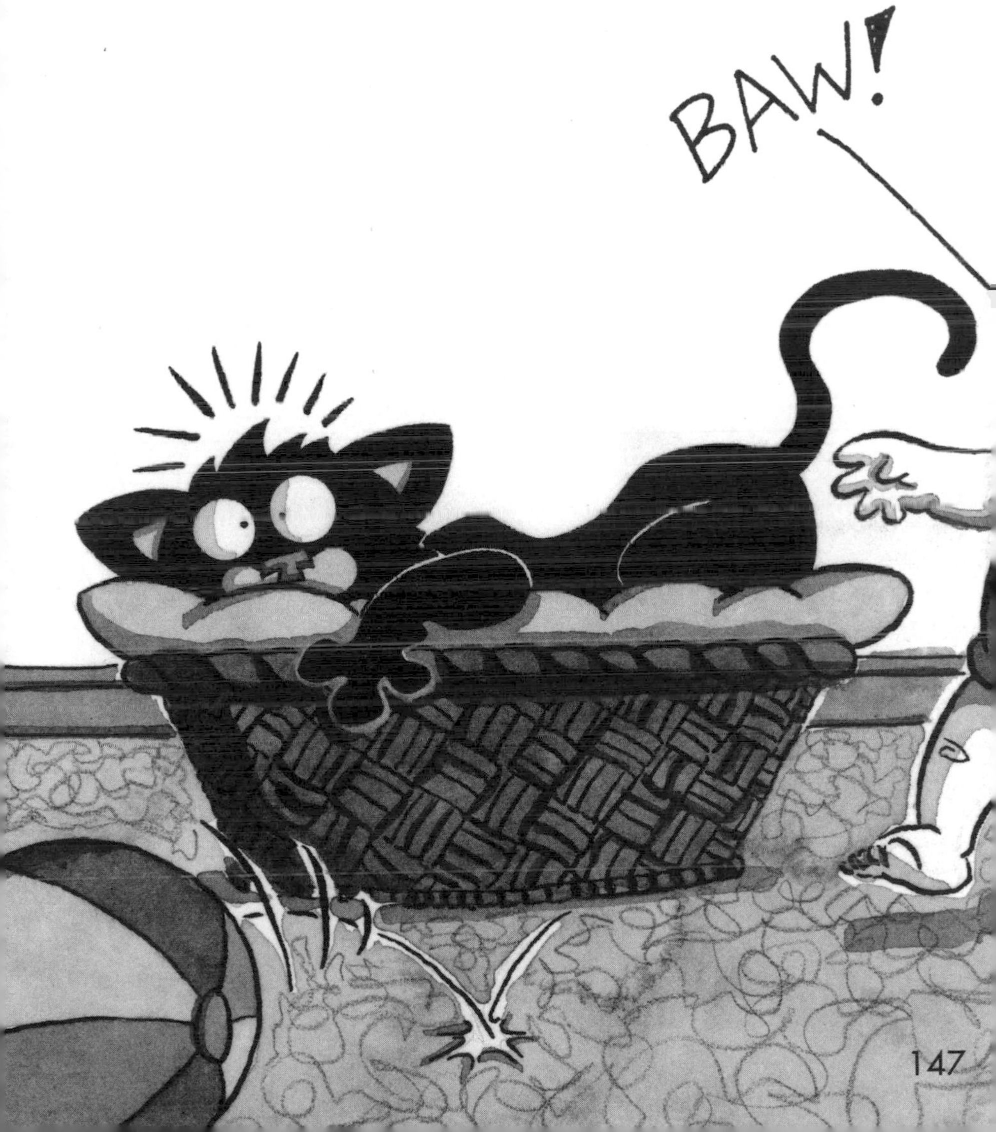
BAW!

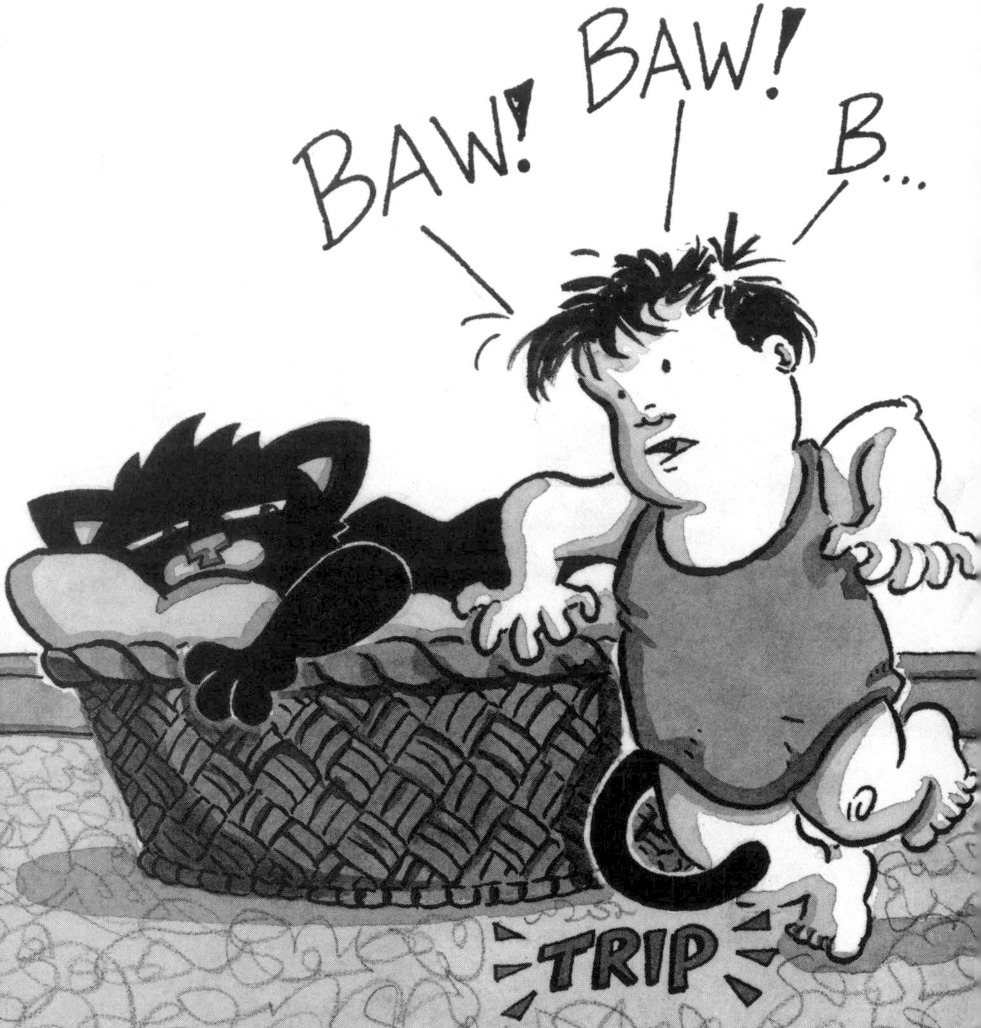
BAW! BAW!
B...
TRIP

KITTY!

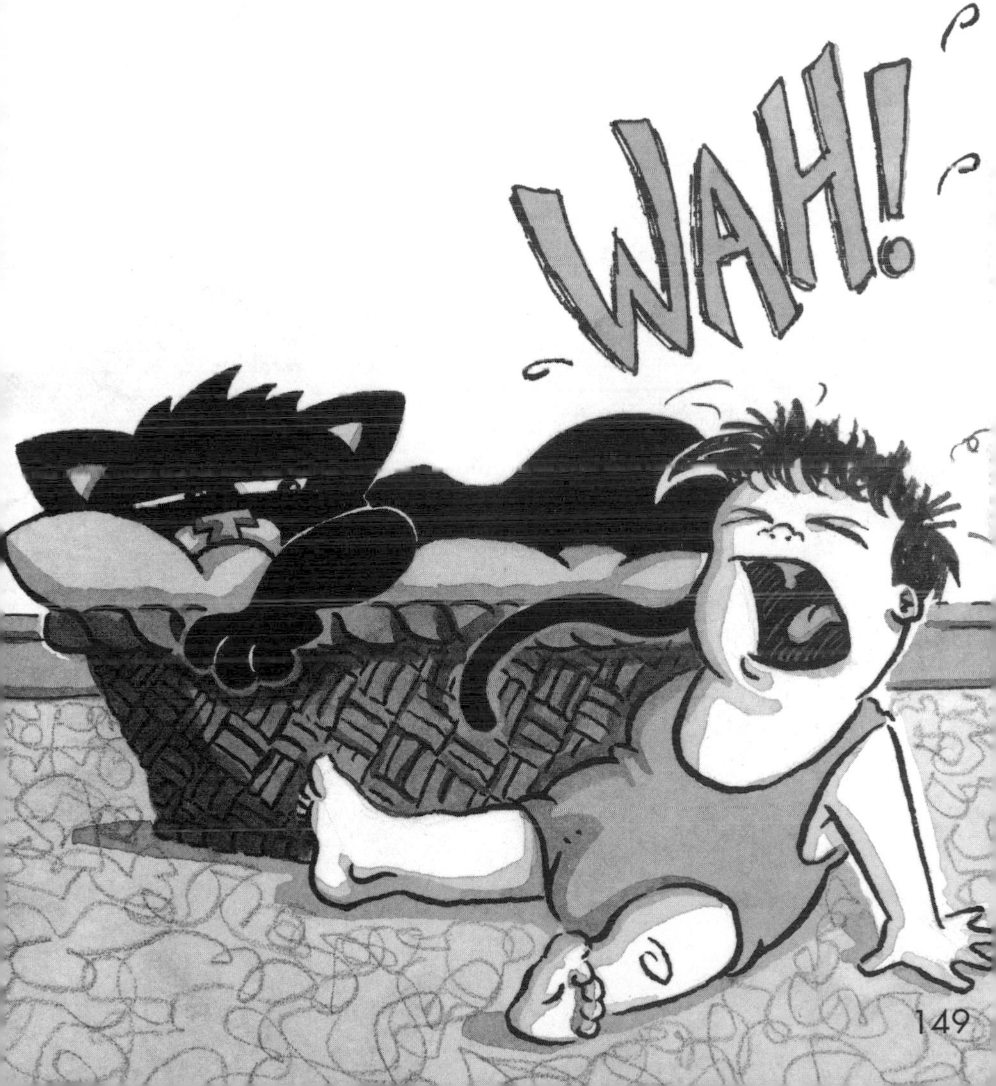
WAH!

③

IS THERE A REVERSE SETTING ON THAT THING?

IF ONLY YOU USED YOUR POWER FOR GOOD INSTEAD OF EVIL!

WHY?

WELL... THINK ABOUT IT. YOU'D MAKE A FORTUNE!

REALLY?

SURE. YOU COULD TURN ALL SORTS OF JUNK INTO CHEESE LIKE OLD TIRES, SOCKS, BANANA PEELS. AND THEN YOU COULD SELL THE CHEESE!

HMM

HOW ABOUT YOU MAKE A RAY GUN THAT TURNS CHEESE INTO MICE!

HA!

HEY!

4

GREAT! NOW YOU BROKE IT!

YAY! I'M BACK!

BING!

CURSES! I SHALL HAVE TO MAKE GOOD MY ESCAPE!

HEY! WHERE DID DR. LAGOMORPH GO?

BEATS ME!

HEH HEH HEH

I DON'T THINK WE'VE SEEN THE LAST OF THAT FIEND!

GOSH

THE END?

I think I need more muscles.

You have enough. Now hush!

What does "subterranean" mean?

Don't miss BAD KITTY's picture books!

MEOW!

BAD KITTY
Nick Bruel

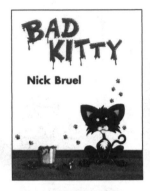

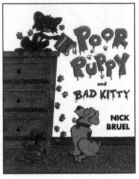

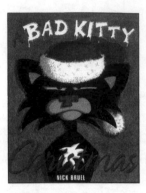

Bad Kitty
ISBN 978-1-59643-069-3
$16.99 US/$18.99 CAN

POOR PUPPY
and
BAD KITTY
NICK BRUEL

Poor Puppy and Bad Kitty
ISBN 978-1-59643-844-6
$16.99 US/$18.99 CAN

BAD KITTY
Christmas
NICK BRUEL

A Bad Kitty Christmas
ISBN 978-1-59643-668-8
$15.99 US/$18.50 CAN

ABOUT THE AUTHOR

NICK BRUEL is the author and illustrator of the phenomenally successful Bad Kitty series including the 2012 CBC Children's Choice Book Award winner *Bad Kitty Meets the Baby.* Nick has also written and illustrated many other picture books including *Who is Melvin Bubble?* and *Bob and Otto.* Nick lives with his wife and daughter in Tarrytown, New York. Visit him at nickbruel.com.

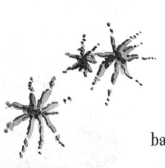

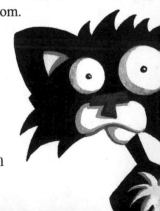

badkittybooks.com
mackids.com

Can't get enough of BAD KITTY?
Read these hilarious companion books!

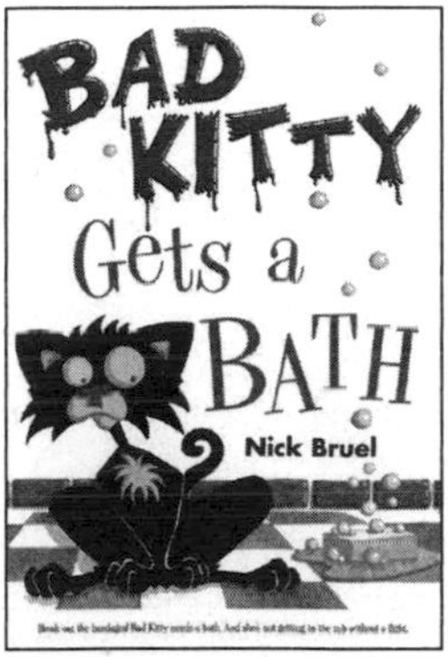
BAD KITTY
Gets a BATH
Nick Bruel

Bad Kitty Gets a Bath

ISBN 978-1-59643-334-1 (hc)
$13.99 US/$15.99 Can
ISBN 978-0-312-58138-1
$6.99 US/$8.99 Can

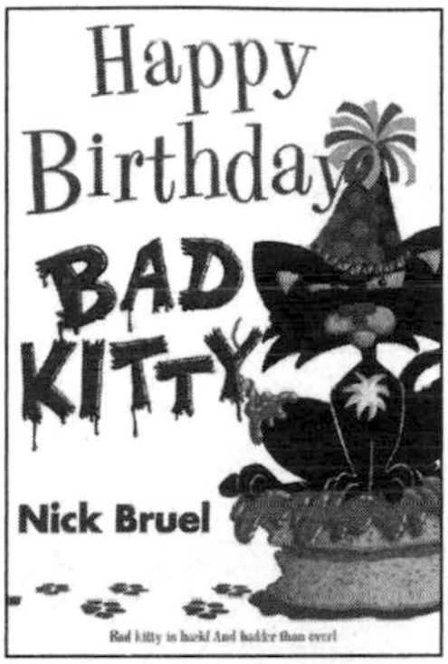
Happy Birthday
BAD KITTY
Nick Bruel
Bad kitty is back! And badder than ever!

Happy Birthday, Bad Kitty

ISBN 978-1-59643-342-7 (hc)
$13.99 US/$15.99 Can
ISBN 978-0-312-62902-1
$6.99 US/$8.50 Can

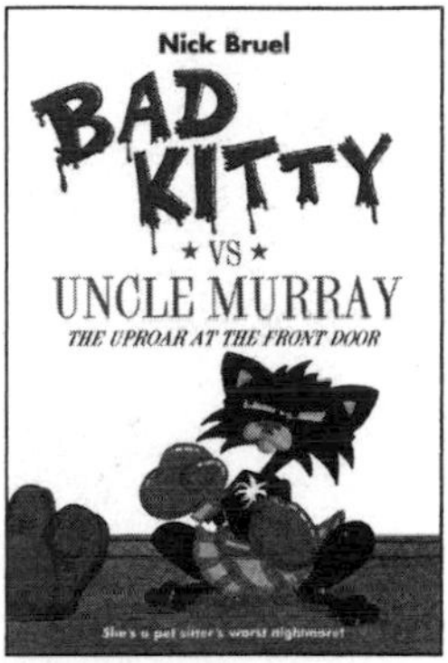
Nick Bruel
BAD KITTY
VS
UNCLE MURRAY
THE UPROAR AT THE FRONT DOOR
She's a pet sitter's worst nightmare!

Bad Kitty vs Uncle Murray

ISBN 978-1-59643-596-4 (hc)
$13.99 US/$15.99 Can
ISBN 978-0-312-67483-0
$6.99 US/$7.99 Can

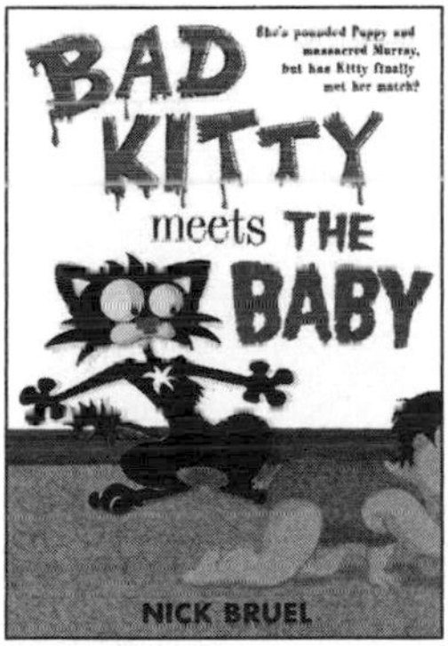
She's pounded Puppy and massacred Murray, but has Kitty finally met her match?
BAD KITTY
meets THE BABY
NICK BRUEL

Bad Kitty Meets the Baby

ISBN 978-1-59643-597-1 (hc)
$13.99 US/$15.99 Can
ISBN 978-0-312-64121-4
$6.99 US/$7.99 Can

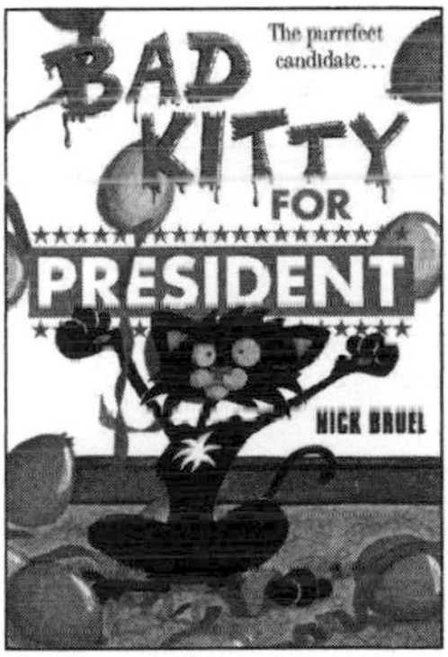
The purrfect candidate...
BAD KITTY
FOR
PRESIDENT
NICK BRUEL

Bad Kitty For President

ISBN 978-1-59643-669-5 (hc)
$13.99 US/$15.99 Can
ISBN 978-1-250-01016-2
$6.99 US/$7.99 Can

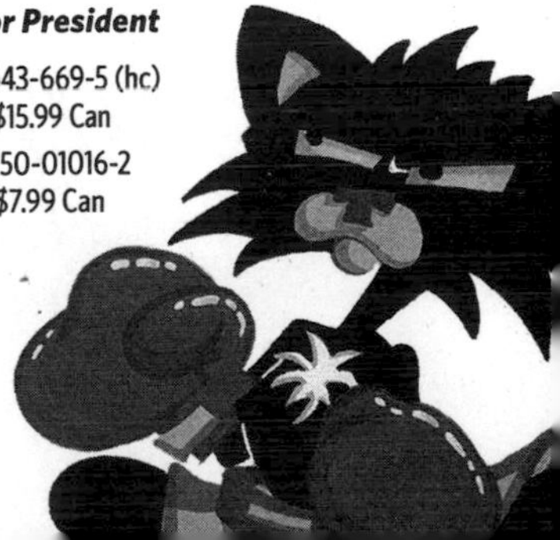

badkittybooks.com

mackids.com